HARUKI MURAKAMI

NORWEGIAN WOOD

Haruki Murakami was born in Kyoto in 1949
and now lives near Tokyo. His work has been
translated into more than fifty languages, and
the most recent of his many international hon-
ors is the Jerusalem Prize, whose previous recip-
ients include J. M. Coetzee, Milan Kundera,
and V. S. Naipaul.

www.harukimurakami.com

VINTAGE

INTERNATIONAL

NORWEGIAN WOOD

NORWEGIAN WOOD

HARUKI MURAKAMI

Translated from the Japanese by Jay Rubin

VINTAGE INTERNATIONAL

Vintage Books

A Division of Random House, Inc.

New York

A VINTAGE INTERNATIONAL ORIGINAL, SEPTEMBER 2000

Copyright © 2000 by Haruki Murakami

All rights reserved under International and Pan-American Copyright Conventions. Published in the United States by Vintage Books, a division of Random House, Inc., New York, and simultaneously in Canada by Random House of Canada Limited, Toronto. Originally published in Japan in two volumes as *Noruwei no mori* by Kodansha Ltd. in 1987. Copyright © 1987 by Haruki Murakami.

Vintage is a registered trademark and Vintage International and colophon are trademarks of Random House, Inc.

Library of Congress Cataloging-in-Publication Data
Murakami, Haruki, 1949–
  [Noruwei no mori. English]
  Norwegian wood / Haruki Murakami ; translated from the Japanese by Jay Rubin.
    p. cm.
  ISBN 0-375-70402-7
    I. Rubin, Jay, 1941–   II. Title.
  PL856.U673 N6713 2000
  895.6'35—dc21
                                        99-053821

Author photograph © Marion Ettlinger
Designed by Suvi Asch

www.vintagebooks.com

Printed in the United States of America
36

for many fêtes

NORWEGIAN WOOD

I WAS THIRTY-SEVEN THEN, STRAPPED IN MY SEAT AS THE HUGE 747 plunged through dense cloud cover on approach to the Hamburg airport. Cold November rains drenched the earth and lent everything the gloomy air of a Flemish landscape: the ground crew in rain gear, a flag atop a squat airport building, a BMW billboard. So—Germany again.

Once the plane was on the ground, soft music began to flow from the ceiling speakers: a sweet orchestral cover version of the Beatles' "Norwegian Wood." The melody never failed to send a shudder through me, but this time it hit me harder than ever.

I bent forward in my seat, face in hands to keep my skull from splitting open. Before long one of the German stewardesses approached and asked in English if I were sick. "No," I said, "just dizzy."

"Are you sure?"

"Yes, I'm sure. Thanks."

She smiled and left, and the music changed to a Billy Joel tune. I straightened up and looked out the plane window at the dark clouds hanging over the North Sea, thinking of what I had lost in the course of my life: times gone forever, friends who had died or disappeared, feelings I would never know again.

The plane reached the gate. People began unlatching their seatbelts and pulling baggage from the storage bins, and all the while I was in the meadow. I could smell the grass, feel the wind on my face, hear the cries of the birds. Autumn 1969, and soon I would be twenty.

The stewardess came to check on me again. This time she sat next to me and asked if I was all right.

"I'm fine, thanks," I said with a smile. "Just feeling kind of blue."

"I know what you mean," she said. "It happens to me, too, every once in a while."

She stood and gave me a lovely smile. "Well, then, have a nice trip. *Auf Wiedersehen.*"

"*Auf Wiedersehen.*"

EIGHTEEN YEARS HAVE GONE BY, and still I can bring back every detail of that day in the meadow. Washed clean of summer's dust by days of gentle rain, the mountains wore a deep, brilliant green. The October breeze set white fronds of head-tall grasses swaying. One long streak of cloud hung pasted across a dome of frozen blue. It almost hurt to look at that far-off sky. A puff of wind swept across the meadow and through her hair before it slipped into the woods to rustle branches and send back snatches of distant barking—a hazy sound that seemed to reach us from the doorway to another world. We heard no other sounds. We met no other people. We saw only two bright, red birds leap startled from the center of the meadow and dart into the woods. As we ambled along, Naoko spoke to me of wells.

Memory is a funny thing. When I was in the scene, I hardly paid it any mind. I never stopped to think of it as something that would make a lasting impression, certainly never imagined that eighteen years later I would recall it in such detail. I didn't give a damn about the scenery that day. I was thinking about myself. I was thinking about the beautiful girl walking next to me. I was thinking about the two of us together, and then about myself again. It was the age, that time of life when every sight, every feeling, every thought came back, like a boomerang, to me. And worse, I was in love. Love with complications. Scenery was the last thing on my mind.

Now, though, that meadow scene is the first thing that comes back to me. The smell of the grass, the faint chill of the wind, the line of the hills, the barking of a dog: these are the first things, and they come with absolute clarity. I feel as if I can reach out and trace them with a fingertip. And yet, as clear as the scene may be, no one is in it. No one. Naoko is not there, and neither am I. Where could we have disappeared to? How could such a thing have happened? Everything that seemed so important back then—Naoko, and the self I was then, and the world I had then: where could they have all gone? It's true, I can't even bring back Naoko's face—

not right away, at least. All I'm left holding is a background, sheer scenery, with no people up front.

True, given time enough, I can bring back her face. I start joining images—her tiny, cold hand; her straight, black hair so smooth and cool to the touch; a soft, rounded earlobe and the microscopic mole just beneath it; the camel's hair coat she wore in the winter; her habit of looking straight into your eyes when asking a question; the slight trembling that would come to her voice now and then (as if she were speaking on a windy hilltop)—and suddenly her face is there, always in profile at first, because Naoko and I were always out walking together, side by side. Then she turns to me, and smiles, and tilts her head just a bit, and begins to speak, and she looks into my eyes as if trying to catch the image of a minnow that has darted across the pool of a limpid spring.

I do need that time, though, for Naoko's face to appear. And as the years have passed, the time has grown longer. The sad truth is that what I could recall in five seconds all too soon needed ten, then thirty, then a full minute—like shadows lengthening at dusk. Someday, I suppose, the shadows will be swallowed up in darkness. There is no way around it: my memory is growing ever more distant from the spot where Naoko used to stand—ever more distant from the spot where my old self used to stand. And nothing but scenery, that view of the meadow in October, returns again and again to me like a symbolic scene in a movie. Each time it appears, it delivers a kick to some part of my mind. "Wake up," it says. "I'm still here. Wake up and think about it. Think about why I'm still here." The kicking never hurts me. There's no pain at all. Just a hollow sound that echoes with each kick. And even that is bound to fade one day. At the Hamburg airport, though, the kicks were longer and harder than usual. Which is why I am writing this book. To think. To understand. It just happens to be the way I'm made. I have to write things down to feel I fully comprehend them.

LET'S SEE, now, what was Naoko talking about that day?

Of course: the "field well." I have no idea whether such a well ever existed. It might have been an image or a sign that existed only inside Naoko, like all the other things she used to spin into existence inside her mind in those dark days. Once she had described it to me, though, I was never able to think of that meadow scene without the well. From that day forward, the image of a thing I had never laid eyes on became inseparably fused to the actual scene of the field that lay before me. I can go so far as to describe the well in minute detail. It lay precisely on the border where the meadow ended and the woods began—a dark opening in the earth a yard across, hidden by the meadow grass. Nothing marked its perimeter—no fence, no stone curb (at least not one that rose above ground level). It was nothing but a hole, a mouth open wide. The stones of its collar had been weathered and turned a strange muddy white. They were cracked and had chunks missing, and a little green lizard slithered into an open seam. You could lean over the edge and peer down to see nothing. All I knew about the well was its frightening depth. It was deep beyond measuring, and crammed full of darkness, as if all the world's darknesses had been boiled down to their ultimate density.

"It's really, *really* deep," said Naoko, choosing her words with care. She would speak that way sometimes, slowing down to find the exact word she was looking for. "But no one knows where it is," she continued. "The one thing I know for sure is that it's around here somewhere."

Hands thrust into the pockets of her tweed jacket, she smiled at me as if to say "It's true!"

"Then it must be incredibly dangerous," I said. "A deep well, but nobody knows where it is. You could fall in and that'd be the end of you."

"The end. Aaaaaaaah, splat. Finished."

"Things like that must actually happen."

"They do, every once in a while. Maybe once in two or three years. Somebody disappears all of a sudden, and they just can't find him. So then the people around here say, 'Oh, he fell in the field well.'"

"Not a nice way to die," I said.

"No, it's a terrible way to die," said Naoko, brushing a cluster of grass seed from her jacket. "The best thing would be to break your neck, but you'd probably just break your leg and then you couldn't do a thing. You'd yell at the top of your lungs, but nobody'd hear you, and you couldn't expect anybody to find you, and you'd have centipedes and spiders crawling all over you, and the bones of the ones who died before are scattered all around you, and it's dark and soggy, and way overhead there's this tiny, tiny circle of light like a winter moon. You die there in this place, little by little, all by yourself."

"Yuck, just thinking about it makes my flesh creep," I said. "Somebody should find the thing and build a wall around it."

"But nobody *can* find it. So make sure you don't go off the path."

"Don't worry, I won't."

Naoko took her left hand from her pocket and squeezed my hand. "Don't *you* worry," she said. "You'll be O.K. *You* could go running all around here in the middle of the night and you'd *never* fall into the well. And as long as I stick with you, I won't fall in, either."

"Never?"

"Never!"

"How can you be so sure?"

"I just know," she said, increasing her grip on my hand and continuing on for a ways in silence. "I know these things. I'm always right. It's got nothing to do with logic: I just feel it. For example, when I'm really close to you like this, I'm not the least bit scared. Nothing dark or evil could ever tempt me."

"Well, that answers that," I said. "All you have to do is stay with me like this all the time."

"Do you mean that?"

"Of course I mean it."

Naoko stopped short. So did I. She put her hands on my shoulders and peered into my eyes. Deep within her own pupils a heavy, black liquid swirled in a strange whirlpool pattern. Those beautiful eyes of hers were looking inside me for a long, long time. Then she stretched to her full height and touched her cheek to mine. It was a marvelous, warm gesture that stopped my heart for a moment.

"Thank you," she said.

"My pleasure," I answered.

"I'm so happy you said that. Really happy," she said with a sad smile. "But it's impossible."

"Impossible? Why?"

"It would be wrong. It would be terrible. It—"

Naoko clamped her mouth shut and started walking again. I could tell that all kinds of thoughts were whirling around in her head, so rather than intrude on them I kept silent and walked by her side.

"It would just be wrong—wrong for you, wrong for me," she said after a long pause.

"Wrong how?" I murmured.

"Don't you see? It's just not possible for one person to watch over another person for ever and ever. I mean, say we got married. You'd have to go to work during the day. Who's going to watch over me while you're away? Or say you have to go on a business trip, who's going to watch over me then? Can I be glued to you every minute of our lives? What kind of equality would there be in that? What kind of relationship would that be? Sooner or later you'd get sick of me. You'd wonder what you were doing with your life, why you were spending all your time babysitting this woman. I couldn't stand that. It wouldn't solve any of my problems."

"But your problems are not going to continue for the rest of your life," I said, touching her back. "They'll end eventually. And when they do, we'll stop and think about how to go on from there. Maybe *you* will have to help *me*. We're not running our lives according to some account book. If you need me, use me. Don't you see? Why do you have to be so rigid? Relax, let your guard down. You're all tensed up so you always expect the worst. Relax your body, and the rest of you will lighten up."

"How can you say that?" she asked in a voice drained of feeling.

Naoko's voice alerted me to the possibility that I had said something I shouldn't have.

"Tell me how you could say such a thing," she said, staring down at the ground beneath her feet. "You're not telling me anything I don't know already. 'Relax your body, and the rest of you will lighten up.' What's the point of saying that to me? If I relaxed my body now, I'd fall apart. I've always lived like this, and it's the only way I know how to go on living. If I relaxed for a second, I'd never find my way back. I'd go to pieces, and the pieces would be blown away. Why can't you see that? How can you talk about watching over me if you can't see that?"

I said nothing in return.

"I'm confused. Really confused. And it's a lot deeper than you think. Deeper . . . darker . . . colder. But tell me something. How could you have slept with me that time? How could you have done such a thing? Why didn't you just leave me alone?"

Now we were walking through the frightful silence of a pine wood. The desiccated corpses of cicadas that had died at the end of the summer littered the surface of the path, crunching beneath our shoes. As if searching for something we'd lost, Naoko and I continued slowly down the path in the woods.

"I'm sorry," she said, taking my arm and shaking her head. "I didn't mean to hurt you. Try not to let what I said bother you. Really, I'm sorry. I was just angry at myself."

"I guess I don't really understand you yet," I said. "I'm not all that smart. It takes me a while to understand things. But if I *do* have the time, I *will* come to understand you—better than anyone else in the world ever can."

We came to a stop and stood in the silent woods, listening. I tumbled pinecones and cicada shells with the toe of my shoe, then looked up at the patches of sky showing through the pine branches. Hands thrust in her jacket pockets, Naoko stood there thinking, her eyes focused on nothing in particular.

"Tell me something, Toru," she said. "Do you love me?"

"You know I do," I answered.

"Will you do me two favors?"

"You may have up to three wishes, madame."

Naoko smiled and shook her head. "No, two will be enough. One is for you to realize how grateful I am that you came to see me here. I hope you'll understand how happy you've made me. I know it's going to save me if anything will. I may not show it, but it's true."

"I'll come to see you again," I said. "And what is the other wish?"

"I want you always to remember me. Will you remember that I existed, and that I stood next to you here like this?"

"Always," I said. "I'll always remember."

She walked on ahead without speaking. The autumn light filtering through the branches danced over the shoulders of her jacket. A dog barked again, closer than before. Naoko climbed a small mound of a hill, stepped out of the pine wood, and hurried down a gentle slope. I followed two or three steps behind.

"Come over here," I called toward her back. "The well might be around here somewhere." Naoko stopped and smiled and took my arm. We walked the rest of the way side by side.

"Do you really promise never to forget me?" she asked in a near whisper.

"I'll never forget you," I said. "I *could* never forget you."

EVEN SO, my memory has grown increasingly distant, and I have already forgotten any number of things. Writing from memory like this, I often feel a pang of dread. What if I've forgotten the most important thing?

What if somewhere inside me there is a dark limbo where all the truly important memories are heaped and slowly turning into mud?

Be that as it may, it's all I have to work with. Clutching these faded, fading, imperfect memories to my breast, I go on writing this book with all the desperate intensity of a starving man sucking on bones. This is the only way I know to keep my promise to Naoko.

Once, long ago, when I was still young, when the memories were far more vivid than they are now, I often tried to write about Naoko. But I was never able to produce a line. I knew that if that first line would come, the rest would pour itself onto the page, but I could never make it happen. Everything was too sharp and clear, so that I could never tell where to start—the way a map that shows too much can sometimes be useless. Now, though, I realize that all I can place in the imperfect vessel of writing are imperfect memories and imperfect thoughts. The more the memories of Naoko inside me fade, the more deeply I am able to understand her. I know, too, why she asked me not to forget her. Naoko herself knew, of course. She knew that my memories of her would fade. Which is precisely why she begged me never to forget her, to remember that she had existed.

The thought fills me with an almost unbearable sorrow. Because Naoko never loved me.

two

ONCE UPON A TIME, MANY YEARS AGO—JUST TWENTY YEARS AGO, in fact—I was living in a dormitory. I was eighteen and a freshman. I was new to Tokyo and new to living alone, and so my anxious parents found a private dorm for me to live in rather than the kind of single room that most students took. The dormitory provided meals and various facilities and would probably help their unworldly eighteen-year-old to survive. Expenses were also a consideration. A dorm cost far less than a private room. As long as I had bedding and a lamp, there was no need to buy a lot of furnishings. For my part, I would have preferred to rent an apartment and live in comfortable solitude, but knowing what my parents had to spend on matriculation fees and tuition at the private university I was attending, I was in no position to insist. And besides, I really didn't care where I lived.

Located on a hill with open views in the middle of the city, the dormitory compound sat on a large quadrangle surrounded by a concrete wall. A huge, towering zelkova tree stood just inside the front gate. People said it was at least a hundred and fifty years old. Standing at its base, you could look up and see nothing of the sky through its dense cover of green leaves.

The paved road leading from the gate curved around the tree and continued on long and straight across a broad quadrangle, two three-story concrete dorm buildings facing each other on either side of the road. These were large buildings with lots of windows, and they gave the impression of being either apartment houses that had been converted into jails or jails that had been converted into apartment houses. There was nothing dirty about them, however, nor did they feel dark. You could hear radios playing through open windows, all of which had the same cream-colored curtains that could not be faded by the sun.

11

Beyond the two dormitories, the road led up to the entrance of a two-story common building, the first floor of which contained a dining hall and bath facility, the second consisting of an auditorium, meeting rooms, and even guest rooms, whose use I could never fathom. Next to the common building stood a third dormitory, also three stories high. Broad green lawns filled the quadrangle, and circulating sprinklers caught the sunlight as they turned. Behind the common building there was a field used for baseball and soccer, and six tennis courts. The complex had everything you could want.

There was just one problem with the place: its political smell. The complex was run by some kind of fishy foundation that centered on some kind of extreme right-wing guy, and there was something strangely twisted—as far as I was concerned—about the way they ran the place. You could see it in the pamphlet they gave to new students and in the dorm rules. The proclaimed "founding spirit" of the dormitory was "to strive to nurture human resources of service to the nation through the ultimate in educational fundamentals," and many financial leaders who endorsed this "spirit" had contributed their private funds to the construction of the facility. This was the public face of the project, though what lay behind it was vague in the extreme. Some said it was a tax dodge, while others saw it as a publicity stunt for the contributors, and still others claimed that the construction of the dormitory was a cover for swindling the public out of a prime piece of real estate. One thing was certain, though: in the dorm complex there existed a privileged club composed of elite students from various universities. They formed "study groups" that met several times a month and that included some of the founders. Any member of the club could be assured of a good job upon graduation. I had no idea which—if any—of these theories was correct, but all shared the assumption that there was "something fishy" about the place.

In any case, I spent two years—from the spring of 1968 to the spring of 1970—living in this "fishy" dormitory. Why I put up with it so long, I can't really say. In terms of everyday life, it made no practical difference to me whether the place was right wing or left wing or anything else.

Each day at the complex began with the solemn raising of the flag. They played the national anthem, too, of course. You can't have one without the other. The flagpole stood in the very center of the compound, where it was visible from every window of all three dormitories.

The head of the east dormitory (my building) was in charge of the flag. He was a tall, eagle-eyed man in his late fifties or early sixties. His bristly hair was flecked with gray, and his sunburned neck bore a long scar. People whispered that he was a graduate of the wartime Nakano spy school, but no one knew for sure. Next to him stood a student who acted as his assistant. No one really knew this guy, either. He had the world's shortest crewcut and always wore a navy blue student uniform. I didn't know his name or which room he lived in, never saw him in the dining hall or the bath. I'm not even sure he was a student, though you would think he must have been, given the "Uniform," which quickly became his nickname. In contrast to Sir Nakano, Uniform was short, pudgy, and pasty-faced. This creepy couple would raise the banner of the Rising Sun every morning at six.

When I first entered the dormitory, the sheer novelty of the event would often prompt me to get up in the morning to observe this patriotic ritual. The two would appear in the quadrangle at almost the exact moment the radio beeped the six o'clock signal. Uniform was wearing his uniform, of course, with black leather shoes, and Nakano wore a short jacket and white training shoes. Uniform held a ceremonial box of unfinished paulownia wood, while Nakano carried a Sony tape player at his side. Nakano set the player at the base of the flagpole. Uniform opened the box to reveal a neatly folded banner. This he reverentially proffered to Nakano, who would clip it to the rope on the flagpole, revealing the bright red circle of the rising sun on a field of pure white. Then Uniform pressed the switch for the playing of the anthem.

"May Our Lord's Reign . . ."

And up the flag would climb.

"Until pebbles turn to boulders . . ."

It would reach halfway up the pole.

"And be covered with moss."

Now it was at the top. The two stood at rigid attention, looking up at the flag. This was quite a sight on clear days when the wind was blowing.

The lowering of the flag at dusk was carried out with the same ceremonial reverence, but in reverse. Down the banner would come and find its place in the box. The national flag does not fly at night.

I did not know why the flag had to be taken down at night. The nation continued to exist after dark, and plenty of people worked the whole night through—track construction crews and taxi drivers and bar hostesses and firemen and night watchmen: it seemed unfair to me that such people were denied the protection of the flag. Or maybe it didn't matter all that much and nobody really cared—aside from me. Not that I really cared, either. It was just something that happened to cross my mind.

The rules for room assignments put freshmen and sophomores in doubles while juniors and seniors had single rooms. Double rooms were a little longer and narrower than nine-by-twelve, with an aluminum-framed window in the wall opposite the door and two desks by the window arranged so the inhabitants of the room could study back-to-back. To the left of the door stood a steel bunk bed. The supplied furniture was sturdy and simple in the extreme and included a pair of lockers, a small coffee table, and some built-in shelves. Even the most well-disposed observer would have had trouble calling this setting poetic. The shelves of most rooms carried such items as transistor radios, hair dryers, electric carafes and cookers, instant coffee, tea bags, sugar lumps, and simple pots and bowls for preparing instant *ramen*. The walls bore pinups from girlie magazines or stolen porno movie posters. One guy had a photo of pigs mating, but this was a far-out exception to the usual naked women or girl pop singers or actresses. Bookshelves on the desks held textbooks and dictionaries and novels.

The filth of these all-male rooms was horrifying. Moldy mandarin orange skins clung to the bottoms of wastebaskets. Empty cans used for ashtrays held mounds of cigarette butts, and when these started to smolder they'd be doused with coffee or beer and left to give off a sour stink. Blackish grime and bits of indefinable matter clung to all the bowls and dishes on the shelves, and the floors were littered with *ramen* wrappers and empty beer cans and lids from one thing or another. It never occurred to anyone to sweep up and throw these things in a wastebasket. Any wind that blew through would raise clouds of dust. Each room had its own horrendous smell, but the components of that smell were the same: sweat and body odor and garbage. Dirty clothes would pile up under the beds, and without anyone bothering to air the mattresses on a regular basis, these sweat-impregnated pads would give off odors beyond redemption. In retrospect, it seems amazing that these shit piles gave rise to no killer epidemics.

My room, on the other hand, was as sanitary as a morgue. The floor and window were spotless, the mattresses were aired each week, all pencils stood in the pencil holders, and even the curtains were laundered once a month. My roommate was clean crazy. None of the others in the dorm believed me when I told them about the curtains. They didn't know that curtains *could* be laundered. They believed, rather, that curtains were semipermanent parts of the window. "There's something wrong with that guy," they'd say, labeling him a Nazi or a storm trooper.

We didn't even have pinups. No, we had a photo of an Amsterdam canal. I had put up a nude shot, but my roommate had pulled it down. "Hey, Watanabe," he said, "I, I'm not too crazy about this kind of thing," and up went the canal photo instead. I wasn't especially attached to the nude, so I didn't protest.

"What the hell's *that*?" was the universal reaction to the Amsterdam photo whenever any of the other guys came to my room.

"Oh, Storm Trooper likes to jerk off to this," I said.

I meant it as a joke, but they all took me seriously—*so* seriously that I began to believe it myself.

Everybody sympathized with me for having pulled Storm Trooper as a roommate, but I really wasn't that upset about it. He left me alone as long as I kept my area clean, and in fact having him as my roommate made things easier for me in many ways. He did all the cleaning, he took care of sunning the mattresses, he threw out the trash. He'd give a sniff and suggest a bath for me if I'd been too busy to wash for a few days. He'd even point out when it was time for me to go to the barber's or trim my nose hair. The one thing that bothered me was the way he'd spray clouds of insecticide if he noticed a single bug in the room, because then I had to take refuge in a neighboring shit pile.

Storm Trooper was majoring in geography at a national university.

As he said it the first time we met, "I'm studying muh-muh-maps."

"You like maps?" I asked.

"Yup. When I graduate, I'm going to work for the Geographical Survey Institute and make muh-muh-maps."

I was impressed anew by the variety of dreams and goals that life could offer. This was one of the very first new impressions I received when I came to Tokyo for the first time. The thought struck me that society *needed* a few people—just a few—who were interested in and even passionate about map making. Odd, though, that someone who wanted to work for the government's Geographical Survey Institute should stutter every time he said the word *map*. Storm Trooper often didn't stutter at all, except when he pronounced the word *map*, for which it was a 100-percent certainty.

"Wha-what are *you* going to major in?" he asked me.

"Drama," I said.

"Gonna put on plays?"

"Nah, just read scripts and do research. Racine, Ionesco, Shakespeare, like that."

He said he had heard of Shakespeare but not the others. I hardly knew anything about the others myself, had just seen their names in lecture handouts.

"You like plays?" he asked.

"Not especially," I said.

This confused him, and when he was confused, his stuttering got worse. I felt sorry I had done that to him.

"I could have picked anything," I said. "Ethnology, Asian history. I just happened to pick drama, that's all," which was not the most convincing explanation I could have come up with.

"I don't get it," he said, looking as if he really didn't get it. "I like muh-muh-maps, so I decided to come to Tokyo and get my parents to se-send me money so I could study muh-muh-maps. But not you, huh?"

His approach made more sense than mine. I gave up trying to explain myself to him. Then we drew lots (matchsticks) to choose bunks. He got the upper bunk, I got the lower.

Tall, with a crewcut and high cheekbones, he always wore the same outfit: white shirt, black pants, black shoes, navy blue sweater. To these he would add a uniform jacket and black briefcase when he went to his school: a typical right-wing student. Which is why everybody called him Storm Trooper. But in fact he was 100-percent indifferent to politics. He wore a uniform because he didn't want to be bothered choosing clothes. What interested him were things like changes in the coastline or the completion of a new rail tunnel. Nothing else. He'd go on for hours once he got started on a subject like that, until you either ran away or fell asleep.

He was up at six each morning with the strains of "May Our Lord's Reign." Which is to say that that ostentatious flag-raising ritual was not entirely useless. He'd get dressed, go to the bathroom, and wash his face — forever. I sometimes got the feeling he must be taking out each tooth and washing it, one at a time. Back in the room, he would snap the wrinkles out of his towel and lay it on the radiator to dry, then return his toothbrush and soap to the shelf. Finally he'd do Radio Calisthenics with the rest of the nation.

I was used to reading late at night and sleeping until eight o'clock, so even when he started shuffling around the room and exercising, I stayed unconscious—until the part where the jumping started. He took his jumping seriously and made the bed bounce every time he hit the floor. I stood it for three days because they had told us that communal life called for a certain degree of resignation, but by the morning of the fourth day, I couldn't take it anymore.

"Hey, can you do that on the roof or someplace?" I said. "I can't sleep."

"But it's already six-thirty!" he said, open-mouthed.

"Yeah, I *know* it's six-thirty. I'm still supposed to be asleep. I don't know how to explain it exactly, but that's how it works for me."

"Anyhow, I can't do it on the roof. Somebody on the third floor would complain. Here, we're over a storeroom."

"So go out on the quad. On the lawn."

"That's no good, either. I don't have a transistor radio. I need to plug it in. And you can't do Radio Calisthenics without music."

True, his radio was an old piece of junk without batteries. Mine was a transistor portable, but it was strictly FM, for music.

"O.K., let's compromise," I said. "Do your exercises but cut out the jumping part. It's so damned noisy. Whaddya say?"

"Juh-jumping? What's that?"

"Jumping is jumping. Bouncing up and down."

"But there isn't any jumping."

My head was starting to hurt. I was ready to give up, but at least I wanted to finish making my point. I got out of bed and started bouncing up and down and singing the opening melody of NHK's Radio Calisthenics. "I'm talking about *this*," I said.

"Oh, *that*. I guess you're right. I never noticed."

"See what I mean?" I said, sitting on the edge of the bed. "Just cut out that part. I can put up with the rest. Stop jumping and let me sleep."

"But that's impossible," he said matter-of-factly. "I can't leave anything out. I've been doing the same thing every day for ten years, and once I start I do the whole routine unconsciously. If I left something out, I wouldn't be able to do any of it."

There was nothing more for me to say. What *could* I have said? The quickest way to put a stop to this was to wait for him to leave the room and throw his goddamn radio out the goddamn window, but I knew if I did that all hell would break loose. Storm Trooper treasured everything he owned. He smiled when he saw me sitting on the bed at a loss for words, and he tried to comfort me.

"Gee, Watanabe, why don't you just get up and exercise with me?" And he went off to breakfast.

NAOKO CHUCKLED when I told her the story of Storm Trooper and his Radio Calisthenics. I hadn't been trying to amuse her, but I ended up laughing myself. Though her smile vanished in an instant, I enjoyed seeing it for the first time in a long while.

We had left the train at Yotsuya and were walking along the embankment by the station. It was a Sunday afternoon in the middle of May. The brief off-and-on showers of the morning had cleared up before noon, and a south wind had swept away the low-hanging clouds. The cherry trees' brilliant green leaves stirred in the air and splashed sunlight in all directions. This was an early summer day. The people we passed had their sweaters or jackets over their shoulders or in their arms. Everyone looked happy in the warm Sunday afternoon sun. The young men playing tennis in the courts beyond the embankment had stripped down to their short pants. Only where two nuns in winter habits sat talking on a bench did the summer light seem not to reach, though both wore looks of satisfaction as they enjoyed chatting in the sun.

Fifteen minutes of walking and I was sweaty enough to take off my thick cotton shirt and go with a T-shirt. Naoko had rolled the sleeves of her light gray sweatshirt up to her elbows. The shirt was nicely faded, having obviously been laundered many times. I felt as if I had seen her in that shirt long before. This was just a feeling I had, not a clear memory. I didn't have that much to remember about Naoko at the time.

"How do you like communal living?" she asked. "Is it fun to live with a lot of other people?"

"I don't know, I've only been doing it a month or so. I guess it's not that bad, I can stand it."

She stopped at a fountain and took a sip, wiping her mouth with a white handkerchief she took from her pants pocket. Then she bent over and carefully retied her shoes.

"Do you think I could do it?"

"What? Live in a dorm?"

"Uh-huh."

"I guess it's all a matter of attitude. You could let a lot of things bother you if you wanted to—the rules, the jerks who think they're hot shit, the roommates doing Radio Calisthenics at six-thirty in the morning. But if you figure it's pretty much the same anywhere you go, you can manage."

"I guess so," she said with a nod. She seemed to be turning something over in her mind. Then she looked straight into my eyes as if peering at some unusual object. Now I saw that her eyes were so deep and clear they made my heart thump. I realized that I had never had occasion to look into her eyes like this. It was the first time the two of us had ever gone walking together or talked at such length.

"Are you thinking about living in a dorm or something?" I asked.

"Uh-uh," she said. "I was just wondering what communal life would be like. And . . ." She seemed to be trying—and failing—to find exactly the right word or expression. Then she sighed and looked down. "Oh, I don't know. Never mind."

That was the end of the conversation. She continued walking east, and I followed just behind.

Almost a year had gone by since I had last seen Naoko, and in that time she had lost so much weight as to look like a different person. The plump cheeks that had been a special feature of hers were all but gone, and her neck had become delicate and slender. Not that she was bony now or unhealthy looking: there was something natural and serene about the way she had slimmed down, as if she had been hiding in some long, narrow space until she herself had become long and narrow. And a lot prettier than I remembered. I wanted to tell her that, but couldn't find a good way to put it.

We had not planned to meet but had run into each other on the Chuo commuter line. She had decided to see a movie by herself, and I was headed for the bookstores in Kanda—nothing urgent in either case. She had suggested that we leave the train, which we happened to do in Yot-suya, where the green embankment makes for a nice place to walk by the old castle moat. Alone together, we had nothing in particular to talk about, and I wasn't quite sure why Naoko had suggested we get off the train. We had never really had much to say to each other.

Naoko started walking the minute we hit the street, and I hurried after her, keeping a yard behind. I could have closed the distance between us, but something held me back. I walked with my eyes on her shoulders and her straight black hair. She wore a big, brown barrette, and when she turned her head I caught a glimpse of a small, white ear. Now and then she would look back and say something. Sometimes it would be a remark I might have responded to, and sometimes it would be something to which I had no way to reply. Other times, I simply couldn't hear what she was saying. She didn't seem to care one way or another. Once she had finished saying whatever she wanted to say, she'd face front again and keep on walking. Oh, well, I told myself, it was a nice day for a stroll.

This was no mere stroll for Naoko, though, judging from that walk. She turned right at Iidabashi, came out at the moat, crossed the intersection at Jinbocho, climbed the hill at Ochanomizu, and came out at Hongo. From there she followed the trolley tracks to Komagome. It was a challenging route. By the time we reached Komagome, the sun was sinking and the day had become a soft spring evening.

"Where are we?" asked Naoko as if noticing our surroundings for the first time.

"Komagome," I said. "Didn't you know? We made this big arc."

"Why did we come here?"

"*You* brought us here. I was just following you."

We went to a shop by the station for a bowl of noodles. Thirsty, I had a whole beer to myself. From the time we gave our order until the time we finished eating, neither of us said a word. I was exhausted from all that walking, and she just sat there with her hands on the table, mulling something over again. All the leisure spots were crowded on this warm Sunday, they were saying on the TV news. And we just walked from Yotsuya to Komagome, I said to myself.

"Well, *you're* in good shape," I said when I had finished my noodles.

"Surprised?"

"You bet."

"I was a long-distance runner in junior high, I'll have you know. I used to do ten or fifteen kilometers. And my father took me mountain climbing on Sundays ever since I can remember. You know our house—right there, next to the mountain. I've always had strong legs."

"It doesn't show," I said.

"I know," she answered. "Everybody thinks I'm this delicate little girl. But you can't tell a book by its cover." To which she added a momentary smile.

"And that goes for me, too," I said. "I'm worn out."

"Oh, I'm sorry, I've been dragging you around all day."

"Still, I'm glad we had a chance to talk. We've never done that before, just the two of us," I said, trying without success to recall what we had talked *about*.

She was playing with the ashtray on the table.

"I wonder . . ." she began, "if you wouldn't mind . . . I mean, if it really wouldn't be any bother to you . . . Do you think we could see each other again? I know I don't have any right to be asking you this."

"Any *right*?" What do you mean by that?"

She blushed. My reaction to her request might have been a little too strong.

"I don't know . . . I can't really explain it," she said, tugging the sleeves of her sweatshirt up over the elbows and down again. Her arms shone a lovely golden down color in the lights of the shop. "I didn't mean to say *right* exactly. I was looking for another way to put it."

Elbows on the table, she stared at the calendar on the wall, almost as if she were hoping to find the proper expression there. Failing, she sighed and closed her eyes and played with her barrette.

"Never mind," I said. "I think I know what you're getting at. I'm not sure how to put it, either."

"I can never say what I want to say," continued Naoko. "It's been like this for a while now. I try to say something, but all I get are the wrong words—the wrong words or the exact *opposite* words from what I mean. I try to correct myself, and that only makes it worse. I lose track of what I was trying to say to begin with. It's like I'm split in two and playing tag with myself. One half is chasing the other half around this big, fat post. The *other* me has the right words, but this me can't catch her."

Naoko raised her face and looked into my eyes. "Does this make any sense to you?"

"Everybody feels like that to some extent," I said. "They're trying to express themselves and it bothers them when they can't get it right."

Naoko looked disappointed with my answer. "No, that's not it either," she said without further explanation.

"Anyhow, I'd be glad to see you again," I said. "I'm always free on Sundays, and walking would be good for me."

We boarded the Yamanote Line, and Naoko transferred to the Chuo Line at Shinjuku. She was living in a tiny apartment way out in the western suburb of Kokubunji.

"Tell me," she said as we parted. "Has anything changed about the way I talk?"

"I think so," I said, "but I'm not sure what. Tell you the truth, I know I saw you a lot back then, but I don't remember talking to you much."

"I guess that's true," she said. "Anyhow, can I call you on Saturday?"

"Sure. I'll be expecting to hear from you."

I FIRST MET NAOKO in the spring of my second year of high school. She was also in her second year and attending a refined girls' high school run by one of the Christian missions. The school was so refined you were considered *un*refined if you studied too much. Naoko was the girlfriend of my best (and only) friend, Kizuki. The two of them had been close almost from birth, their houses not two hundred yards apart.

As with most couples who have been together since childhood, there was a casual openness about the relationship of Kizuki and Naoko and little sense that they wanted to be alone together. They were always visiting each other's homes and eating or playing mah-jongg with each other's families. I double-dated with them any number of times. Naoko would bring a classmate for me and the four of us would go to the zoo or the pool or a movie. The girls she brought were always pretty, but a little too refined for my taste. I got along better with the somewhat cruder girls from my own public high school who were easier to talk to. I could never tell what was going on inside the pretty heads of the girls that Naoko brought along, and they probably couldn't understand me, either.

After a while, Kizuki gave up trying to arrange dates for me, and instead the three of us would do things together. Kizuki and Naoko and I: odd, but that was the most comfortable combination. Introducing a fourth person into the mix would always make things a little awkward. We were like a TV talk show, with me the guest, Kizuki the talented host, and Naoko his assistant. He was good at occupying that central position. True, he had a sarcastic side that often impressed people as arrogant, but in fact he was a considerate and fair-minded person. He would distribute his remarks and jokes fairly to Naoko and to me, taking care to see that neither of us felt left out. If one or the other stayed quiet too long, he would steer his conversation in that direction and get the person to talk. It probably looked harder than it was: he knew how to monitor and adjust the air around him on a second-by-second basis. In addition, he had a rare talent for finding the interesting parts of someone's generally uninteresting comments so that, when speaking to him, you felt that you were an exceptionally interesting person with an exceptionally interesting life.

And yet he was not the least bit sociable. I was his only real friend at school. I could never understand why such a smart and capable talker did not turn his talents to the broader world around him but remained satisfied to concentrate on our little trio. Nor could I understand why he picked me to be his friend. I was just an ordinary kid who liked to read books and listen to music and didn't stand out in any way that would prompt someone like Kizuki to pay attention to me. We hit it off right away, though. His father was a dentist, known for his professional skill and his high fees.

"Wanna double-date Sunday?" he asked me just after we met. "My girlfriend goes to a girls' school, and she'll bring along a cute one for you."

"Sure," I said, and that was how I met Naoko.

The three of us spent a lot of time together, but whenever Kizuki left the room, Naoko and I had trouble talking to each other. We never knew what to talk *about*. And in fact there was no topic of conversation that we held in common. Instead of talking, we'd drink water or toy with something on the table and wait for Kizuki to come back and start the conversation up again. Naoko was not particularly talkative, and I was more of a listener than a talker, so I felt uncomfortable when I was left alone with her. Not that we were incompatible: we just had nothing to talk about.

Naoko and I saw each other exactly once after Kizuki's funeral. Two weeks after the event, we met at a coffee house to take care of some minor matter, and when that was finished we had nothing more to say. I tried raising several different topics, but none of them led anywhere. And when Naoko did talk, there was a certain edge to her voice. She seemed angry with me, but I had no idea why. We never saw each other again until that day we happened to meet on the Chuo Line in Tokyo a year later.

NAOKO MIGHT HAVE BEEN ANGRY with me because I, and not she, had been the last one to see Kizuki alive. That may not be the best way to put it, but I more or less understood how she felt. I would have traded places with her if I could have, but finally what had happened had happened, and there was nothing I could do about it.

It had been a nice afternoon in May. After lunch, Kizuki suggested we cut classes and go play pool or something. I had no special interest in my afternoon classes, so together we left school, ambled down the hill to a billiards parlor on the harbor, and shot four games. When I won the first, easygoing game, he got serious and won the other three. This meant that I paid, according to our custom. Kizuki made not a single wisecrack as we played, which was most unusual. We had a smoke afterward.

"Why so serious?" I asked.

"I didn't want to lose today," said Kizuki with a satisfied smile.

He died that night in his garage. He led a rubber hose from the exhaust pipe of his N-360 to a window, taped over the gap in the window, and revved the engine. I have no idea how long it took him to die. His parents had been out visiting a sick relative, and when they opened the garage to put their car away, he was already dead. His radio was going, and a gas station receipt was tucked under the windshield wiper.

Kizuki had left no suicide note, and had no motive that anyone could think of. Because I had been the last one to see him, I was called in for questioning by the police. I told the investigating officer that Kizuki had given no indication of what he was about to do, that he had been exactly the same as always. The policeman had obviously formed a poor impression of both Kizuki and of me, as if it was perfectly natural for the kind of person who would skip classes and shoot pool to commit suicide. A small article in the paper brought the affair to a close. Kizuki's parents got rid of his red N-360. For a time, a white flower marked his homeroom desk.

In the ten months between Kizuki's death and graduation, I was unable to find a place for myself in the world around me. I started sleeping with one of the girls at school, but that didn't last six months. Nothing about her really got to me. I applied to a private university in Tokyo, the kind of school with an entrance exam for which I wouldn't have to study much, and I passed without exhilaration. The girl asked me not to go to Tokyo— "It's five hundred miles from here!" she pleaded—but I had to get away from Kobe at any cost. I wanted to begin a new life where I didn't know a soul.

"You don't give a damn about me anymore, now that you've slept with me," she said, crying.

"That's not true," I insisted. "I just need to get away from this town." But she was not prepared to understand me. And so we parted. Thinking about all the things that made her so much nicer than the other girls at home, I sat on the bullet train to Tokyo feeling terrible about what I'd done, but there was no way to undo it. I would try to forget her.

There was only one thing for me to do when I started my new life in the dorm: stop taking everything so seriously; establish a proper distance between myself and everything else. Forget about green-felt pool tables and red N-360s and white flowers on school desks; about smoke rising from tall crematorium smokestacks, and chunky paperweights in police interrogation rooms. It seemed to work at first. I tried hard to forget, but there remained inside me a vague knot-of-air kind of thing. And as time went by, the knot began to take on a clear and simple form, a form that I am able to put into words, like this:

Death exists, not as the opposite but as a part of life.

Translated into words, it's a cliché, but at the time I felt it not as words but as that knot of air inside me. Death exists—in a paperweight, in four red and white balls on a billiard table—and we go on living and breathing it into our lungs like fine dust.

Until that time, I had understood death as something entirely separate from and independent of life. The hand of death is bound to take us, I had felt, but until the day it reaches out for us, it leaves us alone. This had seemed to me the simple, logical truth. Life is here, death is over there. I am here, not over there.

The night Kizuki died, however, I lost the ability to see death (and life) in such simple terms. Death was not the opposite of life. It was already here, within my being, it had always been here, and no struggle would permit me to forget that. When it took the seventeen-year-old Kizuki that night in May, death took me as well.

I lived through the following spring, at eighteen, with that knot of air in my chest, but I struggled all the while against becoming serious. Becoming serious was not the same thing as approaching truth, I sensed, however vaguely. But death was a fact, a serious fact, no matter how you looked at it. Stuck inside this suffocating contradiction, I went on endlessly spinning in circles. Those were strange days, now that I look back at them. In the midst of life, everything revolved around death.

three

NAOKO CALLED ME THE FOLLOWING SATURDAY, AND THAT SUNDAY we had a date. I suppose I can call it a date. I can't think of a better word for it.

As before, we walked the streets. We stopped someplace for coffee, walked some more, had supper in the evening, and said good-bye. Again, she talked only in snatches, but this didn't seem to bother her, and I made no special effort to keep the conversation going. We talked about whatever came to mind—our daily routines, our colleges; each a little fragment that led nowhere. We said nothing at all about the past. And mainly, we walked—and walked, and walked. Fortunately, Tokyo is such a big city, we could never have covered it all.

We kept on walking like this almost every weekend. She would lead, and I would follow close behind. Naoko had a variety of barrettes and always wore them with her right ear exposed. I remember her most clearly this way, from the back. She would toy with her barrette whenever she felt embarrassed by something. And she was always dabbing at her mouth with a handkerchief. She did this whenever she had something to say. The more I observed these habits of hers, the more I came to like her.

Naoko went to a girls' college on the rural western edge of Tokyo, a nice little school famous for its teaching of English. Nearby was a narrow irrigation canal with clean, clear water, and Naoko and I would often walk along its banks. Sometimes she would invite me up to her apartment and cook for me. It never seemed to concern her that the two of us were in such close quarters together. The room was small and neat and so lacking in frills that only the stockings drying in the corner by the window gave any hint that a girl lived there. She led a spare, simple life with hardly any friends. No one who had known her in high school could have imagined her like this. Back then, she had dressed with real flair and surrounded herself with a million friends. When I saw her room, I realized that, like me, she had wanted to go away to college and begin a new life far from anyone she knew.

"Know why I chose this school?" she said with a smile. "Because nobody from home was coming here. We were all supposed to go some-place more chic. You know what I mean."

My relationship with Naoko was not without its progress, though. Little by little, she grew more accustomed to me, and I to her. When summer vacation ended and the new term started, Naoko began walking next to me as if it were the most natural thing in the world to do. She saw me as a friend now, I concluded, and walking side by side with such a beautiful girl was by no means painful for me. We kept walking all over Tokyo in the same undirected way, climbing hills, crossing rivers and rail lines, just walking and walking with no destination in mind. We forged straight ahead, as if our walking were a religious ritual meant to heal our wounded spirits. If it rained, we used umbrellas, but in any case we walked.

Then came autumn, and the dormitory grounds were buried in zelkova leaves. The fragrance of a new season arrived when I put on my first sweater. Having worn out one pair of shoes, I bought some new ones, of suede.

I can't seem to recall what we talked about then. Nothing special, I would guess. We continued to avoid any mention of the past and rarely mentioned Kizuki. We could face each other over coffee cups in total silence.

Naoko liked to hear me tell stories about Storm Trooper. Once he had a date with a classmate (a girl in geography, of course) but came back in the early evening looking glum. "Tell me, Wa-Wa-Watanabe, what do you talk about with gir-gir-girls?" I don't remember how I answered him, but he had picked the wrong guy to ask. In July, somebody in the dorm had taken down Storm Trooper's Amsterdam canal scene and put up a photo of the Golden Gate Bridge instead. He told me he wanted to know if Storm Trooper could masturbate to the Golden Gate Bridge. "He loved it," I "reported" later, which prompted someone else to put up an iceberg. Each time the photo changed in his absence, Storm Trooper became upset.

"Who-who-who the hell is doing this?" he asked.

"I wonder," I said. "But what's the difference? They're all nice pictures. You should be grateful."

"Yeah, I guess so, but it's weird."

My stories of Storm Trooper always made Naoko laugh. Not many things succeeded in doing that, so I talked about him often, though I was not exactly proud of myself for using him this way. He just happened to be the youngest son in a not-too-wealthy family who had grown up a little too serious for his own good. Making maps was the one small dream of his one small life. Who had the right to make fun of him for that?

By then, however, "Storm Trooper jokes" had become an indispensable source of dormitory talk, and there was no way for me to undo what I had done. Besides, the sight of Naoko's smiling face had become my own special source of pleasure. I went on supplying everyone with new stories.

Naoko asked me one time—just once—if I had a girl I liked. I told her about the one I had left behind in Kobe. "She was nice," I said, "I enjoyed sleeping with her, and I miss her every now and then, but finally, she didn't move me. I don't know, sometimes I think I've got this hard kernel in my heart, and nothing much can get inside it. I doubt if I can really love anybody."

"Have you ever *been* in love?" Naoko asked.

"Never," I said.

She didn't ask me more than that.

When autumn ended and cold winds began tearing through the city, Naoko would often walk pressed against my arm. I could sense her breathing through the thick cloth of her duffle coat. She would entwine her arm with mine, or cram her hand in my pocket, or, when it was really cold, cling tightly to my arm, shivering. None of this had any special meaning. I just kept walking with my hands shoved in my pockets. Our rubber-soled shoes made hardly any sound on the pavement, except for the dry crackling when we trod the broad, withered leaves of sycamore on the roads. I felt sorry for Naoko whenever I heard that sound. My arm was not the one she needed, but the arm of someone else. My warmth was not what she needed, but the warmth of someone else. I felt almost guilty being me.

As the winter deepened, the transparent clarity of Naoko's eyes seemed to increase. It was a clarity that had nowhere to go. Sometimes Naoko would lock her eyes on mine for no apparent reason. She seemed to be searching for something and this would give me a strange, lonely, helpless sort of feeling.

I wondered if she was trying to convey something to me, something she could not put into words—something prior to words that she could not grasp within herself and which therefore had no hope of ever turning into words. Instead, she would fiddle with her barrette, dab at the corners of her mouth with a handkerchief, or look into my eyes in that meaningless way. I wanted to hold her tight when she did these things, but I would hesitate and hold back. I was afraid I might hurt her if I did that. And so the two of us kept walking the streets of Tokyo, Naoko searching for words in space.

The guys in the dorm would always razz me when I got a call from Naoko or went out on a Sunday morning. They assumed, naturally enough, that I had found a girlfriend. There was no way to explain the truth to them, and no need to explain it, so I let them think what they wanted to. I had to face a barrage of stupid questions in the evening—what position had we used? What was she like down there? What color underwear had she been wearing that day? I gave them the answers they wanted.

AND SO I WENT from eighteen to nineteen. Each day the sun would rise and set, the flag would be raised and lowered. Each Sunday I would have a date with my dead friend's girl. I had no idea what I was doing or what I was going to do. For my courses I would read Claudel and Racine and Eisenstein, but they meant almost nothing to me. I made no friends in classes, and hardly knew anyone in the dorm. The others in the dorm thought I wanted to be a writer, because I was always alone with a book, but I had no such ambition. There was nothing I wanted to be.

I tried to talk about this feeling with Naoko. She, at least, would be able to understand what I was feeling with some degree of precision, I thought. But I could never find the words to express myself. Strange, I seemed to have caught her word-searching sickness.

On Saturday nights I would sit by the phone in the lobby, waiting for Naoko to call. Most of the others were out on Saturday nights, so the lobby was usually deserted. I would stare at the grains of light suspended in that silent space, struggling to see into my own heart. What did I want? And what did others want from me? But I could never find the answers. Sometimes I would reach out and try to grasp the grains of light, but my fingers touched nothing.

I READ A LOT, but not a lot of different books: I like to read my favorites again and again. Back then it was Truman Capote, John Updike, Scott

Fitzgerald, Raymond Chandler, but I didn't see anyone else in my classes or the dorm reading writers like that. They liked Kazumi Takahashi, Kenzaburo Oe, Yukio Mishima, or contemporary French novelists, which was another reason I didn't have much to say to anybody but kept to myself and my books. With my eyes closed, I would touch a familiar book and draw its fragrance deep inside me. This was enough to make me happy.

At eighteen my favorite book was John Updike's *The Centaur*, but after I had read it any number of times, it began to lose some of its initial luster and yielded first place to *The Great Gatsby*. *Gatsby* stayed in first place for a long time after that. I would pull it off the shelf when the mood hit me and read a section at random. It never once disappointed me. There wasn't a boring page in the whole book. I wanted to tell people what a wonderful novel it was, but no one around me had read *The Great Gatsby* or was likely to. Urging others to read F. Scott Fitzgerald, if not a reactionary act, was not something one could do in 1968.

When I did finally meet the one person in my world who had read *Gatsby*, he and I became friends because of it. His name was Nagasawa. He was two years older than I, and because he was majoring in legal studies at the prestigious Tokyo University, he was on the fast track to national leadership. We lived in the same dorm and knew each other only by sight, until one day when I was reading *Gatsby* in a sunny spot in the dining hall. He sat down next to me and asked what I was reading. When I told him, he asked if I was enjoying it. "This is my third time through," I said, "and every time I find something new that I like even more than the last time."

"This man says he has read *The Great Gatsby* three times," he said as if to himself. "Well, any friend of *Gatsby* is a friend of mine."

And so we became friends. This happened in October.

The better I got to know Nagasawa, the stranger he seemed. I had met a lot of strange people in my day, but none as strange as Nagasawa. He was a far more voracious reader than I, but he made it a rule never to touch a book by any author who had not been dead at least thirty years. "That's the only kind of book I can trust," he said.

"It's not that I don't believe in contemporary literature," he added, "but I don't want to waste valuable time reading any book that has not had the baptism of time. Life is too short."

"What kind of authors *do* you like?" I asked, speaking in respectful tones to this man two years my senior.

"Balzac, Dante, Joseph Conrad, Dickens," he answered without hesitation.

"Not exactly fashionable."

"That's why I read them. If you only read the books that everyone else is reading, you can only think what everyone else is thinking. That's the world of hicks and slobs. Real people would be ashamed of themselves doing that. Haven't you noticed, Watanabe? You and I are the only real ones in the dorm. The other guys are crap."

This took me off guard. "How can you say that?"

" 'Cause it's true. I know. I can see it. It's like we have marks on our foreheads. And besides, we've both read *The Great Gatsby.*"

I did some quick calculating. "But Fitzgerald's been dead only twenty-eight years," I said.

"So what? Two years? Fitzgerald's advanced."

No one else in the dorm knew that Nagasawa was a secret reader of classic novels, nor would it have mattered if they had. Nagasawa was known for being smart. He breezed into Tokyo University, he got good grades, he would take the Civil Service Exam, join the Foreign Ministry, and become a diplomat. He came from a super family. His father owned a big hospital in Nagoya, and his brother had also graduated from Tokyo, gone on to medical school, and would one day inherit the hospital. Nagasawa always had plenty of money in his pocket, and he carried himself with real dignity. People treated him with respect, even the dorm head. When he asked someone to do something, the person would do it without protest. There was no choice in the matter.

Nagasawa had a certain inborn quality that drew people to him and made them follow him. He knew how to stand at the head of the pack, to assess the situation, to give precise and tactful instructions that others would obey. Above his head hung an aura that revealed his powers like an angel's halo, the mere sight of which would inspire awe in people for this superior being. Which is why it shocked everyone that Nagasawa chose me, a person with no distinctive qualities, to be his special friend. People I hardly knew treated me with a certain respect because of it, but what they did not seem to realize was that the reason for my having been chosen was a simple one, namely that I treated Nagasawa with none of the adulation he received from other people. I had a definite interest in the strange, complex aspects of his nature, but none of those other things—his grades, his aura, his looks—impressed me. This must have been something new for him.

There were sides to Nagasawa's personality that conflicted in the extreme. Even I would be moved by his kindness at times, but he could, just as easily, be malicious and cruel. He was both a spirit of amazing loftiness and an irredeemable man of the gutter. He could charge forward, the optimistic leader, even as his heart writhed in a swamp of loneliness. I saw these paradoxical qualities of his from the start, and I could never understand why they weren't just as obvious to everyone else. He lived in his own special hell.

Still, I think I always managed to view him in the most favorable light. His greatest virtue was his honesty. Not only would he never lie, he would always acknowledge his shortcomings. He never tried to hide things that might embarrass him. And where I was concerned, he was unfailingly kind and supportive. Had he not been, my life in the dorm would have been far more unpleasant than it was. Still, I never once opened my heart to him, and in that sense my relationship with Nagasawa stood in stark contrast to my relationship with Kizuki. The first time I saw Nagasawa drunk and tormenting a girl, I promised myself never, under any circumstances, to open myself up to him.

There were several "Nagasawa legends" that circulated through the dorm. According to one, he supposedly once ate three slugs. Another gave him a huge penis and had him sleeping with over a hundred girls.

The slug story was true. He told me so himself. "Three big mothers," he said. "Swallowed 'em whole."

"What the hell for?"

"Well, it happened the first year I came to live here," he said. "There was some shit between the freshmen and the upperclassmen. Started in April and finally came to a head in September. I went to work things out with the upperclassmen as freshman representative. Real right-wing assholes. They had these wooden kendo swords, and 'working things out' was probably the last thing they wanted to do. So I said, 'All right, let's put an end to this. Do what you want to me, but leave the other guys alone.' So they said, 'O.K., let's see you swallow a couple of slugs.' 'Fine,' I said, 'let's have 'em.' The sons of bitches went out and got three huge slugs. And I swallowed 'em."

"What was it like?"

"'What was it like?' You have to swallow one yourself. The way it slides down your throat and into your stomach . . . it's cold, and it leaves this disgusting aftertaste . . . yuck, I get chills just thinking about it. I wanted to puke but I fought it. I mean, if I had puked 'em up, I would have just had to swallow 'em all over again. So I kept 'em down. All three of 'em."

"Then what happened?"

"I went back to my room and drank a bunch of salt water. What else could I do?"

"Yeah, I guess so."

"But after that, nobody could say a thing to me. Not even the upperclassmen. I'm the only guy in this place who can swallow three slugs."

"I bet you are."

Finding out about his penis size was easy enough. I just went to the dorm's communal bath with him. He had a big one, all right. But a hundred girls was probably an exaggeration. "Maybe seventy-five," he said. "I can't remember them all, but I'm sure it's at least seventy." When I told him I had slept with only one, he said, "Oh, we can fix that, easy. Come with me next time. I'll get you one like nothing."

I didn't believe him, but he turned out to be right. It was easy. Almost too easy, with all the excitement of stale beer. We went to a bar in Shibuya or Shinjuku (he had his favorites), found a pair of girls (the world was full of pairs of girls), talked to them, drank, went to a hotel, and had sex with them. He was a great talker. Not that he had anything great to say, but girls would get carried away listening to him, they'd drink too much and end up sleeping with him. I guess they enjoyed being with somebody so nice and handsome and clever. And the most amazing thing was that, just because I was with him, I seemed to become as fascinating to them as he was. Nagasawa would urge me to talk, and girls would respond to me with the same smiles of admiration they gave him. His magic did it, a real talent he had that impressed me every time. Compared with Nagasawa, Kizuki's conversational gift was child's play. This was a whole different level of accomplishment. As much as I found myself caught up in Nagasawa's power, though, I still missed Kizuki. I felt a new admiration for his sincerity. Whatever talents he had he would share with Naoko and me alone, while Nagasawa was bent on disseminating his considerable gifts to all around him. Not that he was dying to sleep with the girls he found: it was just a game to him.

I was not too crazy about sleeping with girls I didn't know. It was an easy way to take care of my sex drive, of course, and I did enjoy all the holding and touching, but I hated the morning after. I'd wake up and find this strange girl sleeping next to me, and the room would reek of alcohol, and the bed and the lighting and the curtains had that special "love hotel" garishness, and my head would be in a hungover fog. Then the girl would wake up and start groping around for her underwear and while she was putting on her stockings she'd say something like, "I hope you used one last night. It's the worst day of the month for me." Then she'd sit in front of a mirror and start grumbling about her aching head or her uncooperative makeup as she redid her lipstick or attached her false eyelashes. I would have preferred not to spend the whole night with them, but you can't worry about a midnight curfew while you're seducing women (which runs counter to the laws of physics anyway), so I'd go out with an overnight pass. This meant I had to stay put until morning and go back to the dorm filled with self-loathing and disillusionment, sunlight stabbing my eyes, mouth coated with sand, head belonging to someone else.

When I had slept with three or four girls this way, I asked Nagasawa, "After you've done this seventy times, doesn't it begin to seem kind of pointless?"

"That proves you're a decent human being," he said. "Congratulations. There is absolutely nothing to be gained from sleeping with one strange woman after another. It just tires you out and makes you disgusted with yourself. It's the same for me."

"So why the hell do you keep it up?"

"Hard to say. Hey, you know that thing Dostoyevsky wrote on gambling? It's like that. When you're surrounded by endless possibilities, one of the hardest things you can do is pass them up. See what I mean?"

"Sort of."

"Look. The sun goes down. The girls come out and drink. They wander around, looking for something. I can give them that something. It's the easiest thing in the world, like drinking water from a spigot. Before you know it, I've got 'em down. It's what they expect. That's what I mean by possibility. It's all around you. How can you ignore it? You have a certain ability and the opportunity to use it: can you keep your mouth shut and let it pass?"

"I don't know, I've never been in a situation like that," I said with a smile. "I can't imagine what it's like."

"Count your blessings," Nagasawa said.

His womanizing was the reason Nagasawa lived in a dorm despite his affluent background. Worried that Nagasawa would do nothing else if allowed to live alone in Tokyo, his father had compelled him to live all four years of college in the dormitory. Not that it mattered much to Nagasawa himself. He was not going to let a few rules bother him. Whenever he felt like it, he would get overnight permission and go girl hunting or spend the night in his girlfriend's apartment. These permissions were not easy to get, but for him they were like free passes—and for me, too, as long as he did the asking.

Nagasawa did have a steady girlfriend, one he'd been going out with since his freshman year. Her name was Hatsumi, and she was the same age as Nagasawa. I had met her a few times and found her to be a very nice girl. She didn't have the kind of looks that immediately attracted attention, and in fact she was so ordinary that when I first met her I had to wonder why Nagasawa couldn't do better, but anyone who talked to her took an immediate liking to her. Quiet, intelligent, funny, caring, she always dressed with wonderful good taste. I liked her a lot and knew that if I could have a girlfriend like Hatsumi, I wouldn't be sleeping around with a bunch of easy marks. She liked me, too, and tried hard to fix me up with a freshman in her club so we could go out on double dates, but I would make up excuses to keep from repeating my past mistakes. Hatsumi went to the absolute top girls' college in the country, and there was no way I was going to be able to talk to one of those super-rich princesses.

Hatsumi had a pretty good idea that Nagasawa was sleeping around, but she never complained to him. She was seriously in love with him, but she never made demands.

"I don't deserve a girl like Hatsumi," Nagasawa once said to me. I had to agree with him.

THAT WINTER I FOUND a part-time job in a little record store in Shinjuku. It didn't pay much, but the work was easy—just watching the place three nights a week—and they let me buy records cheap. For Christmas I bought Naoko a Henry Mancini record with a track of her favorite, "Dear Heart." I wrapped it myself and added a bright red ribbon. She gave me a pair of woolen gloves that she had knitted herself. The thumbs were a little short, but the gloves did keep my hands warm.

"Oh, I'm sorry," she said, blushing. "What a bad job!"

"Don't worry, they fit fine," I said, holding my gloved hands out to her.

"Well, at least you won't have to shove your hands in your pockets, I guess."

Naoko didn't go home to Kobe for break that winter. I sort of stuck around Tokyo, too, working in the record store right up to the end of the year. I didn't have anything especially fun to do in Kobe or anyone I wanted to see. With the dorm's dining hall closed for the holiday, I went to Naoko's apartment for my meals. On New Year's Eve we had rice cakes and soup like everybody else.

A lot happened in late January and February that year, 1969.

At the end of January, Storm Trooper went to bed with a raging fever, which meant I had to stand Naoko up that day. I had gone to a lot of trouble to get my hands on some free tickets for a concert. Naoko had been especially eager to go because the orchestra was performing one of her favorites, Brahms's fourth symphony. But with Storm Trooper tossing around in bed on the verge of what looked like an agonizing death, I couldn't just go off and leave him, and I couldn't find anyone crazy enough to nurse him in my place. I bought some ice and used several layers of vinyl bags to hold it on his forehead, wiped his sweat with cold towels, took his temperature every hour, and even changed his undershirt for him. The fever stayed high for a full day, but on the morning of the second day he jumped out of bed and started exercising as if nothing had happened, and his temperature was absolutely normal. It was hard to believe he was a human being.

"Weird," said Storm Trooper. "I've never run a fever in my life." It was almost as if he were blaming me.

This made me mad. "But you *did* have a fever," I insisted, showing him the two wasted tickets.

"Good thing they were free," he said. I wanted to grab his radio and throw it out the window, but instead I went back to bed with a headache.

It snowed several times in February.

Near the end of the month I got into a stupid fight with one of the upperclassmen on my floor and took a punch at him. He hit his head against the concrete wall, but he wasn't badly injured, and Nagasawa straightened things out for me. Still, I was called into the dorm head's office and given a warning, after which I grew increasingly uncomfortable living in the dormitory.

The academic year ended in March, but I came up a few credits short.

My grades were mediocre—mostly Cs and Ds with a few Bs. Naoko had all the credits she needed to begin the spring term as a full-fledged sophomore. We had completed one full cycle of the seasons.

HALFWAY THROUGH APRIL Naoko turned twenty. She was seven months older than I was, my own birthday being in November. There was something strange about Naoko's becoming twenty. I felt as if the only thing that made sense, whether for Naoko or for me, was to keep going back and forth between eighteen and nineteen. After eighteen would come nineteen, and after nineteen, eighteen. Of course. But she turned twenty. And in the fall, I would do the same. Only the dead stay seventeen forever.

It rained on her birthday. After classes I bought a cake nearby and took the streetcar to her apartment. We ought to have a celebration, I had said. I probably would have wanted the same thing if our positions had been reversed. It must be hard to pass your twentieth birthday alone. The streetcar had been packed, and it had pitched wildly, so that by the time I arrived at Naoko's room the cake was looking more like the Roman Colosseum than anything. Still, once I had managed to stand up the twenty candles I had brought along, light them, close the curtains, and turn out the lights, we had the makings of a birthday party. Naoko opened a bottle of wine. We drank, had some cake, and enjoyed a simple dinner.

"I don't know, it's stupid being twenty," she said. "I'm just not ready. It feels weird. Like somebody's pushing me from behind."

"I've got seven months to get ready," I said with a laugh.

"You're so lucky! Still nineteen!" said Naoko with a hint of envy.

While we ate I told her about Storm Trooper's new sweater. Until then he had had only one, a navy blue high school sweater, so two was a big move for him. The sweater itself was a nice one, red and black with a knitted deer motif, but on him it made everybody laugh. He couldn't figure out what was going on.

"Wha-what's so funny, Watanabe?" he asked, sitting next to me in the dining hall. "Is something stuck to my forehead?"

"Nothing," I said, trying to keep a straight face. "There's nothing funny. Nice sweater."

"Thanks," he said, beaming.

Naoko loved the story. "I *have* to meet him," she said. "Just once."

"No way," I said. "You'd laugh in his face."

"You think so?"

"I'd bet on it. I see him every day, and still I can't help laughing sometimes."

We cleared the table and sat on the floor, listening to music and drinking the rest of the wine. She drank two glasses in the time it took me to finish one.

Naoko was unusually talkative that night. She told me about her childhood, her school, her family. Each episode was a long one, done with the painstaking detail of a miniature. I was amazed at the power of her memory, but as I sat listening it began to dawn on me that there was something wrong with the way she was telling these stories: something strange, even warped. Each tale had its own internal logic, but the link from one to the next was odd. Before you knew it, story A had turned into story B contained in A, and then came C from something in B, with no end in sight. I found things to say in response at first, but after a while I stopped trying. I put on a record, and when it ended I lifted the needle and put on another one. After the last record I went back to the first. She had only six all together. The cycle started with *Sgt. Pepper's Lonely Hearts Club Band* and ended with Bill Evans's *Waltz for Debbie*. Rain fell past the window. Time moved slowly. Naoko went on talking by herself.

It eventually dawned on me what was wrong: Naoko was taking great care as she spoke not to touch on certain things. One of those things was Kizuki, of course, but there was more than Kizuki. And though she had certain subjects she was determined to avoid, she went on endlessly and in incredible detail about the most trivial and inane things. I had never heard her speak with such intensity before, and so I did nothing to interrupt her.

Once the clock hit eleven, though, I began to feel nervous. She had been talking nonstop for over four hours. I had to worry about the last train, and my midnight curfew. I saw my chance and cut in.

"Time for the troops to go home," I said, looking at my watch. "Last train's coming."

My words did not seem to reach her, though. Or, if they did, she was unable to grasp their meaning. She clamped her mouth shut for a split second, then went on with her story. I gave up and, shifting to a more comfortable position, drank what was left of the second bottle of wine. I figured I had better let her talk herself out. The curfew and the last train would have to take care of themselves.

She did not go on for long, though. Before I knew it, she had stopped talking. The ragged end of the last word she spoke seemed to float in the air, where it had been torn off. She had not actually finished what she was saying. Her words had simply evaporated. She had been trying to go on, but had come up against nothing. Something was gone now, and I was probably the one who had destroyed it. My words might have finally reached her, taken their time to be understood, and obliterated whatever energy it was that had kept her talking so long. Lips slightly parted, she turned her half-focused eyes on mine. She looked like some kind of machine that had been humming along until someone pulled the plug. Her eyes appeared clouded, as if covered by a thin, translucent membrane.

"Sorry to interrupt," I said, "but it's getting late, and . . ."

One big tear spilled from her eye, ran down her cheek, and splattered on a record jacket. Once that first tear broke free, the rest followed in an unbroken stream. Naoko bent forward where she sat on the floor and pressing her palms to the mat, she began to cry with the force of a person vomiting on all fours. Never in my life had I seen anyone cry with such intensity. I reached out and placed a hand on her trembling shoulder. Then, all but instinctively, I took her in my arms. Pressed against me, her whole body trembling, she continued to cry without a sound. My shirt became damp—and then soaked—with her tears and hot breath. Soon her fingers began to move across my back as if in search of something, some important something that had always been there. Supporting her weight with my left arm, I used my right hand to caress her soft straight hair. And I waited. In that position, I waited for Naoko to stop crying. And I went on waiting. But Naoko's crying never stopped.

I SLEPT WITH NAOKO that night. Was it the right thing to do? That I cannot tell. Even now, almost twenty years later, I can't be sure. I guess I'll never know. But at the time, it was all I could do. She was in a heightened state of tension and confusion, and she made it clear that she wanted me to give her release. I turned the lights down and began, one piece at a time, and with the gentlest touch I could manage, to remove her clothes. Then I took off my own. It was warm enough, that rainy April night, for us to cling to each other's nakedness without a sense of chill. We explored each other's bodies in the darkness without words. I kissed her and enfolded her soft breasts in my hands. She clutched at my erection. Her opening was warm and wet and asking for me.

And yet, when I went inside her, Naoko tensed with pain. Was this her first time? I asked, and she nodded. Now it was my turn to be confused. I had assumed that Naoko had been sleeping with Kizuki all that time. I went in as far as I could and stayed that way for a long time, holding Naoko, without moving. And then, as she began to seem more calm, I allowed myself to move inside her, taking a long time to come to climax, with slow, gentle movements. Her arms tightened around me at the end, when at last she broke her silence. Her cry was the saddest sound of orgasm I had ever heard.

When everything had ended, I asked Naoko why she had never slept with Kizuki. This was a mistake. No sooner had I asked the question than she took her arms from me and started crying soundlessly again. I pulled her bedding from the closet, spread it on the mat floor, and put her in beneath the covers. Smoking, I watched the endless April rain beyond the window.

THE RAIN HAD STOPPED when morning came. Naoko was sleeping with her back to me. Or maybe she hadn't slept at all. Whether she was awake or asleep, all words had left her lips, and her body now seemed stiff, almost frozen. I tried several times to talk to her, but she would not answer or move. I stared for a long time at her naked shoulder, but in the end I lost all hope of eliciting a response and decided to get up.

The floor was still littered with record jackets and glasses and wine bottles and the ashtray I had been using. Half the caved-in birthday cake remained on the table. It was as if time had come to a sudden stop here. I picked up the things off the floor and drank two glasses of water at the sink. On Naoko's desk lay a dictionary and a French verb chart. On the wall above the desk hung a calendar, one without an illustration or photo of any kind, just the numbers of the days of the month. Neither were there memos or marks written next to any of the figures.

I picked my clothes up off the floor and put them on. The front of my shirt was still damp and chilly. It had Naoko's smell. On the notepad lying on the desk I wrote, "I'd like to have a good, long talk with you once you've calmed down. Please call me soon. Happy Birthday." I took one last look at Naoko's shoulder, stepped outside, and quietly shut the door.

A WEEK WENT BY, but no call came. Naoko's apartment house had no system for summoning people to the phone, and so on Sunday morning I took the train out to Kokubunji. She was not there, and the name had been removed from her door. The windows and storm shutters were closed up tight. The manager told me that Naoko had moved out three days earlier. Where she had moved to, he had no idea.

I went back to the dorm and wrote a long letter addressed to Naoko at her home in Kobe. Wherever she was, they would forward it to her at least.

I gave her an honest account of my feelings. There was a lot I still didn't understand, I said, and though I was trying hard to understand, it would take time. Where I would be once that time had gone by, it was impossible for me to say now, which is why it was impossible for me to make promises or demands, or to set down pretty words. For one thing, we knew too little of each other. If, however, she would grant me the time, I would give it my best effort, and the two of us would come to know each other better. In any case, I wanted to see her once again and have a good, long talk. When I lost Kizuki, I lost the one person to whom I could speak honestly of my feelings, and I imagined it had been the same for Naoko. She and I had probably needed each other more than either of us knew, which is probably why our relationship had taken such a major detour and become, in a sense, warped. "I probably should not have done what I did, and yet I believe that it was all I could do. The warmth and closeness I felt for you at that moment was something I had never experienced before. I need you to answer this letter. Whatever that answer may be, I need to have it."

The answer did not come.

Something inside me had dropped away, and nothing came in to fill the cavern. There was an abnormal lightness to my body, and sounds had a hollow echo to them. I went to classes more faithfully than ever. The lectures were boring, and I never talked to my classmates, but I had nothing else to do. I would sit by myself in the very front row of the lecture hall, speak to no one, and eat alone. I quit smoking.

The student strike started at the end of May. "Dismantle the university," they all screamed. Go ahead, do it, I thought. Dismantle it. Tear it apart. Crush it to bits. I don't give a damn. A breath of fresh air for me. I'm ready for anything. I'll help if you need it. Just go ahead and do it.

With the campus blockaded and lectures suspended, I started to work at a trucking company. Riding shotgun, loading and unloading trucks, that kind of stuff. It was tougher than I thought. At first I could hardly get out of bed in the morning with the pain. The money was good, though, and as long as I kept my body moving I could forget about the emptiness inside. I worked on the truck five days a week, and three nights a week I continued my job at the record store. Nights without work I spent with whiskey and books. Storm Trooper wouldn't touch whiskey and couldn't stand the smell, so when I was sprawled on my bed chugging it down straight, he would complain that the fumes made it impossible for him to study and ask me to take my bottle outside.

"*You* get the hell out," I growled at him.

"But you know drinking in the dorm is a-a-against the rules."

"I don't give a shit. *You* get out."

He stopped complaining, but now I was annoyed. I went to the roof and drank alone.

In June I wrote Naoko another long letter, addressing it again to her house in Kobe. It said pretty much the same thing as the first letter, but at the end I added this: "Waiting for your answer is one of the most painful things I have ever been through. At least let me know whether or not I hurt you." When I dropped it in the mail, I felt as if the cavern inside me had grown again.

Also during June I went out with Nagasawa twice again to sleep with girls. It was easy both times. The first girl put up a terrific struggle when I tried to get her undressed and into the hotel bed, but when I began reading alone in bed because it just wasn't worth it, she came over and started nuzzling me. And after I had done it with the second one, she started asking me all kinds of personal questions—how many girls had I slept with? Where was I from? Which school did I go to? What kind of music did I like? Had I ever read any novels by Osamu Dazai? Where would I like to go if I could travel abroad? Did I think her nipples were too big? I made up some answers and went to sleep, but next morning she said she wanted to have breakfast with me, and she kept up the stream of questions over the tasteless eggs and toast and coffee. What kind of work did my father do? Did I have good grades in high school? What month was I born? Had I ever eaten frogs? She was giving me a headache, so as soon as we had finished eating I said I had to go to work.

"Will I ever see you again?" she asked with a sad look.

"Oh, I'm sure we'll meet again somewhere before long," I said, and left. What the hell am I doing? I started wondering as soon as I was alone and feeling disgusted with myself. And yet it was all I *could* do. My body was hungering for women. All the time I was sleeping with those girls, I thought about Naoko, about the white shape of her naked body in the darkness, her sighs, the sound of the rain. The more I thought about these things, the hungrier my body grew. I went up to the roof with my whiskey and asked myself where I thought I was heading.

Finally, at the beginning of July, a letter came from Naoko. A short letter.

Please forgive me for not answering sooner. But try to understand. It took me a very long time before I was in any condition to write, and I have started this letter at least ten times. Writing is a painful process for me.

Let me begin with my conclusion. I have decided to take a year off from school. Officially, it's a leave of absence, but I suspect that I will never be going back. This will no doubt come as a surprise to you, but in fact I had been thinking about doing this for a very long time. I tried a few times to mention it to you, but I was never able to make myself begin. I was afraid even to pronounce the words.

Try not to be so worked up about things. Whatever happened—or didn't happen—the end result would have been the same. This may not be the best way to put it, and I'm sorry if it hurts you. What I am trying to tell you is, I don't want you to blame yourself for what happened with me. It is something I have to take on all by myself. I had been putting it off for more than a year, and so I ended up making things very difficult for you. There is probably no way to put it off any longer.

After I moved out of my apartment, I came back to my family's house in

Kobe and was seeing a doctor for a while. He tells me there is a place in the hills outside Kyoto that would be perfect for me, and I'm thinking of spending a little time there. It's not exactly a hospital, more a sanatorium kind of thing with a far freer style of treatment. I'll leave the details for another letter. What I need now is to rest my nerves in a quiet place cut off from the world.

I feel grateful in my own way for the year of companionship you gave me. Please believe that much even if you believe nothing else. You are not the one who hurt me. I myself am the one who did that. This is truly how I feel.

For now, however, I am not prepared to see you. It's not that I don't *want* to see you: I'm simply not prepared for it. The moment I feel ready, I will write to you. Perhaps then we can get to know each other better. As you say, this is probably what we should do: get to know each other better.

Good-bye

I read Naoko's letter again and again, and each time I read it I would be filled with that same unbearable sadness I used to feel whenever Naoko herself stared into my eyes. I had no way to deal with it, no place I could take it to or hide it away. Like the wind passing over my body, it had neither shape nor weight, nor could I wrap myself in it. Objects in the scene would drift past me, but the words they spoke never reached my ears.

I continued to spend my Saturday nights in the lobby. There was no hope of a phone call, but I didn't know what else to do with the time. I would switch on the baseball game and pretend to watch it as I cut the empty space between me and the television set in two, then cut each half in two again, over and over, until I had fashioned a space small enough to hold in my hand.

I would switch the set off at ten, go back to my room, and go to sleep.

AT THE END OF THE MONTH, Storm Trooper gave me a firefly. It was in an instant coffee jar with air holes in the lid and containing some blades of grass and a little water. In the bright room the firefly looked like an ordinary black bug you'd find by a pond somewhere, but Storm Trooper insisted that it was the real thing. "I know a firefly when I see one," he said, and I had no reason or basis to dispute him.

"Fine," I said. "It's a firefly." It had a sleepy look on its face, but it kept trying to climb up the slippery glass walls of the jar and falling back.

"I found it in the quad," he said.

"Here? By the dorm?"

"Sure. You know the hotel down the street? They release fireflies in their garden for summer guests. This one made it over here."

Storm Trooper was busy stuffing clothes and notebooks into his black Boston bag as he spoke.

We were several weeks into summer vacation, and Storm Trooper and I were almost the only ones left in the dorm. I had continued my jobs rather than go back to Kobe, and he had stayed on for a practical training session. Now that the training had ended, he was going back to the mountains of Yamanashi.

"You could give this to your girlfriend," he said. "I'm sure she'd love it."

"Thanks," I said.

After dark the dorm was hushed, like a ruin. The flag had been lowered and the lights glowed in the windows of the dining hall. With so few students left, they turned on only half the lights in the place, keeping the right half dark and the left half lighted. Still, the smell of dinner drifted up to us—some kind of cream stew.

I took my bottled firefly to the roof. No one else was up there. A white undershirt hung on a clothesline where someone had forgotten to take it in, waving in the evening breeze like the discarded shell of some huge insect. I climbed a steel ladder in the corner of the roof to the top of the dormitory's water tank. The tank was still warm with the heat of the sunlight it had absorbed during the day. I sat in the narrow space atop the tank, leaning against the handrail and coming face-to-face with a white moon only slightly short of full. The lights of Shinjuku glowed to the right, and Ikebukuro to the left. Car headlights flowed in brilliant streams from one pool of light to the other. A dull roar of jumbled sounds hung over the city like a cloud.

The firefly made a faint glow in the bottom of the jar, its light too weak, its color too pale. I hadn't seen a firefly in years, but the ones in my memory sent a far more intense light into the summer darkness, and that brilliant, burning image was the one that had stayed with me all that time.

Maybe this firefly was on the verge of death. I gave the jar a few shakes. The firefly bumped against the glass walls and tried to fly, but its light remained dim.

I tried to recall when I had last seen fireflies, and where it might have been. I could see the scene in my mind, but was unable to recall the time or place. I could hear the sound of water in the darkness and see an old-fashioned brick sluice. It had a handle you could turn to open and close the gate. The stream it controlled was small enough to be hidden by the grass on its banks. The night was dark, so dark I couldn't see my feet when I turned out my flashlight. Hundreds of fireflies drifted over the pool of water held back by the sluice gate, their hot glow reflected in the water like a shower of sparks.

I closed my eyes and steeped myself in that long-ago darkness. I heard the wind with unusual clarity. Far from strong, the wind swept past me, leaving strangely brilliant trails in the darkness. I opened my eyes to find the darkness of the summer night a few degrees deeper than it had been.

I twisted open the lid of the jar and took the firefly out, setting it on the two-inch lip of the water tank. It seemed not to grasp its new surroundings. It hobbled around the head of a steel bolt, catching its legs on curling scabs of paint. It moved to the right until it found its way blocked, then circled back to the left. Finally, with some effort, it mounted the head of the bolt and crouched there for a while, unmoving, as if it had taken its last breath.

Still leaning against the handrail, I studied the firefly. Neither I nor it made a move for a very long time. The wind continued sweeping past the two of us while the numberless leaves of the zelkova tree rustled in the darkness.

I waited forever.

Only much later did the firefly take to the air. As if some thought had suddenly come to it, the firefly spread its wings, and in a moment it had flown past the handrail to float in the pale darkness. It traced a swift arc by the side of the water tank as if trying to bring back a lost interval in time. And then, after hovering there for a few seconds as if to watch its curved line of light blend into the wind, it finally flew off to the east.

Long after the firefly had disappeared, the trail of its light remained inside me, its pale, faint glow hovering on and on in the thick darkness behind my eyelids like a lost soul.

More than once I tried stretching my hand out in that darkness. My fingers touched nothing. The faint glow remained, just beyond their grasp.

four

DURING SUMMER BREAK THE UNIVERSITY CALLED IN THE RIOT police, who broke down the barricades and arrested the students inside. This was nothing special. It's what all the schools were doing at the time. The universities were not so easily "dismantled." Massive amounts of capital had been invested in them, and they were not about to dissolve just because a few students had gone wild. And in fact those students who had sealed the campus had not wanted to dismantle the university either. All they had really wanted was to shift the balance of power within the university structure, a matter about which I could not have cared less. And so, when the strike was crushed, I felt nothing.

I went to the campus in September expecting to find rubble. The place was untouched. The library's books had not been carted off, the professors' offices had not been destroyed, the student affairs office had not been burned to the ground. I was thunderstruck. What the hell had those guys been doing behind the barricades?

When the strike was defused and lectures started up again under police occupation, the first ones to take their seats in the classrooms were those assholes who had led the strike. As if nothing had ever happened, they sat there taking notes and answering "here" when roll was called. I found this incredible. After all, the strike resolution was still in effect. There had been no declaration bringing it to an end. All that had happened was that the university had called in the riot police and torn down the barricades, but the strike itself was supposed to be continuing. The assholes had screamed their heads off at the time of the strike resolution, denouncing students who opposed the strike (or even expressed their doubts about it), at times even trying them in their own kangaroo courts. I made a point of visiting those former leaders and asking why they were attending classes instead of continuing the strike, but they couldn't give me a straight answer. What could they have said? That they were afraid of losing college credits through inadequate attendance? To think that these idiots had been the ones screaming for the dismantling of the university! What a joke. Let the wind change direction a little bit, and their cries turned to whispers.

Hey, Kizuki, I thought, you're not missing a damn thing. This world is a piece of shit. The assholes are earning their college credits and helping to create a society in their own disgusting image.

For a while I attended classes but refused to answer when they called the roll. I knew it was a pointless gesture, but I felt so bad I had no choice. All I managed to do was to isolate myself more than ever from my class-mates. By remaining silent when my name was called, I made everyone uncomfortable for a few seconds. None of the other students spoke to me, and I spoke to none of them.

By the second week in September I reached the conclusion that a college education was meaningless. I decided to think of it as a period of training in techniques for dealing with boredom. I had nothing I especially wanted to accomplish in society that would require me to quit school right away, and so I went to my classes each day, took lec-ture notes, and spent my free time in the library reading or looking things up.

AND THOUGH THAT SECOND WEEK in September had rolled around, there was no sign of Storm Trooper. More than unusual, this was an earth-shaking development. His university had started up again, and it was inconceivable that Storm Trooper would cut classes. A thin layer of dust clung to his desk and radio. His plastic cup and toothbrush, tea can, insec-ticide spray, and such stood in a neat row on his shelf.

I kept the room clean in his absence. I had picked up the habit of neat-ness over the past year and a half, and without him there to take care of the room, I had no choice but to do it. I swept the floor each day, wiped the window every third day, and aired my mattress once a week, waiting for him to come back and tell me what a great job I had done.

But he never came back. I returned from classes one day to find all his stuff gone and his name tag removed from the door. I went to the dorm head's room and asked what had happened.

"He's withdrawn from the dormitory," he said. "You'll be alone in the room for the time being."

I couldn't get him to tell me why Storm Trooper had disappeared. This was a man whose greatest joy in life was to control everything and keep others in the dark.

Storm Trooper's iceberg poster stayed on the wall for a time, but I eventually took it down and replaced it with Jim Morrison and Miles Davis. This made the room seem a little more like my own. I used some of the money I had saved from work to buy a small stereo. At night I would drink alone and listen to music. I thought about Storm Trooper every now and then, but I enjoyed living alone.

AT ELEVEN-THIRTY one Monday, after a lecture on Euripides in History of Drama, I took a ten-minute walk to a little restaurant and had an omelette and salad for lunch. The place was on a quiet back street and it had somewhat higher prices than the student dining hall, but you could relax there, and they knew how to make a good omelette. "They" were a married couple who rarely spoke to each other, and they had one part-time waitress. As I sat there eating by the window, a group of four students came in, two men and two women, all rather neatly dressed. They took the table near the door, spent some time looking over the menu and discussing their options, until one of them reported their choices to the waitress.

Before long I noticed that one of the girls kept glancing in my direction. She had extremely short hair and wore dark sunglasses and a white cotton minidress. I had no idea who she was, so I went on with my lunch, but she soon slipped out of her seat and came over to where I was sitting. With one hand on the edge of my table, she said, "You're Watanabe, aren't you?"

I raised my head and looked at her more closely. Still I could not recall ever having seen her. She was the kind of girl you notice, so if I had met her before I should have been able to recognize her immediately, and there weren't that many people in my university that knew me by name.

"Mind if I sit down?" she asked. "Or are you expecting somebody?"

Still uncertain, I shook my head. "No, nobody's coming. Please."

With a wooden clunk, she dragged a chair out and sat down across from me, staring straight at me through her sunglasses, then glancing down at my plate.

"Looks good," she said.

"It is good. Mushroom omelette and green pea salad."

"Damn," she said. "Oh, well, I'll get it next time. I already ordered something else."

"What'd you order?"

"Macaroni and cheese."

"Their macaroni and cheese is not bad, either," I said. "By the way, do I know you? I can't seem to remember."

"Euripides," she said "*Electra.* 'No god hearkens to my helpless cry.' You know—the class just ended."

I stared at her hard. She took off her sunglasses. At last I remembered her—a freshman I had seen in History of Drama. A striking change in hairstyle had kept me from recognizing her.

"Oh," I said, touching a spot a few inches below my shoulder, "your hair was down to here before summer break."

"You're right," she said. "I had a perm this summer, and it was *just awful.* I was ready to kill myself. I looked like a corpse on the beach with seaweed stuck to my head. So I figured as long as I was ready to die, I might as well cut it all off. At least it's cool in the summer." She ran her hand through her pixie cut and gave me a smile.

"It looks good, though," I said, still munching on my omelette. "Let me see your profile."

She turned away and held the pose for a few seconds.

"Yeah, I thought so. It really looks good on you. Nicely shaped head. Pretty ears, too, uncovered like that."

"So I'm *not* crazy after all! I thought I looked good myself once I cut it all off. Not one guy likes it, though. They all tell me I look like a first-grader or a concentration camp survivor. What's this thing that guys have for girls with long hair? Fascists, the whole bunch of them! Why do guys all think girls with long hair are the classiest, the sweetest, the most feminine? I mean, I myself know at least two hundred and fifty *un*classy girls with long hair. Really."

"I think you look better now than you did before," I said. And I meant it. As far as I could recall, with long hair she had been just another cute coed. From the girl who sat before me now, though, surged a fresh and physical life force. She was like a small animal that has popped into the world with the coming of spring. Her eyes moved like an independent organism with joy, laughter, anger, amazement, and despair. I hadn't seen a face so vivid and expressive in ages, and I enjoyed watching it live and move.

"Do you mean it?" she asked.

I nodded, still munching on my salad.

She put her dark sunglasses on and looked at me from behind them. "You're not lying, are you?"

"I like to think of myself as an honest man," I said.

"Far out."

"So tell me: why do you wear such dark glasses?"

"I felt defenseless when my hair got short all of a sudden. Like somebody threw me into a crowd all naked."

"Makes sense," I said, eating the last of my omelette. She watched me with intense interest.

"You don't have to go back to them?" I asked, motioning toward her three companions.

"Nah. I'll go back when they serve the food. Am I interrupting your meal?"

"There's nothing left to interrupt," I said, ordering coffee when she showed no sign of leaving. The wife took my dishes and brought cream and sugar.

"Now *you* tell *me*," she said. "Why didn't you answer today when they called the roll? You *are* Watanabe, aren't you? Toru Watanabe?"

"That's me."

"So why didn't you answer?"

"I just didn't feel like it today."

She took her sunglasses off again, set them on the table, and looked at me as if she were staring into the cage of some rare animal at the zoo. "'I just didn't feel like it today.' You talk like Humphrey Bogart. Cool. Tough."

"Don't be silly. I'm just an ordinary guy. Like everybody else."

The wife brought my coffee and set it on the table. I took a sip without adding sugar or cream.

"Look at that. You drink it black."

"It's got nothing to do with Humphrey Bogart," I explained patiently, "I just don't happen to like sweets. I think you've got me all wrong."

"Why are you so tanned?"

"I've been hiking around the last couple of weeks. Backpack. Sleeping bag."

"Where'd you go?"

"Kanazawa. Noto Peninsula. Up to Niigata."

"Alone?"

"Alone," I said. "Found some company here and there."

"Some romantic company? New women in far-off places."

"Romantic? Now I *know* you've got me wrong. How's a guy with a sleeping bag on his back and his face all stubbly supposed to have romance?"

"Do you always travel alone like that?"

"Uh-huh."

"You enjoy solitude?" she asked, leaning her cheek on her hand. "Traveling alone, eating alone, sitting off by yourself in lecture halls . . ."

"Nobody likes being alone that much. I don't go out of my way to make friends, that's all. It just leads to disappointment."

The tip of one earpiece in her mouth, sunglasses dangling down, she mumbled, "'Nobody likes being alone. I just hate to be disappointed.' You can use that line if you ever write your autobiography."

"Thanks," I said.

"Do you like green?"

"Why do you ask?"

"You're wearing a green polo shirt."

"Not especially. I'll wear anything."

"'Not especially. I'll wear anything.' I love the way you talk. Like spreading plaster nice and smooth. Has anybody ever told you that?"

"Nobody," I said.

"My name's Midori," she said. "'Green.' But green looks terrible on me. Weird, huh? It's like I'm cursed, don't you think? My sister's name is Momoko: 'Peach Girl.'"

"Does she look good in pink?"

"She looks *great* in pink! She was *born* to wear pink. It's totally unfair."

The food arrived at Midori's table, and a guy in a madras jacket called out to her, "Hey, Midori, come 'n' get it!" She waved at him as if to say "I know."

"Say, tell me," she said, "do you take lecture notes? In drama?"

"Sure do."

"I hate to ask, but could I borrow your notes? I've missed twice, and I don't know anybody in the class."

"No problem," I said, and pulled the notebook from my bag. After checking to make sure I hadn't written anything in it I didn't want seen, I handed it to Midori.

"Thanks," she said. "Are you coming to school the day after tomorrow?"

"Sure am."

"Meet me here at noon. I'll give you back your notebook and buy you lunch. I mean . . . it's not like you get an upset stomach or anything if you don't eat alone, right?"

"No way," I said. "But you don't have to buy me lunch just 'cause I'm lending you my notebook."

"Don't worry," she said. "I like to buy people lunch. But anyhow, shouldn't you write it down somewhere? You won't forget?"

"I won't forget. Day after tomorrow. Twelve o'clock. Midori. Green."

From the other table, somebody called out, "Hurry up, Midori, your food's getting cold!"

She ignored the call and asked me, "Have you always talked like that?"

"I think so," I said. "Never noticed before." And in fact no one had ever told me there was anything unusual about the way I spoke.

She seemed to be mulling something over for a few seconds. Then she stood up with a smile and went back to her table. She waved to me as I walked past a few minutes later, but the three others barely glanced in my direction.

At noon on Wednesday there was no sign of Midori in the restaurant. I thought I might wait for her over a beer, but the place started to fill up as soon as the drink came, so I ordered lunch and ate alone. I finished at 12:35, but still no Midori. Paying my bill, I went outside and crossed the street to a little shrine, where I waited on the stone steps for the beer buzz to clear and Midori to come. I gave up at one o'clock and went to read in the library. At two I went to my German class.

When the lecture ended, I went to the student affairs office and looked for Midori's name in the class list for History of Drama. The only Midori in the class was Midori Kobayashi. Next I flipped through the cards of the student files and found the address and phone number of a Midori

Kobayashi who had entered the university in 1969. She lived in a northwest suburb, Toshima, with her family. I slipped into a phone booth and dialed the number.

A man answered: "Kobayashi Bookstore." Kobayashi Bookstore?

"Sorry to bother you," I said, "but I wonder if Midori might be in?"

"No, she's not," he said.

"Do you think she might be on campus?"

"Hmm, no, she's probably at the hospital. Who's calling, please?"

Instead of answering, I thanked him and hung up. The hospital? Could she have been injured or taken sick? But the man had spoken without the least sense of emergency. "She's probably at the hospital," he had said, as easily as he might have said, "She's at the fish store." I thought about a few other possibilities until thinking itself became a bother, then I went back to the dorm and stretched out on my bed, finishing a copy of Conrad's *Lord Jim* that I had borrowed from Nagasawa. When I was through, I went to Nagasawa's room to give it back.

Nagasawa was on his way out to the dining hall, so I went with him and ate supper.

"How'd the exams go?" I asked. The second round of upper-level exams for the Foreign Ministry had been held in August.

"Like always," said Nagasawa as if it had been nothing. "You take 'em, you pass. Group discussions, interviews . . . like screwin' a chick."

"In other words, easy," I said. "When do they let you know?"

"First week of October. If I pass, I'll buy you a big dinner."

"So tell me, what kind of guys make it to round two? All superstars like you?"

"Don't be stupid. They're a bunch of idiots. Idiots or weirdos. I'd say ninety-five percent of the guys who want to be bureaucrats aren't worth shit. I'm not kidding. They can barely read."

"So why are you trying to join the Foreign Ministry?"

"All kinds of reasons," said Nagasawa. "I like the idea of working overseas, for one. But mainly I want to test my abilities. If I'm going to test myself, I want to do it in the biggest field there is—the nation. I want to see how high I can climb, how much power I can exercise in this insanely huge bureaucratic system. See what I mean?"

"Sounds like a game."

"It *is* a game. I don't give a damn about power and money per se.

Really, I don't. I may be a selfish bastard, but I'm incredibly cool about shit like that. I could be a Zen saint. The one thing I do have, though, is curiosity. I want to see what I can do out there in the big, tough world."

"And you have no use for 'ideals,' I suppose."

"None. Life doesn't require ideals. It requires standards of action."

"But there are lots of other ways to live, aren't there?" I asked.

"You like the way I live, don't you?"

"That's beside the point," I said. "I could never get into Tokyo University, I can't sleep with any girl I want whenever I want to, I'm no great talker, people don't look up to me, I haven't got a girlfriend, and the future's not going to open up to me when I get a literature B.A. from a second-rate private college. What does it matter if I like the way you live?"

"Are you saying you *envy* the way I live?"

"No, I don't," I said. "I'm too used to being who I am. And I don't really give a damn about Tokyo University or the Foreign Ministry. The one thing I envy you for is having a terrific girlfriend like Hatsumi."

Nagasawa shut up and ate. When we were finished with supper, he said, "You know, Watanabe, I have this feeling like, maybe ten years or twenty years after we get out of this place, we're going to meet up again somewhere. And one way or another, I think we're going to have some connection."

"Sounds like Dickens," I said with a smile.

"I guess it does," he said, smiling back. "But my hunches are usually right."

The two of us left the dining hall and went out to a bar. We stayed there drinking until after nine.

"Tell me, Nagasawa," I asked, "what is the 'standard of action' in *your* life?"

"You'll laugh if I tell you," he said.

"No I won't."

"All right," he said. "'To be a gentleman.'"

I didn't laugh, but I nearly fell off my chair. "'To be a gentleman'? A *gentleman*?"

"You heard me."

"What does it mean to be a gentleman? How do you define it?"

"A gentleman is someone who does not what he *wants* to do but what he *should* do."

"You're the weirdest guy I've ever met," I said.

"You're the straightest guy I've ever met," he said. And he paid for us both.

I WENT TO THE FOLLOWING week's drama lecture, but still saw no sign of Midori Kobayashi. After a quick survey of the room convinced me she was not there, I took my usual seat in the front row and wrote a letter to Naoko while I waited for the professor to come. I wrote about my summer travels—the roads I had walked, the towns I had passed through, the people I had met. "And every night I would think of you. Now that I can no longer see you, I realize how much I needed you. School is incredibly boring, but as a matter of self-discipline I am going to all my classes and doing all the assignments. Everything seems pointless since you left. I'd like to have a nice, long talk with you. If possible, I'd like to visit your sanatorium and see you for several hours. And, if possible, I'd like to go out walking with you side by side the way we used to. Please try to answer this letter, even a short note, I don't care."

I filled four sheets of letter paper, folded it, slipped it into an envelope, and addressed it to Naoko care of her family.

By then the professor had arrived, wiping the sweat from his brow as he took the roll. He was a small, mournful-looking man who walked with a metal cane. While not exactly fun, the lectures in his course were always well prepared and worthwhile. After remarking that the weather was as hot as ever, the professor began to talk about the use of the deus ex machina in Euripides and explained how the concept of "god" was different in Euripides than it was in Aeschylus or Sophocles. He had been talking for some fifteen minutes when the classroom door opened and in walked Midori. She was wearing a dark blue sport shirt, cream-colored cotton slacks, and her usual sunglasses. After flashing a "sorry I'm late" kind of smile toward the professor, she sat down next to me. Then she took a notebook—my notebook—from her shoulder bag and handed it to me. Inside, I found a note: "Sorry about Wednesday. Are you mad?"

The lecture was about half over and the professor was drawing a sketch of a Greek stage on the blackboard when the door opened again and two students in helmets walked in. They looked like some kind of comedy team, one tall and thin and pale, the other short and round and dark and totally unsuited to the long beard he wore. The tall one carried an arm-load of political agitation handbills. The short one walked up to the professor and said, with a degree of politeness, that they would like to use the second half of his period for political debate and hoped that he would cooperate, adding, "The world is full of problems far more urgent and relevant than Greek tragedy." This was more an announcement than a request. The professor replied, "I rather doubt that the world has problems far more urgent and relevant than Greek tragedy, but you're not going to listen to anything I have to say, so do what you like." Grasping the edge of his table, he set his feet on the floor, picked up his cane, and limped out of the classroom.

While the tall student passed out his handbills, the round one went to the podium and started lecturing. The handbills were full of the usual simplistic sloganeering: "Smash Fraudulent Elections for University President"; "Marshal All Forces for New All-Campus Strike"; "Crush the Imperial-Educational-Industrial Complex." I had no problem with what they were saying, but the writing was lame. It had nothing to inspire confidence or arouse the passions. And the round guy's speech was just as bad—the same old tune with different words. The true enemy of this bunch was not State Power but Lack of Imagination.

"Let's get out of here," said Midori.

I nodded and stood, and the two of us made for the door. The round guy said something to me at that point, but I couldn't catch it. Midori waved to him and said, "See ya later."

"Gee, are we counterrevolutionaries?" Midori asked me when we were outside. "Are we going to be strung up on telephone poles if the revolution succeeds?"

"Let's have lunch first, just in case."

"Good. There's a place I want to take you. It's kinda far, though. Can you spare the time?"

"Sure, I'm O.K. until my two o'clock class."

Midori took me to Yotsuya by bus and showed me to a fancy boxed-lunch specialty shop in a sheltered spot just behind the station. The minute we sat down they served us soup and the lunch of the day in square, red-lacquered boxes. This was a place worth a bus ride to eat at.

"Great food," I said.

"And cheap, too. I've been coming here since high school. My old school's right down the street. They were so strict, we had to sneak out to eat here. They'd suspend you if they caught you eating out."

Without the sunglasses, Midori's eyes looked somewhat sleepier than they had the last time. When she was not playing with the narrow silver bracelet on her left wrist, she would be scratching at the corners of her eyes with the tip of her little finger.

"Tired?" I asked.

"Kinda. I'm not getting enough sleep. But I'm O.K., don't worry," she said. "Sorry about the other day. Something important came up and I just couldn't get out of it. All of a sudden, in the morning. I thought about calling you at the restaurant but I couldn't remember the name, and I didn't know your home number. Did you wait long?"

"No big deal. I've got a lot of time on my hands."

"A lot?"

"Way more than I need. I wish I could give you some to help you sleep."

Midori rested her cheek on her hand and smiled at me. "What a nice guy you are."

"Not nice. Just got time to kill," I said. "By the way, I called your house that day and somebody told me you were at the hospital. Something wrong?"

"You called my house?" she asked with a slight wrinkle forming between her eyebrows. "How did you get my number?"

"Looked it up in the student affairs office. Anybody can do that."

She nodded once or twice and started playing with the bracelet again. "I never would have thought of that. I guess I could have looked your number up. Anyhow, about the hospital, I'll tell you next time. I don't feel like it now. Sorry."

"That's O.K. I didn't mean to pry."

"No, you're not prying. I'm just kinda tired. Like a monkey in the rain."

"Don't you think you ought to go home and get some sleep?"

"Not now. Let's get out of here."

SHE TOOK ME to her old high school a short walk from Yotsuya.

Passing the station, I thought about Naoko and our endless walking. It had all started from there. I realized that if I hadn't run into Naoko on the

train that Sunday in May, my life would have been very different from
what it was now. But then I changed my mind: no, even if we hadn't met
that day, my life might not have been any different. We had met that day
because we were supposed to meet. If we hadn't met then and there, we
would have met somewhere else sometime. I didn't have any basis for
thinking this: it was just a feeling.

Midori Kobayashi and I sat on a park bench together, looking at the
building where she used to go to high school. Ivy clung to the walls, and
pigeons huddled beneath the gables, resting their wings. It was a nice old
building with character. A great oak tree stood in the schoolyard, and a
column of white smoke rose straight up beside it. The fading summer
light gave the smoke a soft and cloudy look.

"Do you know what that smoke is?" Midori asked me without warning.

"No idea," I said.

"They're burning sanitary napkins."

"No kidding." I couldn't think of anything else to say.

"Sanitary napkins, tampons, stuff like that," Midori said with a smile.
"It *is* a girls' school. The old janitor collects them from all the receptacles
and burns them in the incinerator. *That's* the smoke."

"Whoa."

"Yeah, that's what I used to say to myself whenever I was in class and
saw the smoke outside the window. 'Whoa.' Think about it: the school had
almost a thousand girls in junior and senior high. So figure nine hundred
of them have started their periods, and maybe a fifth of those are having
their periods at any one time: one hundred and eighty girls. That's a hundred and eighty girls' worth of napkins in the receptacles every day."

"I bet you're right—though I'm not so sure about the figures."

"Anyhow, it's a lot. One hundred and eighty girls. What do you think it
feels like to collect and burn that much stuff?"

"Can't imagine," I said. How could I have imagined what the old guy
was going through? Midori and I went on watching the smoke.

"I really didn't want to go to this school," Midori said. She gave her
head a little shake. "I wanted to go to an absolutely ordinary public high
school. An ordinary school with ordinary people where I could relax and
have fun like an ordinary teenager. But my parents thought it would look
good for me to go to this fancy place. They're the ones who stuck me in
here. You know: that's what happens when your grades are good in ele-

mentary school. The teacher tells your parents, 'With grades like hers, she ought to go *there*.' So that's where I ended up. Six years I went and I never liked it. All I could think of was getting out. And you know, I've got certificates of merit for never having been late or missed a day of school. That's how much I hated the place. Get it?"

"No, I don't get it."

"It's 'cause I hated the place so much. I wasn't going to let it beat me. I figured, let it get me once and I'd be finished. I was scared I'd just keep slipping down and down. I'd crawl to school with a temperature of a hundred and three. The teacher would ask me if I was sick, but I'd say no. At graduation they gave me certificates for perfect attendance and perfect punctuality, plus a French dictionary. That's why I'm taking German now. I didn't want to owe this school *anything*. I'm not kidding."

"Why did you hate it so much?"

"Did *you* like *your* school?"

"Well, no, but I didn't especially hate it, either. I went to an ordinary public high school but I never thought about it one way or another."

"Well, *this* school," Midori said, scratching the corner of her eye with her little finger, "had nothing but upper-class girls—almost a thousand girls with good backgrounds and good grades. *Rich* girls. They had to be rich to survive. High tuition, endless contributions, expensive school trips. Like, if we went to Kyoto, they'd put us up in a first-class inn and serve us tea-ceremony food on lacquer tables, and they'd take us once a year to the most expensive hotel in Tokyo to study table manners. I mean, this was no ordinary school. Out of a hundred and sixty girls in my class, I was the only one from a middle-class neighborhood like Toshima. I looked at the school register once to see where the others lived, and every single one of them was from a rich area. Well, no, there was one girl from way out in Chiba with the farmers, so I got kinda friendly with her. And she was really nice. She invited me to her house, though she apologized for how far I'd have to travel to get there. I went and it was *incredible*, this giant piece of land you'd have to walk fifteen minutes to get around. It had this amazing garden and two dogs like compact cars they fed *steaks* to. But still, this girl felt embarrassed about living out in Chiba. This is a girl who would be driven to school in a Mercedes Benz if she was late! By a chauffeur! Like right out of the Green Hornet: the hat, the white gloves, the whole deal. And still she had this inferiority complex. Can you believe it?"

I shook my head.

"I was the only one in the whole school who lived in a place like Kita-Otsuka Toshima. And under 'parent's profession' it said, 'bookstore owner.' Everybody in my class thought that was so neat: 'Oh, you're so lucky, you can read any book you like' and stuff. Of course, they were thinking of some monster bookstore like Kinokuniya. They could never have imagined the poor little Kobayashi Bookstore. The door creaks open and you've got nothing but magazines. The steady sellers are the ladies' magazines with illustrated pullout sections on the latest sexual techniques. The local housewives buy them and sit at the kitchen table reading them from cover to cover, and give 'em a try when their husbands get home. And they've got the most incredible positions! Is this what housewives have on their minds all day? The cartoons are the other big seller: *Magazine, Sunday, Jump.* And of course the weeklies. So this 'bookstore' is almost all magazines. Oh, there are a few books, paperbacks, like mysteries and swashbucklers and romances. That's all that sell. And how-to books: how to win at go, how to raise bonsai, how to give wedding speeches, how to have sex, how to quit smoking, you name it. We even sell writing supplies—stacks of ballpoint pens and pencils and notebooks next to the cash register. But that's it. No *War and Peace*, no Kenzaburo Oe, no *Catcher in the Rye*. That's the Kobayashi Bookstore. That's how 'lucky' I am. Do you think I'm lucky?"

"I can just see the place."

"You know what I mean. Everybody in the neighborhood comes there, some of them for years, and we deliver. It's a good business, more than enough to support a family of four, no debts, two daughters in college, but that's it. Nothing to spare for extras. They should never have sent me to a school like that. It was a recipe for heartache. I had to listen to them grumble to me every time the school asked for a contribution, and I was always scared to death I'd run out of money if I went out with my classmates and they wanted to eat someplace expensive. It's a miserable way to live. Is your family rich?"

"My family? No, my parents are absolutely ordinary working people, not rich, not poor. I know it's not easy for them to send me to a private college in Tokyo, but there's just me, so it's not that big a deal. They don't give me much to live on, so I work part-time. We live in a typical house with a little garden and drive a Toyota Corolla."

"What's your job like?"

"I work in a Shinjuku record shop three nights a week. It's easy. I just sit there and mind the store."

"No kidding," said Midori. "I don't know, just looking at you, I kinda figured you had never been hard up for money."

"It's true. I never *have* been hard up for money. Not that we have tons of it, either. I'm like most people."

"Well, 'most people' in my school were *rich*," said Midori, palms up on her lap. "That was the problem."

"So now you'll have plenty of chances to see a world without that problem. More than you want to, maybe."

"Hey, tell me, what d'you think the best thing is about being rich?"

"Beats me."

"Being able to say you don't have any money. Like, if I suggested to a classmate we do something, she could say, 'Sorry, I don't have any money.' Which is something I could *never* say if the situation was reversed. If *I* said 'I don't have any money,' it would *really mean* 'I don't have any money.' It's sad. Like if a pretty girl says 'I look terrible today, I don't want to go out,' that's O.K., but if an ugly girl says the same thing people laugh at her. That's what the world was like for me. For six years, until last year."

"You'll get over it."

"I hope so. College is such a relief! It's full of ordinary people."

She smiled with the slightest curl of her lip and smoothed her short hair with the palm of her hand.

"Do you have a job?" I asked.

"Yeah, I write map notes. You know those little pamphlets that come with maps? With descriptions of the different neighborhoods and population figures and points of interest. Here there's so-and-so hiking trail or such-and-such a legend, or some special flower or bird. I write the texts for those things. It's *so* easy! Takes no time at all. I can write a whole booklet with a day of looking things up in the library. All you have to do is master a couple of secrets and all kinds of work comes your way."

"What kind of secrets?"

"Like you put in some little something that nobody else has written and the people at the map company think you're a literary genius and send you more work. It doesn't have to be anything at all, just some tiny thing. Like, say, when they made a dam in this particular valley, the water covered over a village, but still every spring the birds come up from the south and you can see them flying over the lake. Put in one little episode like that and people love it, it's so graphic and sentimental. The usual part-timer doesn't bother with stuff like that, but I can make myself decent money with what I write."

"Yeah, but you have to find those 'episodes.'"

"True," said Midori with a tilt of the head. "But if you're looking for them, you usually find them. And if you don't, you can always make up something harmless."

"Oh-ho!"

"Peace," said Midori.

She said she wanted to hear about my dormitory, so I told her the usual stories about the raising of the flag and Storm Trooper's Radio Calisthenics. Storm Trooper gave Midori an especially big laugh, as he seemed to do with all the world's people. Midori said she thought it would be fun to have a look at the dorm. There was nothing fun about the place, I told her: "Just a few hundred guys in grubby rooms, drinking and jerking off."

"Does that include you?"

"It includes every man on the face of the earth," I explained. "Girls have periods and boys jerk off. Everybody."

"Even ones with girlfriends? I mean, sex partners."

"It's got nothing to do with that. The Keio student living next door to me jerks off before every date. He says it relaxes him."

"I don't know much about that stuff. I was in a girls' school so long."

"I guess the ladies' magazine supplements don't go into that."

"Not at all!" she said, laughing. "Anyhow, Watanabe, would you have some time this Sunday? Are you free?"

"I'm free every Sunday. Until six, at least. That's when I go to work."

"Why don't you come visit me? At the Kobayashi Bookstore. The store itself will be closed, but I have to hang around there alone all day. I might be getting an important phone call. How about lunch? I'll cook for you."

"I'd like that," I said.

Midori tore a page from a notebook and drew a detailed map of the way to her place. She used a red pen to make a large X where the house stood.

"You can't miss it. There's a big sign: 'Kobayashi Bookstore.' Come at noon. I'll have lunch ready."

I thanked her and put the map in my pocket. "I'd better get back to campus now," I said. "My German class starts at two." Midori said she had someplace to go and took the train from Yotsuya.

SUNDAY MORNING I GOT UP AT NINE, shaved, did my laundry, and hung the clothes on the roof. It was a beautiful day. The first smell of autumn was in the air. Red dragonflies were flitting around the quadrangle, chased by neighborhood kids swinging nets. With no wind, the Rising Sun hung limp on its pole. I put on a freshly ironed shirt and walked from the dorm to the streetcar stop. A student neighborhood on a Sunday morning: the streets were dead, virtually empty, most stores closed. What few sounds there were echoed with special clarity. A girl wearing sabots clip-clopped across the asphalt roadway, and next to the streetcar barn four or five kids were throwing rocks at a line of empty cans. A flower store was open, so I went in and bought some daffodils. Daffodils in the autumn: that was strange. But I had always liked that particular flower.

Three old women were the only passengers on the Sunday morning streetcar. They all looked at me and my flowers. One of them gave me a smile. I smiled back. I sat in the last seat and watched the old houses passing close by the window. The streetcar almost touched the overhanging eaves. The laundry deck of one house had ten potted tomato plants, next to which a big black cat lay stretched out in the sun. In the yard of another house, a little kid was blowing soap bubbles. I heard an Ayumi Ishida song coming from someplace, and could even catch the smell of curry cooking. The streetcar snaked its way through this private back-alley world. A few more passengers got on at stops along the way, but the three old women went on talking intently about something, huddled together face-to-face.

I got off near Otsuka Station and followed Midori's map down a broad street without much to look at. None of the shops along the way seemed to be doing very well, housed as they were in old buildings with gloomy-looking interiors and faded writing on some of the signs. Judging from the age and style of the buildings, this area had been spared the wartime air raids, leaving whole blocks intact. A few of the places had been entirely rebuilt, but just about all had been enlarged or repaired in spots, and it was those additions that tended to look far more shabby than the old buildings themselves.

The whole atmosphere of the place suggested that most of the people who used to live here had become fed up with the cars and the filthy air and the noise and high rents and moved to the suburbs, leaving only cheap apartments and company flats and hard-to-move shops and a few stubborn holdouts who clung to old family properties. Everything looked blurred and grimy as if wrapped in a haze of exhaust gas.

Ten minutes' walk down this street brought me to a corner gas station, where I turned right into a short block of shops, in the middle of which hung the sign for Kobayashi Bookstore. True, it was not a big store, but neither was it as small as Midori's description had led me to imagine. It was just a typical neighborhood bookstore, the same kind I used to run to on the very day the boys' magazines came out. A nostalgic mood overtook me as I stood in front of the place.

The whole front of the store was sealed off by a big, roll-down metal shutter inscribed with a magazine advertisement: "*Weekly Bunshun* Sold Here Thursdays." I still had fifteen minutes to noon, but I didn't want to kill time wandering through the block with a handful of daffodils, so I pressed the doorbell beside the shutter and stepped a few paces back to wait. Fifteen seconds went by without an answer, and I was debating with myself whether to ring again when I heard a window clatter open above me. I looked up to find Midori leaning out and waving.

"Come in," she yelled. "Lift the shutter."

"Is it O.K.? I'm kind of early," I shouted back.

"No problem. Come upstairs. I'm busy in the kitchen." She pulled the window closed.

The shutter made a terrific grinding noise as I raised it three feet from the ground, ducked under, and lowered it again. The shop was pitch black inside. I managed to feel my way to the back stairway, tripping over bound piles of magazines. There I untied my shoes and climbed up to the living area. The interior of the house was dark and gloomy. Where the stairs came up was a simple parlor with a sofa and easy chairs. It was a small room with dim light coming in the window, reminiscent of old Polish movies. There was a kind of storage area on the left and what looked like the door to a bathroom. I had to climb the steep stairway with care to reach the second floor, but once I got there, it was so much brighter than the first floor that I felt a good deal of relief.

"Over here," called Midori's voice. To the right at the top of the stairs was what looked to be a dining room, and beyond that a kitchen. The house itself was old, but the kitchen seemed to have been remodeled recently with new cabinets and a bright, shiny sink and faucet. There I found Midori preparing food. She had a pot bubbling, and the smell of broiled fish filled the air.

"There's beer in the refrigerator," said Midori with a glance in my direction. "Have a seat while I finish this." I took a can and sat at the kitchen table. The beer was so cold it might have been in the refrigerator for the better part of a year. On the table lay a small, white ashtray, a newspaper, and a soy sauce dispenser. There was also a notepad and pen, with a phone number and some figures on the pad that seemed to be calculations connected with shopping.

"I should have this done in ten minutes," she said. "Can you stand the wait?"

"Of course I can," I said.

"Get good and hungry, then. I'm making a lot."

I sipped my beer and focused on Midori as she went on cooking, her back to me. She worked with quick, nimble movements, handling no fewer than four cooking procedures at once. Over here she tested the taste of a boiled dish, and the next second she was at the cutting board, rat-tat-tatting, then she took something out of the refrigerator and piled it in a dish, and before I knew it she had washed a pot she was finished using. From the back, she looked like an Indian percussionist—ringing a bell, tapping a block, striking a water buffalo bone, each movement precise and economical, with perfect balance. I watched in awe.

"Let me know if there's something I can do," I said just in case.

"That's O.K.," said Midori with a smile in my direction. "I'm used to doing everything alone." She wore slim blue jeans and a navy T-shirt. An Apple Records logo nearly covered the back of the shirt. She had incredibly narrow hips, as if she had somehow skipped the growth stage in which the hips are solidified, and this gave her a far more neutral look than most girls have in slim jeans. The light pouring in from the kitchen window gave her shape a kind of vague outline.

"You really didn't have to put together such a feast," I said.

"It's no feast," answered Midori without turning my way. "I was too busy to do any real shopping yesterday. I'm just slapping together a few things I had in the fridge. Really, don't worry. Besides, it's Kobayashi fam-

ily tradition to treat guests well. I don't know what it is, but we like to enter-
tain. It's inborn, a kind of sickness. Not that we're especially nice or people
love us or anything, but if somebody shows up we have to treat them well
no matter what. We've all got the same personality flaw, for better or
worse. Take my father, for example. He himself hardly drinks, but the
house is full of alcohol. What for? To serve guests! So don't hold back:
drink all the beer you want."

"Thanks," I said.

It suddenly dawned on me that I had left the flowers downstairs. I had
set them aside when untying my shoes and forgotten to bring them up
with me. I slipped back downstairs and found the ten bright blossoms
lying in the gloom. Midori took a tall, slim glass from the cupboard and
arranged the flowers in it.

"I love daffodils," said Midori. "I once sang 'Seven Daffodils' in the
high school talent show. Do you know the song?"

"Of course I do.

"We had a folk group. I played guitar."

She sang "Seven Daffodils" as she arranged the food on plates.

MIDORI'S COOKING WAS FAR BETTER than I had imagined it would be,
an amazing assortment of fried, pickled, boiled, and roasted dishes using
eggs, mackerel, fresh greens, eggplant, mushrooms, radishes, and sesame
seeds, all done in the delicate Kyoto style.

"This is *great*," I said with my mouth full.

"O.K., tell me the truth now," Midori said. "You weren't expecting my
cooking to be very good, were you—judging from my looks."

"I guess not," I said honestly.

"You're from the Kansai region, so you like this kind of delicate flavor-
ing, right?"

"Don't tell me you changed style especially for me?"

"Don't be ridiculous! I wouldn't go to that much trouble. No, we
always eat like this."

"So your mother—or your father— is from the Kansai?"

"Nope, my father was born in Tokyo and my mother's from Fukushima.
There's not a single Kansai person among my relatives. We're all from
Tokyo or the northern Kanto."

"I don't get it," I said. "How come you can make this hundred-percent-authentic Kansai-style food? Did somebody teach you?"

"Well, it's kind of a long story," she said, eating a slice of fried egg. "My mother hated housework of any kind, and she almost never cooked anything. And we had the business to think about, so it was always like 'Today we're so busy, let's order out' or 'Let's just buy some croquettes at the butcher shop' and stuff. I hated that even when I was a little kid, I mean like cooking a big pot of curry and eating the same thing three days in a row. So then one day—I was in the third year of middle school—I decided I was going to cook for the family and do it right. I went to the big Kinoku-niya in Shinjuku and bought the biggest, handsomest cookbook I could find, and I mastered it from cover to cover: how to choose a cutting board, how to sharpen knives, how to bone a fish, how to shave fresh bonito flakes, everything. It turned out the author of the book was from the Kansai, so all my cooking is Kansai style."

"You mean you learned how to make all this stuff from a book?!"

"I saved my money and went to eat the real thing. That's how I learned flavorings. I've got pretty good intuition. I'm hopeless as a logical thinker, though."

"It's amazing you could teach yourself to cook so well without having anyone show you."

"It wasn't easy," said Midori with a sigh, "growing up in a house where nobody gave a damn about food. I'd tell them I wanted to buy decent knives and pots and they wouldn't give me the money. 'What we have now is good enough,' they'd say, but I'd tell them that was crazy, you couldn't bone a fish with the kind of flimsy knives we had at home, so they'd say, 'What the hell do you have to bone a fish for?' It was hopeless trying to communicate with them. I saved up my allowance and bought real professional knives and pots and strainers and stuff. Can you believe it? Here's a fifteen-year-old girl pinching pennies to buy strainers and whetstones and tempura pots when all the other girls at school are getting huge allowances and buying beautiful dresses and shoes. Don't you feel sorry for me?"

I nodded, swallowing a mouthful of clear soup with fresh *junsai* greens.

"When I was in my first year of high school, I *had* to have an egg fryer—a long, narrow pan for making this *dashimaki* style of fried egg we're eating. I bought it with money I was supposed to use for a new bra. For *three months* I had to live with *one bra*. Can you believe it? I'd wash my bra at night, go crazy trying to dry it, and wear it the next day. And if it didn't dry right, I had a tragedy to deal with. The saddest thing in the world is wearing a damp bra. I'd walk around with tears pouring from my eyes. To think I was suffering this for an egg fryer!"

"I see what you mean," I said with a laugh.

"I know I shouldn't say this, but actually it was kind of a relief to me when my mother died. I could run the family budget *my* way. I could buy what *I* liked. So now I've got a relatively complete set of cooking utensils. My father doesn't know a thing about the budget."

"When did your mother die?"

"Two years ago. Cancer. Brain tumor. She was in the hospital a year and a half. It was terrible. She suffered from beginning to end. Finally lost her mind, had to be doped up all the time, and still she couldn't die, though when she did it was practically a mercy killing. It's the worst kind of death—the person's in agony, the family goes through hell. It took every cent we had. I mean, they'd give her these shots—bang, bang, twenty thousand yen a pop, and she had to have round-the-clock care. I was so busy with her, I couldn't study, had to delay college for a year. And as if that weren't bad enough—" she stopped herself in midsentence, put her chopsticks down, and sighed. "How did this conversation turn so dark all of a sudden?"

"It started with the business about the bras," I said.

"So anyway, eat your eggs and think about what I just told you," Midori said with a solemn expression.

Eating my portion filled me up, but Midori ate far less. "Cooking ruins my appetite," she said. She cleared the table, wiped up the crumbs, brought out a box of Marlboros, put one in her mouth, and lit up with a match. Taking hold of the glass with the daffodils, she studied the blooms for a while.

"I guess I won't switch them to a vase," she said. "If I leave them like this, it's like I just happened to pick them by a pond somewhere and threw them into the first thing I got my hands on."

"I did pick them by the pond at Otsuka Station," I said.

She chuckled. "You *are* a weird one. Making jokes with a perfectly straight face."

Chin in hand, she smoked half her cigarette, then crushed it out in an ashtray. She rubbed her eyes as if smoke had gotten into them.

"Girls are supposed to be a little more elegant when they put their cigarettes out. You did that like a lumberjack. You shouldn't just cram it down in the ashtray but press it lightly around the edges of the ash. Then it doesn't get all bent up. And girls are *never* supposed to blow smoke through their noses. And most girls wouldn't talk about how they wore the same bra for three months when they're eating alone with a man."

"I *am* a lumberjack," Midori said, scratching next to her nose. "I can never manage to be chic. I try it as a joke sometimes, but it never sticks. Any more critiques for me?"

"Girls don't smoke Marlboros," I said.

"What's the difference? One tastes as bad as another." She turned the red Marlboro package over and over in her hand. "I just started smoking last month. It's not like I was dying for tobacco or anything. I just sort of felt like it."

"Why's that?" I asked.

She pressed her hands together atop the table and thought about it a while. "What's the difference? You don't smoke?"

"Quit in June," I said.

"How come?"

"It was a pain. I hated running out of smokes in the middle of the night. I don't like having something control me that way."

"You're very clear about what you like and what you don't like," she said.

"Maybe so," I said. "Maybe that's why people don't like me. Never have."

"It's 'cause you show it," she said. "You make it obvious you don't care whether people like you or not. That makes some people mad." She spoke in a near mumble, chin in hand. "But I like talking to you. The way you talk is so unusual. 'I don't like having something control me that way.'"

I HELPED HER WASH the dishes. Standing next to her, I wiped as she washed, and I piled the things on the counter.

"So," I said, "your family's out today?"

"My mother's in her grave. She died two years ago."

"Yeah, I heard that part."

"My sister's on a date with her fiancé. Probably on a drive. Her boyfriend works for some car company. He loves cars. I *don't* love cars."

Midori stopped talking and washed. I stopped talking and wiped.

"And then there's my father," she said after some time had gone by.

"Right," I said.

"He went off to Uruguay in June of last year and he's been there ever since."

"Uruguay?! Why Uruguay?"

"He was thinking of settling there, believe it or not. An old army buddy of his has a farm there. All of a sudden, my father announces he's going to go too, that there's no limit to what he can do in Uruguay, and he gets on a plane and that's that. We tried hard to stop him, like, 'Why do you want to go to a place like that? You can't speak the language, you've hardly ever left Tokyo.' But he wouldn't listen. Losing my mother was a real shock to him. I mean, it made him a little cuckoo. That's how much he loved her. Really."

There was not much I could say in reply. I stared at Midori with my mouth open.

"What do you think he said to my sister and me when our mother died? 'I would much rather have lost the two of you than her.' It knocked the wind out of me. I couldn't say a word. You know what I mean? You just can't *say* something like that. O.K., he lost the woman he loved, his partner for life. I understand the pain, the sadness, the heartbreak. I pity him. But you don't tell the daughters you fathered 'You should have died in her place.' I mean, that's just too terrible. Don't you agree?"

"Yeah, I see your point."

"That's one wound that will never go away," she said, shaking her head. "But anyhow, everybody in my family's a little different. We've all got something just a little bit strange."

"So it seems," I said.

"Still, it *is* wonderful for two people to love each other, don't you think? I mean, for a man to love his wife so much he can tell his daughters they should have died in her place . . . !"

"Maybe so, now that you put it that way."

"And then he dumps the two of us and runs off to Uruguay."

I wiped another dish without replying. After the last one, Midori put everything back in the cabinets.

"So, have you heard from your father?" I asked.

"One postcard. In March. But what does he write? 'It's hot here,' or 'The fruit's not as good as I expected.' Stuff like that. I mean, give me a break! One stupid picture of a donkey! He's lost his marbles! He didn't even say whether he'd met that guy—that friend of his or whatever. He did add near the end that once he's settled he'll send for me and my sister, but not a word since then. And he never answers our letters."

"What would you do if your father said, 'Come to Uruguay'?"

"I'd go and have a look around at least. It might be fun. My sister says she'd absolutely refuse. She can't stand dirty things and dirty places."

"Is Uruguay dirty?"

"Who knows? *She* thinks it is. Like the roads are full of donkey shit and it's swarming with flies, and the toilets don't work, and lizards and scorpions crawl all over the place. She maybe saw a movie like that. She can't stand bugs, either. All she wants to do is drive through pretty scenery in fancy cars."

"No kidding."

"I mean, what's wrong with Uruguay? I'd go."

"So who's running the store?"

"My sister, but she hates it. We've got an uncle in the neighborhood who helps out and makes deliveries. And I help out when I have time. A bookstore's not exactly hard labor, so we can manage. If it gets to be too much, we'll sell the place."

"Do you like your father?"

Midori shook her head. "Not especially."

"So how can you follow him to Uruguay?"

"I believe in him."

"Believe in him?"

"Yeah, I'm not that fond of him, but I believe in my father. How can I *not* believe in a man who gives up his house, his kids, his work, and runs off to Uruguay from the shock of losing his wife? Do you see what I mean?"

I sighed. "Sort of, but not really."

Midori laughed and patted me on the back. "Never mind," she said. "It really doesn't matter."

ONE STRANGE THING after another came up that Sunday afternoon. A fire broke out near Midori's house and when we went up to the third-floor laundry deck to watch, we sort of kissed. It sounds stupid when I put it that way, but that was how things worked out.

We were drinking coffee after the meal and talking about the university when we heard the sound of sirens. They got louder and louder and seemed to be increasing in number. Lots of people ran by the store, some of them shouting. Midori went to a room that faced the street, opened the window, and looked down. "Wait here a minute," she said, and disappeared, after which I heard feet pounding up stairs.

I sat there drinking coffee alone and trying to remember where Uruguay was. Let's see, Brazil was over here, and Venezuela there, and Colombia somewhere over here, but the location of Uruguay I couldn't manage to recall. Midori came down a few minutes later and urged me to hurry somewhere with her. I followed her to the end of the hall and climbed a steep, narrow stairway to a wooden deck with bamboo laundry poles. The deck was higher than most of the surrounding rooftops and gave a good view of the neighborhood. Huge clouds of black smoke shot up from a place three or four houses away and flowed with the breeze out toward the main street. A burning smell filled the air.

"It's Sakamoto's place," said Midori, leaning over the railing. "They used to make traditional door fittings and stuff. They went out of business, though."

I leaned over the railing with her and strained to see what was going on. A three-story building blocked our view of the exact fire scene, but there seemed to be three or four fire engines over there working on the blaze. No more than two of them could squeeze into the narrow lane where the house was burning, the rest standing by on the main street. The usual crowd of gawkers filled the area.

"Hey, maybe you should gather your valuables together and get ready to evacuate this place," I said to Midori. "The wind's blowing the other way now, but it could change any time, and you've got a gas station right there. I'll help you pack."

"What valuables?" said Midori.

"Well, you must have something you'd want to save—passbooks, seals, legal papers, stuff like that. Emergency cash."

"Forget it. I'm not running away."

"Even if this place burns?"

"You heard me. I don't mind dying."

I looked her in the eye, and she looked straight at me. I couldn't tell if she was serious or joking. We stayed like that for a while, and soon I stopped worrying.

"O.K.," I said. "I get it. I'll stay with you."

"You'll die with me?" Midori asked with shining eyes.

"Hell, no," I said. "I'll run if it gets dangerous. If you want to die, you can do it alone."

"Cold-hearted bastard!"

"I'm not going to die with you just because you made lunch for me. Of course, if it had been dinner . . ."

"Oh, well . . . Anyhow, let's stay here and watch for a while. We can sing songs. And if something bad happens, we can think about it then."

"Sing songs?"

Midori brought two floor pillows, four cans of beer, and a guitar from downstairs. We drank and watched the black smoke rising. Midori strummed and sang. I asked her if she didn't think this might anger the neighbors. Drinking beer and singing while you watched a local fire from the laundry deck didn't seem like the most admirable behavior I could think of.

"Forget it," she said. "We never worry about what the neighbors might think."

She sang some of the folk songs she had played with her group. I would have been hard-pressed to say she was good, but she did seem to enjoy her own music. She went through all the old standards — "Lemon Tree," "Puff (the Magic Dragon)," "Five Hundred Miles," "Where Have All the Flowers Gone?" "Michael, Row the Boat Ashore." At first she tried to get me to sing bass harmony, but I was so bad she gave up and sang alone to her heart's content. I worked on my beer and listened to her sing and kept an eye on the fire. It flared up and died down several times. People were yelling and giving orders. A newspaper helicopter clattered overhead, took pictures, and flew away. I worried that we might be in the picture. A policeman screamed through a loudspeaker for gawkers to pull back. A little kid was crying for his mother. Glass shattered somewhere. Before long the wind started shifting unpredictably, and white ash flakes would fall out of the air around us, but Midori went on sipping and singing. After she had gone through most of the songs she knew, she sang an old one that she said she had written herself.

I'd love to cook a stew for you
But I have no pot.
I'd love to knit a scarf for you
But I have no wool.
I'd love to write a poem for you
But I have no pen.

"It's called 'I Have Nothing,'" Midori announced. It was a truly terrible song, both words and music.

I listened to this musical mess with thoughts of how the house would blow apart in the explosion if the gas station caught fire. Tired of singing, Midori put her guitar down and slumped against my shoulder like a cat in the sun.

"How did you like my song?" she asked.

I answered cautiously, "It was unique and original and very expressive of your personality."

"Thanks," she said. "The theme is that I have nothing."

"Yeah, I kinda thought so."

"You know," she said, "when my mother died . . ."

"Yeah?"

"I didn't feel the least bit sad."

"Oh."

"And I didn't feel sad when my father left, either."

"Yeah?"

"It's true. Don't you think I'm terrible? Cold-hearted?"

"I'm sure you've got your reasons."

"My reasons. Hmm. Things were pretty complicated in this house. But I always thought, I mean, they're my mother and father, of course I'd be sad if they died or I never saw them again. But it didn't happen that way. I didn't feel anything. Not sad, not lonely. I hardly even think of them. Sometimes I'll have dreams, though. Sometimes my mother will be glaring at me out of the darkness and she'll accuse me of being happy she died. But I'm *not* happy she died. I'm just not very sad. And to tell the truth, I never shed a single tear. I cried all night when my cat died, though, when I was little."

Why so much smoke? I wondered. I couldn't see flames, and the burning area didn't seem to be spreading. There was just this column of smoke winding up into the sky. What could have kept burning so long?

"But I'm not the only one to blame," Midori continued. "It's true I've got a cold streak. I recognize that. But if they—my father and mother—had loved me a little more, I would have been able to feel more—to feel real sadness, for example."

"Do you think you weren't loved enough?"

She tilted her head and looked at me. Then she gave a sharp, little nod. "Somewhere between 'not enough' and 'not at all.' I was always hungry for love. Just once, I wanted to know what it was like to get my fill of it—to be fed so much love I couldn't take any more. Just once. But they never gave that to me. Never, not once. If I tried to cuddle up and beg for something, they'd just shove me away and yell at me. 'No! That costs too much!' It's all I ever heard. So I made up my mind I was going to find someone who would love me unconditionally three hundred and sixty-five days a year. I was still in elementary school at the time—fifth or sixth grade—but I made up my mind once and for all."

"Wow," I said. "And did your search pay off?"

"That's the hard part," said Midori. She watched the rising smoke for a while, thinking. "I guess I've been waiting so long I'm looking for perfection. That makes it tough."

"Waiting for the perfect love?"

"No, even I know better than that. I'm looking for selfishness. Perfect selfishness. Like, say I tell you I want to eat strawberry shortcake. And you stop everything you're doing and run out and buy it for me. And you come back out of breath and get down on your knees and hold this strawberry shortcake out to me. And I say I don't want it anymore and throw it out the window. That's what I'm looking for."

"I'm not sure that has anything to do with love," I said with some amazement.

"It does," she said. "You just don't know it. There are times in a girl's life when things like that are incredibly important."

"Things like throwing strawberry shortcake out the window?"

"Exactly. And when I do it, I want the man to apologize to me. 'Now I see, Midori. What a fool I've been! I should have known that you would lose your desire for strawberry shortcake. I have all the intelligence and sensitivity of a piece of donkey shit. To make it up to you, I'll go out and buy you something else. What would you like? Chocolate mousse? Cheesecake?'"

"So then what?"

"So then I'd give him all the love he deserves for what he's done."

"Sounds crazy to me."

"Well, to *me*, that's what love is. Not that anyone can understand me, though." Midori gave her head a little shake against my shoulder. "For a certain kind of person, love begins from something tiny or silly. From something like that or it doesn't begin at all."

"I've never met a girl who thinks like you."

"A lot of people tell me that," she said, digging at a cuticle. "But it's the only way I know how to think. Seriously. I'm just telling you what I believe. It's never crossed my mind that my way of thinking is different from other people's. I'm not *trying* to be different. But when I speak out honestly, everybody thinks I'm kidding or playacting. When that happens, I feel like everything's such a pain!"

"And you want to let yourself die in a fire?"

"Hey, no, that's different. It's just a matter of curiosity."

"What? Dying in a fire?"

"No, I just wanted to see how you'd react," Midori said. "But dying itself, I'm not afraid of. Really. Like here, I'd just be overcome with smoke and lose consciousness and die before I knew it. That doesn't frighten me at all, compared with the way I saw my mother and a few relatives die. *All* my relatives die after suffering with some terrible illness. It's in the blood, I guess. It's always a *long, long* process, and at the end you almost can't tell whether the person is alive or dead. All that's left is pain and suffering."

Midori put a Marlboro between her lips and lit it.

"That's the kind of death that frightens me. The shadow of death slowly, slowly eats away at the region of life, and before you know it everything's dark and you can't see, and the people around you think of you as more dead than alive. I hate that. I couldn't stand it."

ANOTHER HALF HOUR, and the fire was out. They had apparently kept it from spreading and prevented any injuries. All but one of the fire engines returned to base, and the crowd dispersed, buzzing with conversation. One police car remained to direct traffic, its rooftop light spinning. Two crows had settled onto nearby light poles to observe the activity below.

Midori seemed drained of energy. Limp, she stared off at the sky, and she hardly spoke.

"Tired?" I asked.

"Not really," she said. "I just sort of let myself go limp and spaced out. First time in a long time."

She looked into my eyes, and I into hers. I put my arm around her and kissed her. The slightest twinge went through her shoulders, and then she relaxed and closed her eyes for several seconds. The early autumn sun cast the shadow of her lashes on her cheek, and I could see it trembling in outline.

It was a soft and gentle kiss, one not meant to lead beyond itself. I would probably not have kissed Midori that day if we hadn't spent the afternoon on the laundry deck in the sun, drinking beer and watching a fire, and she probably felt the same. After a long time of watching the glittering rooftops and the smoke and the red dragonflies and other things, we had felt something warm and close, and we both probably wanted, half-consciously, to preserve that mood in some form. It was that kind of kiss. But as with all kisses, it was not without a certain element of danger.

The first to speak was Midori. She held my hand and told me, with what seemed like some difficulty, that she was seeing someone. I said that I had sensed as much.

"Do you have a girl you like?" she asked.

"I do," I said.

"But you're always free on Sundays, right?"

"It's very complicated," I said.

And then I realized that the brief spell of the early autumn afternoon had vanished.

AT FIVE I SAID I had to go to work and suggested that Midori go out with me for a snack. She said she had to stay home in case her phone call came.

"I hate waiting at home all day for a call. When I spend the day alone, I feel as if my flesh is rotting little by little—rotting and melting until there's nothing left but a green puddle that gets sucked down into the earth. And all that stays behind are my clothes. That's how it feels to me, waiting indoors all day."

"I'll keep you company next time you have to wait for a call," I said. "As long as lunch is included."

"Great," she said. "I'll fix another fire for dessert."

MIDORI DIDN'T COME to the next day's History of Drama lecture. I went to the cafeteria after class and ate a cold, tasteless lunch alone. Then I sat in the sun and observed the campus scene. Two women students next to me were carrying on a long conversation, standing the whole time. One cradled a tennis racquet to her breast with all the loving care she might give a baby, while the other held some books and a Leonard Bernstein LP. Both girls were pretty and were obviously enjoying talking to each other. From the direction of the student club building came the sound of a bass voice practicing scales. Here and there stood groups of four or five students expressing whatever opinions they happened to hold, laughing and shouting to one another. In the parking lot was a bunch of guys on skateboards. A professor with a leather briefcase in his arms crossed the parking lot, avoiding the skateboarders. In the quadrangle a helmeted girl student knelt on the ground, painting huge characters on a sign with something about American imperialism invading Asia. It was the usual noontime university scene, but as I sat watching it with renewed attention, I became aware of a certain fact. In his or her own way, each person I saw before me looked happy. Whether they were really happy or just looked it, I couldn't tell. But they did look happy on this pleasant early afternoon at the end of September, and because of that I felt a kind of loneliness that was new to me, as if I were the only one here who was not truly part of the scene.

Come to think of it, what scene *had* I been part of in recent years? The last one I could remember was a billiards parlor near the harbor, where Kizuki and I shot pool together in a mood of total friendship. Kizuki died that night, and ever since then a cold, stiffening wind had come between me and the world. This boy Kizuki: what had his existence meant to me? To this question I could find no answer. All I knew—with absolute certainty—was that Kizuki's death had robbed me forever of a part of my adolescence. But what that meant, and what would come from it, were far beyond my understanding.

I sat there for a long time, watching the campus and the people passing through it, and hoping, too, that I might see Midori. But she never appeared, and when the noon break ended, I went to the library to prepare for my German class.

NAGASAWA CAME TO MY ROOM that Saturday afternoon and suggested we have one of our nights on the town. He would arrange an overnight pass for me. I said I would go. I had been feeling especially foggy-brained for the past week and was ready to sleep with anybody, it didn't matter much who.

Late in the afternoon I showered and shaved and put on fresh clothes—a polo shirt and cotton jacket—then had dinner with Nagasawa in the dining hall and the two of us caught a bus to Shinjuku. We walked around a lively section for a while, then went to one of our regular bars and sat there waiting for a likely pair of girls. The girls tended to come in pairs to this bar—except on this particular evening. We stayed there almost two hours, sipping whiskey and sodas at a rate that kept us sober. Finally, two friendly looking girls took seats at the bar, ordering a gimlet and a margarita. Nagasawa approached them right away, but they said they were waiting for their boyfriends. Still, the four of us enjoyed a nice chat until their dates showed up and the girls joined them.

Nagasawa took me to another bar to try our luck, a small place in a kind of cul-de-sac, where most of the customers were already drunk and noisy. A group of three girls occupied a table at the back. We joined them and enjoyed a little conversation, the five of us getting into a nice mood, but when Nagasawa suggested we go to a different place to drink, the girls said it was almost curfew time and they had to go back to their dorms. So much for our "luck." We tried one more place with the same results. For some reason, the girls were just not coming our way.

When eleven-thirty rolled around, Nagasawa was ready to give up. "Sorry I dragged you around for nothing," he said.

"No problem," I said. "It was worth it to me just to see you have your off days sometimes, too."

"Maybe once a year," he admitted.

In fact, I didn't care about getting laid anymore. Wandering around Shinjuku on a noisy Saturday night, observing the mysterious energy created by a mix of sex and alcohol, I began to feel that my own desire was a puny thing.

"What are you going to do now, Watanabe?"

"Maybe go to an all-nighter," I said. "I haven't seen a movie in a long time."

"I'll be going to Hatsumi's, then," said Nagasawa. "Do you mind?"

"Hell, no," I said. "Why should I mind?"

"If you'd like, I could introduce you to a girl who'd let you spend the night."

"Nah, I really am in the mood for some movies."

"Sorry," said Nagasawa. "I'll make it up to you some time." And he disappeared into the crowd. I went into a fast-food place for a cheeseburger and some coffee to kill the buzz, then went to see *The Graduate* in an old rep house. I didn't think it was all that good, but I didn't have anything better to do, so I stayed and watched it again. Emerging from the theater at four in the morning, I wandered along the chilly streets of Shinjuku, thinking.

When I tired of walking, I went to an all-night coffeehouse and waited with a book and a cup of coffee for the morning trains to start. Before long, the place became crowded with people who, like me, were waiting for those first trains. A waiter came to ask me apologetically if I would mind sharing my table. I said it would be all right. It didn't matter to me who sat across from me: I was just reading a book.

My companions at the table turned out to be two girls. They looked to be about my age. Neither of them was a knockout, but they weren't bad. Both were reserved in the way they dressed and made up: they were definitely not the type to be wandering around Shinjuku at five in the morning. I guessed that they had just happened to miss the last train. They seemed relieved to be seated with me: I was neatly dressed, had shaved in the evening, and to top things off I was absorbed in Thomas Mann's *The Magic Mountain*.

One of the girls was on the large side. She wore a gray parka and white jeans, carried a big vinyl pocketbook, and had on big, shell-shaped earrings. Her friend was a small girl with glasses. She wore a blue cardigan over a checked shirt and had a blue turquoise ring. The smaller one seemed to have a habit of taking her glasses off and pressing her eyes with her fingertips.

Both girls ordered café au lait and cake, which it took them some time to consume as they carried on what seemed like a serious discussion in hushed tones. The large girl tilted her head any number of times, while the small one shook hers just as often. I couldn't make out what they were saying because of the loud stereo playing Marvin Gaye or the Bee Gees or something, but it seemed the small girl was angry or upset and the large girl was trying to comfort her. I alternated passages of my book with glances in their direction.

Clutching her shoulder bag to her breast, the smaller girl went off to the ladies' room, at which point her companion spoke to me.

"I'm sorry to bother you, but I wonder if you might know of any bars in the neighborhood that would still be serving drinks?"

Taken off guard, I set my book aside and asked, "After five o'clock in the morning?"

"Yes . . ."

"If you ask me, at five-twenty in the morning, most people are on their way home to get sober and go to bed."

"Yes, I realize that," she said with a good deal of embarrassment, "but my friend says she has to have a drink. It's kind of important."

"There's probably nothing much you can do but go home and drink."

"But I have to catch a seven-thirty train to Nagano."

"So find a vending machine and a nice place to sit. It's about all you can do."

"I know this is asking a lot, but could you come with us? Two girls alone really can't do something like that."

I had had a number of unusual experiences in Shinjuku, but I had never before been invited to have a drink with two strange girls at five-twenty in the morning. Refusing would have been more trouble than it was worth, and time was no problem, so I bought an armload of sake and snacks from a nearby machine, and the three of us went to an empty lot by the west exit of the station to hold an impromptu drinking party.

The girls told me they had become friends while working at a travel agency. Both of them had graduated from junior college this year and taken their first jobs. The small one had a boyfriend she had been seeing for a year, but had recently found out he was sleeping with another girl and she was taking it hard. The bigger one was supposed to have left for the mountains of Nagano last night for her brother's wedding, but she had decided to spend the night with her depressed friend and take the first express on Sunday morning.

"It's too bad what you're going through," I said to the small one, "but how did you figure out your boyfriend was sleeping with someone else?"

Taking little sips of sake, the girl tore at some weeds underfoot. "I didn't have to figure anything out," she said. "I opened his door, and there he was, doing it."

"When was that?"

"The night before last."

"No kidding. The door was unlocked?"

"Right."

"I wonder why he didn't lock it?"

"How the hell should I know?"

"Yeah, how's she supposed to feel?" said the big one, who seemed truly concerned for her friend. "What a shock it must have been for her. Don't you think it's terrible?"

"I really can't say," I answered. "You ought to have a good talk with your boyfriend. Then it's a question of whether you forgive him or not."

"Nobody knows how I feel," spat out the little one, still tearing grass.

A flock of crows sailed out of the west and flew over a big department store. It was full daylight now. The time for the train to Nagano was approaching, so we gave what was left of the sake to a homeless guy downstairs at the west exit, bought platform tickets, and went in to see the big girl off. After the train pulled out of sight, the small girl and I somehow ended up going to a nearby hotel. Neither of us was particularly dying to sleep with the other, but it seemed necessary to bring things to a close.

I got undressed first and sat in the bathtub drinking beer with a vengeance. She got in with me and did the same, the two of us stretched out and guzzling beer in silence. We couldn't seem to get drunk, though, and neither of us was sleepy. Her skin was very fair and smooth, and she had beautiful legs. I complimented her on her legs, but her "Thanks" was little more than a grunt.

Once we were in bed, though, she was like a different person. She responded to the slightest touch of my hands, writhing and moaning. When I went inside her, she dug her nails into my back, and as her orgasm approached she called out another man's name exactly sixteen times. I concentrated on counting them as a way to delay my own orgasm. Then the two of us fell asleep.

She was gone when I woke at twelve-thirty. I found no note of any kind. One side of my head felt strangely heavy from having drunk at an odd time. I took a shower to wake myself up, shaved, and sat in a chair, naked, drinking a bottle of juice from the refrigerator and reviewing in order the events of the night before. Each scene felt unreal and strangely distanced, as if I were viewing it through two or three layers of glass, but the events had undoubtedly happened to me. The beer glasses were still sitting on the table, and a used toothbrush lay by the sink.

I ate a light lunch in Shinjuku and went to a telephone booth to call Midori Kobayashi on the off chance that she might be home alone waiting for a call again today. I let it ring fifteen times but no one answered. I tried again twenty minutes later with the same result. Then I took a bus back to the dorm. A special delivery letter was waiting for me in the mailbox by the entry. It was from Naoko.

five

"Thanks for your letter," wrote Naoko. Her family had forwarded it "here," she said. Far from upsetting her, its arrival had made her very happy, and in fact she had been on the point of writing to me herself.

Having read that much, I opened my window, took off my jacket, and sat on the bed. I could hear pigeons cooing in a nearby roost. The breeze stirred the curtains. Holding the seven pages of letter paper from Naoko, I gave myself up to an endless stream of feelings. It seemed as if the colors of the real world around me had begun to drain away from my having done nothing more than read a few lines she had written. I closed my eyes and spent a long time collecting my thoughts. Finally, after one deep breath, I continued reading.

"It's almost four months since I came here," she went on.

I've thought a lot about you in that time. The more I've thought, the more I've come to feel that I was unfair to you. I probably should have been a better, fairer person when it came to the way I treated you.

This may not be the most normal way to look at things, though. Girls my age *never* use the word *fair*. Ordinary girls as young as I am are basically indifferent to whether things are fair or not. The central question for them is not whether something is fair but whether or not it's beautiful or will make them happy. *Fair* is a man's word, finally, but I can't help feeling that it is also exactly the right word for me now. And because questions of beauty and happiness have become such difficult and convoluted propositions for me now, I suspect, I find myself clinging instead to other standards—like, whether or not something is fair or honest or universally true.

In any case, though, I believe that I have not been fair to you and that, as a result, I must have led you around in circles and hurt you deeply. In doing so, however, I have led myself around in circles and hurt myself just as deeply. I say this not as an excuse or a means of self-justification but because it is true. If I have left a wound inside you, it is not just your wound but mine as well. So please try not to hate me. I am a flawed human being—a far more flawed human being than you realize. Which is precisely why I do not want you to hate me. Because if you were to do that, I would really go to pieces. I can't do what you can do: I can't slip inside my shell and wait for things to pass. I don't know for a fact that you are really like that, but sometimes you give me that impression. I often envy that in you, which may be why I led you around in circles so much.

This may be an overanalytical way of looking at things. Don't you agree? The therapy they perform here is certainly not overanalytical, but when you are under treatment for several months the way I am here, like it or not, you become more or less analytical. "This was caused by that, and that means this, because of which thus-and-such." Like that. I can't tell whether this kind of analysis is trying to simplify the world or subdivide it.

In any case, I myself feel that I am far closer to recovery than I was at one time, and people here tell me this is true. This is the first time in a long time that I have been able to sit down and calmly write a letter. The one I wrote you in July was something I had to wring out of me (though, to tell the truth, I don't remember what I wrote—was it terrible?), but this time I am very, very calm. Clean air, a quiet world cut off from the outside, a daily schedule for living, regular exercise: those are what I needed, it seems. How wonderful it is to be able to write someone a letter! To feel like conveying your thoughts to a person, to sit at your desk and pick up a pen, to put your thoughts into words like this is truly marvelous. Of course, once I *do* put them into words, I find I can only express a fraction of what I want to say, but that's all right. I'm happy just to be able to feel I want to write to someone. And so I am writing to you. It's seven-thirty in the evening, I've had my dinner, and I've just finished my bath. The place is hushed, and it's pitch dark outside. I can't see a single light through the window. I usually have a clear view of the stars from here, but not today, with the clouds. Everyone here knows a lot about the stars, and they tell me, "That's Virgo," or "That's Sagittarius." They probably learn whether they want to or not because there's nothing to do here once the sun goes down. Which is also why they know so much about birds and flowers and insects. Speaking to them, I realize how ignorant I was about such things, which is kind of nice.

The number of people living here is right around seventy. In addition, the staff (doctors, nurses, office staff, etc.) come to just over twenty. It's such a wide-open place, these are not big numbers at all. Far from it: it might be closer to say the place is on the empty side. It's big and filled with nature and everybody lives quietly—so quietly you sometimes feel that this is the normal, real world. Which of course it's not. We can have it this way because we live here under certain preconditions.

I play tennis and basketball. Basketball teams are made up of both staff and (I hate the word, but there's no way around it) patients. When I'm absorbed in a game, though, I lose track of who are the patients and who are staff. This is kind of strange. I know this will *sound* strange, but when I look at the people around me during a game, they all look equally deformed.

I said this one day to the doctor in charge of my case, and he told me that, in a sense, what I was feeling was right, that we are in here not to correct the deformation but to accustom ourselves to it: that one of our problems was our inability to recognize and accept our own deformities. Just as each person has certain idiosyncrasies in the way he or she walks, people have idiosyncrasies in the way they think and feel and see things, and though you might want to correct them, it doesn't happen overnight, and if you try to force the issue in one case, something else might go funny. He gave me a very simplified explanation, of course, and it's just one small part of the problems we have, but I think I understand what he was trying to say. It may well be that we can never fully adapt to our own deformities. Unable to find a place inside ourselves for the very real pain and suffering that these deformities cause, we come here to get away from such things. As long as we are here, we can get by without hurting others or being hurt by them because we know that we are "deformed." That's what distinguishes us from the outside world: most people go about their lives there unconscious of their deformities, while in this little world of ours the deformities themselves are a precondition. Just as Indians wear feathers on their heads to show which tribes they belong to, we wear our deformities in the open. And we live quietly so as not to hurt one another.

In addition to playing sports, all participate in the raising of vegetables: tomatoes, eggplants, cucumbers, watermelon, strawberries, scallions, cabbage, daikon radishes, and on and on. We raise just about everything. We use hot houses, too. The people here know a lot about vegetable farming, and they put a lot of energy into it. They read books on the subject and call in experts and talk from morning to night about which fertilizer to use and the condition of the soil and stuff like that. I have come to love growing vegetables. It's marvelous to watch different fruits and vegetables getting bigger and bigger each day. Have you ever raised watermelon? They swell up, just like some kind of little animals.

We eat freshly picked fruits and vegetables every day. They also serve meat and fish, of course, but when you're living here you feel less and less like eating those because the vegetables are so fresh and delicious. Sometimes we go out and gather wild plants and mushrooms. We have experts on that kind of thing (come to think of it, this place is crawling with experts) who tell us which plants to pick and which to avoid. As a result of all this, I've gained over six pounds since I got here. My weight is just about perfect, thanks to the exercise and the good eating on a regular schedule.

When we're not farming, we read or listen to music or knit. We don't have TV or radio, but we do have a very decent library with books and records. The record collection has everything from Mahler symphonies to the Beatles, and I'm always borrowing records to listen to in my room.

The one real problem with this facility is that once you're here you don't want to leave—or you're afraid to leave. As long as we're here, we feel calm and peaceful. Our deformities seem natural. We think we've recovered. But we can never be sure that the outside world would accept us in the same way.

My doctor says it's time I began having contact with "outside people"— meaning normal people in the normal world. When he says that, the only face I see is yours. To tell the truth, I don't want to see my parents. They're too upset over me, and seeing them puts me in a bad mood. Plus, there are things I have to explain to you. I'm not sure I *can* explain them very well, but they're important things I can't go on avoiding any longer.

Still, you shouldn't feel that I'm a burden to you. The one thing I don't want to be is a burden to anyone. I can sense the good feelings you have for me. They make me very happy. All I am doing in this letter is trying to convey that happiness to you. Those good feelings of yours are probably just what I need at this point in my life. Please forgive me if anything I've written here upsets you. As I said before, I am a far more flawed human being than you realize.

I sometimes wonder: IF you and I had met under absolutely ordinary circumstances, and IF we had liked each other, what would have happened? If I had been normal and you had been normal (which, of course, you are) and there had been no Kizuki, what would have happened? Of course, this "IF" is way too big. I'm trying hard at least to be fair and honest. It's all I can do at this point. I hope to convey some small part of my feelings to you this way.

Unlike an ordinary hospital, this facility has free visiting hours. As long as you call the day before, you can come anytime. You can even eat with me, and there's a place for you to stay. Please come and see me sometime when it's convenient for you. I look forward to seeing you. I'm enclosing a map. Sorry this turned into such a long letter.

I read Naoko's letter all the way through, and then I read it again. After that I went downstairs, bought a Coke from the vending machine, and drank it while reading the letter one more time. I put the seven pages of letter paper back into the envelope and laid it on my desk. My name and address had been written on the pink envelope in perfect, tiny characters that were just a bit too precisely formed for those of a girl. I sat at my desk, studying the envelope. The return address on the back said "Ami Hostel." An odd name. I thought about it for a few minutes, concluding that the "ami" must be from the French word for "friend."

After putting the letter away in my desk drawer, I changed clothes and went out. I was afraid that if I stayed near the letter I would end up reading it ten, twenty, who knew how many times? I walked the streets of Tokyo on Sunday without a destination, as I had always done with Naoko. I wandered from one street to the next, recalling her letter line by line and mulling each sentence over as best I could. When the sun went down, I returned to my dorm and placed a long-distance call to the Ami Hostel. A woman receptionist answered. I asked her if it might be possible for me to visit Naoko the following afternoon. She took my name and said I should call back in half an hour.

The same woman answered when I called back after eating. It would indeed be possible for me to see Naoko, she said. I thanked her, hung up, and put a change of clothes and a few toilet articles in my knapsack. Then I picked up *The Magic Mountain* again, reading and sipping brandy and waiting to get sleepy. Even so, I didn't fall asleep until after one o'clock in the morning.

six

As soon as I woke up at seven o'clock on Monday morning, I washed my face, shaved, and went straight to the dorm head's room without eating breakfast to say that I was going to be gone for two days hiking in the hills. He was used to my taking short trips when I had free time, and reacted without surprise. I took a crowded commuter train to Tokyo Station and bought a bullet-train ticket to Kyoto, literally jumping onto the first *Hikari* express to pull out. I made do with coffee and a sandwich for breakfast and dozed for an hour.

I arrived in Kyoto a few minutes before eleven. Following Naoko's instructions, I took a city bus to a small terminal serving the northern suburbs. The next bus to my destination would not be leaving until 11:35, I was told, and the trip would take a little over an hour. I bought a ticket and went to a bookstore across the street for a map. Back in the waiting room, I studied the map to see if I could find exactly where the Ami Hostel was located. It turned out to be much farther into the mountains than I had imagined. The bus would have to cross several hills in its trek north, then turn around where the canyon road dead-ended and return to the city. My stop would be just before the end of the line. There was a trailhead near the bus stop, according to Naoko, and if I followed the trail for twenty minutes I would reach Ami Hostel. If it was that deep in the mountains, no wonder it was a quiet place!

The bus pulled out with twenty passengers aboard, following the Kamo River through the north end of Kyoto. The tightly packed city streets gave way to more sparse housing, then fields and vacant land. Black tile roofs and vinyl-sided hothouses caught the early autumn sun and sent it back with a glare. When the bus entered the canyon, the driver had to start hauling the steering wheel back and forth to follow the twists and curves of the road, and I began to feel queasy. I could still taste my morning coffee. By the time the number of curves began to decrease to the point where I felt some relief, the bus plunged into a chilling cedar forest. The trees might have been old growth the way they towered over the road, blocking out the sun and covering everything in gloomy shadows. The breeze flowing into the bus's open windows turned suddenly cold, its dampness sharp against the skin. The valley road hugged the riverbank, continuing so long through the trees it began to seem as if the whole world had been buried forever in cedar forest—at which point the forest ended, and we came out to an open basin surrounded by mountain peaks. Broad, green farmland spread out in all directions, and the river by the road looked bright and clear. A single thread of white smoke rose in the distance. Some houses had laundry drying in the sun, and dogs were howling. Each farmhouse had firewood out front piled up to the eaves, usually with a cat resting somewhere on the pile. The road was lined with such houses for a time, but I saw not a single person.

The scenery repeated this pattern any number of times. The bus would enter cedar forest, come out to a village, then go back into forest. It would stop at a village to let people off, but no one ever got on. Forty minutes after leaving the city, the bus reached a mountain pass with a wide-open view. The driver stopped the bus and announced that we would be waiting there for five or six minutes: people could step down from the bus if they wished. There were only four passengers left now, including me. We all got out and stretched or smoked and looked down at the panorama of Kyoto far below. The driver went off to the side for a pee. A suntanned man in his early fifties who had boarded the bus with a big, rope-tied cardboard carton asked me if I was going out to hike in the mountains. I said yes to keep it simple.

Eventually another bus came climbing up from the other side of the pass and stopped next to ours. The driver got out, had a short talk with our driver, and the two men climbed back into their buses. The four of us returned to our seats, and the buses pulled out in opposite directions. It was not immediately clear to me why our bus had had to wait for the other one, but a short way down the other side of the mountain the road narrowed suddenly. Two big buses could never have passed each other on the road, and in fact passing ordinary cars coming in the other direction required a good deal of maneuvering, with one or the other vehicle having to back up and squeeze into the overhang of a curve.

The villages along the road were far smaller now, and the level areas under cultivation far more narrow. The mountain was steeper, its walls pressed closer to the bus windows. They seemed to have just as many dogs as the other places, though, and the arrival of the bus would set off a howling competition.

At the stop where I got off, there was nothing—no houses, no fields, just the bus stop sign, a little stream, and the trail opening. I slung my knapsack over my shoulder and started up the track. The stream ran along the left side of the trail, and a forest of deciduous trees lined the right side. I had been climbing the gentle slope for some fifteen minutes when I came to a road leading into the woods on the right, the opening barely wide enough to accommodate a car. "Ami Hostel. Private. No Trespassing," read the sign by the road.

Sharply etched tire tracks ran up the road through the trees. The occasional flapping of wings echoed in the woods. The sound came through with strange clarity, as if amplified above the other voices of the forest. Once, from far away, I heard what might have been a rifle shot, but it was a small and muffled sound, as if it had passed through several filters.

Beyond the woods I came to a white stone wall. It was no higher than my own height and, lacking additional barriers on top, would have been easy for me to scale. The black iron gate looked sturdy enough, but it was wide open, and there was no one manning the guardhouse. Another sign like the last one stood by the gate: "Ami Hostel. Private. No Trespassing." A few clues suggested the guard had been there until some moments before: the ashtray held three butts, a teacup stood there half empty, a transistor radio sat on a shelf, and the clock on the wall ticked off the time with a dry sound. I waited a while for the person to come back, but when that showed no sign of happening, I gave a few pushes to something that looked as if it might be a bell. The area just inside the gate was a parking lot. In it stood a minibus, a four-wheel-drive Land Cruiser, and a dark blue Volvo. The lot could have held thirty cars, but only those three were parked there now.

Two or three minutes went by, and then a gatekeeper in a navy blue uniform came down the forest road on a yellow bicycle. He was a tall man in his early sixties with a receding hairline. He leaned the yellow bike against the guardhouse and said, "I'm very sorry to have kept you waiting," though he didn't sound sorry at all. The number 32 was painted on the bike's fender in white. When I gave him my name, he picked up the phone and repeated it twice to someone on the other end. Replying, "Yes, uh-huh, I see" to the other person, he hung up.

"Go to the main building, please, and ask for Doctor Ishida," he said to me. "You take this road through the trees to a rotary. Then take your second left—got that? Your *second* left—from the rotary. You'll see an old house. Turn right and go through another bunch of trees to a concrete building. That's the main building. It's easy, just watch for the signs."

I took the second left from the rotary as instructed, and where that leg ended I came to an interesting old building that had obviously been some-one's country house once upon a time. It had a manicured garden with well-shaped rocks and a stone lantern. This property must once have been a country estate. Turning right through the trees, I saw a three-story con-crete building. It stood in a hollowed-out area, and so there was nothing overpowering about its three stories. It was simple in design and gave a strong impression of cleanliness.

The entrance was on the second floor. I climbed the stairs and went in through a big glass door to find a young woman in a red dress at the recep-tion desk. I gave her my name and said I had been instructed to ask for Doctor Ishida. She smiled and gestured toward a brown sofa, suggesting in low tones that I wait there for the doctor to come. Then she dialed the telephone. I lowered my knapsack from my back, sank down into the deep cushions of the sofa, and surveyed the place. It was a clean, pleasant lobby, with ornamental potted plants, tasteful abstract paintings, and a polished floor. As I waited, I kept my eyes on the floor's reflection of my shoes.

At one point the receptionist assured me, "The doctor will be here soon." I nodded. What an incredibly quiet place! There were no sounds of any kind. You would have thought everyone was taking a siesta. People, animals, bugs, plants must all be sound asleep, I thought, it was such a quiet afternoon.

Before long, though, I heard the soft padding of rubber soles, and a mature, bristly haired woman appeared. She swept across the lobby, sat down next to me, crossed her legs, and took my hand. Instead of just shak-ing it, she turned my hand over, examining it front and back.

"You haven't played a musical instrument, at least not for some years now, have you?" were the first words out of her mouth.

"No," I said, taken aback. "You're right."

"I can tell from your hands," she said with a smile.

There was something almost mysterious about this woman. Her face had lots of wrinkles. These were the first thing to catch your eye, but they didn't make her look old. Instead, they emphasized a certain youthfulness in her that transcended age. The wrinkles *belonged* where they were, as if they had been part of her face since birth. When she smiled, the wrinkles smiled with her; when she frowned, the wrinkles frowned, too. And when she was neither smiling nor frowning, the wrinkles lay scattered over her face in a strangely warm, ironic way. Here was a woman in her late thirties who seemed not merely a nice person but whose niceness drew you to her. I liked her from the moment I saw her.

Wildly chopped, her hair stuck out in patches and the bangs lay crooked against her forehead, but the style suited her perfectly. She wore a blue work shirt over a white T-shirt, baggy, cream-colored pants, and tennis shoes. Long and slim, she had almost nothing for breasts. Her lips moved constantly to one side in a kind of ironic curl, and the wrinkles at the corners of her eyes moved in tiny twitches. She looked like a kindly, skilled, but somewhat world-weary woman carpenter.

Chin drawn in and lips curled, she took some time to look me over from head to toe. I imagined that any minute now she was going to whip out her tape measure and start measuring me everywhere.

"*Can* you play an instrument?" she asked.

"Sorry, no," I said.

"Too bad," she said. "It would have been fun."

"I guess it would have been," I said. Why all this talk about musical instruments?

She took a pack of Seven Stars from her breast pocket, put one between her lips, lit it with a cigarette lighter, and began puffing away with obvious pleasure.

"It crossed my mind that I should tell you about this place, Mr.— Watanabe, wasn't it?—before you see Naoko. So I arranged for the two of us to have this little talk. Ami Hostel is kind of unusual—enough so that you might find it a little confusing without any background knowledge. I'm right, aren't I, in supposing that you don't know anything about this place?"

"Almost nothing."

"Well, then, first of all—" she began, then snapped her fingers. "Come to think of it, have you had lunch? I'll bet you're hungry."

"You're right, I am."

"Come with me, then. We can talk over food in the dining hall. Lunchtime is over, but if we go now they can still make us something."

She took the lead, hurrying down a corridor and a flight of stairs to the first-floor dining hall. It was a large room, with enough space for perhaps two hundred people, but only half was in use, the other half closed off with partitions, like a resort hotel in the off-season. The day's menu listed a potato stew with noodles, salad, orange juice, and bread. The vegetables turned out to be as startlingly delicious as Naoko had said in her letter, and I finished everything on my plate.

"You obviously enjoy your food!" said my female companion.

"It's wonderful," I said. "Plus, I've hardly eaten anything all day."

"You're welcome to mine if you like. I'm full. Here, go ahead."

"I will, if you really don't want it."

"I've got a small stomach. It doesn't hold much. I make up for what I'm missing with cigarettes." She lit another Seven Stars. "Oh, by the way, you can call me Reiko. Everybody does."

Reiko seemed to derive great pleasure from watching me while I ate the potato stew she had hardly touched and munched on her bread.

"Are you Naoko's doctor?" I asked.

"Me? Naoko's doctor?!" She squinched up her face. "What makes you think I'm a doctor?"

"They told me to ask for Doctor Ishida."

"Oh, I get it. No no no, I teach music here. It's a kind of therapy for some patients, so for fun they call me the 'Music Doctor' and sometimes 'Doctor Ishida.' But I'm just another patient. I've been here seven years. I work as a music teacher and help out in the office, so it's hard to tell anymore whether I'm a patient or staff. Didn't Naoko tell you about me?"

I shook my head.

"That's strange," said Reiko. "I'm Naoko's roommate. I like living with her. We talk about all kinds of things. Including you."

"What about me?"

"Well, first I have to tell you about this place," said Reiko, ignoring my question. "The first thing you ought to know is that this is no ordinary 'hospital.' It's not so much for treatment as for convalescence. We do have a few doctors, of course, and they give hourly sessions, but they're just checking people's conditions, taking their temperature and things like that, not administering 'treatments' like in a regular hospital. There are no bars on the windows here, and the gate is always wide open. People enter voluntarily and leave the same way. You have to be suited to that kind of convalescence to be admitted here in the first place. In some cases, people who need specialized therapy end up going to a specialized hospital. O.K. so far?"

"I think so," I said. "But what does this 'convalescence' consist of? Can you give me a concrete example?"

Reiko exhaled a cloud of smoke and drank what was left of her orange juice. "Just living here is the convalescence," she said. "A regular routine, exercise, isolation from the outside world, clean air, quiet. Our farmland makes us practically self-sufficient; there's no TV or radio. We're like one of those commune places you hear so much about. Of course, one thing different from a commune is that it costs a bundle to get in here."

"A bundle?"

"Well, it's not ridiculously expensive, but it's not cheap. Just look at these facilities. We've got a lot of land here, a few patients, a big staff, and in my case I've been here a long time. True, I'm almost staff myself, so I get a substantial break, but still . . . Say, how about a cup of coffee?"

I'd like some, I said. She crushed out her cigarette and went over to the counter, where she poured two cups of coffee from a warm pot and brought them back to where we were sitting. She put sugar in hers, stirred it, frowned, and took a sip.

"You know," she said, "this sanatorium is not a profit-making enterprise, so it can keep going without charging as much as it might have to otherwise. The land was a donation. They created a corporation for the purpose. The whole place used to be the donor's summer home, until some twenty years ago. You saw the old house, I'm sure?"

I had, I said.

"That used to be the only building on the property. It's where they did group therapy. That's how it all got started. The donor's son had a tendency toward mental illness and a specialist recommended group therapy for him. The doctor's theory was that if you could have a group of patients living out in the country, helping each other with physical labor, and have a doctor for advice and checkups, you could cure certain kinds of sickness. They tried it, and the operation grew and was incorporated, and they put more land under cultivation, and put up the main building five years ago."

"Meaning, the therapy worked."

"Well, not for everything. Lots of people don't get better. But also a lot of people who couldn't be helped anywhere else managed a complete recovery here. The best thing about this place is the way everybody helps everybody else. Everybody knows they're flawed in some way, and so they try to help each other. Other places don't work that way, unfortunately. Doctors are doctors and patients are patients: the patient looks for help to the doctor and the doctor gives his help to the patient. Here, though, we all help each other. We're all each others' mirrors, and the doctors are part of us. They watch us from the sidelines and they slip in to help us if they see we need something, but it sometimes happens that we help them. Sometimes we're better at something than they are. For example, I'm teaching one doctor to play the piano, and another patient is teaching a nurse French. That kind of thing. Patients with problems like ours are often blessed with special abilities. So everyone here is equal—patients, staff—and you. You're one of us while you're in here, so I help you and you help me." Reiko smiled, gently flexing every wrinkle on her face. "You help Naoko and Naoko helps you."

"What should I do, then? Give me a concrete example."

"First you decide that you want to help and that you need to be helped by the other person. Then you decide to be totally honest. You will not lie, you will not gloss over anything, you will not cover up anything that might prove embarrassing for you. That's all there is to it."

"I'll try," I said. "But tell me, Reiko, why have you been in here for seven years? Talking with you like this, I can't believe there's anything wrong with you."

"Not while the sun's up," she said with a somber look. "But when night comes, I start drooling and rolling on the floor."

"Really?"

"Don't be ridiculous, I'm kidding," she said, shaking her head with a look of disgust. "I'm completely well—for now, at least. I stay here because I enjoy helping other people get well, teaching music, raising vegetables. I like it here. We're all more or less friends. Compared to that, what have I got in the outside world? I'm thirty-eight, going on forty. I'm not like Naoko. There's nobody waiting for me to get out, no family to take me back. I don't have any work to speak of, and almost no friends. And after seven years, I don't know what's going on out there. Oh, I'll read a paper in the library every once in a while, but I haven't set foot outside this property for seven years. I wouldn't know what to do if I left."

"But maybe a new world would open up for you," I said. "It's worth a try, don't you think?"

"Hmm, you may be right," she said, turning her cigarette lighter over and over in her hand. "But I've got my own set of problems. I can tell you all about them sometime if you like."

I nodded in response. "And Naoko," I said, "has she gotten better?"

"Hmm, we think she has. She was pretty confused at first and we had our doubts for a while, but she's calmed down now and she's improved to where she's able to express herself verbally. She's definitely headed in the right direction. But she should have gotten treatment a lot earlier than she did. Her symptoms were already showing up from the time that boyfriend of hers, Kizuki, killed himself. Her family should have seen it, and she herself should have realized that something was wrong. Of course, things weren't right at home, either . . ."

"They weren't?" I shot back.

"You didn't know?" Reiko seemed even more surprised than I was.

I shook my head.

"I'd better let Naoko tell you about that herself. She's ready for some honest talk with you." Reiko gave her coffee another stir and took a sip. "There's one more thing you need to know," she said. "According to the rules here, you and Naoko will not be allowed to be alone together. Visitors can't be alone with patients. An observer always has to be present— which in this case means me. I'm sorry, but you'll just have to put up with me. O.K.?"

"O.K.," I said with a smile.

"But still," she said, "the two of you can talk about anything you'd like. Forget I'm there. I know pretty much everything there is to know about you and Naoko."

"Everything?"

"Pretty much. We have these group sessions, you know. So we learn a lot about each other. Plus Naoko and I talk about everything. We don't have many secrets here."

I looked at Reiko as I drank my coffee. "To tell you the truth," I said, "I'm confused. I still don't know whether what I did to Naoko in Tokyo was the right thing to do or not. I've been thinking about it this whole time, but I still don't know."

"And neither do I," said Reiko. "And neither does Naoko. That's something the two of you will have to decide for yourselves. See what I mean? Whatever happened, the two of you can turn it in the right direction—*if* you can reach some kind of mutual understanding. Maybe, once you've got *that* taken care of, you can go back and think about whether what happened was the right thing or not. What do you say?"

I nodded.

"I think the three of us can help each other—you and Naoko and I—if we really want to, and if we're really honest. It can be incredibly effective when three people work at it like that. How long can you stay?"

"Well, I'd like to get back to Tokyo by early evening the day after tomorrow. I have to work, and I've got a German exam on Thursday."

"Good," she said. "So you can stay with us. That way it won't cost you anything and you can talk without having to worry about the time."

"With '*us*'?" I asked.

"Naoko and me, of course," said Reiko. "We have a separate bedroom, and there's a sofa bed in the living room, so you'll be able to sleep fine. Don't worry."

"Do they allow that?" I asked. "Can a male visitor stay in a woman's room?"

"I don't suppose you're going to come in and rape us in the middle of the night?"

"Don't be silly."

"So there's no problem, then. Stay in our place and we can have some nice, long talks. That would be the best thing. Then we can really understand each other. And I can play my guitar for you. I'm pretty good, you know."

"Are you sure I'm not going to be in the way?"

Reiko put her third Seven Stars between her lips and lit it after screwing up the corner of her mouth. "Naoko and I have already discussed this.

The two of us together are giving you a personal invitation to stay with us. Don't you think you should just politely accept?"

"Of course, I'll be glad to."

Reiko deepened the wrinkles at the corners of her eyes and looked at me for a time. "You've got this funny way of talking," she said. "Don't tell me you're trying to imitate that boy in *Catcher in the Rye?*"

"No way!" I said with a smile.

Reiko smiled too, cigarette in mouth. "You *are* a good person, though. I can tell that much from looking at you. I can tell these things after seven years of watching people come and go here: there are people who can open their hearts and people who can't. You're one of the ones who can. Or, more precisely, you can if you want to."

"What happens when people open their hearts?"

Cigarette dangling from her lips, Reiko clasped her hands together on the table. She was enjoying this. "They get better," she said. Her ashes dropped onto the table, but she paid them no mind.

REIKO AND I LEFT THE MAIN BUILDING, crossed a hill, and passed by a pool, some tennis courts, and a basketball court. Two men—one thin and middle-aged, the other young and fat—were on a tennis court. Both used their racquets well, but to me the game they were playing could not have been tennis. It seemed as if the two of them had a special interest in the bounce of tennis balls and were doing research in that area. They slammed the ball back and forth with a strange kind of concentration. Both were drenched in sweat. The young man, at the end of the court closer to us, noticed Reiko and came over. They exchanged a few words, smiling. Beside the court, a man with no expression on his face was using a large mower to cut the grass.

Moving on, we came to a patch of woods where some fifteen or twenty neat little cottages stood at some distance from one another. The same kind of yellow bike the gatekeeper had been riding was parked at the entrance of almost every house. "Staff members and their families live here," said Reiko.

"We have just about everything we need without going to the city," she said as we walked along. "Where food is concerned, as I said before, we're practically self-sufficient. We get eggs from our own chicken coop. We have books and records and exercise facilities, our own convenience store, and every week barbers and beauticians come to visit. We even have movies on weekends. Anything special we need we can ask a staff member to buy for us in town. Clothing we order from catalogues. Living here is no problem."

"But you can't go into town?"

"No, that we can't do. Of course if there's something special, like we have to go to the dentist, or something, that's another matter, but as a rule we can't go into town. Each person is completely free to leave this place, but once you've left you can't come back. You burn your bridges. You can't go off for a couple of days in town and expect to come back. It only stands to reason, though. Everybody would be coming and going."

Beyond the trees we came to a gentle slope. At irregular intervals along the slope stood a row of two-story wooden houses that had something strange about them. What made them look strange it's hard to say, but that was the first thing I felt when I saw them. My reaction was a lot like what we feel from attempts to paint unreality in a pleasant way. It occurred to me that this was what you might get if Walt Disney did an animated version of a Munch painting. All the houses were exactly the same shape and color, nearly cubical, in perfect left-to-right symmetry, with big front doors and lots of windows. The road twisted its way among them like the artificial practice course of a driving school. Well-manicured flowering shrubbery stood in front of each house. There was no sign of people, and curtains covered all the windows.

"This is called Area C. The women live here. Us! There are ten houses, each containing four units, two people per unit. That's eighty people all together, but at the moment there are only thirty-two of us."

"Quiet, isn't it?"

"Well, there's nobody here now," Reiko said. "I've been given special permission to move around freely like this, but everybody else is off pursuing their individual schedules. Some are exercising, some are gardening, some are in group therapy, some are out gathering wild plants. Each person makes up his or her own schedule. Let's see, what's Naoko doing now? I think she was supposed to be working on new paint and wallpaper. I forget. There are a few jobs like that that go till five."

Reiko walked into the building marked "C-7," climbed the stairs at the far end of the hallway, and opened the door on the right, which was unlocked. She showed me around the apartment, a pleasant, if plain, four-room unit: living room, bedroom, kitchen, and bath. It had no extra furniture or unnecessary decoration, but neither was the place severe. There was nothing special about it, but being there was kind of like being with Reiko: you could relax and let the tension leave your body. The living room had a sofa, a table, and a rocking chair. Another table stood in the kitchen. Both tables had large ashtrays on them. The bedroom had two beds, two desks, and a closet. A small night table stood between the beds with a reading lamp atop it and a paperback turned facedown. The kitchen had a small electric range that matched the refrigerator and was equipped for simple cooking.

"No bathtub, just a shower, but it's pretty impressive, wouldn't you say? Bath and laundry facilities are communal."

"It's almost too impressive. My dorm room has a ceiling and a window."

"Ah, but you haven't seen the winters here," said Reiko, touching my back to guide me to the sofa and sitting down next to me. "They're long and harsh. Nothing but snow and snow and more snow everywhere you look. It gets damp and chills you to the bone. We spend the winter shoveling snow. Mostly you stay inside where it's warm and listen to music or talk or knit. If you didn't have this much space, you'd suffocate. You'll see if you come here in the winter."

Reiko gave a deep sigh as if picturing the winter, and she folded her hands on her knees.

"This will be your bed," she said, patting the sofa. "We'll sleep in the bedroom, and you'll sleep here. You should be O.K., don't you think?"

"I'm sure I'll be fine."

"So, that does it," said Reiko. "We'll be back around five. Naoko and I both have things to do until then. Do you mind staying here alone?"

"Not at all. I'll study my German."

When Reiko left, I stretched out on the sofa and closed my eyes. I lay there steeping myself in the silence when, out of nowhere, I thought of the time Kizuki and I took a motorcycle trip. That had been autumn, too, I realized. Autumn how many years ago? Yes, four years ago. I recalled the smell of Kizuki's leather jacket and the racket made by that red Yamaha 125cc bike. We went to a spot far down the coast, and came back the same evening, exhausted. Nothing special happened on that trip, but I remembered it well. The sharp autumn wind moaned in my ears, and looking up at the sky, my hands clutching Kizuki's jacket, I felt as if I might be swept into outer space.

I lay there for a long time, letting my mind wander from one memory to another. For some strange reason, lying down in this room seemed to bring back old memories that I had rarely if ever recalled before. Some of them were pleasant, but others carried a trace of sadness.

How long did this go on? I was so immersed in that torrent of memory (and it was a torrent, like a spring gushing out of the rocks) that I failed to notice Naoko quietly open the door and come in. I opened my eyes, and there she was. I raised my head and looked into her eyes for a time. She was sitting on the arm of the sofa, looking at me. At first I thought she might be an image spun into existence by my own memories. But it was the real Naoko.

"Sleeping?" she whispered.

"No," I said, "just thinking." I sat up and asked, "How are you?"

"I'm good," she said with a little smile like a pale, distant scene. "I don't have much time, though. I'm not supposed to be here now. I just got away for a minute, and I have to go back right away. Don't you hate my hair?"

"Not at all," I said. "It's cute." Her hair was in a simple, schoolgirl style, one side held in place with a barrette the way she used to have it in the old days. It suited Naoko very well, as if she had always worn her hair that way. She looked like one of the beautiful little girls you see in woodblock prints from the middle ages.

"It's such a pain, I have Reiko cut it for me. Do you really think it's cute?"

"Really."

"My mother hates it." She opened the barrette, let the hair hang down, smoothed it with her fingers, and closed the barrette again. The barrette was shaped like a butterfly.

"I wanted to be sure to see you alone before the three of us get together. Not that I had anything special to say. I just wanted to see your face and get used to having you here. Otherwise, I'd have trouble getting to know you again. I'm so bad with people."

"Well?" I asked. "Is it working?"

"A little," she said, touching her barrette again. "But time's up. I've got to go."

I nodded.

"Toru," she began, "I really want to thank you for coming to see me. It makes me very happy. But if being here is any kind of burden to you, you shouldn't hesitate to tell me so. This is a special place, and it has a special system, and some people can't get into it. So if you feel like that, please be honest and let me know. I won't be crushed. We're honest with each other here. We tell each other all kinds of things with complete honesty."

"I'll tell you," I said. "I'll be honest."

Naoko sat down and leaned against me on the sofa. When I put my arm around her, she rested her head on my shoulder and pressed her face to my neck. She stayed like that for a time, almost as if she were taking my temperature. Holding her, I felt warm in the chest. After a short while, she stood up without saying a word and went out through the door as quietly as she had come in.

With Naoko gone, I went to sleep on the sofa. I hadn't intended to do so, but I fell into the kind of deep sleep I had not had for a long time, filled with a sense of Naoko's presence. In the kitchen were the dishes Naoko ate from, in the bathroom was the toothbrush Naoko used, and in the bedroom was the bed in which Naoko slept. Sleeping soundly in this apartment of hers, I wrung the fatigue from every cell of my body, drop by drop. I dreamed of a butterfly dancing in the half-light.

When I awoke again, the hands of my watch were pointing to 4:35. The light had changed, the wind had died, the shapes of the clouds were different. I had sweated in my sleep, so I dried my face with a small towel from my knapsack and put on a fresh undershirt. Going to the kitchen, I took a drink of water and stood there looking through the window over the sink. This window faced a window of the next building, on the inside of which hung several paper cutouts—a bird, a cloud, a cow, a cat, all done in skillful silhouette and joined together. As before, there was no sign of people present, and there were no sounds of any kind. I felt as if I were living alone in an extremely well-cared-for ruin.

PEOPLE STARTED COMING BACK to Area C a little after five o'clock. Looking out the kitchen window, I saw three women passing by just below. All wore hats that prevented me from telling their ages, but judging from the voices I heard, they were not very young. Shortly after they had disappeared around a corner, four more women appeared from the same direction and, like the first group, they disappeared around the same corner. An evening mood hung over everything. From the living room window I could see trees and the line of hills. Above the ridge floated a border of pale sunlight.

Naoko and Reiko came back together at five-thirty. Naoko and I exchanged proper greetings as if meeting for the first time. She seemed truly embarrassed. Reiko noticed the book I had been reading and asked what it was. Thomas Mann's *The Magic Mountain*, I told her.

"How could you bring a book like that to a place like this?" she demanded to know. She was right, of course.

Reiko then made coffee for the three of us. I told Naoko about Storm Trooper's sudden disappearance and about the last day I saw him, when he gave me the firefly. "I'm so sorry he's gone," she said. "I wanted to hear more stories about him." Reiko asked who this Storm Trooper person was, so I told her about his antics and got a big laugh from her. The world was at peace and filled with laughter as long as stories of Storm Trooper were being told.

At six we went to the dining hall in the main building for supper. Naoko and I had fried fish with green salad, boiled vegetables, rice, and miso soup. Reiko limited herself to pasta salad and coffee, followed by another cigarette.

"You don't need to eat so much as you get older," she said by way of explanation.

Some twenty other people were there in the dining hall. A few new ones arrived as we ate, but meanwhile a few others left. Aside from the variety in people's ages, the scene looked pretty much like that of the dining hall in my dormitory. Where it differed was the uniform volume at which people conversed. There were no loud voices and no whispers, no one laughing out loud or crying out in shock, no one yelling to another person with exaggerated gestures, nothing but quiet conversations, all carried on at the same level. People were eating in groups of three to five. Each group had a single speaker, to whom the others would listen with nods and grunts of interest, and when that person was done speaking, the next would take up the conversation. I could not tell what they were saying, but the way they said it reminded me of the strange tennis game I had seen at noon. I wondered if Naoko spoke like this when she was with them and, strangely enough, I felt a twinge of loneliness mixed with jealousy.

At the table behind me, a balding man in white with the authentic air of a doctor was holding forth to a nervous-looking young man in glasses and a squirrel-faced woman of middle age on the effects of weightlessness on the secretion of gastric juices. The two listened with an occasional "My goodness" or "No kidding," but the longer I listened to the balding man's style of speaking, the less certain I became that, even in his white coat, he really was a doctor.

No one in the dining hall paid me any special attention. No one stared or even seemed to notice I was there. My presence must have been an entirely natural event.

Just once, though, the man in white spun around and asked me, "How long will you be staying?"

"Two nights," I said. "I'll be leaving on Wednesday."

"It's nice here at this time of year, isn't it? But come again in winter. It's *really* nice when everything's white."

"Naoko may be out of here by the time snow comes," said Reiko to the man.

"True, but still, the winter's really nice," he repeated with a somber expression. I felt increasingly unsure as to whether or not he was a doctor.

"What do you people talk about?" I asked Reiko, who seemed not quite to get my meaning.

"What do we talk about? Just ordinary things. What happened today, or books we've read, or tomorrow's weather, you know. Don't tell me you're wondering if people jump to their feet and shout stuff like 'It'll rain tomorrow if a polar bear eats the stars tonight!'"

"No, no, of course not," I said. "I was just wondering what all these quiet conversations were about."

"It's a quiet place, so people talk quietly," said Naoko. She made a neat pile of fish bones at the edge of her plate and dabbed at her mouth with a handkerchief. "There's no need to raise your voice here. You don't have to convince anybody of anything, and you don't have to attract anyone's attention."

"I guess not," I said, but as I ate my meal in these quiet surroundings, I was surprised to find myself missing the buzz of people. I wanted to hear people laughing and shouting for no reason and saying overblown things. That was just the kind of noise I had grown sick of in recent months, but sitting here and eating fish in this unnaturally quiet room, I couldn't relax. The dining hall had all the atmosphere of a specialized-machine-tool trade fair. People with a strong interest in a limited field came together in a limited spot and exchanged information understood only by themselves.

BACK IN THE ROOM AFTER SUPPER, Naoko and Reiko announced that they would be going to the Area C communal bath and that if I didn't mind just a shower, I could use the one in their bathroom. I would do that, I said, and after they were gone I got undressed, showered, and washed my hair. I found a Bill Evans record in the bookcase and was listening to it while drying my hair when I realized that it was the record I had played in Naoko's room on the night of her birthday, the night she cried and I took her in my arms. That had happened only six months earlier, but it felt like something from a much remoter past. Maybe it felt that way because I had thought about it so often — too often, to the point where it had distorted my sense of time.

The moon was so bright, I turned the lights off and stretched out on the sofa to listen to Bill Evans's piano. Streaming in through the window, the moonlight cast long shadows and splashed the walls with a touch of diluted India ink. I took a thin metal flask from my knapsack, let my mouth fill with the brandy it contained, let the warmth move slowly down my throat to my stomach, and from there felt it spreading to every corner of my body. After one more sip, I closed the flask and returned it to my knapsack. Now the moonlight seemed to be swaying with the music.

Twenty minutes later, Naoko and Reiko came back from the bath.

"Oh! It was so dark here, we thought you packed your bags and went back to Tokyo," exclaimed Reiko.

"No way," I said. "I hadn't seen such a bright moon for years. I wanted to look at it with the lights off."

"It's lovely, though," said Naoko. "Reiko, do we still have those candles from the last power outage?"

"Probably, in a kitchen drawer."

Naoko brought a large white candle from the kitchen. I lit it, dripped a little wax into a plate, and stood it up. Reiko used the flame to light a ciga-

rette. As the three of us sat facing the candle amid these hushed surroundings, it began to seem as if we were the only ones left on some far edge of
the world. The still shadows of the moonlight and the swaying shadows of
the candlelight met and melded on the white walls of the apartment.
Naoko and I sat next to each other on the sofa, and Reiko settled into the
rocking chair facing us.

"How about some wine?" Reiko asked me.

"You're allowed to drink?" I asked with some surprise.

"Well, not really," said Reiko, scratching an earlobe with a hint of embarrassment. "But they pretty much let it go. If it's just wine or beer and you
don't drink too much. I've got a friend on the staff who buys me a little
now and then."

"We have our drinking parties," said Naoko with a mischievous air.
"Just the two of us."

"That's nice," I said.

Reiko took a bottle of white wine from the refrigerator, opened it with a
corkscrew, and brought three glasses. The wine had a clear, delicious fla-
vor that seemed almost homemade. When the record ended, Reiko brought
a guitar out from under her bed, and after tuning it with a look of fondness
for the instrument, she began to play a slow Bach fugue. She missed her
fingering every now and then, but it was real Bach, with real feeling—
warm, intimate, and filled with the joy of performance.

"I started playing the guitar here," said Reiko. "There are no pianos in
the rooms, of course. I'm self-taught, and I don't have guitar hands, so I'll
never get very good, but I really love the instrument. It's small and simple
and easy, kind of like a warm little room."

She played one more short Bach piece, something from a suite. Eyes
on the candle flame, sipping wine, listening to Reiko's Bach, I felt the tension inside me slipping away. When Reiko ended the Bach, Naoko asked
her to play a Beatles song.

"Request time," said Reiko, winking at me. "She makes me play Beatles
every day, like I'm her music slave."

Despite her protest, Reiko played a fine "Michelle."

"That's a good one," she said. "I really like that song." She took a sip of
wine and puffed her cigarette. "It makes me feel like I'm in a big meadow
in a soft rain."

Then she played "Nowhere Man" and "Julia." Now and then as she played, she would close her eyes and shake her head. Afterward she would go back to the wine and the cigarette.

"Play 'Norwegian Wood,'" said Naoko.

Reiko brought a porcelain beckoning cat from the kitchen. It was a coin bank, and Naoko dropped a hundred-yen piece from her purse into its slot.

"What's this all about?" I asked.

"It's a rule," said Naoko. "When I request 'Norwegian Wood,' I have to put a hundred yen into the bank. It's my favorite, so I make a point of paying for it. I make a request when I really want to hear it."

"And that way I get my cigarette money!" said Reiko.

Reiko gave her fingers a good flexing and then played "Norwegian Wood." Again she played with real feeling, but never allowed it to become sentimental. I took a hundred-yen coin from my pocket and dropped it into the bank.

"Thank you," said Reiko with a sweet smile.

"That song can make me feel *so* sad," said Naoko. "I don't know, I guess I imagine myself wandering in a deep wood. I'm all alone and it's cold and dark, and nobody comes to save me. That's why Reiko never plays it unless I request it."

"Sounds like *Casablanca!*" Reiko said with a laugh.

She followed "Norwegian Wood" with a few bossa novas while I kept my eyes on Naoko. As she had said in her letter, she looked healthier than before, suntanned, her body firmed up from exercise and outdoor work. Her eyes were the same deep, clear pools they had always been, and her small lips still trembled shyly, but overall her beauty had begun to change to that of a mature woman. Almost gone now was the sharp edge—the chilling sharpness of a thin blade—that could be glimpsed in the shadows of her beauty, in the place of which there hovered now a uniquely soothing, quiet calm. I felt moved by this new, gentle beauty of hers, and amazed to think that a woman could change so much in the course of half a year. I felt as drawn to her as ever, perhaps more than before, but the thought of what she had lost in the meantime also gave me cause for regret. Never again would she have that self-centered beauty that seems to take its own, independent course in adolescent girls and no one else.

Naoko said she wanted to hear about how I was spending my days. I talked about the student strike, and about Nagasawa. This was the first time I had ever said anything to her about him. I found it challenging to give her an accurate account of his odd humanity, his unique philosophy, and his uncentered morality, but Naoko seemed finally to grasp what I was trying to tell her. I hid the fact that I went out hunting girls with him, revealing only that the one person in the dorm I spent any real time with was this unusual guy. All the while, Reiko went through another practice of the Bach fugue she had played before, taking occasional breaks for wine and cigarettes.

"He sounds like a strange person," said Naoko.

"He *is* strange," I said.

"But you like him?"

"I'm not sure," I said. "I guess I can't say I *like* him. Nagasawa is beyond liking or not liking. He doesn't try to be liked. In that sense, he's a very honest guy, even stoic. He doesn't try to fool anybody."

"'Stoic,' sleeping with all those girls? Now *that* is weird," said Naoko, laughing. "How many girls has he slept with?"

"It's probably up to eighty now," I said. "But in his case, the higher the numbers go, the less each individual act seems to mean. Which is what I think he's trying to accomplish."

"And you call that 'stoic'?"

"For him it is."

Naoko thought about my words for a minute. "I think he's a lot sicker in the head that I am," she said.

"So do I," I said. "But he can put all his warped qualities into a logical system. He's brilliant. If you brought him here, he'd be out in two days. 'Oh, sure, I know all that,' he'd say. 'I understand everything you're doing here.' He's that kind of guy. The kind people respect."

"I guess I'm the opposite of brilliant," said Naoko. "I don't understand anything they're doing here — any better than I understand myself."

"It's not because you're not smart," I said. "You're normal. I've got tons of things I don't understand about myself. We're both normal: ordinary."

Naoko raised her feet to the edge of the sofa and rested her chin on her knees. "I want to know more about you," she said.

"I'm just an ordinary guy — ordinary family, ordinary education, ordinary face, ordinary grades, ordinary thoughts in my head."

"You're such a big Scott Fitzgerald fan . . . wasn't he the one who said you shouldn't trust anybody who calls himself an ordinary man? You lent me the book!" said Naoko with a mischievous smile.

"True," I said. "But this is no affectation. I really, truly believe deep down that I'm an ordinary person. Can you find something in me that's *not* ordinary?"

"Of course I can!" said Naoko with a hint of impatience. "Don't you get it? Why do you think I slept with you? Because I was so drunk I would have slept with anyone?"

"No, of course I don't think that," I said.

Naoko remained silent for a long time, staring at her toes. At a loss for words, I took another drink of wine.

"How many girls have *you* slept with, Toru?" Naoko asked in a tiny voice as if the thought had just crossed her mind.

"Eight or nine," I answered truthfully.

Reiko plopped the guitar into her lap. "You're not even twenty years old!" she said. "What kind of life are you leading?"

Naoko kept silent and watched me with those clear eyes of hers. I told Reiko about the first girl I'd slept with and how we had broken up. I had found it impossible to love her, I explained. I went on to tell her about my sleeping with one girl after another under Nagasawa's tutelage.

"I'm not trying to make excuses, but I was in pain," I said to Naoko. "Here I was, seeing you almost every week, and talking with you, and knowing that the only one in your heart was Kizuki. It hurt. It really hurt. And I think that's why I slept with girls I didn't know."

Naoko shook her head for a few moments, and then she raised her face to look at me. "You asked me that time why I had never slept with Kizuki, didn't you? Do you still want to know?"

"I guess it's something I really ought to know," I said.

"I think so, too," said Naoko. "The dead will always be dead, but we have to go on living."

I nodded. Reiko played the same difficult passage over and over, trying to get it right.

"I was ready to sleep with him," said Naoko, unclasping her barrette and letting her hair down. She toyed with the butterfly shape in her hands. "And of course he wanted to sleep with me. So we tried. We tried a lot. But it never worked. We couldn't do it. I didn't know why then, and I still don't know why. I loved him, and I wasn't worried about losing my virginity. I would have been glad to do anything he wanted. But it never worked."

Naoko lifted the hair she had let down and fastened it with the barrette.

"I couldn't get wet," she said in a tiny voice. "I never opened to him. So it always hurt. I was just too dry, it hurt too much. We tried everything we could think of—creams and things—but still it hurt me. So I used my fingers, or my lips. I would always do it for him that way. You know what I mean."

I nodded in silence.

Naoko cast her gaze through the window at the moon, which looked bigger and brighter now than it had before. "I never wanted to talk about any of this," she said. "I wanted to shut it up in my heart. I wish I still could. But I have to talk about it. I don't know the answer. I mean, I was plenty wet the time I slept with you, wasn't I?"

"Uh-huh," I said.

"I was wet from the minute you walked into my apartment the night of my twentieth birthday. I wanted you to hold me. I wanted you to take my clothes off and touch me all over and to get inside me. I had never felt like that before. Why is that? Why do things happen that way? I mean, I really loved him."

"And not me," I said. "You want to know why you felt that way about me even though you didn't love me."

"I'm sorry," said Naoko. "I don't mean to hurt you, but this much you have to understand: Kizuki and I had a truly special relationship. We had been together from the time we were three. It's how we grew up: always together, always talking, understanding each other perfectly. The first time we kissed—it was in the sixth grade—was just wonderful. The first time I had my period, I ran to him and cried like a baby. We were that close. So after he died, I didn't know how to relate to other people. I didn't know what it means to love another person."

She reached for her wineglass on the table but managed only to knock it onto the floor, spilling the wine on the carpet. I crouched down and retrieved the glass, setting it on the table. Did she want to drink some more? I asked. Naoko remained silent for a while, then suddenly burst into tears, trembling all over. Slumping forward, she buried her face in her hands and sobbed with all the suffocating violence she had had that night with me. Reiko laid her guitar down and sat by Naoko, caressing her back. When she put an arm across Naoko's shoulders, Naoko pressed her face against Reiko's chest like a baby.

"You know," Reiko said to me, "it might be a good idea for you to go out for a little walk. Maybe twenty minutes. Sorry, but I think that would help."

I nodded and stood, pulling a sweater on over my shirt. "Thanks for stepping in," I said to Reiko.

"Don't mention it," she said with a wink. "This is not your fault. Don't worry, by the time you come back she'll be O.K."

My feet carried me down the road, which was illuminated by the oddly unreal light of the moon, and into the woods. Beneath that moonlight, all sounds bore a strange reverberation. The hollow sound of my own footsteps seemed to come from another direction as if I were hearing someone walking on the bottom of the sea. Behind me, every now and then, I would hear a crack or a rustle. A heavy pall hung over the forest, as if the animals of the night were holding their breath, waiting for me to pass.

Where the road sloped upward beyond the trees, I sat and looked toward the building where Naoko lived. It was easy to tell which room was hers. All I had to do was find the one window toward the back where a faint light trembled. I focused on that point of light for a long, long time. It made me think of something like the final throb of a soul's dying embers. I wanted to cup my hands over what was left and keep it alive. I went on watching it the way Jay Gatsby watched that tiny light on the opposite shore night after night.

WHEN I WALKED BACK to the front entrance of the building half an hour later, I could hear Reiko practicing the guitar. I padded up the stairs and tapped on the apartment door. Inside I found no sign of Naoko. Reiko sat alone on the carpet, playing her guitar. She pointed toward the bedroom door to let me know Naoko was in there. Then she set the guitar down on the floor and took a seat on the sofa, inviting me to sit next to her and dividing what wine was left between our two glasses.

"Naoko is fine," she said, touching my knee. "Don't worry, all she has to do is rest for a while. She'll calm down. She was just a little upset. How about taking a walk with me in the meantime?"

"Good," I said.

Reiko and I ambled down a road illuminated by streetlamps. When we reached the area by the tennis and basketball courts, we sat on a bench. She picked up a basketball from under the bench and turned it in her hands. Then she asked me if I played tennis. I knew how to play, I said, but I was bad at it.

"How about basketball?"

"Not my strongest sport," I said.

"What *is* your strongest sport?" Reiko asked, wrinkling the corners of her eyes with a smile. "Aside from sleeping with girls."

"I'm not so good at that, either," I said, stung by her words.

"Just kidding," she said. "Don't get mad. But really, though, what *are* you good at?"

"Nothing special. I have things I *like* to do."

"For instance?"

"Hiking trips. Swimming. Reading."

"You like to do things alone, then?"

"I guess so. I could never get excited about games you play with other people. I can't get into them. I lose interest."

"Then you *have* to come here in the winter. We do cross-country ski-ing. I'm sure you'd like that, tramping around in the snow all day, working up a good sweat." Under the streetlamp, Reiko stared at her right hand as if she were inspecting an antique musical instrument.

"Does Naoko get like that often?" I asked.

"Every now and then," said Reiko, now looking at her left hand. "Every once in a while she'll get worked up and cry like that. But that's O.K. She's letting her feelings out. The scary thing is *not* being able to do that. Then your feelings build up and harden and die inside. That's when you're in big trouble."

"Did I say something I shouldn't have?"

"Not a thing. Don't worry. Just speak your mind honestly. That's the best thing. It may hurt a little sometimes, and somebody may get worked up the way Naoko did, but in the long run it's the best thing. That's what you should do if you're serious about making Naoko well again. Like I told you in the beginning, you should think not so much about wanting to help her as wanting to recover yourself by helping her to recover. That's the way it's done here. So you have to be honest and say everything that comes to mind while you're here at least. Nobody does that in the outside world, right?"

"I guess not," I said.

"I've seen all kinds of people come and go in my seven years here," said Reiko, "maybe *too* many people. So I can usually tell by looking at a person whether they're going to get better or not, almost by instinct. But in Naoko's case, I'm not sure. I have absolutely no idea what's going to happen to her. For all I know, she could be a-hundred-percent recovered next month, or she could go on like this for years. So I really can't tell you what to do aside from the most generalized kind of advice: to be honest, or to help each other."

"What makes Naoko such a hard case for you?"

"Probably because I like her so much. I think my emotions get in the way and I can't see her clearly. I mean, I really like her. But aside from that, she has a bunch of different problems that are all tangled up, so it's hard to unravel any one of them. It may take a very long time to undo them all, or something could trigger them to come unraveled all at once. It's kind of like that. Which is why I can't be sure about her."

She picked up the basketball again, twirled it in her hands, and bounced it on the ground.

"The most important thing is not to let yourself get impatient," Reiko said. "This is one more piece of advice I have for you: don't get impatient. Even if things are so tangled up you can't do anything, don't get desperate or blow a fuse and start yanking on one particular thread before it's ready to come undone. You have to figure it's going to be a long process and that you'll work on things slowly, one at a time. Do you think you can do that?"

"I can try," I said.

"It may take a very long time, you know, and even then she may not recover completely. Have you thought about that?"

I nodded.

"Waiting is hard," she said, bouncing the ball. "Especially for someone your age. You just sit and wait for her to get better. Without deadlines or guarantees. Do you think you can do that? Do you love Naoko that much?"

"I'm not sure," I said honestly. "Like Naoko, I'm not really sure what it means to love another person. Though she meant it a little differently. I do want to try my best, though. I have to, or else I won't know where to go.

Like you said before, Naoko and I have to save each other. It's the only way for either of us to be saved."

"And are you going to go on sleeping with girls you pick up?"

"I don't know what to do about that either," I said. "What do you think? Should I just keep waiting and masturbating? I'm not in complete control there, either."

Reiko set the ball on the ground and patted my knee. "Look," she said, "I'm not telling you to stop sleeping with girls. If you're O.K. with that, then it's O.K. It's your life after all, it's something *you* have to decide. All I'm saying is you shouldn't use yourself up in some unnatural form. Do you see what I'm getting at? It would be such a waste. The years nineteen and twenty are a crucial stage in the maturation of character, and if you allow yourself to become warped when you're that age, it will cause you pain when you're older. It's true. So think about it carefully. If you want to take care of Naoko, take care of yourself, too."

I said I would think about it.

"I was twenty once myself. Once upon a time. Would you believe it?"

"I believe it. Of course."

"Deep down?"

"Deep down," I said with a smile.

"And I was cute, too. Not as cute as Naoko, but pretty damn cute. I didn't have all these wrinkles."

I said I liked her wrinkles a lot. She thanked me.

"But don't ever tell another woman that you find her wrinkles attractive," she added. "I like to hear it, but I'm the exception."

"I'll be careful," I said.

She slipped a wallet from her pants pocket and handed me a photo from the card holder. It was a color snapshot of a cute girl around ten years old wearing skis and brightly colored ski clothes and standing on the snow with a sweet smile for the camera.

"Don't you think she's pretty? My daughter," said Reiko. "She sent me this in January. She's in—what?—fourth grade now."

"She's got your smile," I said, returning the photo. Reiko put the wallet back into her pocket and, with a sniff, put a cigarette between her lips and lit up.

"I was going to be a concert pianist," she said. "I had talent, and people recognized it and made a fuss over me while I was growing up. I won competitions and had top grades in the conservatory, and I was set to study in Germany after graduation. Not a cloud on the horizon. Everything worked out perfectly, and when it didn't there was always somebody to fix it. But then one day something happened, and it all blew apart. I was in my senior year at the conservatory and there was a fairly important competition coming up. I practiced for it constantly, but all of a sudden the little finger of my left hand stopped moving. I don't know why, it just did. I tried massaging it, soaking it in hot water, taking off from practice for a few days: nothing worked. So then I got scared and went to the doctor's. They tried all kinds of tests but they couldn't come up with anything. There was nothing wrong with the finger itself, and the nerves were O.K., they said: there was no reason it should stop moving. The problem must be psychological. So I went to a psychiatrist, but he didn't really know what was going on, either. Probably precompetition stress, he figured, and told me to get away from the piano for a while."

Reiko inhaled deeply and let the smoke out. Then she bent her neck to the side a few times.

"So I went to recuperate at my grandmother's place on the coast in Izu. I figured I'd forget about that particular competition and really relax, spend a couple of weeks away from the piano doing anything I wanted. But it was hopeless. Piano was all I could think about. Maybe my finger would never move again. How would I live if that happened? The same thoughts kept going round and round in my brain. And no wonder: piano had been my whole life up to that point. I had started playing when I was four and grew up thinking about the piano and nothing else. I never did housework to make sure I wouldn't injure my fingers. People paid attention to me for that one thing: my talent at the piano. Take the piano away from a girl who's grown up like that, and what's left? So then, *snap!* My mind became a complete jumble. Total darkness."

She dropped her cigarette to the ground and stamped it out, and then she bent her neck a few times again.

"That was the end of my dream of becoming a concert pianist. I spent two months in the hospital. My finger started to move shortly after I went in, so I *was* able to return to the conservatory and graduate, but something inside me had vanished. Some jewel of energy or something had disappeared—evaporated—from inside my body. The doctor said I lacked the mental strength to become a professional pianist and advised me to abandon the idea. So after graduating I took pupils and taught them at home. But the pain I felt was excruciating. It was as if my life had ended. Here I was in my early twenties and the best part of my life had ended. Do you see how terrible that would be? I had had my hands on such potential, and I woke up one day and all of it was gone. No one would applaud me, no one would make a big fuss over me, no one would tell me how wonderful I was. I spent day after day in the house teaching neighborhood children Beyer exercises and sonatinas. I felt so miserable, I cried all the time. To think what I had missed! I would hear about people who were far less talented than I was taking second place in a competition or holding a recital in such-and-such a hall, and the tears would pour out of me.

"My parents walked around me on tiptoe, afraid of hurting me. But I knew how disappointed they were. All of a sudden the daughter they had been so proud of was a returnee from a mental hospital. They couldn't even marry me off. When you're living with people, you sense what they're feeling, and I hated it. I was afraid to go out, afraid the neighbors were talking about me. So then, *snap!* It happened again—the jumble, the darkness. It happened when I was twenty-four, and this time I spent seven months in a sanatorium. Not this place: a regular insane asylum with high walls and locked gates. A filthy place without pianos. I didn't know what to do with myself. All I knew was I wanted to get out of there as soon as I could, so I struggled desperately to get better. Seven months: a *long* seven months. That's when my wrinkles got started."

Reiko smiled, stretching her lips from side to side.

"I hadn't been out of the hospital for long when I met a man and got married. He was a year younger than me, an engineer who worked in an airplane manufacturing company, and one of my pupils. A nice man. He didn't say a lot, but he was warm and sincere. He had been taking lessons from me for six months when all of a sudden he asked me to marry him. Just like that—one day when we were having tea after his lesson. Can you believe it? We had never dated or held hands. He took me totally off guard. I told him I couldn't get married. I said I liked him and thought he was a nice person but that, for certain reasons, I couldn't marry him. He wanted to know what those reasons were, so I explained everything to him with complete honesty—that I had been hospitalized twice for mental breakdowns. I told him *everything*—what the cause had been, my condition, and the possibility that it could happen again. He said he needed time to think, and I encouraged him to take all the time he needed. But when he came for his lesson a week later, he said he still wanted to marry me. I asked him to wait three months. We would see each other for three months, I said, and if he still wanted to marry me at that point, we would talk about it again.

"We dated once a week for three months. We went everywhere, and talked about everything, and I got to like him a lot. When I was with him, I felt as if my life had finally come back to me. It gave me a wonderful sense of relief to be alone with him: I could forget all those terrible things that had happened. So what if I hadn't been able to become a concert pianist? So what if I had spent time in mental hospitals? My life hadn't ended. Life was still full of wonderful things I hadn't experienced. If only for having made me feel that way, I felt tremendously grateful to him. After three months went by, he asked me again to marry him. And this is what I said to him: 'If you want to sleep with me, I don't mind. I've never slept with anybody, and I'm very fond of you, so if you want to make love to me, I don't mind at all. But marrying me is a whole different matter. If you marry me, you take on all my troubles, and they're a lot worse than you can imagine.'

"He said he didn't care, that he didn't just want to sleep with me, he wanted to marry me, to share everything I had inside me. And he meant it. He was the kind of person who would only say what he really meant, and do anything he said. So I agreed to marry him. It was all I could do. We got married, let's see, four months later, I think it was. He fought with his parents over me, and they disowned him. He was from an old family that lived in a rural part of Shikoku. They had my background investigated and found out that I had been hospitalized twice. No wonder they opposed the marriage. So, anyhow, we didn't have a wedding ceremony. We just went to the ward office and registered our marriage and took a trip to Hakone for two nights. That was plenty for us: we were happy. And finally, I remained a virgin until the day I married. I was twenty-five years old! Can you believe it?"

Reiko sighed and picked up the basketball again.

"I figured that as long as I was with him, I would be all right," she went on. "As long as I was with him, my troubles would stay away. That's the most important thing for a sickness like ours: a sense of trust. If I put myself in this person's hands, I'll be O.K. If my condition starts to worsen even the slightest bit—if a screw comes loose—he'll notice right away, and with tremendous care and patience he'll fix it, he'll tighten the screw again, put all the jumbled threads back in place. If we have that sense of trust, our sickness stays away. No more *snap!* I was so happy! Life was so great! I felt as if someone had pulled me out of a cold, raging sea and wrapped me in a blanket and laid me in a warm bed. I had a baby two years after we were married, and then my hands were really full! I practically forgot about my sickness. I'd get up in the morning and do the housework and take care of the baby and feed my husband when he came home from work. It was the same thing day after day, but I was happy. It was probably the happiest time of my life. How many years did it last, I wonder? At least until I was thirty-one. And then, all of a sudden, *snap!* It happened again. I fell apart."

Reiko lit a cigarette. The wind had died down. The smoke rose straight up and disappeared into the darkness of night. Just then I realized that the sky was filled with stars.

"Something happened?" I asked.

"Yes," she said, "something very strange, as if a trap had been set for me. Even now, it gives me a chill just to think about it." Reiko rubbed a temple with her free hand. "I'm sorry, though, making you listen to all this talk about me. You came here to see Naoko, not listen to my story."

"I'd really like to hear it, though," I said. "If you don't mind, I'd like to hear the rest."

"Well," Reiko began, "when our daughter entered kindergarten, I started playing again, little by little. Not for anyone else, but for myself. I started with short pieces by Bach, Mozart, Scarlatti. After such a long blank period, of course, my feel for the music didn't come back right away. And my fingers wouldn't move the way they used to. But I was thrilled to be playing the piano again. With my hands on the keys, I realized how much I had loved music—and how much I had hungered for it. To be able to perform music for yourself is a wonderful thing.

"As I said before, I had been playing from the time I was four years old, but it occurred to me that I had never once played for myself. I had always been trying to pass a test or practice an assignment or impress somebody. Those are all important things, of course, if you are going to master an instrument. But after a certain age you have to start performing for yourself. That's what music *is*. I had to drop out of the elite course and pass my thirty-first birthday before I was finally able to see that. I would send my child off to kindergarten and hurry through the housework, then take an hour or two playing music I liked. So far so good, right?"

I nodded in affirmation.

"Then one day I had a visit from one of the ladies of the neighborhood, someone I at least knew well enough to say hello to on the street, asking me to give her daughter piano lessons. I didn't know about the daughter—though we lived in the same general 'neighborhood' our houses were still pretty far apart—but according to the woman, her daughter used to pass my house and loved to hear me play. She had seen me at some point, too, and now she was pestering her mother to get me to teach her. She was in her second year of middle school and had taken lessons from a number of people, but things had not gone well for one reason or another and now she had no teacher.

"I turned her down. I had had that blank of several years, and while it might have made sense for me to take on an absolute beginner, it would have been impossible for me to pick up with someone who had had lessons for a number of years. Besides, I was too busy taking care of my own child. And though I didn't say this to the woman, nobody can deal with the kind of child who changes teachers constantly. So then the woman asked me to at least do her daughter the favor of meeting her once. This was a fairly pushy lady and I could see she was not going to let me off the hook easily, so I agreed to meet the girl—but *just meet* her. Three days later the girl came to the house by herself. She was an absolute angel, with a kind of pure, sweet, transparent beauty. I had never—and have never—seen such a beautiful little girl. She had long, shiny hair as black as freshly ground India ink, slim, graceful arms and legs, bright eyes, and a soft little mouth that looked as if someone had just made it. I couldn't speak when I first saw her, she was so beautiful. Sitting on my couch, she turned my living room into a gorgeous parlor. It hurt to look straight at her: I had to squint. So, anyhow, that's what she was like. I can still picture her clearly."

Reiko narrowed her eyes as if she were actually picturing the girl.

"Over coffee we talked for a whole hour—talked about all kinds of things: music, her school, just everything. I could see right off she was a smart one. She knew how to hold a conversation: she had clear, sharp opinions and a natural gift for captivating the other person. Frighteningly so. Exactly what it was that made her frightening, I couldn't tell at the time. It just struck me how frighteningly intelligent she was. But in her presence I lost any normal powers of judgment I might have had. She was so young and beautiful, I felt overwhelmed to the point of seeing myself as an inferior specimen, a clumsy excuse for a human being who could only have negative thoughts about her because of my own warped and filthy mind."

Reiko shook her head several times.

"If I were as pretty and smart as she was, I'd have been a more normal human being. What more could you want if you were that smart and that beautiful? Why would you have to torment and walk all over your weaker inferiors if everybody loved you so much? What reason could there possibly be for acting that way?"

"Did she do something terrible to you?"

"Well, let me just say the girl was a pathological liar. She was sick, pure and simple. She made up everything. And while she was making up her stories, she would come to believe them. And then she would change things around her to fit her story. She had such a quick mind, she could always keep a step ahead of you and take care of things that would ordinarily strike you as odd, so it would never cross your mind that she was lying. First of all, no one would ever suspect that such a pretty little girl would lie about the most ordinary things. I certainly didn't. She told me tons of lies for six months before I had the slightest inkling that anything was wrong. She lied about *everything*, and I never suspected. I know it sounds crazy."

"What did she lie about?"

"When I say everything, I mean *everything*." Reiko gave a sarcastic laugh. "When people tell a lie about something, they have to make up a bunch of lies to go with the first one. *Mythomania* is the word for it. When the usual mythomaniac tells lies, they're usually the innocent kind, and most people notice. But not with that girl. To protect herself, she'd tell hurtful lies without batting an eyelash. She'd use everything she could get her hands on. And she would lie either more or less, depending on who she was talking to. To her mother or close friends who would know right away, she hardly ever lied, or if she had to tell one, she'd be really, really careful to tell lies that wouldn't come out. Or if they did come out, she'd find an excuse or apologize in that clingy voice of hers with tears pouring out of her beautiful eyes. No one could stay mad at her then.

"I still don't know why she chose me. Was I another victim to her, or a source of salvation? I just don't know. Of course, it hardly matters now. Now that everything is over. Now that I'm like this."

A short silence followed.

"She repeated what her mother had told me, that she had been moved when she heard me playing as she passed the house. She had seen me on the street a few times, too, and begun to worship me. She actually used that word: *worship*. It made me turn bright red. I mean, to be 'worshiped' by such a beautiful little doll of a girl! I don't think it was an absolute lie, though. I was in my thirties already, of course, and I could never be as beautiful and bright as she was, and I had no special talent, but I must have had something that drew her to me, something that was missing in her, I would guess. Which must have been what got her interested in me to begin with. I believe that now, looking back. And I'm not boasting."

"No, I think I know what you mean."

"She had brought some music with her and asked if she could play for me. So I let her. It was a Bach Invention. Her performance was . . . interesting. Or should I say strange? It just wasn't ordinary. Of course it wasn't polished. She hadn't been going to a professional school, and what lessons she had taken had been an on-and-off kind of thing; she was very much self-taught. Her sound was untrained. She'd have been rejected immediately if this had been a music school audition. But she made it work. Ninety percent was just terrible, but the other ten percent was there—she made it sing: it was music. And this was a Bach Invention! So I got interested in her. I wanted to know what she was all about.

"Needless to say, the world is full of kids who can play Bach way better than she could. Twenty times better. But most of their performances would have nothing to them. They'd be hollow, empty. This girl's technique was bad, but she had that little bit of something that could draw people—or draw me, at least—into her performance. So I decided it might be worthwhile to teach her. Of course, retraining her at that point to where she could become a pro was out of the question. But I felt it might be possible to make her into the kind of happy pianist I was then—and still am—someone who could enjoy making music for herself. This turned out to be an empty hope, though. She was not the kind of person who quietly goes about doing things for herself. This was a child who would make detailed calculations to use every means at her disposal to impress other people. She knew exactly what she had to do to make people admire and praise her. And she knew exactly what kind of performance it would take to draw me in. She had calculated everything, I'm sure, and put everything she had into practicing the most important passages over and over again for my benefit. I can see her doing it.

"Still, even now, after all this came clear to me, I believe it was a wonderful performance, and I would feel the same chills down my spine if I could hear it again. Knowing all I know about her flaws, her cunning and lies, I would still feel it. I'm telling you, there are such things in this world."

Reiko cleared her throat with a dry rasp and broke off her story.

"So, did you take her as a pupil?" I asked.

"Sure I did. One lesson a week. Saturday mornings. Saturday was a day off at her school. She never missed a lesson, she was never late, she was an ideal pupil. She always practiced for her lessons. After every lesson, we'd have some cake and chat."

At that point, Reiko looked at her watch as if suddenly remembering something.

"Don't you think we should be getting back to the room? I'm a little worried about Naoko. I'm sure *you* haven't forgotten about her now, have you?"

"Of course not." I laughed. "It's just that I was drawn into your story."

"If you'd like to hear the rest, I'll tell it to you tomorrow. It's a long story—too long for one sitting."

"You're a regular Scheherazade."

"I know," she said, joining her laughter with mine. "You'll never get back to Tokyo."

We retraced our steps through the path in the woods and returned to the apartment. The candles had been extinguished and the living room lights were out. The bedroom door was open and the lamp on the night table was on, its pale light spilling into the living room. Naoko sat alone on the sofa in the gloom. She had changed into a loose-fitting blue nightgown, its collar pulled tight around her neck, her legs folded under her on the sofa. Reiko approached her and rested a hand on the crown of her head.

"Are you all right now?"

"I'm fine. Sorry," answered Naoko in a tiny voice. Then she turned toward me and repeated her apology. "I must have scared you."

"A little," I said with a smile.

"Come here," she said. When I sat down next to her, Naoko, her legs still folded, leaned toward me until her face was nearly touching my ear, as if she was going to share a secret with me. Then she planted a soft kiss by my ear. "Sorry," she said once more, this time directly into my ear, her voice subdued. Then she moved away from me.

"Sometimes," she said, "I get so confused, I don't know what's happening."

"That happens to me all the time," I said.

Naoko smiled and looked at me.

"If you don't mind," I said, "I'd like to hear more about you. About your life here. What you do every day. The people you meet."

Naoko talked about her daily routine in this place, speaking in short but crystal-clear phrases. Wake up at six in the morning. Breakfast in the apartment. Clean out the birdhouse. Then usually farm work. She took care of the vegetables. Before or after lunch, she would have either an hour-long session with her doctor or a group discussion. In the afternoon she could choose from among courses that might interest her, outside work, or sports. She had taken several courses: French, knitting, piano, ancient history.

"Reiko is teaching me piano," she said. "She also teaches guitar. We all take turns as pupils or teachers. Somebody with fluent French teaches French, one person who used to be in social studies teaches history, another good at knitting teaches knitting: that's a pretty impressive school right there. Unfortunately, I don't have anything I can teach anyone."

"Neither do I," I said.

"I put a lot more energy into my studies here than I ever did in college. I work hard and enjoy it—a lot."

"What do you do after supper?"

"Talk with Reiko, read, listen to records, go to other peoples' apartments and play games, stuff like that."

"I do guitar practice and write my autobiography," said Reiko.

"Autobiography?"

"Just kidding." Reiko laughed. "We go to bed around ten o'clock. Pretty healthy lifestyle, wouldn't you say? We sleep like babies."

I looked at my watch. It was a few minutes before nine. "I guess you'll be getting sleepy soon."

"That's O.K. We can stay up late today," said Naoko. "I haven't seen you in such a long time, I want to talk more. So talk."

"When I was alone before, all of a sudden I started thinking about the old days," I said. "Do you remember when Kizuki and I came to visit you at the hospital? The one on the seashore. I think it was the second year of high school."

"When I had the chest operation," Naoko said with a smile. "Sure, I remember. You and Kizuki came on a motorcycle. You brought me a box of chocolates and they were all melted together. They were so hard to eat! I don't know, it seems like such a long time ago."

"Yeah, really. I think you were writing a poem then, a long one."

"All girls write poems at that age," Naoko tittered. "What reminded you of that all of a sudden?"

"I wonder. The smell of the sea wind, the oleanders: before I knew it, they just popped into my head. Did Kizuki come to see you at the hospital a lot?"

"No way! We had a big fight about that afterward. He came once, and then he came with you, and that was it for him. He was terrible. And that first time he couldn't sit still and he only stayed about ten minutes. He brought me some oranges and mumbled all this stuff I couldn't understand, and he peeled an orange for me and mumbled more stuff and he was out of there. He said he had a thing about hospitals." Naoko laughed. "He was always a kid about that kind of stuff. I mean, nobody likes hospitals, right? That's why people visit people in hospitals—to make them feel better, and perk up their spirits and stuff. But Kizuki just didn't get it."

"He wasn't so bad when the two of us came to see you, though. He was just his usual self."

"Because you were there," said Naoko. "He was always like that around you. He struggled to keep his weaknesses hidden. I'm sure he was very fond of you. He made a point of letting you see only his best side. He wasn't like that with me. He'd let his guard down. He could be really moody. One minute he'd be chattering away, and the next thing he'd be depressed. It happened all the time. He was like that from the time he was little. He did keep trying to change himself, to improve himself, though."

Naoko recrossed her legs atop the sofa.

"He tried hard, but it didn't do any good, and that would make him really angry and sad. There was so much about him that was fine and beautiful, but he could never find the confidence he needed. 'I've got to do that, I've got to change this,' he was always thinking, right up to the end. Poor Kizuki!"

"Still, though," I said, "if it's true that he was always struggling to show me his best side, I'd say he succeeded. His best side was all that I could see."

Naoko smiled. "He'd be thrilled if he could hear you say that. You were his only friend."

"And Kizuki was my only friend," I said. "There was never anybody I could really call a friend, before him or after him."

"That's why I loved being with the two of you. His best side was all that I could see then, too. I could relax and stop worrying when the three of us were together. Those were my favorite times. I don't know how *you* felt about it."

"I used to worry about what *you* were thinking," I said, giving my head a shake.

"The problem was that that kind of thing couldn't go on forever," said Naoko. "Such perfect little circles are impossible to maintain. Kizuki knew it, and I knew it, and so did you. Am I right?"

I nodded.

"To tell you the truth, though," Naoko went on, "I loved his weak side, too. I loved it as much as I loved his good side. There was absolutely nothing mean or sneaky about him. He was weak: that's all. I tried to tell him that, but he wouldn't believe me. He'd always tell me it was because we had been together from the time we were three. I knew him too well, he'd say: I couldn't tell the difference between his strong points and his flaws, they were all the same to me. He couldn't change my mind about him, though. I went on loving him just the same, and I could never be interested in anyone else."

Naoko looked at me with a sad smile.

"Our boy-girl relationship was really unusual, too. It was as if we were physically joined somewhere. If we happened to be apart, some special gravitational force would pull us back together again. It was the most natural thing in the world when we became boyfriend and girlfriend. It was nothing we had to think about or make any choices about. We started kissing at twelve and petting at thirteen. I'd go to his room or he'd come to my room and I'd finish him off with my hands. It never occurred to me that we were being precocious. It just happened as a matter of course. If he wanted to play with my breasts or vagina, I didn't mind at all, or if he had semen he wanted to get rid of, I didn't mind helping with that, either. I'm sure it would have shocked us both if someone had accused us of doing anything wrong. Because we weren't. We were just doing what we were supposed to do. We had always shown each other every part of our bodies. It was almost as if we owned each other's bodies jointly. For a while, at least, we made sure we didn't go any further than what I've said, though. We were afraid of getting me pregnant, and had almost no idea at that point of how you go about preventing it . . . Anyhow, that's how Kizuki and I grew up together, hand in hand, an inseparable pair. We had almost no sense of the oppressiveness of sex or the anguish that comes with the sudden swelling of the ego that ordinary kids experience when they reach puberty. We were totally open about sex, and where our egos were concerned, the way we absorbed and shared each other's, we had no strong awareness of them. Do you see what I mean?"

"I think so," I said.

"We couldn't bear to be apart. So if Kizuki had lived, I'm sure we would have been together, loving each other, and gradually growing unhappy."

"*Un*happy? Why's that?"

With her fingers, Naoko combed her hair back several times. She had taken her barrette off, which made the hair fall over her face when she dropped her head forward.

"Because we would have had to pay the world back what we owed it," she said, raising her eyes to mine. "The pain of growing up. We didn't pay when we should have, so now the bills are due. Which is why Kizuki did what he did, and why I'm in here. We were like kids who grew up naked on a desert island. If we got hungry, we'd just pick a banana; if we got lonely, we'd go to sleep in each other's arms. But that kind of thing doesn't last forever. We grew up fast and had to enter society. Which is why you were so important to us. You were the link connecting us with the outside world. We were struggling through you to fit in with the outside world as best we could. In the end, it didn't work, of course."

I nodded.

"I wouldn't want you to think that we were using you, though. Kizuki really loved you. It just so happened that our connection with you was our first connection with anyone else. And it still is. Kizuki may be dead, but you are still my only link with the outside world. And just as Kizuki loved you, I love you. We never meant to hurt you, but we probably did; we probably ended up making a deep wound in your heart. It never occurred to us that anything like that might happen."

Naoko lowered her head again and fell silent.

"Say, how about a cup of cocoa?" suggested Reiko.

"Good. I'd like some," said Naoko.

"I'd like to have some of the brandy I brought, if you don't mind," I said.

"Oh, absolutely," said Reiko. "Could I have a sip?"

"Sure," I said, laughing.

Reiko brought out two glasses and we toasted each other. Then she went into the kitchen to make cocoa.

"Can we talk about something a little more cheerful?" asked Naoko.

I didn't happen to have anything cheerful to talk about. I thought, If only Storm Trooper were still around! That guy could inspire a string of stories. A few of those would have made everybody feel good. The best I could do was talk at length about the filthy habits of the guys in the dormitory. I felt sick just talking about something so gross, but Naoko and Reiko practically fell over laughing, it was all so new to them. Next Reiko did imitations of mental patients. This was a lot of fun, too. Naoko started looking sleepy once eleven o'clock rolled around, so Reiko let down the sofa back and gave me a pillow, sheets, and blankets.

"If you feel like raping anybody in the middle of the night, don't get the wrong one," said Reiko. "The unwrinkled body in the left bed is Naoko's."

"Liar! Mine's the right bed," said Naoko.

Reiko added, "By the way, I arranged for us to skip some of our afternoon schedule. Why don't the three of us have a little picnic? I know a nice place close by."

"Good idea," I said.

The women took turns brushing their teeth and withdrew to the bedroom. I poured myself a sip of brandy and stretched out on the sofa bed, going over the day's events from morning to night. It felt like an awfully long day. The room continued to glow white in the moonlight. Aside from the occasional slight creak of a bed, hardly a sound came from the bedroom, where Naoko and Reiko lay sleeping. Tiny diagrammatic shapes seemed to float in the darkness when I closed my eyes, and my ears sensed the lingering reverberation of Reiko's guitar, but neither of these lasted any length of time. Sleep came and carried me into a mass of warm mud. I dreamed of willows. Both sides of a mountain road were lined with willows. An incredible number of willows. A fairly stiff breeze was blowing, but the branches of the willow trees never swayed. Why should that be? I wondered, and then I saw that every branch of every tree had tiny birds clinging to it. Their weight kept the branches from stirring. I grabbed a stick and hit a nearby branch with it, hoping to chase the birds off and allow the branch to sway. But the birds would not leave. Instead of flying away, they turned into bird-shaped metal chunks that crashed to the ground.

When I opened my eyes, I felt as if I were seeing the continuation of my dream. The moonlight filled the room with the same soft white glow. As if by reflex, I sat up in bed and started searching for the metal birds, which of course were not there. What I saw instead was Naoko at the foot of the bed, sitting still and alone, staring out through the window. She had drawn her knees up and was resting her chin on them, looking like a hungry orphan. I searched for the watch I had left by my pillow, but it was not in the place where I knew it should be. I figured from the angle of the moonlight that the time must be two or three o'clock in the morning. I felt a violent thirst but I decided to keep still and continue watching Naoko. She was wearing the same blue nightgown I had seen her in earlier, and on one side her hair was held in place by the butterfly barrette, revealing the beauty of her face in the moonlight. Strange, I thought; she had taken the barrette off before going to bed.

Naoko stayed frozen in place, like a small nocturnal animal that has been lured out by the moonlight. The direction of the glow exaggerated the silhouette of her lips. Seeming utterly fragile and vulnerable, the silhouette pulsed almost imperceptibly with the beating of her heart or the motions of her inner heart, as if she were whispering soundless words to the darkness.

I swallowed in hopes of easing my thirst, but in the stillness of the night, the sound I made was huge. As if this were a signal to her, Naoko stood and glided toward the head of the bed, gown rustling faintly. She knelt on the floor by my pillow, eyes fixed on mine. I stared back at her, but her eyes told me nothing. Strangely transparent, they seemed like windows to a world beyond, but however long I peered into their depths, there was nothing I could see. Our faces were no more than ten inches apart, but she was light-years away from me.

I reached out and tried to touch her, but Naoko drew back, lips trembling faintly. A moment later, she brought her hands up and began slowly to undo the buttons of her gown. There were seven in all. I felt as if it were the continuation of my dream as I watched her slim, lovely fingers opening the buttons one by one from top to bottom. Seven small, white buttons: when she had unfastened them all, Naoko slipped the gown from her shoulders and threw it off completely like an insect shedding its skin. She had been wearing nothing under the gown. All she had on was the butterfly barrette. Naked now, and still kneeling by the bed, she looked at me. Bathed in the soft light of the moon, Naoko's body had the heart-breaking luster of newborn flesh. When she moved—and she did so almost imperceptibly—the play of light and shadow on her body shifted subtly. The swelling roundness of her breasts, her tiny nipples, the indentation of her navel, her hipbones and pubic hair, all cast grainy shadows, the shapes of which kept changing like ripples spreading over the calm surface of a lake.

What perfect flesh! I thought. When had Naoko come to possess such a perfect body? What had happened to the body I held in my arms that night last spring?

A sense of imperfection had been what Naoko's body had given me that night as I tenderly undressed her while she cried. Her breasts had seemed hard, the nipples oddly jutting, the hips strangely rigid. She was a beautiful girl, of course, her body marvelous and alluring. It aroused me that night and swept me along with a gigantic force. But still, as I held her and caressed her and kissed her naked flesh, I felt a strange and powerful awareness of the imbalance and awkwardness of the human body. Holding Naoko in my arms, I wanted to explain to her, "I am having intercourse with you now. I am inside you. But really this is nothing. It doesn't matter. It is nothing but the joining of two bodies. All we are doing is telling each other things that can only be told by the rubbing together of two imperfect lumps of flesh. By doing this, we are sharing our imperfection." But of course I could never have said such a thing with any hope of being understood. I just went on holding her tightly. And as I did so, I was able to feel inside her body some kind of stony foreign matter, something extra that I could never draw close to. And that sensation both filled my heart for Naoko and gave my erection a terrifying intensity.

The body that Naoko revealed before me now, though, was nothing like the one I had held that night. This flesh had been through many changes to be reborn in utter perfection beneath the light of the moon. All signs of girlish plumpness had been stripped away since Kizuki's death to be replaced by the flesh of a mature woman. So perfect was Naoko's physical beauty now that it aroused nothing sexual in me. I could only stare, astounded, at the lovely curve from waist to hips, the rounded richness of the breasts, the gentle movement with each breath of the slim belly, and the soft, black pubic shadow beneath.

She exposed her nakedness to me this way for perhaps five minutes until, at last, she wrapped herself in her gown once more and buttoned it from top to bottom. As soon as the last button was in place, she rose and glided toward the bedroom, opened the door silently, and disappeared within.

I stayed fixed in place for a very long time until it occurred to me to leave the bed. I retrieved my watch from where it had fallen on the floor and turned it toward the moonlight. The time was three-forty. I went to the kitchen and drank a few glassfuls of water before stretching out in bed again, but sleep never came for me until the morning sunlight crept into every corner of the room, dissolving all traces of the moon's pale glow. I was somewhere on the edge of sleep when Reiko came and smacked me on the cheek, shouting, "Morning! Morning!"

WHILE REIKO STRAIGHTENED OUT MY SOFA BED, Naoko went to the kitchen and started making breakfast. She smiled at me and said, "Good morning." "Good morning," I said in reply. I stood by and watched Naoko as she put water on to boil and sliced some bread, humming all the while, but I could sense nothing in her manner to suggest that she had revealed her naked body to me the night before.

"Your eyes are red," she said to me as she poured the coffee. "Are you O.K.?"

"I woke up in the middle of the night and couldn't get back to sleep."

"I bet we were snoring," said Reiko.

"Not at all," I said.

"That's good," said Naoko.

"He's just being polite," said Reiko, yawning.

At first I thought that Naoko was embarrassed or acting innocent for Reiko, but her behavior remained unchanged when Reiko momentarily left the room, and her eyes had their usual transparent look.

"How'd you sleep?" I asked Naoko.

"Like a log," she answered with ease. She wore a simple hairpin without any kind of decoration.

I didn't know what to make of this, and I continued to feel that way all through breakfast. Buttering my bread or peeling my egg, I kept glancing across the table at Naoko, in search of a sign.

"Why do you keep looking at me like that?" she asked with a smile.

"I think he's in love with somebody," said Reiko.

"*Are* you in love with somebody?" Naoko asked me.

"Could be," I said, returning her smile. When the two women started joking around at my expense, I gave up trying to think about what had happened in the night and concentrated on my bread and coffee.

After breakfast, Reiko and Naoko said they would be going to feed the birds in the birdhouse. I volunteered to go along. They changed into jeans and work shirts and white rubber boots. Set in a little park behind the tennis courts, the birdhouse had everything in it from chickens and pigeons to peacocks and parrots and was surrounded by flower beds and shrubberies and benches. Two men in their forties, also apparently sanatorium patients, were raking up leaves that had fallen in the pathways. The women walked over to say good morning to the pair, and Reiko got a laugh from them with another of her jokes. Cosmos were blooming in the flower beds, and the shrubberies were extremely well manicured. Spotting Reiko, the birds started chattering and flying about inside the cage.

The women entered the shed by the cage and came out with a bag of feed and a garden hose. Naoko screwed the hose on a spigot and turned on the water. Taking care to prevent any birds from flying out, the two of them slipped into the cage, Naoko hosing down the dirt and Reiko scrubbing the floor with a deck brush. The spray they set up sparkled in the glare of the morning sun. The peacocks flapped around the cage to avoid getting splashed. A turkey raised its head and glowered at me like a crotchety old man, while a parrot on the perch above screeched its displeasure and beat its wings. Reiko meowed at the parrot, which slunk over to the far corner but soon was calling, "Thank you! Crazy! Shithead!"

"I wonder who taught him *that* kind of language?" said Naoko with a sigh.

"Not *me*," said Reiko. "I would never do such a thing." She started meowing again, and the parrot shut up.

Laughing, Reiko explained, "This guy once had a run-in with a cat. Now he's scared to death of them."

When they were through cleaning, the two set their tools down and went around filling each of the feeders. Splashing its way through puddles on the floor, the turkey darted to its feed box and plunged its head in, too obsessed with eating to be bothered by Naoko's smacks on its tail.

"Do you do this every morning?" I asked Naoko.

"Every morning!" she said. "They usually give this job to new women. It's so easy. Like to see the rabbits?"

"Sure," I said. The rabbit hutch was behind the birdhouse. Some ten rabbits lay inside, asleep in the straw. Naoko swept up their droppings, put feed in their box, and picked up one of the babies, rubbing it against her cheek.

"Isn't it precious?" she gushed. She let me hold it. The warm little ball of fur cringed in my arms, twitching its nose.

"Don't worry, he won't hurt you," she said to the rabbit, stroking its head with her finger and smiling at me. It was such a radiant smile, without a trace of shadow, that I couldn't help smiling myself. And what about Naoko last night? I wondered. I knew for certain that it had been the real Naoko and not a dream: she had definitely taken her clothes off and shown her naked body to me.

Reiko whistled a lovely rendition of "Proud Mary" as she stuffed a vinyl bag with the debris they had gathered and tied off the opening. I helped them carry the tools and feed bag to the shed.

"Morning is my favorite time of day," said Naoko. "It's like everything's starting out fresh and new. I begin to get sad around noontime, and I hate it when the sun goes down. I live with those same feelings day after day."

"And while you're living with those feelings, you youngsters get old just like me," said Reiko with a smile. "You're thinking about how it's morning now or night and the next thing you know, you're old."

"But you *like* getting old," said Naoko.

"Not really," said Reiko. "But I sure don't wish I was young again."

"Why not?" I asked.

"Because it's such a pain in the neck!" she said. Then she tossed her broom in and closed the door of the shed, whistling "Proud Mary" all the while.

BACK AT THE APARTMENT, the women changed their rubber boots for tennis shoes and said they'd be going to the farm. Reiko suggested I stay behind with a book or something because the work would be no fun to watch and they would be doing it as part of a group. "And while you're waiting you can wash the pile of dirty underwear we left by the sink," she added.

"You're kidding," I said, taken aback.

"Of course I am." She laughed. "You're so sweet. Isn't he, Naoko?"

"He really is," said Naoko, laughing with her.

"I'll work on my German," I said with a sigh.

"Yeah, do your homework like a good boy," said Reiko. "We'll be back before lunch."

The two of them went out tittering. I heard the footsteps and voices of a number of people walking by downstairs.

I went into the bathroom and washed my face again, then borrowed a nail clipper and trimmed my nails. For a bathroom that was being shared by two women, its contents were incredibly simple. Aside from some neatly arranged bottles of cleansing cream and lip moisturizer and sunblock, there was almost nothing that could be called cosmetics. When I finished trimming my nails, I made myself some coffee and drank it at the kitchen table, German book open. Stripping down to a T-shirt in the sun-filled kitchen, I had set about memorizing all the forms in a grammar chart when I was struck by an odd feeling. It seemed to me that the longest imaginable distance separated irregular German verb forms from this kitchen table.

The two women came back from the farm at eleven-thirty, took turns in the shower, and changed into fresh clothes. The three of us went to the dining hall for lunch, then walked to the front gate. This time the guardhouse had a man on duty. He was sitting at his desk, enjoying a lunch that must have been brought to him from the dining hall.

The transistor radio on the shelf was playing a sentimental old pop tune. He waved to us with a friendly "Hi" as we approached, and we helloed him back.

Reiko explained to him that we were going to walk outside the grounds and return in three hours.

"Great," he said. "Ya lucked out with the weather. Just stay away from the valley road, though. It got washed out in that big rain. No problem anywhere else."

Reiko wrote her name and Naoko's in a furlough registry along with the date and time.

"Enjoy yourselves," said the guard. "And take care."

"Nice guy," I said.

"He's a little strange up here," Reiko said, touching her head.

He had been right about the weather, though. The sky was a fresh-swept blue, with only a trace of white cloud clinging to the dome of heaven like a thin streak of test paint. We walked beside the low stone wall of Ami Hostel for a time, then moved away to climb a steep, narrow trail single file. Reiko led the way, with Naoko in the middle and me bringing up the rear. Reiko climbed with the confident stride of one who knew every stretch of every mountain in the area. We concentrated on walking, with hardly a word among us. Naoko wore blue jeans and a white blouse and carried her jacket in one hand. I watched her long, straight hair sway-ing right and left where it met her shoulders. She would glance back at me now and then, smiling when our eyes met. The trail continued upward so long it was almost dizzying, but Reiko's pace never slackened. Naoko hurried to keep up with her, wiping the sweat from her face. Not having indulged in such outdoor activities for some time, I found myself running short of breath.

"Do you do this a lot?" I asked Naoko.

"Maybe once a week," she answered. "Having a tough time?"

"Kind of," I said.

"We're almost there," said Reiko. "This is about two-thirds of the way. Come on, you're a boy, aren't you?"

"Yeah, but I'm out of shape."

"Playing with girls all the time," muttered Naoko as if to herself.

I wanted to answer her, but I was too winded to speak. Every now and then, red birds with tufts on their heads would flit across our path, brilliant against the blue of the sky. The fields around us were filled with white and blue and yellow flowers, and bees buzzed everywhere. Moving ahead one step at a time, I thought of nothing but the scene passing before my eyes.

The slope gave out after another ten minutes, and we entered a level plateau. We rested there, wiping the sweat off, catching our breath, and drinking from our water bottles. Reiko found a leaf and used it to make a whistle.

The trail entered a gentle downward grade amid tall, waving thickets of plume grass. We continued on for some fifteen minutes before passing through a village. There were no signs of humanity here, and the dozen or so houses were all in varying states of decay. Waist-high grass grew among the houses, and dry, white gobs of pigeon droppings clung to holes in the walls. Only the pillars survived in the case of one collapsed building, while others looked ready to be lived in as soon as you opened the storm shutters. These dead, silent houses pressed against either side of the road as we slipped through.

"People lived in this village until seven or eight years ago," Reiko informed me. "This was farmland around here. But they all cleared out. Life was just too hard. They'd be trapped when the snow piled up in the winter. And the soil is not particularly fertile. They could make a better living in the city."

"What a waste," I said. "Some of the houses look perfectly usable."

"Some hippies tried living here at one point, but they gave up. Couldn't take the winters."

A little beyond the village we came to a big fenced area that seemed to be a pasture. Way over on the other side, I caught sight of a few horses grazing. We followed the fence line, and a big dog came running over to us, tail wagging. It stood up, leaning on Reiko, sniffing her face, then jumped playfully on Naoko. I whistled and it came over to me, licking my hand with its long tongue.

Naoko patted the dog's head and explained that the animal belonged to the pasture. "I'll bet he's close to twenty," she said. "His teeth are so bad, he can't eat much of anything hard. He sleeps in front of the shop all day, and he comes running when he hears footsteps."

Reiko took a scrap of cheese from her knapsack. Catching its scent, the dog bounded over to her and chomped down on it.

"We won't be able to see this fellow much longer," said Reiko, patting the dog's head. "In the middle of October they put the horses and cows in trucks and take 'em down to the barn. The only time they let 'em graze is the summer, when they open a little coffeehouse kind of thing for the tourists. The 'tourists'! Maybe twenty hikers in a day. Say, how about something to drink?"

"Good idea," I said.

The dog led the way to the coffeehouse, a small, white house with a front porch and a faded sign in the shape of a coffee cup hanging from the eaves. He led us up the steps and stretched out on the porch, narrowing his eyes. When we took our places around a table on the porch, a girl with a ponytail and wearing a sweatshirt and white jeans came out and greeted Reiko and Naoko like old friends.

"This is a friend of Naoko's," said Reiko, introducing me.

"Hi," she said.

"Hi," I answered.

While the three women traded small talk, I stroked the neck of the dog under the table. This was the hard, stringy neck of an old dog. When I scratched the lumpy spots, the dog closed his eyes and sighed with pleasure.

"What's his name?" I asked the girl.

"Pepe," she said.

"Hey, Pepe," I said to the dog, but he didn't budge.

"He's hard of hearing," said the girl. "You have to talk loud or he can't hear."

"Pepe!" I shouted. The dog opened his eyes and snapped to attention with a bark.

"Never mind, Pepe," said the girl. "Sleep more and live longer." Pepe flopped down again at my feet.

Naoko and Reiko ordered cold glasses of milk and I asked for a beer.

"Let's hear the radio," said Reiko. The girl switched on an amplifier and tuned in an FM station. Blood, Sweat and Tears came on with "Spinning Wheel."

Reiko looked pleased. "Now *this* is what we're here for! We don't have radios in our rooms, so if I don't come here once in awhile, I don't have any idea what's playing out there."

"Do you sleep in this place?" I asked the girl.

"No way!" she laughed. "I'd die of loneliness if I spent the night here.

The pasture guy drives me into town and I come out again in the morning." She pointed toward a four-wheel-drive truck parked in front of the nearby pasture office.

"You've got a vacation coming up soon, too, right?" asked Reiko.

"Yeah, we'll be shutting up this place before too long," said the girl. Reiko offered her a cigarette, and the two had a smoke.

"I'll miss you," said Reiko.

"I'll be back in May, though," said the girl with a laugh.

Cream came on the radio with "White Room." After a commercial, it was Simon and Garfunkel's "Scarborough Fair."

"I *like* that," said Reiko when it was over.

"I saw the movie," I said.

"Who's in it?"

"Dustin Hoffman."

"I don't know him," she said with a sad little shake of the head. "The world changes like mad, and I don't know what's happening."

She asked the girl for a guitar. "Sure," said the girl, switching off the radio and bringing out an old guitar. The dog raised its head and sniffed the instrument.

"You can't eat this," Reiko said with mock sternness. A grass-scented breeze swept over the porch. The mountains lay spread out before us, ridgeline sharp against the sky.

"It's like a scene from *The Sound of Music*," I said to Reiko as she tuned up.

"What's that?" she asked.

She strummed the guitar in search of the opening chord of "Scarborough Fair." This was apparently her first attempt at the song, but after a few false starts she got to where she could play it through without hesitating. She had it down pat the third time and even started adding a few flourishes. "Good ear," she said to me with a wink. "I can usually play just about anything if I hear it three times."

Softly humming the melody, she did a full rendition of "Scarborough Fair." The three of us applauded, and Reiko responded with a decorous bow of the head.

"I used to get more applause for a Mozart concerto," she said.

Her milk was on the house if she would play the Beatles' "Here Comes the Sun," said the girl. Reiko gave her a thumbs-up and launched into the song. Hers was not a full voice, and too much smoking had given it a husky edge, but it was lovely, with real presence. I almost felt as if the sun really were coming up again as I sat there listening and drinking beer and looking at the mountains. It was a soft, warm feeling.

Reiko gave the guitar back and asked for more radio. Then she suggested to Naoko and me that we take an hour and hike around the area.

"I want to listen to the radio some more and hang out with her. If you come back by three, that should be O.K."

"Is it all right for us to be alone together so long?"

"Well, actually, it's against the rules, but what the hell. I'm not a chaperone, after all. I could use a break. And you came all the way from Tokyo, I'm sure you've got a pile of stuff you want to talk about."

Reiko lit another cigarette as she spoke.

"Let's go," said Naoko, standing up.

I stood and started after her. The dog woke up and followed us a ways, but it soon lost interest and went back to its place on the porch. We strolled down a level road that followed the pasture fence. Naoko would take my hand every now and then or slip her arm under mine.

"This is kind of like the old days, isn't it?" she said.

"That wasn't 'the old days,' " I laughed. "It was spring of this year! If that was 'the old days,' ten years ago was ancient history."

"It feels like ancient history," said Naoko. "But anyhow, sorry about last night. I don't know, I was a bundle of nerves. I really shouldn't have done that after you came here all the way from Tokyo."

"Never mind," I said. "Both of us have a lot of feelings we need to get out in the open. So if you want to take those feelings and smash somebody with them, smash me. Then we can understand each other better."

"So if you understand me better, what then?"

"You don't get it, do you?" I said. "It's not a question of 'what then.' Some people get a kick out of reading railroad timetables and that's all they do all day. Some people make huge model boats out of matchsticks. So what's wrong if there happens to be one guy in the world who enjoys trying to understand you?"

"Kind of like a hobby?" she said, amused.

"Sure, I guess you could call it a hobby. Most normal people would call it friendship or love or something, but if you want to call it a hobby, that's O.K., too."

"Tell me," said Naoko, "you liked Kizuki, too, didn't you?"

"Of course," I said.

"How about Reiko?"

"I like her a lot," I said. "She's really nice."

"How come you always like people like that—people like *us*, I mean? We're all kinda weird and twisted and drowning—me and Kizuki and Reiko. Why can't you like more normal people?"

"Because I don't see you like that," I said after giving it some thought. "I don't see you or Kizuki or Reiko as 'twisted' in any way. The guys *I* think of as twisted are out there running around."

"But we *are* twisted," said Naoko. "*I* can see that."

We walked for a while in silence. The road left the fence and came out to a circular grassy field, ringed with trees as if it were a pond.

"Sometimes I wake up in the middle of the night *so* scared," said Naoko, pressing up against my arm. "I'm scared I'll never get better again. I'll always stay twisted like this and grow old and waste away here. I get so chilled it's like I'm all frozen inside. It's horrible . . . so cold . . ."

I put my arm around her and drew her close.

"I feel like Kizuki is reaching out for me from the darkness, calling to me, 'Hey, Naoko, we can't stay apart.' When I hear him saying that, I don't know what to do."

"What *do* you do?"

"Well . . . don't take this the wrong way, now."

"O.K., I won't."

"I ask Reiko to hold me. I wake her up and crawl into her bed and let her hold me tight. And I cry. And she strokes me until the ice melts and I'm warm again. Do you think it's sick?"

"No, it's not sick. I wish *I* could be the one to hold you, though," I said.

"So hold me. Now. Right here."

We sat down on the dry grass of the meadow and put our arms around each other. The tall grass surrounded us, and we could see nothing but the sky and clouds above. I gently lay Naoko down and took her in my arms. She was soft and warm and her hands reached out for me. We kissed with real feeling.

"Tell me something, Toru," Naoko whispered in my ear.

"What's that?" I asked.

"Do you want to sleep with me?"

"Of course I do," I said.

"Can you wait?"

"Of course I can wait."

"Before we do it again, I want to get myself a little righter. I want to make myself into a person righter for that hobby of yours. Will you wait for me to do that?"

"Of course I'll wait."

"Are you hard now?"

"You mean the soles of my feet?"

"Silly," Naoko tittered.

"If you're asking whether I have an erection, of course I do."

"Will you do me a favor and stop saying 'Of course'?"

"O.K., I'll stop."

"Is it difficult?"

"What?"

"To be all hard like that."

"Difficult?"

"I mean, are you suffering?"

"Well, it's all in how you look at it."

"Want me to help you get rid of it?"

"With your hand?"

"Uh-huh. To tell you the truth," said Naoko, "it's been sticking into me ever since we lay down. It hurts."

I pulled my hips away. "Better?"

"Thanks."

"You know?" I said.

"What?"

"I wish you would do it."

"O.K.," she said with a nice smile. Then she unzipped my pants and took my stiff penis in her hand.

"It's warm," she said.

She started to move her hand, but I stopped her and unbuttoned her blouse, reaching around to undo her bra strap. I kissed her soft, pink nipples. She closed her eyes and slowly started moving her fingers.

"Hey, you're pretty good at that," I said.

"Be a good boy and shut up," said Naoko.

AFTER I CAME, I held her in my arms and kissed her again. Naoko redid her bra and blouse, and I closed my zipper.

"Will that make it easier for you to walk?" she asked.

"I owe it all to you."

"Well, then, sir, if it suits you, shall we walk a little farther?"

"By all means."

We cut across the meadow, through a stand of trees, and across another meadow. Naoko talked about her dead sister, explaining that although she had hardly said anything about this to anyone, she felt she ought to tell me.

"She was six years older than me, and our personalities were *totally* different, but still we were very close. We never fought, not once. It's true. Of course, with such a big difference in our ages, there was nothing much for us to fight about."

Her sister was one of those girls who are tops in everything—a super student, a super athlete, popular, a leader, kind, straightforward, the boys liked her, her teachers loved her, her walls were covered with certificates of merit. There's always one girl like that in any public school. "I'm not saying this because she's my sister, but she never let any of this spoil her or make her the least bit stuck-up or a show-off. It's just that, no matter what you gave her to do, she would naturally do it better than anyone else.

"So when I was little, I decided that I was going to be the sweet little girl." Naoko twirled a frond of plume grass as she spoke. "I mean, you know, I grew up hearing everybody talking about how smart she was and how good she was at sports and how popular she was. Of course I'm going to figure there's no way I could ever compete with her. My face, at least, was a little prettier than hers, so I guess my parents decided they'd bring me up cute. Right from the start they put me in *that* kind of school. They dressed me in velvet dresses and frilly blouses and patent leather shoes and gave me piano lessons and ballet lessons. This just made my sister even crazier about me—you know: I was her cute little sister. She'd give me these cute little presents and take me everywhere with her and help me with my homework. She even took me along on dates. She was the best big sister anyone could ask for.

"Nobody knew why she killed herself. The same as with Kizuki. Exactly the same. She was seventeen, too, and she never gave the slightest hint she was going to commit suicide. She didn't leave a note, either. Really, it was exactly the same, don't you think?"

"Sounds like it."

"Everybody said she was too smart or she read too many books. And she *did* read a lot. She had tons of books. I read a bunch of them after she died, and it was so sad. They had her comments in the margins and flowers pressed between the pages and letters from boyfriends, and every time I came across something like that I'd cry. I cried a lot."

Naoko fell silent for a few seconds, twirling the grass again.

"She was the kind of person who took care of things by herself. She'd never ask anybody for advice or help. It wasn't a matter of pride, I think. She just did what seemed natural to her. My parents were used to this and figured she'd be O.K. if they left her alone. I would go to my sister for advice and she was always ready to give it, but she never went to anybody else. She did what needed to be done, on her own. She never got angry or moody. This is all true, I mean it, I'm not exaggerating. Most girls, when they have their period or something, will get grumpy and take it out on other people, but she never even did that. Instead of going into a bad mood, she would become very subdued. Maybe once in two or three months this would happen to her: she'd shut herself up in her room and stay in bed, take off from school, hardly eat a thing, turn the lights off, and space out. She wouldn't be in a bad mood, though. When I came home from school, she'd call me into her room and sit me down next to her and ask me about my day. I'd tell her all the little things—like what kinds of games I played with my friends or what the teacher said or my test grades, stuff like that. She'd take in every detail and make comments and suggestions, but as soon as I left—to play with a friend, say, or go for a ballet lesson—she'd space out again. After two days, she'd snap out of it just like that and go off to school. This kind of thing went on for, I don't know, maybe four years. My parents were worried at first and I think they went to a doctor for advice, but, I mean, she'd be perfectly fine after the two days went by, so they figured it'd work itself out if they left her alone, she was such a bright, steady girl.

"After she died, though, I heard my parents talking about a younger brother of my father's who had died long before. He had also been very bright, but he had stayed shut up in the house for *four years*—from the time he was seventeen until he was twenty-one. And then suddenly one day he left the house and jumped in front of a train. My father said, 'Maybe it's in the blood—from my side.'"

While Naoko was speaking, her fingers unconsciously teased the tassel of the plume grass, scattering its fibers to the wind. When the shaft was bare, she wound it around her fingers.

"I was the one who found my sister dead," she went on. "In autumn when I was in the sixth grade. November. On a dark, rainy day. My sister was a senior in high school at the time. I came home from my piano lesson at six-thirty and my mother was fixing dinner. She told me to tell my sister that dinner was ready. I went upstairs and knocked on her door and yelled, 'Dinner's ready,' but there was no answer. Her room was absolutely silent. I thought this was strange, so I knocked again and opened the door and peeked inside. I figured she was probably sleeping. She wasn't in bed, though. She was standing by the window, staring outside, with her neck bent at a kind of angle like this. Like she was thinking. The room was dark, the lights were out, and it was hard to see anything. 'What are you doing?' I said to her. 'Dinner is ready.' That's when I noticed that she looked taller than usual. What was going on? I wondered: it was so strange! Did she have high heels on? Was she standing on something? I moved closer and was just about to speak to her again when I saw it: there was a rope above her head. It came straight down from a beam in the ceiling—I mean it was amazingly straight, like somebody had drawn a line in space with a ruler. My sister had a white blouse on—yeah, a simple white blouse like this one—and a gray skirt, and her toes were pointing down like a ballerina's, except there was a space between the tip of her toes and the floor of maybe seven or eight inches. I took in every detail. Her face, too. I looked at her face. I couldn't help it. I thought: I've got to go right downstairs and tell my mother. I've got to scream. But my body ignored me. It moved on its own, separately from my conscious mind. It was trying to lower her from the rope while my mind was telling me to hurry downstairs. Of course, there was no way a little girl could have the strength to do such a thing, and so I just stood there, spacing out, for maybe five or six minutes, a total blank, like something inside me had died. I just stayed that way, with my sister, in that cold, dark place until my mother came up to see what was going on."

Naoko shook her head.

"For three days after that I couldn't talk. I just lay in bed like a dead person, eyes wide open and staring into space. I didn't know what was happening." Naoko pressed against my arm. "I told you in my letter, didn't I? I'm a far more flawed human being than you realize. My sickness is a lot worse than you think: it has far deeper roots. And that's why I want you to go on ahead of me if you can. Don't wait for me. Sleep with other girls if you want to. Don't let thoughts of me hold you back. Just do what you want to do. Otherwise, I might end up taking you with me, and that is the one thing I don't want to do. I don't want to interfere with your life. I don't want to interfere with anybody's life. Like I said before, I want you to come to see me every once in a while, and always remember me. That's all I want."

"It's *not* all *I* want, though," I said.

"You're wasting your life being involved with me."

"I'm not wasting anything."

"But I might never recover. Will you wait for me forever? Can you wait ten years, twenty years?"

"You're letting yourself be scared by too many things," I said. "The dark, bad dreams, the power of the dead. You have to forget them. I'm sure you'll get well if you do."

"If I can," said Naoko, shaking her head.

"If you can get out of this place, will you live with me?" I asked. "Then I can protect you from the dark and from bad dreams. Then you'd have me instead of Reiko to hold you when things got difficult."

Naoko pressed still more firmly against me. "That would be wonderful," she said.

WE GOT BACK TO THE COFFEEHOUSE a little before three. Reiko was reading a book and listening to Brahms's second piano concerto on the radio. There was something wonderful about Brahms playing at the edge of a grassy meadow without a sign of people as far as the eye could see. Reiko was whistling along with the cello passage opening the third movement.

"Backhaus and Böhm," she said. "I wore this record out once, a long time ago. Literally. I wore the grooves out listening to every note. I sucked the music right out of it."

Naoko and I ordered coffee.

"Do a lot of talking?" asked Reiko.

"Tons," said Naoko.

"Tell me all about his, uh, you know, later."

"We didn't do any of that," said Naoko, reddening.

"Really?" Reiko asked me. "Nothing?"

"Nothing," I said.

"Bo-o-o-ring!" she said with a bored look on her face.

"True," I said, sipping my coffee.

THE SCENE IN THE DINING HALL was the same as it had been the day before—the mood, the voices, the faces. Only the menu had changed. The balding man in white who, yesterday, had been talking about the secretion of gastric juices under weightless conditions joined the three of us at our table and talked for a long time about the correlation of brain size to intelligence. As we ate our soybean hamburger steaks, we heard all about the volume of Bismarck's brain and Napoleon's. He pushed his plate aside and used a ballpoint pen and notepaper to draw sketches of brains. He would start to draw, declare, "No, that's not quite it," and start a new one. This happened any number of times. When he was through, he carefully put the remaining notepaper away in a pocket of his white jacket and slipped the pen into his breast pocket. He had a total of three pens in that pocket, along with pencils and a ruler. When he was through eating, he repeated what he had told me the day before, "The winters here are nice. Make sure you come back when it's winter," and left the dining hall.

"Is that guy a doctor or a patient?" I asked Reiko.

"Which do you think?"

"I really can't tell. In either case, he doesn't seem all that normal."

"He's a doctor," said Naoko. "Doctor Miyata."

"Yeah," said Reiko, "but I bet he's the craziest one here."

"Mr. Omura, the gatekeeper, is pretty crazy, too," answered Naoko.

"True," said Reiko, nodding as she stabbed her broccoli. "He does these wild calisthenics every morning, screaming nonsense at the top of his lungs. And before you came, Naoko, there was a girl in the business office, Miss Kinoshita, who tried to kill herself. And last year they fired a male nurse, Tokushima, who had a terrible drinking problem."

"Sounds like patients and staff could trade places," I said.

"Right on," said Reiko, waving her fork in the air. "I guess you're finally starting to figure out how things work here."

"I guess."

"What makes us most normal," said Reiko, "is knowing that we're not normal."

BACK IN THE ROOM, Naoko and I played cards while Reiko practiced Bach on her guitar.

"What time are you leaving tomorrow?" Reiko asked me, taking a break and lighting a cigarette.

"Right after breakfast," I said. "The bus comes after nine. That way I can get back in time for tomorrow night's work."

"Too bad. It'd be nice if you could stay longer."

"If I hung around too long, I might end up living here," I said, laughing.

"Maybe so," Reiko said. Then, to Naoko, she said, "Oh, yeah, I've got to go get some grapes at Oka's. I totally forgot."

"Want me to go with you?" asked Naoko.

"How about letting me borrow your young Mr. Watanabe here?"

"Fine," said Naoko.

"Good. Let's just the two of us go for another nighttime stroll," said Reiko, taking my hand. "We were almost there yesterday. Let's go all the way tonight."

"Fine," said Naoko, tittering. "Do what you like."

The night air was cool. Reiko wore a pale blue cardigan over her shirt and walked with her hands shoved in the pockets of her jeans. Looking up at the sky, she sniffed the breeze like a dog. "Smells like rain," she said. I tried sniffing, too, but couldn't smell anything. True, there were lots of clouds in the sky obscuring the moon.

"If you stay here long enough, you can pretty much tell the weather by the smell of the air," said Reiko.

We entered the wooded area where the staff houses stood. Reiko told me to wait a minute and walked over to the front door of one house, where she rang the bell. A woman came to the door—no doubt the lady of the house—and stood there chatting and chuckling with Reiko. Then she ducked inside and came back with a large plastic bag. Reiko thanked her and said goodnight before returning to the spot where I was standing.

"Look," she said, opening the bag.

The bag held a huge pile of grapes in clusters.

"Do you like grapes?"

"I sure do."

She handed me the topmost bunch. "It's O.K. to eat them. They're washed."

We walked along eating grapes and spitting the skins and seeds on the ground. The fruit was fresh and delicious.

"I give their boy piano lessons once in a while, and they give me different stuff. The wine we had was from them. I sometimes ask them to do a little shopping for me in town."

"I'd like to hear the rest of the story you were telling me yesterday," I said.

"Fine," said Reiko. "But if we keep coming home late, Naoko might start getting suspicious."

"I'm willing to risk it."

"O.K., then. I want a roof, though. It's a little chilly tonight."

She turned left as we approached the tennis courts. We went down a narrow stairway and came out to a spot where several storehouses stood like a block of row houses. Reiko opened the door of the nearest one, stepped in, and turned on the lights. "Come in," she said. "It's a nothing kind of place, though."

The storehouse contained neat rows of cross-country skis, boots, and poles, and on the floor were piled snow removal equipment and bags of rock salt.

"I used to come here all the time for guitar practice—when I wanted to be alone. Nice and cozy, isn't it?"

Reiko sat on the bags of rock salt and invited me to sit next to her. I did as I was told.

"Not much ventilation here, but mind if I smoke?"

"Sure, go ahead," I said.

"This is one habit I can't seem to break," she said with a frown, but she lit up with obvious enjoyment. Not many people enjoy tobacco as much as Reiko did. I ate my grapes, carefully peeling them one at a time and tossing the skins and seeds into a tin that served as a wastebasket.

"Now, let's see, how far did we get last night?" Reiko asked.

"It was a dark and stormy night, and you were climbing the steep cliff to grab the bird's nest."

"You're amazing, the way you can joke around with such a straight face," said Reiko. "Let's see, I think I had gotten to where I was giving piano lessons to the girl every Saturday morning."

"That's it."

"Assuming you can divide everybody in the world into two groups— those who are good at teaching things to people, and those who are not— I pretty much belong to the first group," said Reiko. "I never thought so when I was young, and I guess I didn't want to think of myself that way, but I realized it was true when I had attained a degree of self-knowledge after I had reached a certain age. I'm good at teaching people things. Really good."

"I'll bet you are."

"I have a lot more patience for others than I have for myself, and I'm much better at bringing out the best in others than in myself. That's just the kind of person I am. I'm the scratchy stuff on the side of the matchbox. But that's fine with me. I don't mind at all. Better to be a first-class matchbox than a second-class match. I got this clear in my own mind, I'd say, after I started teaching the girl. I had taught a few others when I was younger, strictly as a sideline, without seeing this about myself. It was only after I started teaching her that I started thinking of myself that way. Hey—I'm *good* at teaching people. That's how well the lessons went.

"As I said yesterday, the girl was nothing special when it came to technique, and there was no question of her becoming a professional musician, so I could take it easy. Plus she was going to the kind of girls' school where anybody with half-decent grades automatically got into college, which meant she didn't have to kill herself studying, and her mother was all for taking it easy with the lessons, too. So I didn't push her to do anything. I knew the first time I met her that she was the kind of girl you *couldn't* push to do anything, that she was the kind of child who would be all sweetness and say, 'Yes, yes,' and *absolutely refuse* to do anything she didn't want to do. So the first thing I did was let her play a piece the way she wanted to—one hundred percent her own way. Then I would play the same piece all different ways for her, and the two of us would discuss which way was better or which way she liked better. Then I'd have her play the piece again, and her performance would be ten times better than the first time through. She would see for herself what worked best and bring those features into her own playing."

Reiko paused for a moment, looking at the glowing end of her cigarette. I went on eating my grapes without a word.

"I know I have a pretty good sense for music, but she was better than me. I used to think it was such a waste! I thought, 'If only she had started out with a good teacher and gotten the proper training, she'd be so much further along!' But I was wrong about that. She was not the kind of child who could stand proper training. There just happen to be people like that. They're blessed with this marvelous talent, but they can't make the effort to systematize it. They end up squandering it in little bits and pieces. I've seen my share of people like that. At first you think they're amazing. Like, they can sight-read some terrifically difficult piece and do a damn good job playing it all the way through. You see them do it, and you're overwhelmed. You think, 'I could never do that in a million years.' But that's as far as they go. They can't take it any further. And why not? Because they won't put in the effort. Because they haven't had the discipline pounded into them. They've been spoiled. They have just enough talent so they've been able to play things well without any effort and they've had people telling them how great they are from the time they're little, so hard work looks stupid to them. They'll take some piece another kid has to work on for three weeks and polish it off in half the time, so the teacher figures they've put enough into it and lets them go to the next thing. And they do *that* in half the time and go on to the *next* piece. They never find out what it means to be hammered by the teacher; they lose out on a certain element required for character building. It's a tragedy. I myself had tendencies like that, but fortunately I had a very tough teacher, so I kept them in check.

"Anyhow, it was a joy to teach her. Like driving down the highway in a high-powered sports car that responds to the slightest touch—maybe responds too quickly, sometimes. The trick to teaching children like that is not to praise them too much. They're so used to praise it doesn't mean anything to them. You've got to dole it out wisely. And you can't force anything on them. You have to let them choose for themselves. And you don't let them rush ahead from one thing to the next: you make them stop and think. But that's about it. If you do those things, you'll get good results."

Reiko dropped her cigarette butt on the floor and stamped it out. Then she took a deep breath as if to calm her emotions.

"When her lessons ended, we'd have tea and chat. Sometimes I'd show her certain jazz piano styles—like, this is Bud Powell, or this is Thelonious Monk. But mostly she talked. And what a talker she was! She could draw you right in. As I told you yesterday, I think most of what she said was made up, but it was *interesting*. She was a keen observer, a precise user of language, sharp-tongued and funny. She could stir your emotions. Yes, really, that's what she was so good at—stirring people's emotions, *moving* you. And she *knew* she had this power. She tried to use it as skillfully and effectively as possible. She could make you feel whatever she wanted—angry or sad or sympathetic or disappointed or happy. She would manipulate people's emotions for no other reason than to test her own powers. Of course, I only realized this later. At the time, I had no idea what she was doing to me."

Reiko shook her head and ate a few grapes.

"It was a sickness," she said. "The girl was sick. She was like the rotten apple that ruins all the other apples. And no one could cure her. She'll have that sickness until the day she dies. In that sense, she was a sad little creature. I would have pitied her, too, if I hadn't been one of her victims. I would have seen *her* as a victim."

Reiko ate a few more grapes. She seemed to be thinking of how best to go on with her story.

"Well, anyhow, I enjoyed her for a good six months. Sometimes I'd find something she said a little surprising or odd. Or she'd be talking and I'd have this rush of horror to realize that the intensity of her hatred for some person went way beyond reason, or it would occur to me that she was just way too clever, and I'd wonder what she was really thinking. But, after all, everybody has their flaws, right? And finally, what business was it of mine to question her personality or character? I was just her piano teacher. All I had to care about was whether she practiced or not. And besides, the truth of the matter is that I liked her. I liked her a lot.

"Still, I was careful not to tell her anything too personal about myself. I just had this instinctive sense I'd better avoid talking about such things. She asked me hundreds of questions—she was dying to know more about me—but I told her only the most harmless kind of stuff, like things about my girlhood or where I'd gone to school, stuff like that. She said she wanted to know more about me, but I told her there was nothing to tell: I'd had a boring life, I had an ordinary husband, an ordinary child, and a ton of housework. 'But I like you so *much*,' she'd say, and look me right in the eye in this clingy sort of way. It sent a thrill through me when she did that—a *nice* thrill. But even so, I never told her more than I had to.

"And then one day—a day in May, I think it was—in the middle of her lesson, she said she felt sick. I saw she was pale and sweating and asked if she wanted to go home, but she said she thought she'd feel better if she could just lie down a while. So I took her—almost carried her—to the bedroom. We had such a small sofa, the bed was the only place she *could* lie down. She apologized for being a bother, but I assured her it was no bother and asked if she wanted anything to drink. She said no, she just wanted me to stay near her a while, which I said I'd be glad to do.

"A few minutes later she asked me to rub her back. She sounded as if she was really suffering, and she was sweating like crazy, so I started to give her a good massage. Then she apologized and asked me if I'd mind taking off her bra, it was hurting her. So, I don't know, I did it. She was wearing a skintight blouse, and I had to unbutton that and reach behind and undo the bra hooks. She had big breasts for a thirteen-year-old. Twice as big as mine. And she wasn't wearing any starter bra but a real adult model, an expensive one. Of course I'm not paying all that much attention at the time, and like an idiot I just keep on rubbing her back. She keeps apologizing in this pitiful voice like she's really sorry, and I keep telling her it's O.K., it's O.K."

Reiko tapped the ashes from her next cigarette to the floor. By then I had stopped eating grapes and was giving all my attention to her story.

"After a while she starts sobbing. 'What's wrong?' I ask her. 'Nothing,' she says. 'It's obviously not nothing,' I say. 'Tell me the truth. What's bothering you?' So she says, 'I just get like this sometimes. I don't know what to do. I'm so lonely and sad, and I can't talk to anybody, and nobody cares about me. And it hurts so much, I just get like this. I can't sleep at night, and I don't feel like eating, and coming here for my lesson is the only thing I have to look forward to.' So I say, 'You can talk to *me*. Tell me why this happens to you.' Things are not going well at home, she says. She can't love her parents, and they don't love her. Her father is seeing another woman and hardly ever comes home, and that makes her mother half crazy and she takes it out on the girl; she beats her almost every day and she hates to go home. So now the girl is really wailing, and her eyes are full of tears, those beautiful eyes of hers. The sight is enough to make a god blubber. So I tell her, if it's so terrible to go home, she can come to my place anytime she likes. When she hears that, the girl throws her arms around me and says, 'Oh, I'm so sorry, but if I didn't have you I wouldn't know what to do. Please don't turn your back on me. If you did that, I'd have nowhere to go.'

"So, I don't know, I hold her head against me and I'm caressing her and saying, 'There there,' and she's got her arms around me and she's stroking my back, and soon I'm starting to feel very strange, my whole body is kind of hot. I mean, here's this picture-perfect beautiful girl and I'm on the bed with her, and we're hugging, and her hands are caressing my back in this incredibly sensual way that my own husband couldn't begin to match, and I feel all the screws coming loose in my body every time she touches me, and before I know it she's got my blouse and bra off and she's stroking my breasts. So that's when it finally hits me that she's an absolute dyed-in-the-wool lesbian. This had happened to me once before, in high school, one of the upperclass girls. So then I tell her to stop.

"'Oh, please,' she says, 'just a little more. I'm so lonely. I'm so lonely, please believe me, you're the only one I have, oh please, don't turn your back on me,' and she takes my hand and puts it on her breast—her very nicely shaped breast, and, sure, I'm a woman, but this electric something goes through me when my hand makes contact. I have no idea what to do. I just keep repeating no no no no no like an idiot. I'm like paralyzed, I can't move. I had managed O.K. to push the girl away in high school, but now I can't do a thing. My body won't take orders. She's holding my right hand against her with her left hand, and she's kissing and licking my nipples, and her right hand is caressing my back and side and bottom. So here I am in the bedroom with the curtains closed and a thirteen-year-old girl has me practically naked—she's been taking my clothes off somehow all along—and touching me all over and I'm writhing with the pleasure of it. Looking back on it now, it seems incredible. I mean, it's crazy, don't you think? But at the time it was like she had cast a spell on me."

Reiko paused to take a puff on her cigarette.

"You know, this is the first time I've ever told a man about this," she said, looking at me. "I'm telling it to you because I think I ought to, but I'm finding it awfully embarrassing."

"I'm sorry," I said, because I didn't know what else to say.

"This went on for a while, and then her right hand started to move down, and she touched me through my panties. By then, I was absolutely soaking wet. I'm ashamed to say it, but I've never been so wet before or since. I had always thought of myself as kind of indifferent to sex, so I was astounded to be getting so worked up. So then she puts these slim, soft fingers of hers inside my panties, and . . . well, you know, I can't bring myself to put it into words. I mean, it was totally different from when a man puts his clumsy hands on you there. It was amazing. Really. Like feathers or down. I thought all the fuses in my head were going to pop. Still, somewhere in my fogged-over brain, the thought occurred to me that I had to put a stop to this. If I let it happen once, I'd never stop, and if I had to carry around a secret like that inside me, my head was going to get completely messed up again. I thought about my daughter, too. What if she saw me like this? She was supposed to be at my parents' house until three on Saturdays, but what if something happened and she came home unexpectedly? This helped me to gather my strength and raise myself on the bed. 'Stop it now, please stop!' I shouted.

"But she wouldn't stop. Instead, she yanked my panties down and started using her tongue. I had rarely let even my husband do that, I found it so embarrassing, but now I had a thirteen-year-old girl licking me all over down there. I just gave up. All I could do was cry. And it was absolutely paradise.

" 'Stop it!' I yelled one more time, and smacked her on the side of the face. As hard as I could. Finally, she stopped and raised herself up and looked into my eyes. The two of us were stark naked, on our knees, in bed, staring at each other. She was thirteen, I was thirty-one, but, I don't know, looking at that body of hers, I felt totally overwhelmed. The image is still vivid in my mind. I could hardly believe I was looking at the body of a thirteen-year-old girl, and I still can't believe it. By comparison, what I had for a body was enough to make you cry. Believe me."

There was nothing I could say, and so I said nothing.

" 'What's wrong?' she says to me. 'You like it this way, don't you? I knew you would the first time I met you. I know you like it. It's way better than doing it with a man—isn't it? Look how wet you got. I can make you feel even better if you'll let me. It's true. I can make you feel like your body's melting away. You want me to do it, don't you?' And she was right. Doing this with her was much better than doing it with my husband. And I *did* want her to do it even more! But I couldn't let it happen, 'Let's do this once a week,' she said. 'Just once a week. Nobody will find out. It'll be our little secret.'

"But I got out of bed and put on my robe and told her to leave and never come back. She just looked at me. Her eyes were absolutely flat. I had never seen them that way before. It was as if they had been painted on cardboard. They had no depth. After she stared at me for a while, she gathered up her clothing without a word and, as slowly as she could, as if she was making a show of it, she put on each piece, one at a time. Then she went back into the room where the piano was and took a brush from her bag. She brushed her hair and wiped the blood from her lips with a handkerchief, put on her shoes, and went out. As she was leaving, she said, 'You're a lesbian, you know. It's true. You may try to hide it, but you'll be a lesbian until the day you die.'

"Is it true?" I asked.

Reiko curved her lips and thought for a while. "Well, it is and it isn't. I definitely felt better with her than with my husband. That's a fact. I had a time there when I really agonized over the question. Maybe I really was a lesbian and just hadn't noticed until then. But I don't think so anymore. Which is not to say I don't have the tendencies. I probably do have them. But I'm not a lesbian in the proper sense of the term. I never feel desire when I look at a woman. Know what I mean?"

I nodded.

"Certain kinds of girls, though, do respond to me, and I can feel it when that happens. Those are the only times it comes out in me. I can hold Naoko in my arms, though, and feel nothing special. We go around in the apartment practically naked when the weather is hot, and we take baths together, sometimes even sleep in the same bed, but nothing happens. I don't feel a thing. I can see that she has a beautiful body, but that's all. Actually, Naoko and I played a game once. We made believe we were lesbians. Want to hear about it?"

"Sure. Tell me."

"When I told her the story I just told you—we tell each other everything, you know—Naoko tried an experiment. The two of us got undressed and she tried caressing me, but it didn't work at all. It just tickled. I thought I was going to die laughing. Just thinking about it makes me itchy. She was so clumsy! I'll bet you're glad to hear *that*."

"Yes, I am, to tell the truth."

"Well, anyway, that's about it," said Reiko, scratching near an eyebrow with the tip of her little finger. "After the girl left my house, I found a chair and sat there spacing out for a while, wondering what to do. I could hear the dull beating of my heart from deep inside my body. My arms and legs seemed to weigh a ton, and my mouth felt as if I had eaten a moth or something, it was so dry. I dragged myself to the bathtub, though, knowing my daughter would be back soon. I wanted to clean those places where the girl had touched and licked me. I scrubbed myself with soap, over and over, but I couldn't seem to get rid of the slimy feeling she had left behind. I knew I was probably imagining it, but that didn't help. That night, I asked my husband to make love to me, kind of as a way to get rid of the defilement. Of course, I didn't tell him anything—l couldn't. All I said to him was that I wanted him to take it slow, to give it more time than usual. And he did. He really concentrated on every little detail, he really took a long, long time, and the way I came that night, oh yes, it was nothing I had ever experienced before, never once in all our marriage. And why do you think that was? Because the touch of that girl's fingers was still there in my body. That's all it was.

"Oh, man, is this embarrassing! Look, I'm sweating! I can't believe I'm saying these things—he 'made love' to me, I 'came'!" Reiko smiled, her lips curved again.

"But even this didn't help. Two days went by, three, and her touch was still there. And her last words seemed to keep echoing and echoing in my head.

"She didn't come to my house the following Saturday. My heart was pounding all day long while I waited, wondering what I would do if she showed up. I couldn't concentrate on anything. She never did come, though. Of course. She was a proud young thing, and she had failed with me in the end. She didn't come the next week, either, nor the week after that, and soon a month went by. I figured that I would be able to forget about what had happened when enough time went by, but I couldn't forget. When I was alone in the house, I would feel her presence and my nerves would be on edge. I couldn't play the piano, I couldn't think, I couldn't do anything during that first month. And then one day I realized that something was wrong whenever I left the house. The people in the neighborhood were looking at me in a strange new way. There was a new distance in their eyes. They were as polite as ever with their greetings, but there was something different in their tone of voice and in their behavior toward me. The woman next door, who used to pay me an occasional visit, seemed to be avoiding me. I tried not to let these things bother me, though. Start noticing things like that, and you've got the first signs of illness.

"Then one day I had a visit from another housewife I was on friendly terms with. We were the same age, and she was the daughter of a friend of my mother's, and her child went to the same kindergarten as mine, so we were fairly close. She just showed up one day and asked me if I knew about a terrible rumor that was going around about me. I said I did not.

" 'What kind of rumor?' I asked.

" 'I almost can't say it, it's so awful,' she said.

" 'Well, you've gone this far, you have to tell me the rest.'

"Still she resisted telling me, but I finally got it all out of her. I mean, her whole purpose in coming to see me was to tell me what she had heard, so of course she was going to spit it out eventually. According to her, people were saying that I was a card-carrying lesbian and had been in and out of mental hospitals for it. They said that I had stripped the clothes off my piano pupil and tried to do things to her and when she had resisted I had smacked her so hard her face swelled up. They had turned the story on its head, of course, which was bad enough, but what really shocked me was that people knew I had been hospitalized.

"My friend said she was telling everyone that she had known me forever and that I was not like that, but the girl's parents believed *her* version and were spreading it around the neighborhood. In addition, they had investigated my background and found that I had a history of mental problems.

"The way my friend heard it, the girl had come home from her lesson one day—*that* day, of course—with her face all bloated, her lip split and bloody, buttons missing from her blouse, and even her underwear torn. Can you believe it? She had done all this to back up her story, of course, which her mother had to drag out of her. I can just see her doing it— putting blood on her blouse, tearing buttons off, ripping the lace on her bra, making herself cry until her eyes were red, messing up her hair, telling her mother a bucket of lies.

"Not that I'm blaming people for believing her. I would have believed her, too, this beautiful doll with a devil's tongue. She comes home crying, she refuses to talk because it's too embarrassing, but then she spills it out. Of *course* people are going to believe her. And to make matters worse, it's true, I *do* have a history of hospitalization for mental problems, I *did* smack her in the face as hard as I could. Who's going to believe *me*? Maybe my husband, is all.

"A few more days went by while I wrestled with the question of whether to tell him or not, but when I did, he believed me. Of course. I told him everything that had happened that day—the kind of lesbian things she did to me, the way I smacked her in the face. Of course, I didn't tell him what I had felt. There's no way I could have told him that. So anyway, he got furious and insisted that he was going to go straight to the girl's family. He said, 'You're a married woman, after all. You're married to *me*. And you're a mother. There's no way you're a lesbian. What a goddam joke!'

"But I wouldn't let him go. All he could do was make things worse. Really, I knew. I knew she was sick. I had seen hundreds of sick people, so I knew. The girl was rotten inside. Peel off a layer of that beautiful skin, and you'd find nothing but rotten flesh. I know it's a terrible thing to say, but it's true. And I knew that ordinary people could never know the truth about her, that there was no way we could win. She was an expert at manipulating the emotions of the adults around her, and we had nothing to prove our case. First of all, who's going to believe that a thirteen-year-old girl set a homosexual trap for a woman in her thirties? No matter what we said, people would believe what they wanted to believe. The more we struggled, the more vulnerable we'd be.

"There was only one thing for us to do, I said: we had to move. If I stayed in that neighborhood any longer, the stress would get to me; my mind would snap again. It was happening already. We had to get out of there, go someplace far away where nobody knew me. My husband was not ready to go, though. It hadn't dawned on him yet how critical I was. And the timing was terrible: he was loving his work, and he had finally succeeded in settling us into our own house (we lived in a little prefab), and our daughter was comfortable in her kindergarten. 'Wait a minute,' he said, 'we can't just pick up and move. I can't find a job just like that. We'd have to sell the house, and we'd have to find another kindergarten. It'll take two months, at least.'

" 'I can't wait two months,' I told him. 'This is going to finish me off once and for all. I'm not kidding. Believe me, I know what I'm talking about.' The symptoms were starting already: my ears were ringing, and I was hearing things, and I couldn't sleep. So he suggested that I leave first, go somewhere by myself, and he would follow after he had taken care of what needed to be done.

" 'No,' I said, 'I don't want to go anywhere alone. I'll fall apart if I don't have you. I need you. Please, don't leave me alone.'

"He held me and pleaded with me to hang on a little longer. Just a month, he said. He would take care of everything—leave his job, sell the house, make arrangements for kindergarten, find a new job. There might be a position he could take in Australia, he said. He just wanted me to wait one month, and everything would be O.K. I couldn't say anything more to that. If I tried to object, it would only isolate me even more."

Reiko sighed and looked at the ceiling light.

"I couldn't hold on for a month, though. One day, it happened again: *snap!* And this time it was really bad. I took sleeping pills and turned on the gas. I woke up in a hospital bed, and it was all over. It took a few months before I had calmed down enough to think, and then I asked my husband to divorce me. I told him it would be the best thing for him and for our daughter. He said he had no intention of divorcing me.

" 'We can make a new start,' he said. 'We can go someplace new, just the three of us, and begin all over again.'

" 'It's too late,' I told him. 'Everything ended when you asked me to wait a month. If you really wanted to start again, you shouldn't have said that to me. Now, no matter where we go, no matter how far away we move, the same thing will happen all over again. And I'll ask you for the same thing, and make you suffer. I don't want to do that anymore.'

"And so we divorced. Or should I say, I divorced him. He married again two years ago, though. I'm still glad I made him leave me. Really. I knew I'd be like this for the rest of my life, and I didn't want to drag anyone down with me. I didn't want to force anyone to live in constant fear that I might lose my mind at any moment.

"He had been wonderful to me, an ideal husband, faithful, strong, and patient, someone I could put my complete trust in. He had done everything he could to heal me, and I had done everything I could to *be* healed, both for his sake and for our daughter's sake. And I had believed in my recovery. I was happy for six years from the time we were married. He got me ninety-nine percent of the way there, but the other one percent went crazy. *Snap!* Everything we had built up came crashing down. In one split second, everything turned into nothing. And that girl was the one who did it."

Reiko collected the cigarette butts she had crushed underfoot and tossed them into the tin can.

"It's a terrible story. We worked so hard, so hard, building our world one brick at a time. And when it fell apart, it happened just like that. Everything was gone before you knew it."

Reiko stood up and thrust her hands in her pants pockets. "Let's go back. It's late."

The sky was darker, the cloud cover thicker than before, the moon invisible. Now, I realized, like Reiko I could smell the rain. And with it mixed the fresh smell of the grapes in the bag I was holding in my hand.

"That's why I can't leave this place," she said. "I'm afraid to leave and get involved with the outside world. I'm afraid to meet new people and feel new feelings."

"I understand," I said. "But I think you can do it. I think you can go outside and make it."

Reiko smiled, but she didn't say a thing.

NAOKO WAS ON THE SOFA with a book. She had her legs crossed, and she pressed her hand against her temple as she read. Her fingers almost seemed to be touching and testing each word that entered her head. Scattered drops of rain were beginning to tap on the roof. The lamplight enveloped Naoko, hovering around her like fine dust. After my long talk with Reiko, Naoko's youthfulness struck me in a whole new way.

"Sorry we're so late," said Reiko, patting Naoko's head.

"Enjoy yourselves?" asked Naoko, looking up.

"Of course," said Reiko.

"Doing what?" Naoko asked me "—just the two of you."

"Not at liberty to say, Miss," I answered.

Naoko chuckled and set her book down. Then the three of us ate grapes to the sound of the rain.

"When it's raining like this," said Naoko, "it feels as if we're the only ones in the world. I wish it would just keep raining so the three of us could stay together."

"Oh, sure," said Reiko, "and while the two of you are going at it, I'm supposed to be fanning you or playing background music on my guitar like some dumb slave. No, thanks!"

"Oh, I'd let you have him once in a while," said Naoko, laughing.

"O.K, then, count me in," said Reiko. "C'mon, rain, pour down!"

THE RAIN DID POUR DOWN, and kept pouring. Thunder shook the place from time to time. When we finished the grapes, Reiko went back to her cigarettes and pulled the guitar out from under her bed and started to play—first, "Desafinado" and "The Girl from Ipanema," then some Bacharach and a few Lennon and McCartney songs. Reiko and I sipped wine again, and when that was gone we shared the brandy that was left in my flask. A warm, close mood took hold as the three of us talked into the night, and I began to wish, with Naoko, that the rain would keep on falling.

"Will you come to see me again?" Naoko asked, looking at me.

"Of course I will," I said.

"And will you write?"

"Every week."

"And will you add a few lines for me?" Reiko asked.

"That I will," I said. "I'd be glad to."

At eleven o'clock, Reiko folded the sofa down and made a bed for me as she had the night before. We said goodnight and turned out the lights and went to bed. Unable to sleep, I took *The Magic Mountain* and a flashlight from my knapsack and read for a while. Just before midnight, the bedroom door edged open and Naoko came and crawled in next to me. Unlike the night before, Naoko was the usual Naoko. Her eyes were in focus, her movements brisk. Bringing her mouth to my ear, she whispered, "I don't know, I can't sleep."

"I can't either," I said. Setting my book down and turning out the flashlight, I took her in my arms and kissed her. The darkness and the sound of the rain enfolded us.

"How about Reiko?"

"Don't worry, she's sound asleep. And when she sleeps, she *sleeps*." Then Naoko asked, "Will you really come to see me again?"

"I will, for sure."

"Even if I can't do anything for you?"

I nodded in the darkness. I could feel the full shape of her breasts against me. I traced the outline of her body through her gown with the flat of my hand. From shoulder to back to hips, I slid my hand again and again, driving the line and the softness of her body into my brain. After we had been in this gentle embrace for a while, Naoko touched her lips to my forehead and slipped out of bed. I could see her pale blue gown flash in the darkness like a fish.

"Good-bye," she called in a tiny voice.

Listening to the rain, I dropped into a gentle sleep.

IT WAS STILL RAINING the following morning—a fine, almost invisible autumn rain unlike the previous night's downpour. You knew it was raining only because of the ripples on puddles and the sound of dripping from the eaves. I woke to see a milky white mist enclosing the window, but as the sun rose a breeze carried the mist away, and the surrounding woods and hills began to emerge.

As we had done the day before, the three of us ate breakfast and headed out to service the birdhouse. Naoko and Reiko wore yellow vinyl rain capes with hoods. I put on a sweater and a waterproof windbreaker. The outside air was damp and chilly. The birds, too, seemed to be avoiding the rain, huddled together at the back of the cage.

"Gets cold here when it rains, doesn't it?" I said to Reiko.

"Now, every time it rains it'll be a little colder, until it turns to snow," she said. "The clouds from the Sea of Japan dump tons of snow when they pass through here."

"What do you do with the birds in winter?"

"Bring 'em inside, of course. What are we supposed to do—dig them out of the snow in spring all frozen? We defrost 'em and bring 'em back to life and yell, O.K., everybody, come and get it!"

I poked the wire mesh and the parrot flapped its wings and screamed, "Shithead! Thank you! Crazy!"

"Now, *that* one I'd like to freeze," Naoko said with a melancholy look. "I really think I *will* go crazy if I have to hear that every morning."

After cleaning the birdhouse, we went back to the apartment. While I packed my things, the women put their farm gear on. We left the building together and parted a short way beyond the tennis court. They turned right and I continued straight ahead. We called good-bye to each other, and I promised I would come again. Naoko gave a little smile and disappeared around the corner.

I passed a number of people on my way to the gate, all of them wearing the same yellow rain capes that Naoko and Reiko had on, all with hoods up. Colors shone with exceptional clarity in the rain. The ground was a deep black, the pine branches a brilliant green, the people wrapped in yellow looking like special spirits that were allowed to wander over the earth on rainy mornings only. They floated over the earth in silence, carrying farm tools and baskets and some kind of sack.

The gatekeeper remembered my name and marked it on the list of visitors when I went out. "I see you're from Tokyo," the old fellow said. "I went there once. Just once. They serve great pork."

"They do?" I asked, uncertain how to answer him.

"I didn't like much of what I ate in Tokyo, but the pork was delicious. I guess they've got some special way of raisin' 'em, eh?"

I said I didn't know, it was the first time I'd heard of it. "When was that, by the way, when you went to Tokyo?"

"Hmm, let's see," he said, cocking his head, "was it the time His Majesty the crown prince got married? My son was in Tokyo and said I ought to see the place at least once. That time. Nineteen fifty-nine."

"Oh, well then, sure, pork must have been good in Tokyo back then," I said.

"How about these days?" he asked.

I wasn't sure, I said, but I hadn't heard anything special about it. This seemed to disappoint him somewhat. He gave every sign of wanting to continue our conversation, but I told him I had to catch a bus and started walking in the direction of the road. Patches of fog remained floating on the road where it skirted the stream, but the breeze carried them over to the steep flanks of a nearby mountain. Every now and then as I walked along I would stop and turn and heave a sigh for no particular reason. I felt almost as if I had come to a planet where the gravity was a little different. Yes, of course, I told myself, feeling sad: I was in the outside world now.

BACK AT THE DORM BY FOUR-THIRTY, I changed right away and left for the record shop in Shinjuku to put in my hours. I minded the store from six o'clock to ten-thirty and sold a few records, but mainly I sat there in a daze, watching the incredible variety of people streaming by outside. There were families and couples and drunks and gangsters and lively looking girls in short skirts and bearded hippies and bar hostesses and some indefinable types. Whenever I put on hard rock, hippies and run-away kids would gather outside to dance and sniff paint thinner or just sit on the ground doing nothing in particular, and when I put on Tony Bennett, they would disappear.

Next door was a shop where a middle-aged, sleepy-eyed guy sold "adult toys." I couldn't imagine why anyone would want the kind of sex paraphernalia he had there, but he seemed to do a lot of business. In the alley diagonally across from the record store I saw a drunken student vomiting. In the games center across from us at another angle, the cook from a local eatery was killing his break time with a game of bingo that took cash bets. Beneath the eaves of a shop that had closed for the night, a dark-faced homeless guy was crouching, motionless. A girl with pale pink lipstick who couldn't have been more than junior-high school age came in and asked me to play the Rolling Stones' "Jumpin' Jack Flash." When I found the disk and put it on for her, she started snapping her fingers to the rhythm and shaking her hips as she danced around the shop. Then she asked me for a cigarette. I gave her one of the manager's, which she smoked with obvious pleasure, and when the record ended she left the shop without so much as a "thank you." Every fifteen minutes or so I would hear the siren of an ambulance or cop car. Three drunken company employees in suits and ties came by, laughing at the tops of their voices every time they yelled "Piece of ass!" at a pretty, long-haired girl in a telephone booth.

The more I watched, the more mixed-up my head became. What the hell was this all about? I wondered. What could it possibly mean?

The manager came back from dinner and said to me, "Hey, know what, Watanabe? Night before last I made it with the boutique chick." For some time now he had had his eye on the girl who worked in a nearby boutique, and every once in a while he would take a record from the shop as a gift for her.

"Good for you," I said to him, whereupon he told me every last detail of his conquest.

"If ya really wanna make a chick, here's what ya gotta do," he began, very pleased with himself. "First, ya gotta give 'er presents. Then ya gotta get 'er drunk. I mean really drunk. Then ya just gotta do it. It's *easy*. See what I mean?"

Head mixed up as ever, I boarded the commuter train and went back to my dorm. Closing the curtains, I doused the lights, stretched out in bed, and felt as if Naoko might come crawling in beside me at any moment. With my eyes closed, I could feel the soft swell of her breasts on my chest, hear her whispering to me, and feel the outline of her body in my hands. In the darkness, I returned to that small world of hers. I smelled the meadow grass, heard the rain at night. I thought of her naked, as I had seen her in the moonlight, and pictured her cleaning the birdhouse and caring for the vegetables with that soft, beautiful body of hers wrapped in the yellow rain cape. Clutching my erection, I thought of Naoko until I came. This seemed to clear my brain somewhat, but it didn't help me sleep. I felt exhausted, even desperate for sleep, but it simply refused to cooperate.

I got out of bed and stood at the window, my unfocused eyes wandering out toward the flagpole. Without the national flag attached to it, the pole looked like a gigantic white bone thrusting up into the darkness of night. What was Naoko doing now? I wondered. Of course, she must be sleeping, sleeping deeply, wrapped in the darkness of that strange little world of hers. Let her be spared from anguished dreams, I found myself hoping.

seven

In P.E. class the next morning, Thursday, I swam several lengths of the fifty-meter pool. The hard exercise cleared my head somewhat and gave me an appetite. After downing a good-size lunch at a student eatery known for its good-size lunches, I was headed for the literature department library to do some research when I bumped into Midori Kobayashi. She had someone with her, a petite girl with glasses, but when she spotted me, she approached me alone.

"Where you going?" she asked.

"Lit Library," I said.

"Why don't you forget it and come have lunch with me?"

"I already ate."

"So what? Eat again."

We ended up going to a nearby café where she had a plate of curry and I had a cup of coffee. She wore a white long-sleeved shirt under a yellow woollen vest with a fish knitted into the design, a narrow gold necklace, and a Disney watch. She seemed to love the curry and drank three glasses of water with it.

"Where've you been all this time?" Midori asked. "I don't know how many times I called."

"Was there something you wanted to talk to me about?"

"Nothing special. I just called."

"I see."

"You see what?"

"Nothing. Just 'I see,'" I said. "Any fires lately?"

"That was fun, wasn't it? It didn't do much damage, but all that smoke made it kind of like reality. Great stuff." Midori chugged down another glass of water, took a breath, and studied my face for a while. "Hey, what's wrong with you?" she asked. "You've got this spaced-out look. Your eyes aren't focused."

"I'm O.K.," I said. "I just got back from a trip and I'm kinda tired."

"You look like you've just seen a ghost."

"I see."

"Hey, do you have classes this afternoon?"

"German and religion."

"Can you skip 'em?"

"Not German. I've got a test today."

"When's it over?"

"Two."

"O.K. How about going into the city with me after that for some drinks?"

"Drinks at two o'clock in the afternoon?!"

"For a change, why not? You look so spaced. C'mon, go drinking with me and get a little life into you. That's what I want to do—drink with you and get some life into myself. Whaddya say?"

"O.K., let's go," I said with a sigh. "I'll look for you in the lit quad at two."

AFTER GERMAN we caught a bus to Shinjuku and went to an underground bar called DUG behind the Kinokuniya bookstore. We each started with two vodka and tonics.

"I come here once in a while," she said. "They don't embarrass you about drinking in the afternoon."

"Do you drink in the afternoon a lot?"

"Sometimes," she said, rattling the ice in her glass. "Sometimes, when the world gets hard to live in, I come here for a vodka and tonic."

"Does the world get hard to live in?"

"Sometimes," said Midori. "I've got my own special little problems."

"Like what?"

"Like family, like boyfriends, like irregular periods. Stuff."

"So have another drink."

"I will."

I waved the waiter over and ordered two more vodka and tonics.

"Remember how, when you came over that Sunday, you kissed me?" Midori asked. "I've been thinking about it. That was nice. Really nice."

"That's nice."

"'That's nice,'" she mimicked me. "The way you talk is so weird!"

"It is?"

"Anyhow, I was thinking, that time. I was thinking how great it would be if that had been the first time in my life a boy had kissed me. If I could switch around the order of my life, I would absolutely absolutely make that my first kiss. And then I would live the rest of my life thinking stuff like, Hey, I wonder whatever happened to that boy named Watanabe I gave my first kiss to on the laundry deck, now that he's fifty-eight? Wouldn't that be great?"

"Yeah, really," I said, cracking open a pistachio nut.

"Hey, what is it with you? Why are you so spaced out? You still haven't answered me."

"I probably still haven't completely adapted to the world," I said after giving it some thought. "I don't know, I feel like this isn't the real world. The people, the scene: they just don't seem real to me."

Midori rested an elbow on the bar and looked at me. "There was something like that in a Jim Morrison song, I'm pretty sure."

"'People are strange when you're a stranger.'"

"Peace," said Midori.

"Peace," I said.

"You really ought to go to Uruguay with me," Midori said, still leaning on the bar. "Girlfriend, family, school—just dump 'em all."

"Not a bad idea," I said, laughing.

"Don't you think it would be wonderful to get rid of everything and everybody and just go someplace where you don't know a soul? Sometimes I feel like doing that. I really really want to do it sometimes. So, like, say you whisked me away somewhere far far away. I'd make a pile of babies for you as tough as little bulls. And we'd all live happily ever after, rolling on the floor."

I laughed and drank down my third vodka and tonic.

"I guess you don't really want a pile of babies as tough as little bulls yet," said Midori.

"I'm tremendously interested," I said. "I'd like to see what they look like."

"That's O.K., you don't have to want them," said Midori, eating a pistachio. "Here I am, drinking in the afternoon, saying whatever pops into my head: 'I wanna dump everything 'n' run off somewhere.' What's the point of going to Uruguay? All they've got there is donkey shit."

"You may be right."

"Donkey shit everywhere. Here a shit, there a shit, the whole world is donkey shit. Hey, I can't open this. You take it." Midori handed me a pistachio with an uncracked shell. I struggled with it until I got it open. "But oh, gee, what a *relief* it was last Sunday! Going up to the laundry deck with you, watching the fire, drinking beer, singing songs. I don't know *how* long it's been since I had such a total sense of *relief*. People are always trying to *force* stuff on me. The minute they see me they start telling me what to do. At least you don't try to force stuff on me."

"I don't know you well enough to force stuff on you."

"You mean, if you knew me better, you'd force stuff on me like everybody else?"

"It's possible," I said. "That's how people live in the real world: forcing stuff on each other."

"You wouldn't do that. I can tell. I'm an expert when it comes to forcing stuff and having stuff forced on you. You're just not that type. That's why I can relax with you. Do you have any idea how many people there are in the world who *like* to force stuff on people and have stuff forced on them? *Tons!* And then they make a big fuss, like, 'I forced her,' 'You forced me'! That's what they like. But *I* don't like it. I just do it 'cause I have to."

"What kind of stuff do you force on people or do they force on you?"

Midori put a piece of ice in her mouth and sucked on it for a while.

"Do you want to get to know me better?" she asked.

"Yeah, kind of."

"Hey, look, I just asked you, 'Do you want to get to know me better?' What the hell kind of answer is that?"

"Yes, Midori, I would like to get to know you better," I said.

"Really?"

"Yes, really."

"Even if you had to turn your eyes away from what you saw?"

"Are you that bad?"

"Well, in a way," Midori said with a frown. "I want another drink."

I called the waiter and ordered a fourth round of drinks. Until they came, Midori cupped her chin in her hand with her elbow on the bar. I kept quiet and listened to Thelonious Monk playing "Honeysuckle Rose." There were five or six other customers in the place, but we were the only ones drinking alcohol. The rich smell of coffee gave the gloomy interior an intimate atmosphere.

"Are you free this Sunday?" Midori asked.

"I think I told you before, I'm always free on Sunday. Until I go to work at six."

"O.K., then, *this* Sunday, will you hang out with me?"

"Sure," I said.

"I'll pick you up at your dorm Sunday morning. I'm not sure exactly what time, though. Is that O.K.?"

"Fine," I said. "No problem."

"Now, let me ask you: do you have any idea what I would like to do right now?"

"I can't imagine."

"Well, first of all, I want to lie down on a big, wide, fluffy bed. I want to get all comfy and drunk and not have any donkey shit anywhere nearby, and I want to have you lying down next to me. And then, little by little, you take my clothes off. *Sooo* tenderly. The way a mother takes a little child's clothing off. *Sooo* softly."

"Hmmm . . ."

"And I'm just spacing out and feeling really nice until, all of a sudden, I realize what's happening and I yell at you, 'Stop it, Watanabe!' And then I say, 'I really like you, Watanabe, but I'm seeing someone else. I can't do this. I'm very proper about these things, believe it or not, so please stop.' But you don't stop."

"But I *would* stop," I said.

"I know that. Never mind, this is just my fantasy," said Midori. "So then you show it to me. Your thing. Sticking way up. I immediately cover my eyes, of course, but I can't help seeing it for a split second. And I say, 'Stop it! Don't *do* that! I don't want anything so big and hard!'"

"It's not so big. Just ordinary."

"Never mind, this is a fantasy. So then you put on this really sad face, and I feel sorry for you and try to comfort you. 'There there, poor thing.'"

"And you're telling me that's what you want to do now?"

"That's it."

"Oh, brother."

WE LEFT THE BAR after five rounds of vodka and tonic. When I tried to pay, Midori slapped my hand and paid with a brand-new ten-thousand-yen bill she took from her purse.

"It's O.K.," she said. "I just got paid, and I invited you. Of course, if you're a card-carrying fascist and you refuse to let a woman buy you a drink . . ."

"No no, I'm O.K."

"And I didn't let you put it in, either."

"Because it's so big and hard," I said.

"Right," said Midori. "Because it's so big and hard."

A little drunk, Midori missed one step, and we almost fell back down the stairs. The layer of clouds that had darkened the sky before was gone now, and the late-afternoon sun poured its gentle light on the city streets. Midori and I strolled those streets for a time. Midori said she wanted to climb a tree, but unfortunately there were no climbable trees in Shinjuku, and the Shinjuku Imperial Gardens were closing.

"Too bad," said Midori. "I love to climb trees."

We continued walking and window-shopping, and soon the street scene seemed realer to me than it had before.

"I'm glad I ran into you," I said. "I think I'm a little more adapted to the world now."

Midori stopped short and peered at me. "It's true," she said. "Your eyes are much more in focus than they were. See? Hanging out with me does you good."

"No doubt about it," I said.

At five-thirty Midori said she had to go home and make dinner. I said I would take a bus back to my dorm, and I saw her as far as the station.

"Know what I want to do now?" Midori asked me as she was leaving.

"I have absolutely no idea what you could be thinking," I said.

"I want you and me to be captured by pirates. Then they strip us and press us together face to face all naked and wind these ropes around us."

"Why would they do a thing like that?"

"Perverted pirates," she said.

"You're the perverted one," I said.

"So then they lock us in the hold and say, 'In one hour, we're gonna throw you into the sea, so have a good time until then.'"

"And . . . ?"

"And so we enjoy ourselves for an hour, rolling all over the place and twisting our bodies."

"And that's the main thing you want to do now?"

"That's it."

"Oh, brother," I said, shaking my head.

MIDORI CAME TO PICK ME UP at nine-thirty on Sunday morning. I had just awakened and hadn't washed my face yet. Somebody pounded on my door and yelled, "Hey, Watanabe, it's a woman!" I went down to the lobby to find Midori wearing an incredibly short jeans skirt and sitting there with her legs crossed, yawning. Every guy passing through on his way to break-fast slowed down to stare at her long, slim legs. She did have really nice legs.

"Am I too early?" she asked. "I bet you just woke up."

"Can you give me fifteen minutes? I'll wash my face and shave."

"I don't mind waiting, but all these guys are staring at my legs."

"What'd you expect, coming into a men's dorm in such a short skirt? Of course they're gonna stare at you."

"Oh, well, it's O.K. I'm wearing really cute panties today—all pink and frilly and lacy."

"That just makes it worse," I said with a sigh. I went back to my room and washed and shaved as fast as I could, put on a blue button-down shirt and a gray tweed sports coat, then went back down and hurried Midori out through the dorm gate. I was in a cold sweat.

"Tell me, Watanabe," Midori said, looking up at the dorm buildings, "do all the guys in here masturbate, rub-a-dub-dub?"

"Probably," I said.

"Do guys think about girls when they do that?"

"I guess so. I kinda doubt that anybody thinks about the stock market or verb conjugations or the Suez Canal when they masturbate. Nah, I'm pretty sure just about everybody thinks about girls."

"The Suez Canal?"

"For example, I mean."

"So I guess they think about *particular* girls, right?"

"Shouldn't you be asking your boyfriend about that?" I said. "Why should I have to explain stuff like that to you on a Sunday morning?"

"I was just curious," she said. "Besides, he'd get mad if I asked him about stuff like that. He'd say girls aren't supposed to ask all those questions."

"A perfectly normal point of view, I'd say."

"But I want to know. This is pure curiosity. Do guys think about particular girls when they masturbate?"

I gave up trying to avoid the question. "Well, *I* do, at least. I don't know about anybody else."

"Have you ever thought about *me* when you were doing it? Tell me the truth. I won't get mad."

"No, I haven't, to tell you the truth," I answered honestly.

"Why not? Aren't I attractive enough?"

"Oh, you're plenty attractive, all right. You're cute, and sexy outfits look good on you."

"So why don't you think about me?"

"Well, first of all, I think of you as a friend, so I don't want to get you involved in my sexual fantasies, and second—"

"You've got somebody else you're supposed to be thinking about."

"That's about the size of it," I said.

"You have good manners even when it comes to something like this," Midori said. "That's what I like about you. Still, couldn't you allow me just one brief appearance? I want to be in one of your sexual fantasies or daydreams or whatever you call them. I'm asking you because we're friends. Who else can I ask for something like that? I can't just walk up to anyone and say, 'When you masturbate tonight, will you please think of me for a second?' It's *because* I think of you as a friend that I'm asking. And I want you to tell me later what it was like. You know, what you did and stuff."

I let out a sigh.

"You can't put it in, though. 'Cause we're just friends. Right? As long as you don't put it in, you can do anything you like, think anything you want."

"I don't know, I've never done it with so many restrictions before," I said.

"Will you just think about me?"

"All right, I'll think about you."

"You know, Watanabe, I don't want you to get the wrong impression— that I'm a nymphomaniac or frustrated or a tease or anything. I'm just *inter-*

ested in that stuff. I want to *know* about it. I grew up surrounded by nothing but girls in a girls' school, you know that. I want to find out what guys are thinking and how their bodies are put together. And not just from pull-out sections in the women's magazines but in actual *case studies.*"

"Case studies?" I groaned.

"But my boyfriend doesn't like it when I want to know things or try things. He gets mad, calls me a nympho or crazy. He won't even let me give him a blow job. Now, that's one thing I'm dying to study."

"Uh-huh."

"Do *you* hate getting blow jobs?"

"No, not really, I don't hate it."

"Would you say you *like* it?"

"Yeah, I'd say that. But can we talk about this next time? Here it is, a really nice Sunday morning, and I don't want to ruin it talking about masturbation and blow jobs. Let's talk about something else. Is your boyfriend in the same university with us?"

"Nope, he goes to another one, of course. We met in high school during a club activity. I was in a girls' school, and he was in a boys' school, and you know how they do those things, joint concerts and stuff. We got serious after graduation, though. Hey, Watanabe."

"What?"

"You only have to do it once. Just think about me, O.K.?"

"O.K., I'll give it a try, next time," I said, throwing in the towel.

WE TOOK A COMMUTER TRAIN to Ochanomizu. When we transferred at Shinjuku I bought a thin sandwich at a stand in the station to take the place of the breakfast I hadn't eaten. The coffee I had with it tasted like boiled printer's ink. The Sunday morning trains were filled with couples and with families on outings. A group of boys with baseball bats and matching uniforms scampered around inside the car. Several of the girls on the train had short skirts on, but none as short as Midori's. Midori would yank on hers every now and then to bring it lower. Some of the men stared at her thighs, which made me feel uneasy, but she didn't seem to mind.

"Know what I'd like to do right now?" Midori whispered to me when we had been riding for some ten minutes.

"No idea," I said. "But please, don't talk about that stuff here. Somebody'll hear you."

"Too bad. This one's kind of wild," Midori said with obvious disappointment.

"Anyhow, why are we going to Ochanomizu?"

"Just come along, you'll see."

With all the cram schools around Ochanomizu Station, on Sunday the area was full of junior high and high school kids on their way to practice exams or classes. Midori plunged through the crowds clutching her shoulder-bag strap with one hand and my hand with the other.

Without warning, she asked me, "Hey, Watanabe, can you explain the difference between the English subjunctive present and the subjunctive past?"

"I think I can," I said.

"Let me ask you, then, what purpose does stuff like that serve in daily life?"

"None at all," I said. "It may not serve any concrete purpose, but it *does* give you some kind of training to help you grasp things in general more systematically."

Midori took a moment to give that some serious thought. "You're amazing," she said. "That never occurred to me before. I always thought of things like the subjunctive case and differential calculus and chemical symbols as totally useless. A pain in the neck. So I've always ignored them. Now I have to wonder if my whole life has been a mistake."

"You've ignored them?"

"Yeah. Like, for me, they didn't exist. I don't have the slightest idea what 'sine' and 'cosine' mean."

"That's incredible! How'd you graduate from high school? How'd you get into college?"

"Don't be silly," said Midori. "You don't have to know anything to pass college entrance exams! All you need is a little intuition—and I have great intuition. 'Choose the correct answer from the following three.' I know immediately which one is right."

"My intuition's not as good as yours, so I have to learn systematic thinking to some extent. Like the way a crow collects chunks of glass in a hollow tree."

"Does it serve some purpose?"

"I wonder. It probably makes it easier to do some kinds of things."

"What kinds of things? Give me an example."

"Metaphysical thought, say. Mastering several languages."

"What good does that do?"

"It depends on the person who does it. It serves a purpose for some, and not for others. But mainly it's training. Whether it serves a purpose or not is another question. Like I said."

"Hmmm," said Midori, seemingly impressed. She led me by the hand down the hill. "You know, Watanabe, you're really good at explaining things to people."

"I wonder," I said.

"It's true. I've asked hundreds of people what good the English subjunctive is, and not one of them gave me a good, clear answer like yours. Not even English teachers. They either got confused or angry or laughed it off. Nobody gave me a decent answer before. If somebody like you had been around when I asked my question, and given me a proper explanation, even I might have been interested in the subjunctive. Damn!"

"Hmmm," I said.

"Have you ever read *Das Kapital*?"

"Yup. Not the whole thing, of course, but parts, like most people."

"Did you understand it?"

"I understood some parts, not others. You have to acquire the necessary intellectual apparatus to read a book like *Das Kapital*. I think I understand the general idea of Marxism, though."

"Do you think a college freshman who hasn't read books like that can understand *Das Kapital* just by reading it?"

"That's pretty nearly impossible, I'd say."

"You know, when I entered the university, I joined a folk music club. I just wanted to sing songs. But the members were a pack of phonies. I get chills just thinking about them. The first thing they tell you when you enter the club is you have to read Marx. 'Prepare page so-and-so to such-and-such for next time.' Somebody lectured on how folk songs have to be deeply involved with society and the radical movement. So, what the hell, I went home and tried as hard as I could to read it, but I didn't understand a thing. It was worse than the subjunctive. I gave up after three pages. So I went to the next week's meeting like a good little scout and said I had read it but that I couldn't understand it. From that point on they treated me like an idiot. I had no critical awareness of the class struggle, they said, I was a social cripple. I mean, this was serious. And all because I said I couldn't understand a piece of writing. Don't you think they were terrible?"

"Uh-huh," I said.

"And their so-called discussions were terrible, too. Everybody would use big words and pretend they knew what was going on. But I would ask questions whenever I didn't understand something. 'What is this imperialist exploitation stuff you're talking about? Is it connected somehow to the East India Company?' 'Does smashing the educational-industrial complex mean we're not supposed to work for a company after we graduate from college?' And stuff like that. But nobody was willing to explain anything to me. Far from it—they got *mad* at me. Can you believe it?"

"Yeah, I can," I said.

"One guy yelled at me, 'You stupid bitch, how do you live like that with nothing in your brain?' Well, that did it as far as I was concerned. I wasn't going to put up with it. O.K., so I'm not so smart. I'm working class. But it's the working class that keeps the world running, and it's the working class that gets exploited. What the hell kind of revolution have you got just tossing out big words that working-class people can't understand? What the hell kind of social revolution is that? I mean, *I'd* like to make the world a better place, too. If somebody's really being exploited, we've got to put a stop to it. That's what I believe, and that's why I ask questions. Am I right, or what?"

"You're right."

"So that's when it hit me. These guys are a bunch of phonies. All they've got on their minds is impressing the new girls with the big words they're so proud of and sticking their hands up their skirts. And when they're seniors, they cut their hair short and go trooping to work for Mitsubishi or IBM or Fuji Bank. They marry pretty wives who've never read Marx and have kids they give fancy new names to that are enough to make you puke. Smash *what* educational-industrial complex? Don't make me laugh! And the new members were just as bad. They didn't understand a thing either, but they made believe they did and they were laughing at me. After the meeting, they told me, 'Don't be silly! So what if you don't understand? Just agree with everything they say.' Hey, Watanabe, I've got stuff that made me even madder than that. Wanna hear?"

"Sure, why not?"

"Well, one time they called a late-night political meeting, and they told the girls to make twenty rice balls each for midnight snacks. I mean, talk about sex discrimination! I decided to keep quiet for a change, though, and showed up like a good girl with my twenty rice balls, complete with *umeboshi* inside and nori outside. And what do you think I got for my efforts? Afterward people complained because my rice balls had *only umeboshi* inside, and I hadn't brought along anything to go with them! The other girls stuffed theirs with cod roe and salmon, and they included nice, thick slices of fried egg. I got so mad I couldn't talk! Where the hell do these 'revolution' mongers get off making a fuss over rice balls? They should be grateful for *umeboshi* and nori. Think about the children starving in India!"

I laughed. "So then what happened with your club?"

"I quit in June, I was so damn mad," Midori said. "Most of these university types are total phonies. They're scared to death somebody's gonna find out they don't know something. They all read the same books and they all throw around the same words, and they get off listening to John Coltrane and seeing Pasolini movies. You call that 'revolution'?"

"Hey, don't ask me, I've never actually seen a revolution."

"Well, if that's revolution, you can have it. They'd probably shoot me for putting *umeboshi* in my rice balls. They'd shoot you, too, for understanding the subjunctive."

"It could happen."

"Believe me, I know what I'm talking about. I'm working class. Revolution or no, the working class is going to have to keep scraping by in the same old shit holes. And what *is* a revolution? It sure as hell isn't just changing the name on city hall. But those guys don't know that—those guys with their big words. Tell me, Watanabe, have you ever seen a tax man?"

"Never have."

"Well *I* have. Lots of times. They come barging in and acting big. 'What's *this* ledger for?' 'Hey, you keep pretty sloppy records.' 'You call this a *business* expense?' 'I want to see all your receipts *right now*.' Meanwhile, we're crouching in the corner, and when suppertime comes we've gotta treat them to sushi deluxe—home delivered. Let me tell you, though, my father never once cheated on his taxes. That's just how he is, a real old-fashioned straight arrow. But tell that to the tax man. All he can do is dig and dig and dig and dig. 'Income's a little low here, don'tcha think?' Well, of *course* the income's low when you're not making any money! I wanted to scream! 'Go do this where they've got some money!' Do you think the tax man's attitude would change if there was a revolution?"

"Highly doubtful, highly doubtful."

"That does it for me, then. I'm not going to believe in any damned revolution. Love is all I'm going to believe in."

"Peace," I said.

"Peace," said Midori.

"Say, where are we headed?" I asked.

"The hospital," she said. "My father's there. It's my turn to stay with him all day."

"Your father?! I thought he was in Uruguay!"

"That was a lie," said Midori as if it was nothing at all. "He's been screaming about going to Uruguay forever, but he could never do that. He can hardly get himself out of Tokyo."

"How bad is he?" I asked.

"It's just a matter of time," she said.

We moved several paces ahead without a word.

"I know what I'm talking about. It's the same thing my mother had. A brain tumor. Can you believe it? It's hardly been two years since a brain tumor killed her, and now he's got one."

THE UNIVERSITY HOSPITAL CORRIDORS WERE NOISY and crowded with weekend visitors and patients who had less serious symptoms, and everywhere hung that special hospital smell, a cloud of disinfectant and visitors' bouquets and urine and mattresses, through which nurses surged back and forth with a dry clattering of heels.

Midori's father was in a semiprivate room, in the bed nearer the door. Stretched out, he looked like some tiny creature with a fatal wound. He lay on his side, limp, the drooping left arm inert, jabbed with an intravenous needle. He was a skinny little man who gave the impression that he would get only skinnier and littler. A white bandage encircled his head, and his pasty white arms were dotted with the wounds left by injections or intravenous feedings. His half-open eyes stared at a fixed point in space, but the bloodshot spheres twitched in our direction when we entered the room. For some ten seconds they stayed focused on us, then drifted back to that fixed point in space.

He was going to die soon, you knew when you saw those eyes. There was no sign of life in his flesh, just the barest traces of what had once been a life. His body was like a dilapidated old house from which all furniture and fixtures have been removed and which awaited now only its final demolition. Around the dry lips sprouted clumps of whiskers like so many weeds. So, I thought, even after so much of his life force had been lost, a man's beard continued to grow.

Midori said hello to the ample-fleshed man in the bed by the window. He nodded and smiled, apparently unable to talk. He coughed a few times and, after sipping some water from a glass by his pillow, he shifted his weight in bed and rolled on his side, turning his gaze out the window. Beyond the window could be seen only a utility pole and some power lines, nothing more, not even a cloud in the sky.

"How are you feeling, Daddy?" said Midori, speaking into her father's ear as if testing a microphone. "How are you today?"

Her father moved his lips. <Not good>, he said, not so much speaking the words as forming them from dried air at the back of his throat. <Head>, he said.

"You have a headache?" Midori asked.

<Yuh>, he said, seemingly incapable of pronouncing more than a syllable or two at a time.

"Well, no wonder," she said. "You've just had your head cut open. Of course it hurts. Too bad, but try to stand it a little more. This is my friend Watanabe."

"Glad to meet you," I said. Midori's father opened his lips partway, then closed them again.

Midori gestured toward a vinyl stool near the foot of the bed and suggested that I sit. I did as I was told. Midori gave her father a drink of water and asked if he'd like a piece of fruit or some jelled fruit dessert. <No>, he said, and when Midori insisted that he had to eat something, he said, <I ate>.

A night table stood near the head of the bed, holding a water bottle, a glass, a dish, and a small clock. From a large paper bag under the table, Midori took some fresh pajamas, underwear, and other things, straightened them out, and put them into the locker that stood by the door. Food for the patient lay in the bottom of the bag: two grapefruits, fruit jelly, and three cucumbers.

"Cucumbers?! What are *these* doing in here?" Midori asked. "I can't imagine what my sister was thinking. I told her on the phone exactly what I wanted her to buy, and I'm sure I never mentioned cucumbers! She was supposed to bring kiwifruit."

"Maybe she misunderstood you," I suggested.

"Yeah, maybe, but if she had thought about it she would have realized that cucumbers couldn't be right. I mean, what's a hospital patient supposed to do? Sit in bed chewing on raw cucumbers? Hey, Daddy, want a cucumber?"

<No>, said Midori's father.

Midori sat by the head of the bed, telling her father bits and pieces of news from home. The TV picture had gone bad and she'd called the repairman; their aunt from Takaido had said she would come to visit in a few days; the druggist, Mr. Miyawaki, had fallen off his bike: stuff like that. Her father responded with grunts.

"Are you sure you don't want anything to eat?"

<No>, her father answered.

"How about you, Watanabe? Some grapefruit?"

"No," I answered.

A few minutes later, Midori took me to the TV room and smoked a cigarette on the sofa. Three patients in pajamas were also smoking there and watching some kind of political discussion show.

"Hey," whispered Midori with a twinkle in her eye. "That old guy with the crutches has been looking at my legs ever since we came in here. The one with glasses in the blue pajamas."

"What do you expect, wearing a skirt like that?"

"It's nice, though. I bet they're all bored. It probably does them good. Maybe the excitement helps them get well faster."

"As long as it doesn't have the opposite effect, I suppose."

Midori stared at the smoke rising straight up from her cigarette.

"You know," she said, "my father's not such a bad guy. I get mad at him sometimes because he says terrible things, but deep down he's honest and he really loved my mother. In his own way, he's lived life with all the intensity he could muster. He's a little weak, maybe, and he has absolutely *no* head for business, and people don't like him very much, but he's a hell of a lot better than the cheats and liars who go around smoothing things over 'cause they're so slick. I'm as bad as he is about not backing down once I've said something, so we fight a lot, but really, he's not a bad guy."

Midori took my hand, as if she were picking up something someone had dropped in the street, and placed it on her lap. Half my hand lay atop the cloth of her skirt, while the other half was touching her thigh. She looked into my eyes for a while.

"Sorry to bring you to a place like this," she said, "but would you mind staying with me a little longer?"

"I'll stay with you all day if you want," I said. "Until five. I like spending time with you, and I've got nothing else to do."

"How do you usually spend your Sundays?"

"Doing laundry," I said. "And ironing."

"I guess you don't want to tell me too much about her . . . your girl-friend?"

"No, I guess not. It's complicated, and I, kind of, don't think I could explain it very well."

"That's O.K. You don't have to explain anything," said Midori. "But do you mind if I tell you what I imagine is going on?"

"No, go ahead. I suspect anything you'd imagine would have to be interesting."

"I think she's a married woman."

"You do?"

"Yeah, she's thirty-two or -three and she's rich and beautiful and she wears fur coats and Charles Jourdan shoes and silk underwear and she's hungry for sex and she likes to do really yucky things. The two of you meet on weekday afternoons and devour each other's bodies. But her husband's home on Sundays, so she can't see you. Am I right?"

"Very, very interesting."

"She has you tie her up and blindfold her and lick every square inch of her body. Then she makes you put weird things inside her and she gets into these incredible positions like a contortionist and you take pictures of her with a Polaroid camera."

"Sounds like fun."

"She's dying for it all the time, so she does everything she can think of. And she thinks about it every day. She's got nothing but free time, so she's always planning: Hmm, next time Watanabe comes, we'll do this, or we'll do that. You get in bed and she goes crazy, trying all these positions and coming three times in every one. And she says to you. 'Don't I have a sensational body? You can't be satisfied with young girls anymore. Young girls won't do *this* for you, will they? Or *this*. Feel good? But don't come yet!' "

"You've been seeing too many porno flicks," I said with a laugh.

"You think so? I was kinda worried about that. But I *love* porno flicks. Take me to one next time, O.K.?"

"Fine," I said. "Next time you're free."

"Really? I can hardly wait. Let's go to a real S and M one, with whips and, like, they make the girl pee in front of everybody. That's my favorite."

"We'll do it."

"You know what I like best about porno theaters?"

"I couldn't begin to guess."

"Whenever a sex scene starts, you can hear this 'Gulp!' sound when everybody swallows all at once," said Midori. "I *love* that 'Gulp!' It's so sweet!"

BACK IN THE HOSPITAL ROOM, Midori aimed a stream of talk at her father again, and he would either grunt in response or say nothing. Around eleven the wife of the man in the other bed came to change her husband's pajamas and peel fruit for him and such. She had a round face and seemed like a nice person, and she and Midori shared a lot of small talk. A nurse showed up with a new intravenous feeding bottle and talked a little while with Midori and the wife before she left. I let my eyes wander around the room and out the window to the power lines. Sparrows would show up every now and then and perch on the lines. Midori talked to her father and wiped the sweat from his brow and let him spit phlegm into a tissue and chatted with the neighbor's wife and the nurse and sent an occasional remark my way and checked the intravenous contraption.

The doctor came on rounds at eleven-thirty, so Midori and I stepped outside to wait in the corridor. When he came out, Midori asked him how her father was doing.

"Well, he's just come out of surgery, and we've got him on painkillers so, well, he's pretty drained," said the doctor. "I'll need another two or three days to evaluate the results of the operation. If it went well, he'll be O.K., and if it didn't, we'll have to make some decisions at that point."

"You're not going to open his head up again, are you?"

"I really can't say until the time comes," said the doctor. "Wow, that's some short skirt you're wearing!"

"Nice, huh?"

"What do you do on stairways?" the doctor asked.

"Nothing special. I let it all hang out," said Midori. The nurse chuckled behind the doctor.

"Incredible. You ought to come and let us open *your* head one of these days to see what's going on in there. Do me a favor and use the elevators while you're in the hospital. I can't afford to have any more patients. I'm way too busy as it is."

Soon after the doctor's rounds it was lunchtime. A nurse pushing a cart loaded with meals was circulating from room to room. Midori's father was given potage, fruit, boiled deboned fish, and vegetables that had been ground into some kind of jelly. Midori turned him on his back and raised him up using the crank at the foot of the bed. She fed him the soup with a spoon. After five or six swallows, he turned his face aside and said, <No more>.

"You've got to eat at least this much," Midori said.

<Later>, he said.

"You're hopeless—if you don't eat properly, you'll never get your strength back," she said. "Don't you have to pee yet?"

<No>, he said.

"Hey, Watanabe, let's go down to the cafeteria."

I agreed to go, but in fact I didn't feel much like eating. The cafeteria was crammed with doctors and nurses and visitors. Long lines of chairs and tables filled the huge, windowless underground cavern where every mouth seemed to be eating and talking—about sickness, no doubt, the voices echoing and reechoing as in a tunnel. Now and then the P. A. system would break through the reverberation with calls for a doctor or nurse. While I laid claim to a table, Midori bought two set meals and carried them over on an aluminum tray. Croquettes with cream sauce, potato salad, shredded cabbage, boiled vegetables, rice, and miso soup: these were lined up in the tray in the same white plastic dishes they used for patients. I ate about half of mine and left the rest. Midori seemed to enjoy her meal to the last mouthful.

"You're not too hungry?" she asked, sipping hot tea.

"Not really," I said.

"It's the hospital," she said, scanning the cafeteria. "This always happens when people aren't used to the place. The smells, the sounds, the stale air, patients' faces, stress, irritation, disappointment, pain, fatigue—

all those things are what do it. They grab you in the stomach and kill your appetite. Once you get used to them, though, they're no problem at all. Plus, you can't really take care of a sick person unless you eat right. It's true. I know what I'm talking about because I've done it with my grandfather, my grandmother, my mother, and now my father. You never know when you're going to have to miss your next meal, so it's important to eat when you can."

"I see what you mean," I said.

"Relatives come to visit and they eat with me here, and they always leave half their food, just like you. And they always say, 'Oh, Midori, it's wonderful you've got such a healthy appetite. I'm too upset to eat.' But get serious, *I'm* the one who's actually here taking care of the patient! They just have to stop by and show a little sympathy. *I'm* the one who wipes the shit and takes the phlegm and dries the bodies off. If sympathy was all it took to clean up shit, I'd have fifty times as much sympathy as anybody else! Instead, they see me eating all my food and they give me this look and say, 'Oh, Midori, you've got such a healthy appetite.' What do they think I am, a donkey pulling a cart? They're old enough to know how the world really works, so why are they so stupid? It's easy to talk big, but the important thing is whether or not you clean up the shit. I can be hurt, you know. I can get as exhausted as anybody else. I can feel so bad I want to cry, too. I mean, *you* try watching a gang of doctors get together and cut open somebody's head when there's no hope of saving them, and stirring things up in there, and doing it again and again, and every time they do it it makes the person worse and a little bit crazier, and see how *you* like it! And on top of it, you see your savings go to hell. I don't know if I can keep going to school another three and a half years, and there's no way my sister can afford a wedding ceremony at this rate."

"How many days do you come here in a week?" I asked.

"Usually four," said Midori. "This place claims they offer total nursing care, and the nurses themselves are great, but there's just too much for them to do. Some member of the family has to be around to take up the slack. My sister's watching the store, and I've got my classes. Still, she manages to get here three days a week, and I come four. And we sneak in a little time for a date now and then. Believe me, it's a full schedule!"

"How can you spend time with me if you're so busy?"

"I like spending time with you," said Midori, playing with a plastic teacup.

"Get out of here for a couple of hours and go take a walk," I said. "I'll take care of your father for a while."

"Why?"

"You need to get away from the hospital and relax by yourself—not talk to anybody, just clear your mind out."

Midori thought about it for a minute and nodded. "Hmm, you may be right. But do you know what to do? How to take care of him?"

"I've been watching. I've pretty much got it. You check the intravenous thing, give him water, wipe the sweat off, and help him spit phlegm. The bedpan's under the bed, and if he gets hungry I feed him the rest of his lunch. Anything I can't figure out I'll ask the nurse."

"I think that should do it," Midori said with a smile. "There's just one thing, though. He's starting to get a little funny in the head, so he says weird things once in a while—things that nobody can understand. Don't let it bother you if he does that."

"I'll be fine." I said.

BACK IN THE ROOM, Midori told her father she had some business to take care of and that I would be watching him while she was out. He seemed to have nothing to say to this. It might have meant nothing to him. He just lay there on his back, staring at the ceiling. If he hadn't been blinking every once in a while, he could have passed for dead. His eyes were bloodshot, as if he had been drinking, and each time he took a deep breath his nose swelled the slightest bit. Otherwise, he didn't move a muscle, and he made no effort to reply to Midori. I couldn't begin to grasp what he might be thinking or feeling in the murky depths of his consciousness.

After Midori left, I thought about trying to speak to her father, but I had no idea what to say to him or how to say it, and so I just kept quiet. Before long, he closed his eyes and went to sleep. I sat on the stool by the head of the bed and studied the occasional twitching of his nose, hoping all the while that he might not die on the spot. How strange it would be, I thought, if this man were to breathe his last with me by his side. After all, I had just met him for the first time in my life, and the only thing binding us together was Midori, a girl I happened to know from my History of Drama class.

He was not dying, though, just sleeping soundly. Bringing my ear close to his face, I could hear his faint breathing. This allowed me to relax and chat with the wife of the man in the next bed. She talked of nothing but Midori on the assumption that I was her boyfriend.

"She's really a wonderful girl," she said. "She takes wonderful care of her father; she's kind and gentle and sensitive and solid, and on top of all that, she's pretty. You'd better treat her right. Don't ever let her go. You won't find another one like her."

"I'll treat her right," I said without elaborating.

"I have a son and daughter at home. He's seventeen and she's twenty-one, and neither of them would ever think of coming to the hospital. The minute school lets out, they're off surfing or dating or whatever. They're terrible. They squeeze me for all the pocket money they can get and then they disappear."

At one-thirty the Mrs. left the hospital room to do some shopping. Both men were sound asleep. Gentle afternoon sunlight flooded the room, and I felt as though I might drift off at any moment atop the stool on which I was perched. White and yellow chrysanthemums in a vase on the table by the window announced to people that it was autumn. In the air floated the sweet smell of boiled fish left untouched from lunch. The nurses continued to clip clop up and down the hall, talking to one another in clear, penetrating voices. They would peek into the room now and then and flash me a smile when they saw that both patients were sleeping. I wished I had something to read, but there were no books or magazines or newspapers in the room, just a calendar on the wall.

I thought about Naoko. I thought about her naked, wearing only her barrette. I thought about the curve of her waist and the dark shadow of her pubic hair. Why had she shown herself to me like that? Had she been sleepwalking? Or was it just a fantasy of mine? As time went by and that little world receded into the distance, I grew increasingly unsure that the events of that night had actually happened. If I told myself they were real, I believed they were real, and if I told myself they were a fantasy, they seemed like a fantasy. They were too clear and detailed to have been a fantasy, and too whole and beautiful to have been real: Naoko's body and the moonlight.

Midori's father suddenly woke and started coughing, which put a stop to my daydreaming. I let him spit his phlegm into a tissue, and wiped the sweat from his brow with a towel.

"Would you like some water?" I asked, to which he gave a four-millimeter nod. I held the small glass water bottle so that he could sip a little bit at a time, dry lips trembling, throat twitching. He drank every bit of the seemingly lukewarm water in the bottle.

"Would you like some more?" I asked. He seemed to be trying to speak, so I brought my ear close.

<That's enough>, he said in a small, dry voice—a voice even smaller and dryer than before.

"Why don't you eat something? You must be hungry." He answered with a slight nod. As Midori had done, I cranked his bed up and started feeding him, alternating spoonfuls of vegetable jelly and boiled fish. It took an incredibly long time to get through half his food, at which point he gave his head a little shake to signal that he had had enough. The movement was almost imperceptible; it apparently hurt him to make larger movements.

"What about the fruit?" I asked him.

<No>, he said. I wiped the corners of his mouth with a towel and made the bed level again before putting the dishes out in the corridor.

"Was that good?" I asked him.

<Awful>, he answered.

"Yeah," I said with a smile. "It looked pretty bad." Midori's father could not seem to decide whether to open his eyes further or close them as he lay there silently, staring at me. I wondered if he knew who I was. He seemed more relaxed when alone with me than when Midori was present. He might have been mistaking me for someone else. Or at least that was how I preferred to think of it.

"Beautiful day out there," I said, perching on the stool and crossing my legs. "It's autumn, Sunday, great weather, and crowded everywhere you go. Relaxing indoors like this is the best thing you can do on such a nice day. It's exhausting to get into those crowds. And the air is bad. I mostly do laundry on Sundays—wash the stuff in the morning, hang it out on the roof of my dorm, take it in before the sun goes down, do a good job of ironing it. I don't mind ironing at all. There's a special satisfaction in making wrinkled things smooth. And I'm pretty good at it, too. Of course, I was lousy at it at first. I put creases in everything. After a month of practice, though, I knew what I was doing. So Sunday is my day for laundry and ironing. I couldn't do it today, of course. Too bad: wasted a perfect laundry day.

"That's O.K., though. I'll wake up early and take care of it tomorrow. Don't worry. I've got nothing else to do on a Sunday.

"After I do my laundry tomorrow morning and hang it out to dry, I'll go to my ten o'clock class. It's the one I'm in with Midori, History of Drama. I'm working on Euripides. Are you familiar with Euripides? He was an ancient Greek—one of the 'Big Three' of Greek tragedy along with Aeschylus and Sophocles. He supposedly died when a dog bit him in Macedonia, but not everybody buys this. Anyhow, that's Euripides. I like Sophocles better, but I suppose it's a matter of taste. I really can't say which is better.

"What marks his plays is the way things get so mixed up the characters are trapped. Do you see what I mean? A bunch of different people appear, and they've all got their own situations and reasons and excuses, and each one is pursuing his or her own brand of justice or happiness. As a result, nobody can do anything. Obviously. I mean, it's basically impossible for *everybody's* justice to prevail or *everybody's* happiness to triumph, so chaos takes over. And then what do you think happens? Simple—a god appears in the end and starts directing traffic. 'You go over *there*, and *you* come *here*, and *you* get together with *her*, and *you* just sit still for a while.' Like that. He's kind of a fixer, and in the end everything works out perfectly. They call this 'deus ex machina.' There's almost always a deus ex machina in Euripides, and that's the point where critical opinion divides over him.

"But think about it—what if there were a deus ex machina in real life? Everything would be so easy! If you felt stuck or trapped, some god would swing down from up there and solve all your problems. What could be easier than that? Anyhow, that's History of Drama. This is more or less the kind of stuff we study at the university."

Midori's father said nothing, but he kept his vacant eyes on me the whole time I was talking. Of course, I couldn't tell from those eyes whether he understood anything at all I was saying.

"Peace," I said.

After all that talk, I felt starved. I had had next to nothing for breakfast and had eaten only half my lunch. Now I was sorry I hadn't done a better job on lunch, but feeling sorry wasn't going to do me any good. I looked in a cabinet for something to eat, but found only a can of nori, some Vicks cough drops, and soy sauce. The paper bag was still there with cucumbers and grapefruit.

"I'm going to eat some cucumbers if you don't mind," I said to Midori's father. He didn't answer. I washed three cucumbers in the sink and dribbled a little soy sauce into a dish. Then I wrapped a cucumber in nori, dipped it in soy sauce, and gobbled it down.

"Mmm, great!" I said to Midori's father. "Fresh, simple, smells like life. Really good cucumbers. A far more sensible food than kiwifruit."

I polished off one cucumber and attacked the next. The sickroom echoed with the lilt of cucumbers crunching. Only after finishing the second whole cucumber was I ready to take a break. I boiled some water on the gas burner in the hall and made myself some tea.

"Would you like something to drink? Water? Juice?" I asked Midori's father.

<Cucumber>, he said.

"Great," I said with a smile. "With nori?"

He gave a little nod. I cranked the bed up again. Then I cut a bite-size piece of cucumber, wrapped it with a strip of nori, stabbed the combination with a toothpick, dipped it into soy sauce, and delivered it to the patient's waiting mouth. With almost no change of expression, Midori's father crunched down on the piece again and again and finally swallowed it.

"How was that? Good, huh?"

<Good>, he said

"It's good when food tastes good," I said. "It's kind of like proof you're alive."

He ended up eating the entire cucumber. When he had finished it, he wanted water, so I gave him a drink from the bottle. A few minutes later, he said he needed to pee, so I took the urine jar from under the bed and held it by the tip of his penis. Afterward I emptied the jar into the toilet and washed it out. Then I went back to the sickroom and finished my tea.

"How are you feeling?" I asked.

<My . . . head>, he said.

"Hurts?"

<A little>, he said with a slight frown.

"Well, no wonder, you've just had an operation. Of course, I've never had one, so I don't know what it's like."

<Ticket>, he said.

"Ticket? What ticket?"

<Midori>, he said. <Ticket>.

I had no idea what he was talking about, and just kept quiet. He stayed silent for a time, too. Then he seemed to say <Please.> He opened his eyes wide and looked at me hard. I guessed that he was trying to tell me something, but I couldn't begin to imagine what it was.

<Ueno>, he said. <Midori>.

"Ueno Station?"

He gave a little nod.

I tried to summarize what he was getting at: "Ticket, Midori, please, Ueno Station," but I had no idea what it meant. I assumed his mind was muddled, but compared with before his eyes now had a terrible clarity. He raised the arm that was free of the intravenous contraption and stretched it toward me. This must have been a major effort for him, the way the hand trembled in midair. I stood and grasped his frail, wrinkled hand. He returned my grasp with what little strength he could muster and said again, <Please>.

"Don't worry," I said. "I'll take care of the ticket and Midori, too." He let his hand drop back on the bed and closed his eyes. Then, with a loud rush of breath, he fell asleep. I checked to make sure he was still alive, then went out to boil more water for tea. As I was sipping the hot liquid, I realized that I had developed a kind of liking for this little man on the verge of death.

THE WIFE OF THE OTHER PATIENT came back a few minutes later and asked if everything was O.K. I assured her it was. Her husband, too, was sound asleep, breathing deeply.

Midori came back after three.

"I was in the park, spacing out," she said. "I did what you told me, didn't talk to anybody, just let my head go empty."

"How was it?"

"Thanks, I feel much better. I still have that draggy, tired feeling, but my body feels way lighter than before. I guess I was way more tired than I realized."

With her father sound asleep, there was nothing for us to do, so we bought coffee from a vending machine and drank it in the TV room. I reported to Midori on what had happened in her absence—that her father had had a good sleep, then woke up and ate some of what was left of his lunch, then saw me eating a cucumber and asked for one himself, ate the whole thing, and peed.

"Watanabe, you're amazing," said Midori. "We're all going crazy trying to get him to eat anything, and you got him to eat a whole cucumber! Incredible!"

"I don't know, I think he just saw me enjoying my own cucumber."

"Or maybe you just have this knack for relaxing people."

"No way," I said with a laugh. "A lot of people will tell you just the opposite about me."

"What do you think about my father?"

"I like him. Not that we had all that much to say to each other. But, I don't know, he seems nice."

"Was he quiet?"

"Very."

"You should have seen him a week ago. He was awful," Midori said, shaking her head. "Kind of lost his marbles and went wild. Threw a glass at me and yelled terrible stuff—'I hope you die, you stupid bitch!' This sickness can do that to people. They don't know why, but it can make people get really mean all of a sudden. It was the same with my mother. What do you think she said to me? 'You're not my daughter! I hate your guts!' The whole world turned black for me for a second when she said that. But that kind of thing is one of the features of this particular sickness. Something presses on a part of the brain and makes people say all kinds of nasty things. You *know* it's just part of the sickness, but still, it hurts. What do you expect? Here I am, working my fingers to the bone for them, and they're saying all this terrible stuff to me."

"I know what you mean," I said. Then I remembered the strange fragments that Midori's father had mumbled to me.

"Ticket? Ueno Station?" Midori said. "I wonder what that's all about?"

"And then he said, 'Please,' and 'Midori.'"

"'Please take care of Midori?'"

"Or maybe he wants you to go to Ueno and buy a ticket. The order of the four words is such a mess, who knows what he means? Does Ueno Station mean anything special to you?"

"Hmm, Ueno Station." Midori thought about it for a while. "The only thing I can think of is the two times I ran away. In the third grade and in the fifth grade. Both times I took a train from Ueno to Fukushima. Bought the tickets with money I took from the cash register. Somebody at home made me really mad, and I did it to get even. I had an aunt in Fukushima, I kind of liked her, so I went to her house. My father was the one who brought me home. Came all the way to Fukushima to get me—a hundred miles! We ate boxed lunches on the train to Ueno. My father told me all kinds of stuff while we were riding, just little bits and pieces with long spaces in between. Like about the big earthquake of nineteen twenty-three or about the war or about the time I was born, stuff he didn't usually talk about. Come to think of it, those were the only times my father and I had something like a good, long talk, just the two of us. Say, can you believe this?—my father was smack dab in the middle of Tokyo during one of the biggest earthquakes in history and he didn't even notice it!"

"No way!"

"It's true! He was riding through Koishikawa with a cart attached to his bike, and he didn't feel a thing. When he got home, all the tiles had fallen off the roofs in the neighborhood, and everybody in the family was hugging pillars and quaking in their boots. He still didn't get it and, the way he tells it, he asked, 'What the hell's going on here?' That's my father's 'fond recollection' of the Great Kanto Earthquake!" Midori laughed. "All his stories of the old days are like that. No drama whatsoever. They're all just a little bit off center. I don't know, when he tells those stories, you kinda get the feeling like nothing important has happened in Japan for the past fifty or sixty years. The young officers' uprising of nineteen thirty-six, the Pacific War, they're all kinda 'Oh yeah, now that you mention it, I guess something like that once happened' kinda things. It's so funny!

"So, anyway, on the train, he'd tell me these stories in bits and pieces while we were riding from Fukushima to Ueno. And at the end, he'd always say, 'So that goes to show you, Midori, it's the same wherever you go.' I was young enough to be impressed by stuff like that."

"So is that *your* 'fond recollection' of Ueno Station?" I asked.

"It sure is," said Midori. "Did you ever run away from home, Watanabe?"

"Never did."

"Why not?"

"Lack of imagination. It never occurred to me to run away."

"You are *so weird!*" Midori said, cocking her head as though truly impressed.

"I wonder," I said.

"Well, anyhow, I think my father was trying to say he wanted you to look after me."

"Really?"

"Really! I understand things like that. Intuitively. So tell me, what was your answer to him?"

"Well, I didn't understand what he was saying, so I just said O.K., don't worry. I'd take care of both you and the ticket."

"You promised my father that? You said you'd take care of me?" She looked me straight in the eye with a dead-serious expression on her face.

"Not like *that*," I hastened to correct her. "I really didn't know *what* he was saying, and—"

"Don't worry. I'm just kidding," she said with a smile. "I love that about you."

Midori and I finished our coffee and went back to the room. Her father was still sound asleep. If you leaned close you could hear his steady breathing. As the afternoon deepened, the light outside the hospital window changed to the soft, gentle color of autumn. A flock of birds perched on the electric wire outside, then flew on. Midori and I sat in a corner of the room, talking quietly the whole time. She read my palm and predicted that I would live to a hundred and five, marry three times, and die in a traffic accident. Not a bad life, I said.

When her father woke just after four o'clock, Midori went to sit by his pillow, wiped the sweat from his brow, gave him water, and asked him about the pain in his head. A nurse came and took his temperature, recorded the number of his urinations, and checked the intravenous equipment. I went to the TV room and watched a little soccer.

At five I told Midori I would be leaving. To her father I explained, "I have to go to work now. I sell records in Shinjuku from six to ten-thirty."

He turned his eyes to me and gave a little nod.

"Hey, Watanabe, I don't know how to put this, but I *really* want to thank you for today," Midori said to me when she saw me to the front lobby.

"I didn't do that much," I said. "But if I can be of any help, I'll come next week, too. I'd like to see your father again."

"Really?"

"Well, there's not that much for me to do in the dorm, and if I come here I get to eat cucumbers."

Midori folded her arms and tapped the linoleum with the heel of her shoe.

"I'd like to go drinking with you again," she said, cocking her head slightly.

"How about the porno flicks?"

"We'll do that first and *then* go drinking. And we'll talk about all the usual disgusting things."

"*I'm* not the one who talks about disgusting things," I protested. "It's *you.*"

"Anyhow, we'll talk about things like that and get plastered and go to bed."

"And you know what happens next," I said with a sigh. "I try to do it, and you don't let me. Right?"

She laughed through her nose.

"Anyhow," I said, "pick me up again next Sunday morning. We'll come here together."

"With me in a little longer skirt?"

"Definitely," I said.

I DIDN'T GO TO THE HOSPITAL that next Sunday, though. Midori's father died on Friday morning.

She called at six-thirty in the morning to tell me that. The buzzer letting me know I had a phone call went off, and I ran down to the lobby with a cardigan thrown over my pajamas. A cold rain was falling silently. "My father died a few minutes ago," Midori said in a small, quiet voice. I asked her if there was anything I could do.

"Thanks," she said. "There's really nothing. We're used to funerals. I just wanted to let you know."

A kind of sigh escaped her lips.

"Don't come to the funeral, O.K.? I hate stuff like that. I don't want to see you there."

"I get it," I said.

"Will you really take me to a porno movie?"

"Of course I will."

"A really disgusting one."

"I'll research the matter thoroughly."

"Good. I'll call you," Midori said, and hung up.

A WEEK WENT BY, though, without a word from Midori. No calls, no sign of her in the classroom. I kept hoping for a message from her whenever I went back to the dorm, but there were never any. One night, I tried to keep my promise by thinking of her when I masturbated, but it didn't work. I tried switching over to Naoko, but not even Naoko's image was any help that time. It seemed so ridiculous, I gave up. Instead, I took a swig of whiskey, brushed my teeth, and went to bed.

I WROTE A LETTER to Naoko on Sunday morning. One thing I told her about was Midori's father. "I went to the hospital to visit the father of a girl in one of my classes and ate some cucumbers in his room. When he heard me crunching on them, he wanted some, too, and he ate his with the same crunching sound. Five days later, though, he died. I still have a vivid memory of the tiny crunching he made when he chewed his pieces of cucumber. People leave strange little memories of themselves behind when they die." My letter went on:

I think of you and Reiko and the birdhouse while I lie in bed after waking up in the morning. I think about the peacock and pigeons and parrots and turkeys—and about the rabbits. I remember the yellow rain capes that you and Reiko wore with the hoods up that rainy morning. It feels good to think about you when I'm warm in bed. I feel as if you're curled up there beside me, fast asleep. And I think how great it would be if it were true.

I miss you something awful sometimes, but in general I go on living with all the energy I can muster. Just as you take care of the birds and the fields every morning, every morning I wind my own spring. I give it some thirty-six good twists by the time I've gotten up, brushed my teeth, shaved, eaten breakfast, changed my clothes, left the dorm, and arrived at the university. I tell myself, "O.K., let's make this day another good one." I hadn't noticed before, but they tell me I talk to myself a lot these days. Probably mumbling to myself while I wind my spring.

It's hard not being able to see you, but my life in Tokyo would be a lot worse if it weren't for you. It's because I think of you when I'm in bed in the morning that I can wind my spring and tell myself I have to live another good day. I know I have to give it my best here just as you are doing there.

Today's Sunday, though, a day I don't wind my spring. I've done my laundry, and now I'm in my room, writing to you. Once I've finished this letter and put a stamp on it and dropped it into the mailbox, there's nothing for me to do until the sun goes down. I don't study on Sundays, either. I do a good enough job studying between classes in the library on weekdays, so that I don't have anything left to do on Sundays. Sunday afternoons are quiet, peaceful, and, for me, lonely. I read books or listen to music. Sometimes I think back on the different routes we used to take in our Sunday walks around Tokyo. I can come up with a pretty clear picture of the clothes you were wearing on any particular walk. I remember all kinds of things on Sunday afternoons.

Say hi from me to Reiko. I really miss her guitar at night.

When I had finished the letter, I walked a couple of blocks to a mailbox, then went to a nearby bakery where I bought an egg sandwich and a Coke. These I had for lunch while I watched a Little League game from a bench in a local playground. The deepening of autumn had brought an increased blueness and depth to the sky. I glanced up to find two vapor trails heading off to the west in perfect parallel like streetcar tracks. A foul ball came rolling my way, and when I threw it back to them the young players doffed their caps with a polite "Thank you, sir." As in most Little League games, there were lots of walks and stolen bases.

After noon I went back to my room to read but couldn't concentrate on my book. Instead I found myself staring at the ceiling and thinking about Midori. I wondered if her father had really been trying to ask me to look after her when he was gone, but I had no way of telling what had been on his mind. He had probably confused me with somebody else. In any case, he had died on a Friday morning when a cold rain was falling, and now it was impossible to know the truth. I imagined that, in death, he had shriveled up smaller than ever. And then they had burned him in an oven until he was nothing but ashes. And what had he left behind? A nothing-much bookstore in a nothing-much neighborhood and two daughters, at least one of whom was more than a little strange. What kind of life was that? I wondered. Lying in that hospital bed with his cut-open head and his muddled brain, what had been on his mind as he looked at me?

Thinking thoughts like this about Midori's father put me in such a miserable mood that I had to bring the laundry down from the roof before it was really dry and head off to Shinjuku to kill time walking the streets. The Sunday crowds gave me some relief. The Kinokuniya bookstore was as jam-packed as a rush-hour train. I bought a copy of Faulkner's *Light in August* and went to the noisiest jazz café I could think of, reading my new book while listening to Ornette Coleman and Bud Powell and drinking hot, thick, foul-tasting coffee. At five-thirty I closed my book, went outside, and ate a light supper. How many Sundays—how many hundreds of Sundays like this—lay ahead of me? "Quiet, peaceful, and lonely," I said aloud to myself. On Sundays, I didn't wind my spring.

eight

HALFWAY THROUGH THAT WEEK I MANAGED TO CUT MY PALM OPEN on a piece of broken glass. I hadn't noticed that one of the glass partitions in a record shelf was cracked. I could hardly believe how much blood gushed out of me, turning the floor at my feet bright red. The store manager found a bunch of towels and tied them tightly over the wound. Then he made a telephone call to locate an all-night emergency room. He was a pretty useless guy most of the time, but this he did with great dispatch. The hospital was nearby, fortunately, but by the time I got there the towels were soaked in red, and the blood they couldn't soak up had been dripping on the asphalt. People scurried out of the way for me. They seemed to think I had been injured in a fight. I felt no pain to speak of, but the blood wouldn't stop.

The doctor was cool as he removed the blood-soaked towels, stopped the bleeding with a tourniquet on my wrist, disinfected the wound and sewed it up, telling me to come again the next day. Back at the record shop, the manager told me to go home: he would put me down as having worked. I took a bus to the dorm and went straight to Nagasawa's room. With my nerves on edge over the cut, I wanted to talk to somebody, and I felt I hadn't seen Nagasawa for a long time.

I found him in his room, drinking a can of beer and watching a Spanish lesson on TV. "What the hell happened to you?" he asked when he saw my bandage. I said I had cut myself but that it was nothing much. He asked if I wanted a beer, and I said no thanks.

"Just wait. This'll be over in a minute," said Nagasawa, and he went on practicing his Spanish pronunciation. I boiled some water and made myself a cup of tea with a tea bag. A Spanish woman recited example sentences: "I have never seen such terrible rain! Many bridges were washed away in Barcelona." Nagasawa read the text aloud in Spanish. "What awful sentences!" he said. "This kind of shit is all they ever give you."

When the program ended, Nagasawa turned off the TV and took another beer from his small refrigerator.

"Are you sure I'm not in the way?" I asked.

"Hell, no. I was bored out of my mind. Sure you don't want a beer?"

"No, I really don't," I said.

"Oh, yeah, they posted the exam results the other day. I passed!"

"The Foreign Ministry exam?"

"That's it. Officially, it's called the 'Foreign Affairs Public Service Personnel First Class Service Examination.' What a joke!"

"Congratulations!" I said, and gave him my left hand to shake.

"Thanks."

"Of course, I'm not surprised you passed."

"No, neither am I." Nagasawa laughed. "But it's nice to have it official."

"Think you'll go to a foreign country once you get in?"

"Nah, first they give you a year of training. Then they send you overseas for a while."

I sipped my tea, and he drank his beer with obvious enjoyment.

"I'll give you this refrigerator when I get out of here," said Nagasawa. "You'd like to have it, wouldn't you? It's great for beer."

"Sure, I'd like to have it, but won't you need it? You'll be living in an apartment or something."

"Don't be stupid! When I get out of this place, I'm buying myself a big refrigerator. I'm gonna live the high life! Four years in a shit hole like this is long enough. I don't want to have to *look* at anything I used in this place. You name it, I'll give it to you—the TV, the Thermos bottle, the radio . . ."

"I'll take anything you want to give me," I said. I picked up the Spanish textbook on his desk and stared at it. "You're starting Spanish?"

"Yeah. The more languages you know the better. And I've got a knack for them. I taught myself French and it's practically perfect. Languages are like games. You learn the rules for one, and they all work the same way. Like women."

"Ah, the reflective life!" I said with a sarcastic edge.

"Anyhow, let's go out to eat sometime soon."

"You mean cruising for women?"

"No, a real dinner. You, me, and Hatsumi at a good restaurant. To celebrate my new job. My old man's paying, so we'll go someplace really expensive."

"Shouldn't it just be you and Hatsumi?"

"No, it'd be better with you there. I'd be more comfortable, and so would Hatsumi."

Oh no, it was Kizuki, Naoko, and me all over again.

"I'll spend the night at Hatsumi's afterward, so join us just for the meal."

"O.K., if you both really want me to," I said. "But, anyhow, what are you planning to do about Hatsumi? When you're through with your training, you'll be assigned overseas, and you probably won't come back for years. What's going to happen to her?"

"That's her problem, not mine."

"I don't get it," I said.

Feet on his desk, Nagasawa took a swig of beer and yawned.

"Look, I'm not planning to get married. I've made that perfectly clear to Hatsumi. If she wants to marry somebody, she should go ahead and do it. I won't stop her. If she wants to wait for me, let her wait. That's what I mean."

"I've gotta hand it to you," I said.

"You think I'm a shit, don't you?"

"I do."

"Look, the world is an inherently unfair place. I didn't write the rules. It's always been that way. I have never once deceived Hatsumi. She knows I'm a shit and that she can leave me anytime she decides she can't take it. I told her that straight out."

Nagasawa finished his beer and lit a cigarette.

"Isn't there anything about life that frightens you?" I asked.

"Hey, I'm not a total idiot," said Nagasawa. "Of *course* life frightens me sometimes. I don't happen to take that as the premise for everything else, though. I'm going to give it a hundred percent and go as far as I can. I'll take what I want and leave what I don't want. That's how I intend to live my life, and if things go bad, I'll stop and reconsider at that point. If you think about it, an unfair society is a society that makes it possible for you to exploit your abilities to the limit."

"Sounds like a pretty self-centered way to live," I said.

"Maybe so, but I'm not just looking up at the sky and waiting for the fruit to drop. In my own way, I'm working hard. I'm working ten times harder than you are."

"That's probably true," I said.

"I look around me sometimes and I get sick to my stomach. Why the hell don't these bastards *do* something? I wonder. They don't do a damn thing, and then they bitch."

Amazed at the harshness of his tone, I looked at Nagasawa. "The way I see it, people *are* working hard. They're working their fingers to the bone. Or am I looking at things wrong?"

"That's not hard work. It's just manual labor," Nagasawa said with finality. "The 'hard work' I'm talking about is more self-directed and purposeful."

"You mean, like studying Spanish when the job season ends and everybody else is taking it easy?"

"That's it. I'm going to have Spanish mastered by next spring. I've got English and German and French down pat, and I'm most of the way there with Italian. You think things like that happen without hard work?"

Nagasawa puffed on his cigarette while I thought about Midori's father. There was one man who had probably never even thought about starting Spanish lessons on TV. He had probably never thought about the difference between hard work and manual labor, either. He was probably too busy to think about such things—busy with work, and busy bringing home a daughter who had run away to Fukushima.

"So, about that dinner of ours," said Nagasawa. "Would this Saturday be O.K. for you?"

"Fine," I said.

NAGASAWA PICKED A FANCY French restaurant in a quiet backstreet of Azabu. He gave his name at the door and the two of us were shown to a secluded private room. Some fifteen prints hung on the walls of the small chamber. While we waited for Hatsumi to arrive, Nagasawa and I sipped a delicious wine and chatted about the novels of Joseph Conrad. He wore an expensive-looking gray suit. I had on an ordinary blue blazer.

Hatsumi arrived fifteen minutes later. She was carefully made up and wore gold earrings, a beautiful deep blue dress, and tasteful red pumps.

When I complimented her on the color of the dress, she told me it was called midnight blue.

"What an elegant restaurant!" said Hatsumi.

"My old man always eats here when he comes to Tokyo," said Nagasawa. "I came here with him once. I'm not crazy about these snooty places."

"It doesn't hurt to eat in a place like this once in a while," said Hatsumi. Turning to me, she asked. "Don't you agree?"

"I guess so. As long as I'm not paying."

"My old man usually brings his woman here," said Nagasawa. "He's got one in Tokyo, you know."

"Really?" asked Hatsumi.

I took a sip of wine, as if I had never heard anything.

Eventually a waiter came and took our orders. After choosing hors d'oeuvres and soup, Nagasawa ordered duck, and Hatsumi and I ordered sea bass. The food arrived at a leisurely pace, which allowed us to enjoy the wine and conversation. Nagasawa spoke first of the Foreign Ministry exam. Most of the examinees were scum who might as well be thrown into a bottomless pit, he said, though he supposed there were a few decent ones in the bunch. I asked if he thought the proportion of good ones to scum was higher or lower than in society in general.

"It's the same," he said. "Of course." It was the same everywhere, he added: an immutable law.

Nagasawa ordered a second bottle of wine when we had finished the first, and for himself he ordered a double scotch.

Hatsumi then began talking about a girl she wanted to fix me up with. This was a perpetual topic for the two of us. She was always telling me about some "cute freshman in my club," and I was always running away.

"She's *really* nice, though, and *really* cute. I'll bring her along next time. You ought to talk to her. I'm sure you'll like her."

"It's a waste of time, Hatsumi," I said. "I'm too poor to go out with girls from your school. I can't talk to them."

"Don't be silly," she said. "This girl is simple and natural and unaffected."

"Come on, Watanabe," said Nagasawa. "Just meet her. You don't have to screw her."

"I should say *not!*" said Hatsumi. "This one's a virgin."

"Like you used to be," said Nagasawa.

"Exactly," said Hatsumi with a bright smile. "Like I used to be. But really," she said to me, "don't give me that stuff about being 'too poor.' It's got nothing to do with anything. Sure, there are a few super stuck-up girls in every class, but the rest of us are just ordinary people. We all eat lunch in the school cafeteria for two hundred fifty yen—"

"Now wait just a minute, Hatsumi," I said, interrupting her. "In *my* school the cafeteria has three lunches: A, B, and C. The A Lunch is a hundred and twenty yen, the B Lunch is a hundred yen, and the C Lunch is eighty yen. Everybody gives me dirty looks when I eat the A Lunch, and guys who can't afford the C Lunch eat *ramen* noodles for sixty yen. That's the kind of school I go to. You still think I can talk to girls from your school?"

Hatsumi could hardly stop laughing. "That's so *cheap!*" she said. "Maybe I should go there for lunch! But really, Toru, you're such a nice guy, I'm sure you'd get along with this girl. She might even like the hundred-and-twenty-yen lunch."

"No way," I said with a laugh. "*Nobody* eats that stuff because they like it; they eat it because they can't afford anything else."

"Anyhow, don't judge a book by its cover. It's true we go to this hoity-toity girls' school, but lots of us there are serious people who think serious thoughts about life. Not *everybody* is looking for a boyfriend with a sports car."

"I know that much," I said.

"Watanabe's got a girl. He's in love," said Nagasawa. "But he won't say a word about her. He's as tight-lipped as they come. A riddle wrapped in an enigma."

"Really?" Hatsumi asked me.

"Really," I said. "But there's no riddle involved here. It's just that the situation is a complicated one, and hard to talk about."

"An illicit love? Ooh! You can talk to *me!*"

I took a sip of wine to avoid answering.

"See what I mean?" said Nagasawa, at work on his third whiskey. "Tight-lipped. When this guy decides he's not going to talk about something, nobody can drag it out of him."

"What a shame," said Hatsumi as she cut a small slice of terrine and brought it to her mouth. "If you had gotten along with her, we could have gone on double dates."

"Yeah, we could've gotten drunk and done a little swapping," said Nagasawa.

"Enough of that kind of talk," said Hatsumi.

"Whaddya mean 'that kind of talk'? Watanabe's got his eye on you," said Nagasawa.

"That has nothing to do with what I'm talking about," Hatsumi murmured. "He's not that kind of person. He's sincere and caring. I can tell. That's why I've been trying to fix him up."

"Oh, sure, he's sincere. Like the time we swapped women once, way back when. Remember, Watanabe?" Nagasawa said this with a blasé look on his face, then slugged back the rest of his whiskey and ordered another one.

Hatsumi set her knife and fork down and dabbed at her mouth with her napkin. Then, looking at me, she asked, "Toru, did you really do that?"

I didn't know how to answer her, and so I said nothing.

"Tell her," said Nagasawa. "What the hell." This was turning ugly. Nagasawa could get nasty when he was drunk, but tonight his nastiness was aimed at Hatsumi, not at me. Knowing that made it all the more difficult for me to go on sitting there.

"I'd like to hear about that," said Hatsumi. "It sounds *very* interesting!"

"We were drunk," I said.

"That's all right, Toru. I'm not blaming you. I just want you to tell me what happened."

"The two of us were drinking in a bar in Shibuya, and we got friendly with this pair of girls. They went to some junior college, and they were pretty plastered, too. So, anyhow, we, uh, went to a hotel and slept with them. Our rooms were right next door to each other. In the middle of the night, Nagasawa knocked on my door and said we should change girls, so I went to his room and he came to mine."

"Didn't the girls mind?"

"No, they were drunk too."

"Anyway, I had a good reason for doing it," said Nagasawa.

"A good reason?"

"Well, the girls were too different. One was really good-looking, but the other one was a dog. It seemed unfair to me. I got the pretty one, but Watanabe got stuck with the other one. That's why we swapped. Right, Watanabe?"

"Yeah, I guess so," I said. But in fact, I had liked the not-pretty one. She was fun to talk to, and she was a nice person. After we had sex, we were enjoying talking to each other in bed when Nagasawa showed up and suggested we change partners. I asked the girl if she minded, and she said it was O.K. with her if that's what we wanted. She probably figured I wanted to do it with the pretty one.

"Was it fun?" Hatsumi asked me.

"Switching, you mean?"

"The whole thing."

"Not especially. It's just something you do. Sleeping with girls that way is not all that much fun."

"So why do you do it?"

"Because of me," said Nagasawa.

"I'm asking Toru," Hatsumi shot back to Nagasawa. "Why do you do something like that?"

"Because sometimes I have this tremendous desire to sleep with a girl."

"If you're in love with someone, can't you manage one way or another with her?" Hatsumi asked after a few moments' thought.

"It's complicated."

Hatsumi sighed.

At that point the door opened and the waiters brought the food in. Nagasawa was presented with his roast duck, and Hatsumi and I received our sea bass. The waiters heaped fresh-cooked vegetables on our plates and dribbled sauce on them before withdrawing and leaving the three of us alone again. Nagasawa cut a slice of duck and ate it with gusto, followed by more whiskey. I took a forkful of spinach. Hatsumi didn't touch her food.

"You know, Toru," she said, "I have no idea what makes your situation so 'complicated,' but I do think that the kind of thing you just told me about is not right for you. You're not that kind of person. What do you think?" She set her hands on the table and looked me in the eye.

"Well," I said, "I've felt that way myself sometimes."

"So why don't you stop?"

"Because sometimes I have a need for human warmth," I answered honestly. "Sometimes, if I can't feel something like the warmth of a woman's skin, I get so lonely I can't stand it."

"Here, let me summarize what I think it's all about," interjected Nagasawa. "Watanabe's got this girl he likes, but for certain complicated reasons, they can't do it. So he tells himself 'Sex is just sex,' and he takes care of his need with somebody else. What's wrong with that? It makes perfect sense. He can't just stay locked in his room jerking off all the time, can he?"

"But if you really love her, Toru, shouldn't it be possible for you to control yourself?"

"Maybe so," I said, bringing a piece of sea bass in cream sauce to my mouth.

"You just don't understand a man's sexual need," said Nagasawa to Hatsumi. "Look at me, for example. I've been with you for three years, and I've slept with plenty of women in that time. But I don't remember a thing about them. I don't know their names, I don't remember their faces. I slept with each of them exactly once. Meet 'em, do it, so long. That's it. What's wrong with that?"

"What I can't stand is that arrogance of yours," said Hatsumi in a soft voice. "Whether you sleep with other women or not is beside the point. I've never really gotten angry at you for fooling around, have I?"

"You can't even call what I do fooling around. It's just a game. Nobody gets hurt," said Nagasawa.

"*I* get hurt," said Hatsumi. "Why am I not enough for you?"

Nagasawa kept silent for a moment and swirled the whiskey in his glass. "It's not that you're not enough for me. That's another phase, another question. It's just a hunger I have inside me. If I've hurt you, I'm sorry. But it's not a question of whether or not you're enough for me. I can only live with that hunger. That's the kind of man I am. That's what makes me *me*. There's nothing I can do about it, don't you see?"

At last Hatsumi picked up her silverware and started eating her fish. "At least you shouldn't drag Toru into your 'games.'"

"We're a lot alike, though, Watanabe and me," said Nagasawa. "Neither of us is interested, essentially, in anything but ourselves. O.K., so I'm arrogant and he's not, but neither of us is able to feel any interest in anything other than what we ourselves think or feel or do. That's why we can think about things in a way that's totally divorced from anybody else. That's what I like about him. The only difference is that he hasn't realized this about himself, and so he hesitates and feels hurt."

"What human being *doesn't* hesitate and feel hurt?" Hatsumi demanded. "Are you trying to say that *you* have never felt those things?"

"Of course I have, but I've disciplined myself to where I can minimize them. Even a rat will choose the least painful route if you shock him enough."

"But rats don't fall in love."

"'Rats don't fall in love.'" Nagasawa looked at me. "That's great. We should have background music for this—a full orchestra with two harps and—"

"Don't make fun of me. I'm serious."

"We're eating," said Nagasawa. "And Watanabe's here. It might be more civil for us to confine 'serious' talk to another occasion."

"I can leave," I said.

"No," said Hatsumi. "Please stay. It's better with you here."

"At least have dessert," said Nagasawa.

"I don't mind, really."

The three of us went on eating in silence for a time. I finished my fish. Hatsumi left half of hers. Nagasawa had finished his duck long before and now was concentrating on his whiskey.

"This was excellent sea bass," I offered, but no one took me up on it. I might as well have thrown a rock down a deep shaft.

The waiters took our plates away and brought lemon sherbet and espresso. Nagasawa barely touched his dessert and coffee, moving directly to a cigarette. Hatsumi ignored her sherbet. "Oh, boy," I thought to myself as I finished my sherbet and coffee. Hatsumi stared at her hands on the table. Like everything she had on, her hands looked chic and elegant and expensive. I thought about Naoko and Reiko. What would they be doing now? I wondered. Naoko could be lying on the sofa reading a book, and Reiko might be playing "Norwegian Wood" on her guitar. I felt an intense desire to go back to that little room of theirs. What the hell was I doing in this place?

"Where Watanabe and I are alike is, we don't give a damn if nobody understands us," Nagasawa said. "That's what makes us different from everybody else. They're all worried about whether the people around them understand them. But not me, and not Watanabe. We just don't give a damn. Self and others are separate."

"Is this true?" Hatsumi asked me.

"No way," I said. "I'm not that strong. I don't feel it's O.K. if nobody understands me. I've got people I want to understand and be understood by. But aside from those few, well, I figure it's kind of hopeless. I don't agree with Nagasawa. I *do* care if people understand me."

"That's practically the same thing as what I'm saying," said Nagasawa, picking up his coffee spoon. "It *is* the same! It's the difference between a late breakfast or an early lunch. Same time, same food, different name."

Now Hatsumi spoke to Nagasawa. "Don't you care whether *I* understand you or not?"

"I guess you don't get it. Person A understands Person B because the *time* is right for that to happen, not because Person B *wants to be understood* by Person A."

"So is it a mistake for me to feel that I want to be understood by someone—by *you*, for example?"

"No, it's not a mistake," answered Nagasawa. "Most people would call that love, if you think you want to understand me. My system for living is way different from other people's system for living."

"So what you're saying is you're not in love with me, is that it?"

"Well, my system and your—"

"To hell with your fucking system!" Hatsumi shouted. That was the first and last time I ever heard her shout.

Nagasawa pushed the button by the table, and the waiter came in with the check. Nagasawa handed him a credit card.

"Sorry about this, Watanabe," said Nagasawa. "I'm going to see Hatsumi home. You go back to the dorm alone, O.K.?"

"You don't have to apologize to me. Great meal," I said, but no one said anything in response.

The waiter brought the card, and Nagasawa signed with a ballpoint pen after checking the amount. Then the three of us stood and went outside. Nagasawa started to step into the street to hail a cab, but Hatsumi stopped him.

"Thanks, but I don't want to spend any more time with you today. You don't have to see me home. Thank you for dinner."

"Whatever," said Nagasawa.

"I want Toru to see me home."

"Whatever," said Nagasawa. "But Watanabe's practically the same as me. He may be a nice guy, but deep down in his heart he's incapable of loving anybody. There's always some part of him somewhere that's wide awake and detached. He just has that hunger that won't go away. Believe me, I know what I'm talking about."

I flagged down a cab and let Hatsumi in first. "Anyhow," I said to Naga-sawa, "I'll make sure she gets home."

"Sorry to put you through this," said Nagasawa, but I could see that he was already thinking about something else.

Once inside the cab, I asked Hatsumi, "Where do you want to go? Back to Ebisu?" Her apartment was in Ebisu.

She shook her head.

"O.K. Want to go for a drink somewhere?"

"Yes," she said with a nod.

"Shibuya," I told the driver.

Folding her arms and closing her eyes, Hatsumi sank back into the corner of the seat. Her small gold earrings caught the light as the taxi swayed. Her midnight blue dress seemed to have been made to match the darkness of the cab. Every now and then her thinly daubed, beautifully formed lips would quiver slightly as if she had caught herself on the verge of talking to herself. Watching her, I could see why Nagasawa had chosen her as his special companion. There were any number of women more beautiful than Hatsumi, and Nagasawa could have made any of them his. But Hatsumi had some quality that could send a tremor through your heart. It was nothing forceful. The power she exerted was a subtle thing, but it called forth deep resonances. I watched her all the way to Shibuya, and wondered, without ever finding an answer, what this emotional reverberation that I was feeling could be.

IT FINALLY HIT ME some dozen or so years later. I had come to Santa Fe to interview a painter and was sitting in a local pizza parlor, drinking beer and eating pizza and watching a miraculously beautiful sunset. Everything was soaked in brilliant red—my hand, the plate, the table, the world—as if some special kind of fruit juice had splashed down on everything. In the midst of this overwhelming sunset, the image of Hatsumi flashed into my mind, and in that moment I understood what that tremor of the heart had been. It was a kind of childhood longing that had always remained—and would forever remain—unfulfilled. I had forgotten the existence of such innocent, all-but-seared-in longing: forgotten for years to remember that such feelings had ever existed inside me. What Hatsumi had stirred in me was a part of my very self that had long lain dormant. And when the realization struck me, it aroused

such sorrow I almost burst into tears. She had been an absolutely special woman. Someone should have done something—anything—to save
her.

But neither Nagasawa nor I could have managed that. As so many of
those I knew had done, Hatsumi reached a certain stage in life and
decided—almost on the spur of the moment—to end it. Two years after
Nagasawa left for Germany, she married, and two years after that she
slashed her wrists with a razor blade.

It was Nagasawa, of course, who told me what had happened. His letter
from Bonn said this: "Hatsumi's death has extinguished something. This
is unbearably sad and painful, even to me." I ripped his letter to shreds and
threw it away. I never wrote to him again.

HATSUMI AND I WENT to a small bar and downed several drinks. Neither
of us said much. Like a bored, old married couple, we sat opposite each
other, drinking in silence and munching peanuts. When the place began
to fill up, we went out for a walk. Hatsumi said she would pay the bill, but
I insisted on paying because the drinks had been my idea.

There was a deep chill in the night air. Hatsumi wrapped herself in her
pale gray cardigan and walked by my side in silence. I had no destination
in mind as we ambled through the nighttime streets, my hands shoved
deep into my pockets. This was just like walking with Naoko, it occurred
to me.

"Do you know someplace we could shoot pool around here?" Hatsumi
asked me without warning.

"Pool?! You shoot pool?"

"Yeah, I'm pretty good. How about you?"

"I play a little four-ball. Not that I'm very good at it."

"O.K. then. Let's go."

We found a pool hall nearby and went in. It was a small place at the far
end of an alley. The two of us—Hatsumi in her chic dress and I in my
blue blazer and regimental tie—clashed with the scruffy pool hall, but
this didn't seem to concern Hatsumi at all as she chose and chalked her
cue. She pulled a barrette from her bag and held her hair aside at one
temple to keep it from interfering with her game.

We played two rounds of four-ball. Hatsumi was as good as she had claimed to be, while my own game was hampered by the thick bandage I still wore on my cut hand. She crushed me.

"You're great," I said in admiration.

"You mean appearances can be deceiving?" she asked as she sized up a shot, smiling.

"Where'd you learn to play like that?"

"My grandfather—my father's father—was an old playboy. He had a table in his house. I used to shoot pool with my brother just for fun, and when I got a little bigger my grandfather taught me the right moves. He was a wonderful guy—stylish, handsome. He's dead now, though. He always used to boast how he once met Deanna Durbin in New York."

She got three in a row, then missed on the fourth try. I managed to squeeze in a ball, then missed an easy shot.

"It's the bandage," said Hatsumi to comfort me.

"No, it's because I haven't played in such a long time," I said. "Two years and five months."

"How can you be so sure of the time?"

"My friend died that night after our last game together," I said.

"So you quit shooting pool?"

"No, not really," I said after giving it some thought. "I just never had the opportunity to play after that. That's all."

"How did your friend die?"

"Traffic accident," I said.

She made several more shots, aiming with deadly seriousness and adjusting the cue ball's speed with precision. Watching her in action—her carefully set hair swept back out of her eyes, golden earrings sparkling, pumps set firmly on the floor, lovely, slender fingers pressing the felt as she took her shot—I felt as if her area of the scruffy pool parlor had been transformed into part of some elegant social event. I had never spent time with her alone before, and this was a marvelous experience for me, as if I had been drawn up to a higher plane of life. At the end of the third game—in which, of course, she crushed me again—my cut began to throb, and so we stopped playing.

"I'm sorry," she said with what seemed like genuine concern, "I should never have suggested this."

"That's O.K.," I said. "It's not a bad cut. I enjoyed playing. Really."

As we were leaving the pool parlor, the skinny woman owner said to

Hatsumi, "You've got a nice stroke, sister." Hatsumi gave her a sweet smile and thanked her as she paid the bill.

"Does it hurt?" she asked when we were outside.

"Not much," I said.

"Do you think it opened?"

"No, it's probably O.K."

"I know! You should come to my place. I'll change your bandage for you. I've got disinfectant and everything. C'mon, I'm right over there."

I told her it wasn't worth worrying about, that I'd be O.K., but she insisted we had to check to see if the cut had opened or not.

"Or is it that you don't like being with me? You want to go back to your room as soon as possible, is that it?" she said with a playful smile.

"No way," I said.

"All right, then. Don't stand on ceremony. It's a short walk."

Hatsumi's apartment was a fifteen-minute walk from Shibuya toward Ebisu. By no means a glamorous building, it was more than decent, with a nice little lobby and an elevator. Hatsumi sat me at the kitchen table and went to the bedroom to change. She came out wearing a Princeton hooded sweatshirt and cotton slacks—and no more gold earrings. Setting a first-aid box on the table, she undid my bandage, checked to see that the wound was still sealed, put a little disinfectant on the area, and tied a new bandage over the cut. She did all this like an expert. "How come you're so good at so many things?" I asked.

"I used to do volunteer work at a hospital. Kind of like playing nurse. That's how I learned."

When she was through with the bandage, Hatsumi went and got two cans of beer from the refrigerator. She drank half of hers, and I drank mine plus the half she left. Then she showed me pictures of the freshman girls in her club. She was right: several of them were cute.

"Anytime you think you want a girlfriend, come to me," she said. "I'll fix you up right away."

"Yes, ma'am."

"All right, Toru, tell me the truth. You think I'm an old matchmaker, don't you?"

"To some extent," I said, telling her the truth, but with a smile. Hatsumi smiled, too. She looked good when she smiled.

"Tell me something else, Toru," she said. "What do you think about Nagasawa and me?"

"What do you mean what do I think? About what?"

"About what I ought to do. From now on."

"It doesn't matter what I think," I said, taking a slug of the well-chilled beer.

"That's all right. Tell me exactly what you think."

"Well, if I were you, I'd leave him. I'd find someone with a more normal way of looking at things and live happily ever after. There's no way in hell you can be happy with that guy. The way he lives, it never crosses his mind to try to make himself happy or to make others happy. Staying with him can only wreck your nervous system. To me, it's already a miracle that you've been with him three years. Of course, I'm very fond of him in my own way. He's a fun guy, and he has lots of great qualities. He has strengths and abilities that I could never hope to match. But finally, his ideas about things and the way he lives his life are not normal. Sometimes, when I'm talking to him, I feel as if I'm going round and round in circles. The same process that takes him higher and higher keeps me going around in circles. It makes me feel so empty! Finally, our very systems are totally different. Do you see what I'm saying?"

"I do," Hatsumi said as she brought me another beer from the refrigerator.

"Plus, after he gets into the Foreign Ministry and does a year of training, he'll be going overseas. What are *you* going to do all that time? Wait for him? He has no intention of marrying anyone."

"I know that, too."

"So I've got nothing else to say."

"I see," said Hatsumi.

I slowly filled my glass with beer.

"You know, when we were shooting pool before, something popped into my mind," I said. "I was an only child, but the whole time I was growing up I never once felt deprived or wished I had brothers or sisters. I was satisfied being alone. But all of a sudden, shooting pool with you, I had this feeling like I wished I had had an elder sister like you—really chic and a knockout in a midnight blue dress and golden earrings and great with a pool cue."

Hatsumi flashed me a happy smile. "That's got to be the nicest thing anybody's said to me in the past year," she said. "Really."

"All I want for you," I said, blushing, "is for you to be happy. It's crazy, though. You seem like someone who could be happy with just about anybody, so how did you end up with Nagasawa, of all people?"

"Things like that just happen. There's probably not much you can do about them. It's certainly true in my case. Of course, Nagasawa would say it's my responsibility, not his."

"I'm sure he would."

"But anyway, Toru, I'm not the smartest girl in the world. If anything, I'm sort of on the stupid side, and old-fashioned. I couldn't care less about 'systems' and 'responsibility.' All I want is to get married and have a man I love hold me in his arms every night and make kids. That's plenty for me. It's all I want out of life."

"And what Nagasawa wants out of life has nothing to do with that."

"People change, though, don't you think?" Hatsumi asked.

"You mean, like, they go out into society and get their butts kicked and grow up kind of thing?"

"Sure. And if he's away from me for a long time, his feelings for me could change, don't you think?"

"Maybe so, if he were an ordinary guy," I said. "But he's different. He's incredibly strong-willed—stronger than you or I can imagine. And he only makes himself stronger with every day that goes by. If something smashes into him, he just works to make himself stronger. He'd eat slugs before he'd back down to anyone. What do you expect to get from a guy like that?"

"But there's nothing I *can* do but wait for him," said Hatsumi with her chin in her hand.

"You love him that much?"

"I do," she answered without a moment's hesitation.

"Oh, brother," I said with a sigh, drinking down the last of my beer. "It must be a wonderful thing to be so sure that you love somebody."

"I'm a stupid, old-fashioned girl," she said. "Have another beer?"

"No, thanks, I've gotta get going. Thanks for the bandage and beer."

As I was standing in the entryway putting on my shoes, the telephone rang. Hatsumi looked at me, looked at the phone, and looked at me again. "Good night," I said, stepping outside. As I shut the door, I caught a glimpse of Hatsumi picking up the receiver. It was the last time I ever saw her.

BY THE TIME I GOT BACK to the dorm, it was eleven-thirty. I went straight to Nagasawa's room and knocked on his door. After the tenth knock it occurred to me that this was Saturday night. Nagasawa always got overnight permission on Saturday nights, supposedly to stay at his relatives' house.

I went back to my room, took off my tie, put my jacket and pants on a hanger, changed into my pajamas, and brushed my teeth. Oh no, I thought, tomorrow is Sunday again. Sundays seemed to be rolling around every four days. Another two Sundays and I would be twenty years old. I stretched out in bed and stared at my calendar as dark feelings came over me.

I SAT AT MY DESK to write my Sunday morning letter to Naoko, drinking coffee from a big cup and listening to old Miles Davis records. A fine rain was falling outside, while my room had the chill of an aquarium. The smell of mothballs lingered in the thick sweater I had just taken out of a storage box. High up on the windowpane clung a huge, fat fly, unmoving. With no wind to stir it, the Rising Sun hung limp against the flagpole like the toga of a Roman senator. A skinny, timid-looking brown dog that had wandered into the quadrangle seemed to be sniffing every blossom in the flower bed. I couldn't begin to imagine why any dog would have to go around sniffing flowers on a rainy day.

My letter was a long one, and whenever my cut right palm began to hurt from holding the pen, I would let my eyes wander out to the rainy quadrangle.

I began by telling Naoko how I had given my right hand a nasty cut while working in the record store, then went on to say that Nagasawa, Hatsumi, and I had had a sort of celebration the night before for Nagasawa's having passed his Foreign Ministry exam. I described the restaurant and the food. The meal was a good one, I said, but the atmosphere changed to something uncomfortable partway through.

I wondered if I should write about Kizuki in connection with having shot pool with Hatsumi and decided to go ahead. It was something I ought to write about, I felt.

I still remember the last shot Kizuki took that day—the day he died. It was a difficult cushion shot that I never expected him to make. Luck seemed to be with him, though: the shot was absolutely perfect, and the white and red balls hardly made a sound as they brushed each other on the green felt for the last point of the game. It was such a beautiful shot, I can still bring back a vivid image of it to this day. For nearly two and a half years after that, I never touched a cue.

The night I played pool with Hatsumi, though, the thought of Kizuki never crossed my mind until the first game ended, and this came as a major shock to me. I had always assumed that I would be reminded of Kizuki whenever I played pool. But not until the first game was over and I bought a Pepsi from a vending machine and started drinking it did I even think of him. It was the Pepsi machine that did it: there had been one in the pool hall we used to play in, and we had often bet drinks on the outcome of our games.

I felt guilty that I hadn't thought of Kizuki right away, as if I had somehow abandoned him. Back in my room, though, I came to think of it this way: two and a half years have gone by since it happened, and Kizuki is still seventeen years old. Not that this means my memory of him has faded. The things that his death gave rise to are still there, bright and clear, inside me, some of them even clearer than when they were new. What I want to say is this: I'm going to turn twenty soon. Part of what Kizuki and I shared when we were sixteen and seventeen has already vanished, and no amount of crying is going to bring that back. I can't explain it any better than this, but I think that you can probably understand what I felt and what I am trying to say. In fact, you are probably the only one in the world who can understand.

I think of you now more than ever. It's raining today. Rainy Sundays make it hard for me. When it rains, I can't do laundry, which means I can't do ironing. I can't go walking, and I can't lie down on the roof. About all I can do is put the record player on auto repeat and listen to *Kind of Blue* over and over while I watch the rain falling in the quadrangle. As I wrote to you earlier, I don't wind my spring on Sundays. That's why this letter is so damn long. I'm stopping now. I'm going to the dining hall for lunch.

Good-bye.

nine

THERE WAS NO SIGN OF MIDORI AT THE NEXT DAY'S LECTURE, either. What was happening with her? Ten days had gone by since I last talked to her on the telephone. I thought about giving her a call, but decided against it. She had said that *she* would call *me*.

That Thursday I saw Nagasawa in the dining hall. He sat down next to me with a tray full of food and apologized for having made our "party" so unpleasant.

"Never mind," I said. "I should be thanking you for a great dinner. I have to admit, though, it was a funny way to celebrate your first job."

"It sure as hell was," he said.

A few minutes went by as we ate in silence.

"I made up with Hatsumi," he said.

"I'm not surprised."

"I was kinda tough on you, too, as I recall it."

"What's with all the apologizing?" I asked. "Are you sick?"

"I may be," he said with a few little nods. "Hatsumi tells me you told her to leave me."

"It only makes sense," I said.

"Yeah, I guess so," said Nagasawa.

"She's a great girl," I said, slurping my miso soup.

"I know," he said with a sigh. "A little too great for me."

I WAS SLEEPING the sleep of death when the buzzer rang to let me know I had a call. It brought me back from the absolute core of sleep in total confusion. I felt as if I had been sleeping with my head soaked in water until my brain swelled up. The clock said 6:15, but I had no idea if that meant A.M. or P.M., and I couldn't remember what day it was. I looked out the window and realized there was no flag on the pole. It was probably P.M. So raising the flag might serve some purpose after all.

"Hey, Watanabe, are you free now?" Midori asked.

"I dunno, what's today?"

"Friday."

"Morning or evening?"

"Evening, of course! You're so weird! Let's see, it's, uh, six-eighteen P.M."

So it *was* P.M. after all! That's right, I had been stretched out on my bed, reading a book, when I dozed off. Friday. I got my head working. I didn't have to go to the record store on Friday nights. "Yeah, I'm free. Where are you?"

"Ueno Station. Why don't you meet me in Shinjuku? I'll leave now."

We set a time and place and hung up.

WHEN I GOT TO DUG, Midori was sitting at the far end of the counter with a drink. She wore a man's wrinkled, white balmacaan coat, a thin yellow sweater, blue jeans, and two bracelets on one wrist.

"What're you drinking?" I asked.

"Tom Collins."

I ordered a whiskey and soda, then realized there was a big suitcase by Midori's feet.

"I took a trip," she said. "Just got back."

"Where'd you go?"

"South to Nara and north to Aomori."

"On the same trip?!"

"Don't be stupid. I may be strange, but I can't go north and south at the same time. I went to Nara with my boyfriend, and then I took off to Aomori alone."

I took a sip of my whiskey and soda, then used a match to light the Marlboro that Midori had in her mouth. "You must have had a hell of a time, with the funeral and all."

"Nah, a funeral's a piece of cake. We've had plenty of practice. You put on a black kimono and sit there like a lady and everybody else takes care of business—an uncle, a neighbor, like that. They bring the sake, order the sushi, say comforting things, cry, carry on, divide up the keepsakes. It's a piece of cake. A picnic. Compared to nursing somebody day after day, it's an absolute picnic. We were drained, my sister and me. We couldn't even cry. We didn't have any tears left. Really. Except, when you do that, they start whispering about you: 'Those girls are cold as ice.' So then, we're *never* going to cry, that's just how the two of us are. I know we could have faked it, but we would never do anything like that. The sons of bitches! The more they wanted to see us cry, the more determined we were not to give them that satisfaction. My sister and I are totally different types, but when it comes to something like that, we're in absolute sync."

Midori's bracelets jangled on her arm as she waved for the waiter and ordered another Tom Collins and a small bowl of pistachios.

"So then, after the funeral ended and everybody went home, the two of us drank sake till the sun went down. Polished off one of those huge half-gallon bottles, and half of another one, and the whole time we were dumping on everybody—this one's an idiot, that one's a shithead, one guy looks like a mangy dog, another one's a pig, so-and-so's a hypocrite, that one's a crook. You have no idea how great it felt!"

"I can imagine."

"We got plastered and went to bed—both of us out cold. We slept for hours, and if the phone rang or something, we just let it go. Dead to the world. Finally, after we woke up, we ordered sushi and talked about what to do. We decided to close the shop for a while and enjoy ourselves. We'd been killing ourselves for months and we deserved a break. My sister just wanted to hang around with her boyfriend for a while, and I decided I'd take mine on a trip for a couple of days and fuck like crazy." Midori clamped her mouth shut and rubbed her ears. "Oops, sorry."

"That's O.K.," I said. "So you went to Nara."

"Yeah, I've always liked that place. The temples, the deer park."

"And did you fuck like crazy?"

"No, not at all, not even once," she said with a sigh. "The second we walked into the hotel room and dumped our bags, my period started. A real gusher."

I couldn't help laughing.

"Hey, it's not funny. I was a week early! I couldn't stop crying when that happened. I think all the stress threw me off. My boyfriend got *sooo* mad!

He's like that: he gets mad right away. It wasn't *my* fault, though. It's not like I *wanted* to get my period. And, well, mine are kind of on the heavy side anyway. The first day or two, I don't want to do *anything*. Make sure you keep away from me then."

"I'd like to, but how can I tell?" I asked.

"O.K., I'll wear a hat for a couple of days after my period starts. A red one. That should work," she said with a laugh. "If you see me on the street and I'm wearing a red hat, don't talk to me, just run away."

"Great. I wish all girls would do that," I said. "So anyhow, what'd you do in Nara?"

"What else *could* we do? We fed the deer and walked all over the place. It was just awful! We had a big fight and I haven't seen him since we got back. I hung around for a couple of days and decided to take a nice trip all by myself. So I went to Aomori. I stayed with a friend in Hirosaki for the first two nights, and then I started traveling around—Shimokita, Tappi, places like that. They're nice. I once wrote a map brochure for the area. Ever been there?"

"Never."

"So anyway," said Midori, taking a sip of her Tom Collins and wrenching open a pistachio, "the whole time I was traveling by myself, I was thinking of you. I was thinking how nice it would be if I could have you with me."

"How come?"

"How come?!" Midori looked at me with eyes focused on nothingness. "Whaddya mean 'How come?'?!"

"Just that. How come you were thinking of me?"

"Maybe because I like you, that's how come! Why else would I be thinking of you? Who would ever think they wanted to be with somebody they didn't like?"

"But you've got a boyfriend," I said. "You don't have to think about me." I took a slow sip of my whiskey and soda.

"Meaning I'm not allowed to think about you if I've got a boyfriend?"

"No, that's not it, I just—"

"Now get this straight, Watanabe," said Midori, pointing at me. "I'm warning you, I've got a whole month's worth of misery crammed inside me and getting ready to blow. So watch what you say to me. Any more of that kind of stuff and I'll flood this place with tears. Once I get started, I'm good for the whole night. Are you ready for that? I'm an absolute animal when I start crying, it doesn't matter *where* I am! I'm not kidding."

I nodded and kept quiet. Ordering a second whiskey and soda, I ate a few pistachios. Somewhere behind the sound of a sloshing shaker and clinking glasses and the scrape of an ice maker, Sarah Vaughan sang an old-fashioned love song.

"Things haven't been right between me and my boyfriend ever since the tampon incident."

"Tampon incident?"

"Yeah, I was out drinking with him and a few of his friends about a month ago and I told them the story of a woman in my neighborhood who blew out a tampon when she sneezed. Funny, right?"

"That *is* funny," I said with a laugh.

"Yeah, all the other guys thought so, too. But he got mad and said I shouldn't be talking about such dirty things. Such a wet blanket!"

"Wow."

"He's a wonderful guy, but he can be really narrow-minded when it comes to stuff like that," said Midori. "Like, he gets mad if I wear anything but white underwear. Don't you think that's narrow-minded?"

"Maybe so," I said, "but it's just a matter of taste." It seemed incredible to me that a guy like that would want a girlfriend like Midori, but I kept the thought to myself.

"So, what have *you* been doing?" she asked.

"Nothing. Same as always," I said, but then I recalled my attempt to masturbate while thinking of Midori as I had promised to do. I told her about it in a low voice that wouldn't carry to the others around us.

Midori's eyes lit up and she snapped her fingers. "How'd it go? Was it good?"

"Nah, I got embarrassed halfway through and quit."

"You mean you lost your erection?"

"Pretty much."

"Damn," she said, shooting a look of annoyance at me. "You can't let yourself get embarrassed. Think about something really sexy. It's O.K., I'm giving you permission. Hey, I know what! Next time I'll get on the phone with you: 'Oh, oh, that's great . . . Oh, I *feel* it . . . Stop, I'm gonna come . . . Oh, don't *do* that!' I'll say stuff like that to you while you're doing it."

"The dormitory phone is in the lobby by the front door, with people coming in and out all the time," I explained. "The dorm head would kill me with his bare hands if he saw me jerking off in a place like that."

"Oh, too bad."

"Never mind," I said. "I'll try again by myself one of these days."

"Give it your best," said Midori.

"Sure thing," I said.

"I wonder if it's me," she said. "Maybe I'm just not sexy. Innately."

"That's not it," I assured her. "It's more a question of attitude."

"You know," she said, "I have this tremendously sensitive back. The soft touch of fingers all over . . . mmmmm."

"I'll keep that in mind."

"Hey, why don't we go now and see a dirty movie?" Midori suggested. "A real, filthy S and M one."

We went from the bar to an eel shop, and from there to one of Shinjuku's most run-down theaters for an adult triple feature. It was the only place we could find in the paper that was showing S&M stuff. Inside, the theater had some kind of undefinable smell. Our timing was good: the S&M feature was just starting as we took our seats. It was the story of a secretary and her high-school-age sister being kidnapped by a bunch of men and subjected to sadistic torture. The men get the older one to do all kinds of awful things by threatening to rape the younger sister, but soon the older sister is transformed into a raging masochist, and the younger one goes crazy from having to watch all the contortions they put her through. It was such a gloomy, repetitive film, I got a little bored after a while.

"If I were the younger sister, I wouldn't go crazy so easily," said Midori. "I'd keep watching."

"I'm sure you would," I said.

"And anyway, don't you think her nipples are too dark for a high school girl—a virgin?"

"Absolutely."

Midori's eyes were glued to the screen. I was impressed: anyone watching a movie with such fierce intensity was getting more than her money's worth. She kept reporting her thoughts to me: "Omigod, will you look at that," or "Three guys at once! They're going to tear her open!" or "I'd like to try that on somebody, Watanabe." I was enjoying Midori a lot more than the movie.

When the lights went up during intermission, I realized there were no other women in the theater. One young guy sitting near us—probably a student—took a look at Midori and changed his seat to the far side.

"Tell me, Watanabe, do you get hard watching this kind of stuff?"

"Well, sure, sometimes," I said. "That's why they *make* these movies."

"So what you're saying is, every time one of those scenes starts, every guy in the theater has his thing standing at attention? Thirty or forty of them standing up all at once? It's so weird if you stop and think about it, don't you think?"

"Yeah, I guess so, now that you mention it."

The second feature was a fairly normal sex flick, which meant it was even more boring than the first. It had lots of oral sex scenes, and every time they started doing fellatio or cunnilingus or sixty-nine the soundtrack would fill the theater with loud sucking or slurping sound effects. Listening to them, I felt strangely moved to think that I was living out my life on this odd planet of ours.

"Who comes up with these sounds, I wonder," I said to Midori.

"I think they're *great!*" she said.

There was also a sound for a penis moving back and forth in a vagina. I had never realized that such sounds even existed. The man was into a lot of heavy breathing, and the woman came up with the usual sort of expressions—"good" or "more"—as she writhed under him. You could also hear the bed creaking. These scenes just went on and on. Midori seemed to be enjoying them at first, but even she got bored after a while and suggested we leave. We went outside and took a few deep breaths. This was the first time in my life the outside air of Shinjuku felt healthy to me.

"That was fun," said Midori. "Let's try it again sometime."

"They just keep doing the same things," I said.

"Well, what else can they do? We all just keep doing the same things." She had a point there.

We found another bar and ordered drinks. I had more whiskey, and Midori drank three or four cocktails of some indefinable sort. Outside again, Midori said she wanted to climb a tree.

"There aren't any trees around here," I said. "And even if there were, you're too wobbly to do any climbing."

"You're always so damn sensible, you ruin everything. I'm drunk 'cause I wanna be drunk. What's wrong with that? And even if I *am* drunk, I can still climb a tree. Hell, I'm gonna climb all the way to the top of a great, big, tall tree and I'm gonna pee all over everybody!"

"You wouldn't happen to be needing to go to the bathroom by any chance?"

"Yup."

I took Midori to a pay toilet in Shinjuku Station, put a coin in the slot and got her inside, then bought an evening paper at a nearby stand and read it while I waited for her to come out. But she didn't come out. I started getting worried after fifteen minutes and was ready to go check on her when she finally emerged looking kind of pale.

"Sorry," she said. "I fell asleep on the toilet."

"Are you O.K.?" I asked, putting my coat over her shoulders.

"Not really," she said.

"I'll take you home. You just have to get home, take a nice, long bath and go to bed. You're exhausted."

"I am *not* going home. What's the point? Nobody's there. I don't want to sleep all by myself in a place like that."

"Terrific," I said. "So what are you going to do?"

"Go to some love hotel around here and sleep with your arms around me all night. Like a log. Tomorrow morning we'll have breakfast somewhere and go to school together."

"You were planning this all along, weren't you? That's why you called me up."

"Of course."

"You should have called your boyfriend, not me. That's the only thing that makes sense. That's what boyfriends are for."

"But I want to be with you."

"You can't be with me," I said. "First of all, I have to be back in the dorm by midnight. Otherwise, I'll break curfew. The one time I did that I had hell to pay. And second, if I go to bed with a girl, I'm going to want to do it with her, and I sure as hell don't want to lie there struggling to restrain myself. I'm not kidding, I might end up forcing you."

"You mean you'd hit me and tie me up and rape me from behind?"

"Hey, look, I'm serious."

"But I'm so lonely! I want to *be* with someone! I know I'm doing terrible things to you, making demands and not giving you anything in return, saying whatever pops into my head, dragging you out of your room and forcing you to take me everywhere, but you're the only one I can *do* stuff like that to! I have never been able to have my own way with anybody, not once in the twenty years I've been alive. My father, my mother, they never paid the slightest attention to me, and my boyfriend, well, he's just not that kind of guy. He gets mad if I try to have my own way. So we end up fighting. You're the only one I can say these things to. And now I'm really really really tired and I want to fall asleep listening to someone tell me how much they like me and how pretty I am and stuff. That's all I want. And when I wake up, I'll be full of energy and I'll never bother you with these kinds of selfish demands again. I swear. I'll be a good girl."

"I hear you, believe me, but there's nothing I can do."

"Oh, please! Otherwise, I'm going to sit right down here on the ground and cry my head off all night long. And I'll sleep with the first guy that talks to me."

That did it. I called the dorm and asked for Nagasawa. When he got on the phone I asked him if he would make it look as if I had come back for the evening. I was with a girl, I explained.

"Fine," he said. "It's a worthy cause, I'll be glad to help you out. I'll just turn over your name tag to the 'in' side. Don't worry. Take all the time you need. You can come in through my window in the morning."

"Thanks. I owe you one," I said, and hung up.

"All set?" Midori asked.

"Pretty much," I said with a sigh.

"Great, let's go to a disco, it's so early."

"Wait a minute, I thought you were tired."

"For something like this, I'm just fine."

"Oh, brother," I said.

AND SHE WAS RIGHT. We went to a disco, and her energy started coming back little by little as we danced. She drank two whiskey and cokes, stayed on the dance floor until her forehead was drenched in sweat.

"This is *so* much *fun!*" she exclaimed when we took a break at a table. "I haven't danced like this in ages. I don't know, when you move your body, it's kind of like your spirit gets liberated."

"*Your* spirit is *always* liberated, I'd say."

"No way," she said, shaking her head and smiling. "Anyhow, now that I'm feeling better, I'm starved! Let's go for pizza."

I took her to a pizza house I knew and ordered draught beer and an anchovy pizza. I wasn't very hungry and ate only four of the twelve slices. Midori finished the rest.

"You sure made a fast recovery," I said. "Not too long ago you were pale and wobbly."

"It's 'cause my selfish demands got through to somebody," she answered. "It unclogged me. Wow, this pizza is great!"

"Tell me, though. Is there really nobody at home?"

"It's true. My sister's staying at her friend's place. Now, that girl's got a *real* case of the creeps. She can't sleep alone in the house if I'm not there."

"Let's forget this love-hotel crap, then. Going to a place like that just makes you feel cheap. Let's go to your house. You must have enough bedding for me?"

Midori thought about it for a minute, then nodded. "O.K., we'll spend the night at my place."

We took the Yamanote Line to Otsuka, and soon we were raising the metal shutter that sealed off the front of the Kobayashi Bookstore. A paper sign on the shutter read "Temporarily Closed." The smell of old paper filled the dark shop, as if the shutter had not been opened for a long time. Half the shelves were empty, and most of the magazines had been tied in bundles for returns. That hollow, chilly feeling I had experienced on my first visit had only deepened. The place looked like a hulk abandoned on the shore.

"You're not planning to open the shop again?" I asked.

"Nah, we're gonna sell it," Midori said. "We'll divide the money and live on our own for a while without anybody's 'protection.' My sister's getting married next year, and I've got three more years of school. We ought to make enough to see us through that much at least. I'll keep my part-time job, too. Once the place is sold, I'll live with my sister in an apartment for a while."

"You think somebody'll want to buy it?"

"Probably. I know somebody who wants to open a yarn shop. She's been asking me recently if I want to sell. Poor Papa, though. He worked *so* hard to get this place, and he was paying off the loan he took out little by little, and in the end he hardly had anything left. It all melted away, like foam on a river."

"He had *you*, though," I said.

"Me?!" Midori said with a laugh. She took a deep breath and let it out. "Let's go upstairs. It's cold down here."

Upstairs, she sat me at the kitchen table and went to warm the bathwater. While she busied herself with that, I put a kettle on to boil and made tea. Waiting for the bath to heat up, we sat across from each other at the kitchen table and drank the tea. Chin in hand, she took a long, hard look at me. There were no sounds other than the ticking of the clock and the hum of the refrigerator motor, turning on and off as the thermostat kicked in and out. The clock showed that midnight was fast approaching.

"Y'know, Watanabe, study it hard enough, and you've got a pretty interesting face."

"Think so?" I asked, somewhat hurt.

"A nice face goes a long way with me," she said. "And yours . . . well, the more I look at it, the more I get to thinking, 'He'll do.'"

"Me, too," I said. "Every once in a while, I think about myself, 'What the hell, I'll do.'"

"Hey, I don't mean that in a bad way. I'm not very good at putting my feelings into words. That's why people misunderstand me. All I'm trying to say is I like you. Have I told you that before?"

"You have," I said.

"I mean, I'm not the only one who has trouble figuring out what men are all about. But I'm working at it, a little at a time."

Midori brought over a box of Marlboros and lit one up. "When you start at zero, you've got a lot to learn."

"I wouldn't be surprised."

"Oh, I almost forgot! You want to burn a stick of incense for my father?"

I followed Midori to the room with the Buddhist altar, lit a stick of incense in front of her father's photo, and brought my hands together.

"Know what I did the other day?" Midori asked. "I got all naked in front of my father's picture. Took off every stitch of clothing and let him have a good, long look. Kind of in a yoga position. Like, 'Here, Daddy, these are my tits, and this is my cunt.'"

"Why in the hell would you do something like that?" I asked.

"I don't know, I just wanted to show him. I mean, half of me comes from his sperm, right? Why shouldn't I show him? 'Here's the daughter you made.' I *was* a little drunk at the time. I suppose that had something to do with it."

"I suppose."

"My sister walked in and fell over. There I was in front of my father's memorial portrait all naked with my legs spread. I guess anybody'd be kinda surprised."

"I guess so."

"I explained why I was doing it and said, 'So take off your clothes and sit down next to me and show him, too, Momo' (her name's Momo), but she wouldn't do it. She went away shocked. She's got this really conservative streak."

"In other words, she's relatively normal, you mean," I said.

"Tell me, Watanabe, what did you think of my father?"

"I'm not good with people I've just met, but it didn't bother me being alone with him. I felt pretty comfortable with him. We talked about all kinds of stuff."

"What kind of stuff?"

"Euripides," I said.

Midori laughed out loud. "You're so *weird*! *Nobody* talks about Euripides with a dying person they've just met!"

"Well, *nobody* sits in front of her father's memorial portrait with her legs spread, either!"

Midori chuckled and gave the altar bell a ring. "G'night, Daddy. We're going to have some fun now, so don't worry and get some sleep. You're not suffering anymore, right? You're dead, right? I'm sure you're not suffering. If you are, you'd better complain to the gods. Tell 'em it's just too cruel. I hope you meet Mommy and the two of you really do it. I saw your wee-wee when I helped you pee. It was pretty impressive! So give it everything you've got. G'night."

WE TOOK TURNS in the bathtub and changed into pajamas. I borrowed a nearly new pair of her father's. They were a little small but better than nothing. Midori spread out a mattress for me on the floor of the altar room.

"You're not scared sleeping in front of the altar?" she asked.

"Not at all. I haven't done anything bad," I said with a smile.

"But you're gonna stay with me and hold me until I fall asleep, right?"

"Right," I said.

Practically falling over the edge of Midori's little bed, I held her in my arms. Nose against my chest, Midori set her hands on my hips. My right arm curled around her back while I tried to keep from falling off by hanging on to the bed frame with my left hand. This was not exactly a situation conducive to sexual excitement. My nose was resting on her head and the short-cut hairs there would give it a tickle every now and then.

"C'mon, *say* something to me," Midori said with her face buried in my chest.

"Whaddya want me to say?"

"Anything. Something to make me feel good."

"You're really cute," I said.

"Midori," she said. "Say my name."

"You're really cute, Midori," I corrected myself.

"Whaddya mean *really* cute?"

"So cute the mountains crumble and the oceans dry up."

Midori lifted her face and looked at me. "You have this special way with words."

"I can feel my heart softening when you say that," I said, smiling.

"Say something even nicer."

"I really like you, Midori. A lot."

"How much is a lot?"

"Like a spring bear," I said.

"A spring bear?" Midori looked up again. "What's that all about? A spring bear."

"You're walking through a field all by yourself one day in spring, and this sweet little bear cub with velvet fur and shiny little eyes comes walking along. And he says to you, 'Hi, there, little lady. Want to tumble with me?' So you and the bear cub spend the whole day in each other's arms, tumbling down this clover-covered hill. Nice, huh?"

"Yeah. *Really* nice."

"That's how much I like you."

"That is the best thing I've ever heard," said Midori, cuddling up against my chest. "If you like me *that* much, you'll do anything I tell you to do, right? You won't get mad, right?"

"No, of course I won't get mad."

"And you'll take care of me always and always."

"Of course I will," I said, stroking her short, soft, boyish hair. "Don't worry, everything is going to be fine."

"But I'm scared," she said.

I held her softly, and soon her shoulders were rising and falling, and I could hear the regular breathing of sleep. I slipped out of her bed and went to the kitchen, where I drank a beer. I wasn't the least bit sleepy, so I thought about reading a book, but I couldn't find anything worth reading nearby. I considered returning to Midori's room to look for one there, but I didn't want to wake her up by rummaging around where she was sleeping.

I sat there staring into space for a while, sipping my beer, when it occurred to me that I was in a bookstore. I went downstairs, switched on the light, and started looking through the paperback shelves. There wasn't much that appealed to me, and most of what did I had read already, but I had to have something to read no matter what. I picked a discolored copy of Hermann Hesse's *Beneath the Wheel* that must have been hanging around the shop unsold for a long time, and left the money for it by the cash register. This was my small contribution to reducing the inventory of the Kobayashi Bookstore.

I sat at the kitchen table, drinking my beer and reading *Beneath the Wheel*. I had first read the novel the year I entered middle school. And now, eight years later, here I was, reading the same book in a girl's kitchen, wearing the undersized pajamas of her dead father. Funny. If it hadn't been for these strange circumstances, I would probably never have reread *Beneath the Wheel*.

The book did have its dated moments, but as a novel it wasn't bad. I moved through it slowly, enjoying it line by line, in the hushed bookstore in the middle of the night. A dusty bottle of brandy stood on a shelf in the kitchen. I poured a little into a coffee cup and sipped it. The brandy warmed me but it did nothing to help me feel sleepy.

I went to check on Midori a little before three, but she was sound asleep. She must have been exhausted. The lights from the block of shops beyond the window cast a soft white glow, like moonlight, over the room. Midori slept with her back to the light. She lay so perfectly still, she might have been frozen stiff. Bending over, I caught the sound of her breathing. She slept just like her father.

The suitcase from her recent travels stood by the bed. Her white coat hung on the back of a chair. Her desktop was neatly arranged, and on the wall over the desk hung a Snoopy calendar. I nudged the curtain aside and looked down at the deserted shops. Every store was closed, their metal shutters down, the vending machines hunched in front of the liquor store the only sign of something waiting for the dawn. The moan of long-distance truck tires sent a deep shudder through the air every now and then. I went back to the kitchen, poured myself another shot of brandy, and went on reading *Beneath the Wheel*.

By the time I finished the book, the sky was growing light. I made myself some instant coffee and used some notepaper and a ballpoint pen I found on the table to write a message to Midori: "I drank some of your brandy. I bought a copy of *Beneath the Wheel*. It got light out, so I'm going home. Good-bye." Then, after some hesitation, I wrote, "You look really cute when you're sleeping." I washed my coffee cup, switched off the kitchen light, went downstairs, quietly lifted the shutter, and went outside. I worried that a neighbor might find me suspicious, but there was no one on the street at five-fifty-something in the morning. Only the crows were on their usual rooftop perch, glaring down at the street. I glanced up at the pale pink curtains in Midori's window, walked to the streetcar stop, rode to the end of the line, and walked to my dorm. On the way I found an open eatery and had myself a breakfast of rice, miso soup, pickled vegetables, and fried eggs. Circling around to the back of the dorm, I gave a little knock on Nagasawa's first-floor window. He let me in right away.

"Coffee?" he asked.

"Nah."

I thanked him, went up to my room, brushed my teeth, took my pants off, got under the covers, and clamped my eyes shut. Finally, a dreamless sleep closed over me like a heavy lead door.

I WROTE TO NAOKO every week, and she often wrote back. None of her letters was very long. Soon there were mentions of the cold November mornings and evenings.

You went back to Tokyo just about the time the fall weather was deepening, so for a time I couldn't tell whether the hole that opened up inside me was from missing you or from the change of season. Reiko and I talk about you all the time. She says be sure to say Hi to you. She is as nice to me as ever. I don't think I would have been able to stand this place if I didn't have her with me. I cry when I'm lonely. Reiko says it's good I can cry. But feeling lonely really hurts. When I'm lonely at night, people talk to me from the darkness. They talk to me the way trees moan in the wind at night. Kizuki; my sister: they talk to me like that all the time. They're lonely too, and looking for someone to talk to.

I often reread your letters at night when I'm lonely and in pain. I get confused by a lot of things that come from outside, but your descriptions of the world around you give me wonderful relief. It's so strange! I wonder why that should be? So I read them over and over, and Reiko reads them too. Then we talk about the things you tell me. I really liked the part about that girl Midori's father. We look forward to getting your letter every week as one of our few entertainments—yes, in a place like this, letters are our entertainments.

I try my best to set aside a time in the week for writing to you, but once I actually sit down in front of the blank piece of letter paper, I begin to feel depressed. I'm really having to push myself to write this letter, too. Reiko's been yelling at me to answer you. Don't get me wrong, though. I have tons of things I want to talk to you about, to tell you about. It's just hard for me to put them into writing. Which is why it's so painful for me to write letters.

Speaking of Midori, she sounds like an interesting person. Reading your letter, I got the feeling she might be in love with you. When I told that to Reiko, she said, "Well, of *course* she is! Even *I* am in love with Watanabe!" We're picking mushrooms and gathering chestnuts and eating them every day. And I do mean *every* day: rice with chestnuts, rice with *matsutake* mushrooms, but they taste so great, we don't get tired of them. Reiko doesn't eat that much, though. For her, it's still one cigarette after another. The birds and the rabbits are doing just fine.

Good-bye.

Three days after my twentieth birthday, a package arrived for me from Naoko. Inside I found a wine-colored crewneck sweater and a letter.

Happy Birthday! I hope you have a happy year being twenty. My own year of being twenty looks as if it's going to end with me as miserable as ever, but I'd really like it if you could have your share of happiness and mine combined. Really. Reiko and I each knit half of this sweater. If I had done it all by myself, it would have taken until next Valentine's Day. The good half is

Reiko's, and the bad half is mine. Reiko is so good at everything she does, I sometimes hate myself when I'm watching her. I mean, I haven't got one single thing I'm really good at!

Good-bye. Be well.

The package had a short note from Reiko, too.

How are you? For you, Naoko may be the pinnacle of happiness, but for me she's just a clumsy girl. Still, we managed to finish this sweater in time for your birthday. Handsome, isn't it? We picked the color and the style. Happy Birthday.

ten

THINKING BACK ON THE YEAR 1969, ALL THAT COMES TO MIND FOR me is a swamp—a deep, sticky bog that feels as if it's going to suck my shoe off each time I take a step. I walk through the mud, exhausted. In front of me, behind me, I can see nothing but an endless swampy darkness.

Time itself slogged along in rhythm with my faltering steps. The people around me had gone on ahead long before, while my time and I hung back, struggling through the mud. The world around me was on the verge of great transformations. Death had already taken John Coltrane, who was joined now by so many others. People screamed there'd be revolutionary changes—which always seemed to be just ahead, at the curve in the road. But the "changes" that came were just two-dimensional stage sets, background without substance or meaning. I trudged along through each day in its turn, looking up only rarely, eyes locked on the endless swamp that lay before me, planting my right foot, raising my left, planting my left foot, raising my right, never sure where I was, never sure I was headed in the right direction, knowing only that I had to keep moving, one step at a time.

I turned twenty, autumn gave way to winter, but in my life nothing changed in any significant way. Unexcited, I went to my classes, worked three nights a week in the record store, reread *The Great Gatsby* now and then, and when Sunday came I would do my wash and write a long letter to Naoko. Sometimes I would go out with Midori for a meal or to the zoo or a movie. The sale of the Kobayashi Bookstore went off as planned, and Midori and her sister moved into a two-bedroom apartment near Myogadani, a more upscale neighborhood. Midori would move out when her sister got married, and take a unit by herself, she said. Meanwhile, she invited me to their new apartment for lunch once. It was a sunny, handsome place, and Midori seemed to enjoy living there far more than she had over the Kobayashi Bookstore.

Every once in a while, Nagasawa would suggest that we go out on one of our excursions, but I always found something I had to do instead. I just didn't want to bother. Not that I didn't like the idea of sleeping with girls: it was just that, when I thought about the whole process I had to go through—drinking on the town, looking for the right kind of girls, talking to them, going to a hotel—it was too much trouble. I had to admire Nagasawa all the more for the way he could continue the ritual without growing sick and tired of it. Maybe what Hatsumi had said to me had had some effect: I could make myself feel far happier just thinking about Naoko than sleeping with some stupid, nameless girl. The sensation of Naoko's fingers bringing me to climax in a grassy field remained vivid inside me.

I wrote to Naoko at the beginning of December to ask if it would be all right for me to come and visit her during winter break. An answer came from Reiko saying they would love to have me. She explained that Naoko was having trouble writing and that she was answering for her. I was not to take this to mean that Naoko was feeling especially bad: there was no need for me to worry. These things came in waves.

When the break came, I stuffed my things into my knapsack, put on snow boots, and set out for Kyoto. The odd doctor had been right: the winter mountains blanketed in snow were incredibly beautiful. As before, I slept two nights in the apartment with Naoko and Reiko, and spent three days with them doing much the same kinds of things as before. When the sun went down, Reiko would play her guitar and the three of us would sit around talking. Instead of our picnic, we went cross-country skiing. An hour of tramping through the woods on skis left us breathless and sweaty. We also joined the residents and staff shoveling snow when there was time. Doctor Miyata popped over to our table at dinner to explain why people's middle fingers are longer than their index fingers while with toes it works the other way. The gatekeeper, Omura, talked to me again about Tokyo pork. Reiko enjoyed the records I brought as gifts from the city. She transcribed a few tunes and figured them out on the guitar.

Naoko was even less talkative than she had been in the fall. When the three of us were together, she would sit on the sofa, smiling, and hardly say a word. Reiko seemed to be gabbing to take up the slack. "But don't worry," Naoko told me. "This is just one of those times. It's a lot more fun for me to listen to you two than to talk myself."

Reiko gave herself some chores that took her out of the apartment so that Naoko and I could get in bed. I kissed her neck and shoulders and breasts, and she used her hands to bring me to climax as before. Afterward, holding her close, I told her how her touch had stayed with me these two months, that I had thought of her and masturbated.

"You haven't slept with anybody else?" Naoko asked.

"Not once," I said.

"All right, then, here's something else for you to remember." She slid down and touched my penis with her lips, then enveloped it in her warmth and ran her tongue all over it, her long, straight hair swaying over my belly and groin with each movement of her lips until I came for a second time.

"Do you think you can remember that?" she asked.

"Of course I can," I said. "I'll always remember it."

I held her tight and slid my hand inside her panties, touching her still-dry vagina. Naoko shook her head and pulled my hand away. We held each other for a time, saying nothing.

"I'm thinking of getting out of the dorm when the school year ends and looking for an apartment," I said. "I've had it with dorm life. If I keep working part-time I can pretty much cover my expenses. How about coming to Tokyo to live with me, the way I suggested before?"

"Oh, Toru, thank you. I'm so happy that you would ask me to do something like that!"

"It's not that I think there's anything wrong with this place," I said. "It's quiet, the surroundings are perfect, and Reiko is a wonderful person. But it's not a place to stay for a long time. It's too specialized for a long stay. The longer you're here, I'm sure, the harder it is to leave."

Instead of answering, Naoko turned her gaze to the outside. Beyond the window, there was nothing to see but snow. Snow clouds hung low and heavy in the sky, with only the smallest gap between clouds and snow-covered earth.

"Take your time, think it over," I said. "Whatever happens, I'm going to move by the end of March. Anytime you decide you want to join me, you can come."

Naoko nodded. I wrapped my arms around her as carefully as if I had been holding a work of art delicately fashioned from glass. She put her arms around my neck. I was naked, and she wore only the briefest white underwear. Her body was so beautiful, I could have enjoyed looking at it all day.

"Why don't I get wet?" Naoko murmured. "That one time was the only time it ever happened. The day of my twentieth birthday, that April. The night you held me in your arms. What is wrong with me?"

"It's strictly psychological, I'm sure," I said. "Give it time. There's no hurry."

"All of my problems are strictly psychological," said Naoko. "What if I never get better? What if I can never have sex for the rest of my life? Can you keep loving me just the same? Will hands and lips always be enough for you? Or will you solve the sex problem by sleeping with other girls?"

"I'm an inborn optimist," I said.

Naoko sat up in bed and slipped on a T-shirt. Over this she put on a flannel shirt, and then she got into her jeans. I put my clothes on, too.

"Let me think about it," Naoko said. "And you think about it too."

"I will," I said. "And speaking of lips, what you did with them just now was great."

Naoko reddened slightly and gave a little smile. "Kizuki used to say that, too."

"He and I had pretty much the same tastes and opinions," I said, smiling.

We sat across from each other at the kitchen table, drinking coffee and talking about the old days. She was beginning to talk more about Kizuki. She would hesitate, and choose her words carefully. Every now and then, the snow would fall for a while and stop. The sky never cleared the whole three days I was there. "I think I can get back here in March," I said as I was leaving. I gave her one last, heavily padded hug with my winter coat on, and kissed her on the lips. "Good-bye," she said.

1970—A YEAR with a whole new sound to it—came along, and that put an end to my teen years. Now I could step ahead into a whole new swamp. Then it was time for final exams, and those I passed with relative ease. If you have nothing else to do and spend all your time going to classes, it takes no special study to get through finals.

Some problems arose in the dorm, though. A few guys active in one of the political factions kept their helmets and iron pipes hidden in their rooms. They had a run-in with some of the jocks under the wing of the dorm head, as a result of which two of them were injured and six expelled from the dorm. The aftershocks of the incident stayed on for a long time, spawning minor fights almost on a daily basis. The atmosphere that hung over the dorm was oppressive, and people's nerves were on edge. I myself was on the verge of getting punched out by one of the jocks when Nagasawa intervened and managed to smooth things over. In any case, it was time for me to get the hell out of there.

Once I had the better part of my exams out of the way, I started looking for an apartment in earnest. After a week of searching, I came up with the right place way out in the suburbs of Kichijoji. The location was not exactly convenient, but it was a house: an independent house—a real find. Originally a gardener's shack or some other kind of cottage, it stood off by itself in the corner of a good-size plot of land, separated from the main house by a large stretch of neglected garden. The landlord would use the front gate, and I the back, which would make it possible for me to preserve my privacy. It had one good-size room, a little kitchen and bathroom, and an unimaginably huge storage closet. It even had a veranda facing the garden. A nice old couple were renting the house at way below market value on condition that the tenant be prepared to move out the following year if their grandson decided to come to Tokyo. They assured me that I could live as I pleased there; they wouldn't be making any demands.

Nagasawa helped me with the move. He managed to borrow a light truck to transfer my stuff, and, as promised, he gave me his refrigerator, TV, and oversize Thermos bottle. He might not need them anymore, but for me they were perfect. He himself was scheduled to move out in two days, to an apartment in the Mita neighborhood.

"I guess we won't be seeing each other for a long time," he said as he left me, "so be well. I'm still sure we'll run across each other in some strange place years from now."

"I'm already looking forward to it," I said.

"And that time we switched girls, the funny-looking one was way better."

"Right on," I said with a laugh. "But anyway, Nagasawa, take care of Hatsumi. Good ones like her are hard to find. And she's a lot more fragile than she looks."

"Yeah, I know," he said, nodding. "That's why I was hoping you would take her when I was through. The two of you would make a great couple."

"Get serious!" I said.

"Just kidding," said Nagasawa. "Anyhow, be happy. I get the feeling a lot of shit is going to come your way, but you're a stubborn son of a bitch, I'm sure you'll handle it. Mind if I give you one piece of advice?"

"Sure, go ahead."

"Don't feel sorry for yourself," he said. "Only assholes do that."

"I'll keep it in mind," I said. We shook hands and went our separate ways, he to his new world, and I back to my swamp.

THREE DAYS AFTER my move, I wrote to Naoko. I described my new house and said how relieved I was to be away from the idiots in the dorm and all their idiotic brainstorms. Now I could start my new life with a new frame of mind.

My window looks out on a big yard, which is used as a meeting place by all the neighborhood cats. I like to stretch out on the veranda and watch them. I'm not sure how many of them get together, but this is one big gang of cats. They take group sun baths. I don't think they're too pleased to see me living here, but when I put out an old chunk of cheese a few of them crept over and took a chance on nibbling it. They'll probably be friends of mine before too long. There's one striped tomcat in the bunch with half-eaten ears. It's amazing how much he looks like my old dorm head. I expect him to start raising the flag any day now.

I'm kind of far from school here, but once I start my major I won't have too many morning classes, so it shouldn't be too bad. It may even be better with the time to read on the train. Now all I have to do is find some easy work out here that I can do three or four days a week. Then I can get back to my spring-winding life.

I don't mean to be rushing you, but April is a good time of year to start new things, and I can't help feeling that the best thing for us would be to begin living together then. You could go back to school, too, if it worked out well. If there's a problem with us actually living together, I could find an apartment for you in the neighborhood. The most important thing is for us to be always near each other. It doesn't *have* to be spring, of course. If you think summer is better, that's fine with me, too. Just let me know what you're thinking, O.K.?"

I'm planning to put some extra time in at work for a while. To cover my moving expenses. I'm going to need a fair amount of money for one thing or another once I start living alone: pots and pans, dishes, stuff like that. I'll be free in March, though, and I definitely want to come to see you. What dates work best for you? I'll plan a trip to Kyoto then. I look forward to seeing you and to receiving your answer.

I spent the next few days buying the things I needed in the nearby Kichijoji shopping district and started cooking simple meals for myself at home. I bought some planks at a local lumberyard and had them cut to size so I could make a desk for myself. I figured I could study on it and, for the time being, eat my meals there, too. I made some shelves and laid in a good selection of spices. A white cat maybe six months old decided she liked me and started eating at my place. I called her Seagull.

Once I had my place fixed up to some extent, I went into town and found a temporary job as a painter's assistant. I filled two solid weeks that way. The pay was good, but the work was murder, and the fumes made my head spin. Every day after work I'd have supper at a cheap eatery, wash it down with beer, go home and play with the cat, and sleep like a dead man. No answer came from Naoko during that time.

I was in the thick of painting when Midori popped into my mind. I hadn't been in touch with her for nearly three weeks, I realized, and hadn't even told her I had moved. I had mentioned to her that I was thinking of moving, and she had said, "Oh, really?" and that was the last time we had talked.

I went to a phone booth and dialed Midori's apartment. The woman who answered was probably her sister. When I gave her my name, she said, "Just a minute," but Midori never came to the phone.

Then the sister, or whoever she was, got back on the line. "Midori says she's too mad to talk to you. You just up and moved and never said a thing to her, right? Just disappeared and never told her where you were going, right? Well, now you've got her boiling mad. And once she gets mad, she stays that way. Like an animal."

"Look, could you just put her on the phone? I can explain."

"She says she doesn't want to hear any explanations."

"Can I explain to *you*, then? I hate to do this to you, but could you listen and tell her what I said?"

"Not *me*, fella! Do it yourself. What kind of man are you? It's *your* responsibility, so *you* do it, and do it right."

It was hopeless. I thanked her and hung up. I really couldn't blame Midori for being mad. What with all the moving and fixing up and working for extra cash, I had never given her a second thought. Not even Naoko had crossed my mind the whole time. This was nothing new for me. Whenever I got involved in something, I shut out everything else.

But then I started thinking how I would have felt if the tables had been turned and Midori had moved somewhere without telling me where or getting in touch with me for three weeks. I would have been hurt—hurt badly, no doubt. No, we weren't lovers, but in a way we had opened ourselves to each other even more deeply than lovers do. The thought caused me a good deal of grief. What a terrible thing it is to wound someone you really care for—and to do it so unconsciously.

As soon as I got home from work, I sat at my new desk and wrote to Midori. I told her how I felt as honestly as I could. I apologized, without explanations or excuses, for having been so careless and insensitive. "I miss you," I wrote. "I want to see you as soon as possible. I want you to see my new house. Please write to me," I said, and sent the letter special delivery.

The answer never came.

This was the beginning of one weird spring. I spent my whole break waiting for letters. I couldn't take a trip, I couldn't go home to see my parents, I couldn't even take a part-time job because there was no telling when a letter might arrive from Naoko saying she wanted me to come see her on such-and-such a date. Afternoons I would spend in the nearby shopping district in Kichijoji, watching double features or reading in a jazz coffeehouse. I saw no one and talked to almost no one. And once a week I would write to Naoko. I never suggested to her that I was hoping for an answer. I didn't want to pressure her in any way. I would tell her about my painting work, about Seagull, about the peach blossoms in the garden, about the nice old lady who sold tofu, about the nasty old lady in the local eatery, about the meals I was making for myself. But still, she never wrote.

Whenever I got sick of reading or listening to records, I would do a little work in the garden. From my landlord I borrowed a rake and broom and pruning shears and spent time pulling weeds and trimming bushes. It didn't take much to make the yard look good. Once the owner invited me to join him for a cup of tea, so we sat on the veranda of the main house drinking green tea and munching on rice crackers and sharing small talk. After retirement, he had taken a job with an insurance company, he said, but he had left that, too, after a couple of years, and now he was taking it easy. The house and land had been in the family for a long time, his children were grown and independent, and he could manage a comfortable old age without working. Which is why he and his wife were always traveling together.

"That's nice," I said.

"No, it's not," he answered. "Traveling is no fun. I'd much rather be working."

He let the yard grow wild, he said, because there were no decent gardeners in the area and because he had developed allergies that made it impossible for him to do the work himself. Cutting grass made him sneeze.

When we had finished our tea, he showed me a storage shed and told me I could use anything I found inside, more or less by way of thanks for my gardening. "We don't have any use for any of this stuff," he said, "so feel free."

And in fact the place was crammed with all kinds of stuff—an old wooden bathtub, a kid's swimming pool, baseball bats. I found an old bike, a handy-size dining table with two chairs, a mirror, and a guitar. "I'd like to borrow these if you don't mind," I said.

"Feel free," he said again.

I spent a day working on the bike: cleaning the rust off, oiling the bearings, pumping up the tires, adjusting the gears, and taking it to a bike repair shop to have a new gear cable installed. It looked like a different bike by the time I was finished. I cleaned a thick layer of dust off the table and gave the piece a new coat of varnish. I replaced the strings of the guitar and glued a section of the body that was coming apart. I took a wire brush to the rust on the tuning pegs and adjusted those. It wasn't much of a guitar, but at least I got it to stay in tune. I hadn't had a guitar in my hands since high school, I realized. I sat on the porch and picked my way through The Drifters' "Up on the Roof" as well as I could. I was amazed to find I still remembered most of the chords.

Next I took a few scraps of lumber and made myself a mailbox. I painted it red, wrote my name on it, and set it out in front of my door. Up until April 3, the only piece of mail that found its way to my box was something that had been forwarded from the dorm: a notice from the reunion committee of my high school class. A class reunion was the last thing I wanted to have anything to do with. That was the class I had been in with Kizuki. I threw the thing into the trash.

I found a letter in the box on the afternoon of April 4. "Reiko Ishida," it said on the back. I made a nice, clean cut across the seal with my scissors and went out to the porch to read it. I had a feeling this was not going to be good news, and I was right.

First Reiko apologized for making me wait so long for an answer. Naoko had been struggling to write me a letter, she said, but she could never seem to write one through to the end.

I offered to send you an answer in her place, but every time I pointed out how wrong it was of her to keep you waiting, she insisted that it was far too personal a matter, that she would write to you herself, which is why I haven't written sooner. I'm sorry, really. I hope you can forgive me.

I know you must have had a difficult month waiting for an answer, but believe me, the month has been just as difficult for Naoko. Please try to understand what she's been going through. Her condition is not good, I have to say in all honesty. She was trying her best to stand on her own two feet, but so far the results have not been good.

Looking back, I see now that the first symptom of her problem was her loss of the ability to write letters. That happened right around the end of November or beginning of December. Then she started hearing things. Whenever she would try to write a letter, she would hear people talking to her, which made it impossible for her to write. The voices would interfere with her attempts to choose her words. It wasn't all that bad until about the time of your second visit, so I didn't take it too seriously. For all of us here, these kinds of symptoms come in cycles, more or less. In her case, they got quite serious after you left. She is having trouble now just holding an ordinary conversation. She can't find the right words to speak, and that puts her into a terribly confused state — confused and frightened. Meanwhile, the "things" she's hearing are getting worse.

We have a session every day with one of the specialists. Naoko and the doctor and I sit around talking and trying to find the exact part of her that's broken. I came up with the idea that it would be good to add you to one of our sessions if possible, and the doctor was in favor of it, but Naoko was against it. I can tell you exactly what her reason was: "I want my body to be clean of all this when I meet him." That was not the problem, I said to her; the problem was to get her well as quickly as possible, and I pushed as hard as I could, but she wouldn't change her mind.

I think I once explained to you that this is not a specialized hospital. We do have medical specialists here, of course, and they provide effective treatments, but concentrated therapy is another matter. The point of this facility is to create an effective environment in which the patient can treat herself or himself, and that does not, properly speaking, include medical treatment. Which means that if Naoko's condition grows any worse, they will probably have to transfer her to some other hospital or medical facility or what have you. Personally, I would find this very painful, but we would have to do it. This is not to say that she could not come back here for treatment on a kind of temporary "furlough." Or, better yet, she could even be cured and finish up with hospitals completely. In any case, we're doing everything we can, and Naoko is doing everything she can. The best thing you can do meanwhile is hope for her recovery and keep sending those letters to her.

The letter was dated March 31. After I had finished reading it, I stayed on the porch and let my eyes wander out to the garden, full now with the freshness of spring. An old cherry tree stood there, its blossoms nearing the height of their glory. A soft breeze blew, and the light of day lent its strangely blurred, smoky colors to everything. Seagull wandered over from somewhere, and after scratching at the boards of the veranda for a while, she stretched out next to me and went to sleep.

I knew I should be doing some serious thinking, but I had no idea how to go about it. And, to tell the truth, thinking was the last thing I wanted to do. The time would come soon enough when I had no choice in the matter, and when that time came I would take a good long time to think things over. Not now, though. Not now.

I spent the day watching the garden, propped against a pillar and stroking Seagull. I felt completely drained. The afternoon deepened, twilight approached, and bluish shadows enveloped the garden. Seagull disappeared, but I went on staring at the cherry blossoms. In the spring gloom, they looked like flesh that had burst through the skin over festering wounds. The garden filled up with the sweet, heavy stench of rotting flesh. And that's when I thought of Naoko's flesh. Naoko's beautiful flesh lay before me in the darkness, countless buds bursting through her skin, green and trembling in an almost imperceptible breeze. Why did such a beautiful body have to be so sick? I wondered. Why didn't they just leave Naoko alone?

I went inside and closed my curtains, but even indoors there was no escape from the smell of spring. It filled everything from the ground up. But the only thing the smell brought to mind for me now was that putrefying stench. Shut in behind my curtains, I felt a violent loathing for spring. I hated what the spring had in store for me; I hated the dull, throbbing ache it aroused inside me. I had never hated anything in my life with such intensity.

I spent three straight days after that all but walking on the bottom of the sea. I could hardly hear what people said to me, and they had just as much trouble catching anything I had to say. My whole body felt enveloped in some kind of membrane, cutting off any direct contact between me and the outside world. I couldn't touch "them," and "they" couldn't touch me. I was utterly helpless, and as long as I remained in that state, "they" were unable to reach out to me.

I sat leaning against the wall, staring up at the ceiling. When I felt hungry I would nibble anything within reach, take a drink of water, and when the sadness of it got to me, I'd knock myself out with whiskey. I didn't bathe, I didn't shave. This is how the three days went by.

A letter came from Midori on April 6. She invited me to meet her on campus and have lunch on the tenth when we had to register for classes. "I put off writing to you as long as I could, which makes us even, so let's make up. I have to admit it, I miss you." I read the letter again and again, four times altogether, and still I couldn't tell what she was trying to say to me. What could it possibly mean? My brain was so fogged over, I couldn't find the connection from one sentence to the next. How would meeting her on registration day make us "even"? Why did she want to have "lunch" with me? I was really losing it. My mind had gone slack, like the soggy roots of a subterranean plant. But somehow I knew I had to snap out of it. And then those words of Nagasawa's came to mind: "Don't feel sorry for yourself. Only assholes do that."

"O.K., Nagasawa. Right, on," I heard myself thinking. I let out a sigh and got to my feet.

I did my laundry for the first time in weeks, went to the public bath and shaved, cleaned my place up, shopped for food and cooked myself a decent meal for a change, fed the starving Seagull, drank only beer, and did thirty minutes of exercise. Shaving, I discovered in the mirror that I was becoming emaciated. My eyes were popping. I could hardly recognize myself.

I went out the next morning on a longish bike ride, and after finishing lunch at home, I read Reiko's letter one more time. Then I did some serious thinking about what I ought to do next. The main reason I had taken Reiko's letter so hard was that it had upset my optimistic belief that Naoko was getting better. Naoko herself had told me, "My sickness is a lot worse than you think: it has far deeper roots." And Reiko had warned me there was no telling what might happen. Still, I had seen Naoko twice, and had been given the impression that she was on the mend. I had assumed that the only problem was whether she could regain the courage to return to the real world, and that if she managed to, the two of us could join forces to make a go of it.

Reiko's letter smashed the illusory castle that I had built on that fragile hypothesis, leaving only a flattened surface devoid of feeling. I would have to do something to regain my footing. It would probably take a long time for Naoko to recover. And even then, she would probably be more debilitated and would have lost even more of her self-confidence than ever. I would have to adapt myself to this new situation. As strong as I might become, though, it would not solve all the problems. I knew that much. But there was nothing else I could do: just keep my own spirits up and wait for her to recover.

Hey, there, Kizuki, I thought. Unlike you, I've chosen to live—and to live the best I know how. Sure, it was hard for you. What the hell, it's hard for *me*. Really hard. And all because you killed yourself and left Naoko behind. But that's something I will never do. I will never, ever turn my back on her. First of all, because I love her, and because I'm stronger than she is. And I'm just going to keep on getting stronger. I'm going to mature. I'm going to be an adult. Because that's what I have to do. I always used to think I'd like to stay seventeen or eighteen if I could. But not anymore. I'm not a teenager anymore. I've got a sense of responsibility now. I'm not the same guy I was when we used to hang out together. I'm twenty now. And I have to pay the price to go on living.

"Shit, Watanabe, what happened to *you?*" Midori asked. "You're all skin and bones!"

"That bad, huh?"

"Too much you-know-what with that married girlfriend of yours, I bet."

I smiled and shook my head. "I haven't slept with a girl since the beginning of October."

"Whew! That can't be true. We're talkin' six months here!"

"You heard me."

"So how'd you lose so much weight?"

"By growing up," I said.

Midori put her hands on my shoulders and looked me in the eye with a twisted scowl that soon turned into a sweet smile. "It's true," she said. "Something's different, kinda. You've changed."

"I told you, I grew up. I'm an adult now."

"You're fantastic, the way your brain works," she said as if genuinely impressed. "Let's go eat. I'm starved."

We went to a little restaurant behind the literature department. I ordered the lunch special and she did the same.

"Hey, Watanabe, are you mad at me?"

"What for?"

"For not answering you, just to get even. Do you think I shouldn't have done that? I mean, you apologized and all."

"Yeah, but it was my fault to begin with. That's just how it goes."

"My sister says I shouldn't have done it. That it was too unforgiving, too childish."

"Yeah, but it made you feel better, didn't it, getting even like that?"

"Uh-huh."

"O.K., then, that's that."

"You *are* forgiving, aren't you?" Midori said. "But tell me the truth, Watanabe, you haven't had sex for six months?"

"Not once."

"So, that time you put me to bed, you must have really wanted it bad."

"Yeah, I guess I did."

"But you didn't do it, did you?"

"Look, you're the best friend I've got now," I said. "I don't want to lose you."

"You know, if you *had* tried to force yourself on me that time, I wouldn't have been able to resist, I was so exhausted."

"But I was too big and hard," I said.

Midori smiled and touched my wrist. "A little before that, I decided I was going to believe in you. A hundred percent. That's how I managed to sleep like that with total peace of mind. I knew I'd be all right, I'd be safe with you there. And I *did* sleep like a log, didn't I?"

"You sure did."

"On the other hand, if you were to say to me, 'Hey, Midori, let's do it. Then everything'll be great,' I'd probably do it with you. Now, don't think I'm trying to seduce you or tease you. I'm just telling you what's on my mind, with total honesty."

"I know, I know."

While we ate lunch, we showed each other our registration cards and found that we had registered for two of the same courses. So I'd be seeing her twice a week at least. With that out of the way, Midori told me about her living arrangements. For a while, neither she nor her sister could get used to apartment life—because it was too easy, she said. They had always been used to running around like crazy every day, taking care of sick people, helping out at the bookstore, and one thing or another.

"We're finally getting used to it, though," she said. "This is the way we should have been living all along—not having to worry about anyone else's needs, just stretching out any way we felt like it. It made us both nervous at first, like our bodies were floating a couple of inches off the floor. It didn't seem real, like real life couldn't really be like that. We were both tense, like everything was gonna get tipped upside down any minute."

"A couple of worrywarts," I said with a smile.

"Well, it's just that life has been too cruel to us till now," Midori said. "But that's O.K. We're gonna get back everything it owes us."

"I'll bet you are," I said, "knowing you. But tell me, what's your sister doing these days?"

"A friend of hers opened this swanky accessory shop a little while ago. My sister goes there to help out three times a week. Otherwise, she's studying cooking, going out on dates with her fiancé, going to the movies, vegging out, and just plain enjoying life."

Midori then asked about my new life. I gave her a description of the layout of the house, and the big yard, and Seagull the cat, and my landlord.

"Are you enjoying yourself?" she asked.

"Pretty much," I said.

"Coulda fooled me," said Midori.

"Yeah, and it's springtime, too," I said.

"And you're wearing that cool sweater your girlfriend knitted for you."

That was a shocker. I glanced down at my wine-colored sweater. "How did you know?"

"You're as honest as they come," said Midori. "I'm guessing, of course! Anyhow, what's wrong with you?"

"I dunno. I'm trying to whip up a little enthusiasm."

"Just remember, life is a box of cookies."

I shook my head a few times and looked at her. "Maybe it's because I'm not so smart, but sometimes I don't know what the hell you're talking about."

"You know how they've got these cookie assortments, and you like some but you don't like others? And you eat up all the ones you like, and the only ones left are the ones you don't like so much? I always think about that when something painful comes up. 'Now I just have to polish these off, and everything'll be O.K.' Life is a box of cookies."

"I guess you could call it a philosophy."

"It's true, though. I've learned it from experience."

WE WERE DRINKING OUR COFFEE when two girls came in. Midori seemed to know them from school. The three of them compared registration cards and talked about a million different things: "What kind of grade did you get in German?" "So-and-so got hurt in the campus riots." "Great shoes, where'd you buy them?" I half-listened, feeling as if their comments were coming from the other side of the world. I sipped my coffee and watched the scene passing by the shop window. It was a typical university springtime scene as the new year was getting under way: a haze hanging in the sky, the cherries blooming, the new students (you could tell at a glance) carrying armloads of new books. I felt myself drifting off a little and thought about Naoko, unable to return to school again this year. A small glass full of anemones stood by the window.

When the other two went back to their table, Midori and I went out to walk around the neighborhood. We visited a few used bookstores, bought some books, went to another coffeehouse for another cup, played some pinball at a games center, and sat on a park bench, talking—or, rather, Midori talked and I grunted in response. When she said she was thirsty, I ran over to a candy store and bought us two colas. I came back to find her scribbling away with her ballpoint pen on some lined paper.

"What's that?" I asked.

"Nothing," she said.

At three-thirty, she announced, "I gotta get going. I'm supposed to meet my sister in the Ginza."

We walked to the subway station and went off in different directions. As she left, Midori stuffed the piece of lined paper, now folded in four, into my pocket. "Read this when you get home," she said. I read it on the train.

I'm writing this letter to you while you're off buying drinks. This is the first time in my life I've ever written a letter to somebody sitting next to me on a bench, but I feel it's the only way I can get through to you. I mean, you're hardly listening to anything I say. Am I right?

Do you realize you did something terrible to me today? You never even noticed that my hairstyle had changed, did you? I've been working on it forever, trying to grow it out, and finally, at the end of last week, I managed to get it into a style you could actually call girlish, but you never even noticed. It was looking pretty good, so I figured I'd give you a little shock when you saw me for the first time after such a long time, but it didn't even register with you. Don't you think that's awful? I'll bet you can't even remember what I was wearing today. Hey, I'm a girl! So what if you've got something on your mind? You can spare me one decent look! All you had to say was "Cute hair," and I would have been able to forgive you for being sunk in a million thoughts, but no!

Which is why I'm going to tell you a lie. It's not true that I have to meet my sister in the Ginza. I was planning to spend the night at your place. I even brought my pajamas with me. It's true. I've got my pajamas and a toothbrush in my bag. I must be an idiot! I mean, you never even invited me over to see your new place. Oh well, what the hell, you obviously want to be alone, so I'll leave you alone. Go ahead and think away to your heart's content!

But don't get me wrong. I'm not totally mad at you. I'm just sad. You were so nice to me when I was having my problems, but now that you're having yours, it seems there's not a thing I can do for you. You're all locked up in that little world of yours, and when I try knocking on the door, you just sort of look up for a second and go right back inside.

So now I see you coming back with our drinks—walking and thinking. I was hoping you'd trip, but you didn't. Now you're sitting next to me chugging down your cola. I was holding out one last hope that you'd notice and say, "Hey, your hair's changed!" but no go. If you had, I would have ripped this letter up and said, "Let's go to your place. I'll make you a nice supper. And afterward we can get in bed and cuddle." But you're about as sensitive as a steel plate. Good-bye.

P.S. Please don't talk to me next time we meet in class.

I rang Midori's apartment from the station when I got off the train in Kichijoji, but there was no answer. With nothing better to do, I ambled around the neighborhood looking for some part-time work I could take after classes started. I would be free all day Saturday and Sunday and could work after five o'clock on Mondays, Wednesdays, and Thursdays, but finding a job that fit my particular schedule was no easy matter. I gave up and went home. When I went out to buy groceries for dinner, I tried Midori's place again. Her sister told me that Midori hadn't come home yet and that she had no idea when she'd be back. I thanked her and hung up.

After eating, I tried to write to Midori, but I gave up after several false starts and wrote to Naoko instead.

Spring was here, I said, and the new school year was beginning. I told her I missed her, that I had been hoping to be able to meet her and talk. "In any case," I said, "I've decided to make myself strong. As far as I can tell, that's all I can do.

"There's one other thing. Maybe it just has to do with me, and you may not care about this one way or the other, but I'm not sleeping with anybody anymore. That's because I don't want to forget the last time you touched me. It meant a lot more to me than you might think. I think about it all the time."

I PUT THE LETTER in an envelope, stuck on a stamp, and sat at my desk a long while staring at it. It was a much shorter letter than usual, but I had the feeling that Naoko might understand me better that way. I poured myself an inch and a half of whiskey, drank it down in two swallows, and went to sleep.

THE NEXT DAY I found a job near Kichijoji Station that I could do on Saturdays and Sundays: waiting on tables at a smallish Italian restaurant. The conditions were nothing much, but transportation and lunches were included. And whenever somebody on the late shift took the day off on a Monday, Wednesday, or Thursday (which happened often) I could take their place. This was perfect for me. The manager said they would raise my pay once I had stayed with them for three months, and they wanted me to start that Saturday. He was a far more decent guy than the clown who ran the record store in Shinjuku.

I TRIED PHONING Midori's apartment again, and again her sister answered. Midori hadn't come back since yesterday, she said, sounding tired, and now she herself was beginning to worry: did I have any idea where she might have gone? All I knew was that Midori had her pajamas and a toothbrush in her bag.

I SAW MIDORI in class on Wednesday. She was wearing a deep green sweater and the dark sunglasses she had often worn that summer. She was seated in the last row, talking with a slightly built girl with glasses I had seen once before. I approached her and said I'd like to talk to her after class. The girl with glasses looked at me first, and then Midori looked at me. Her hairstyle was, in fact, somewhat more womanly than it had been before: more grown-up.

"I have to see somebody," Midori said, cocking her head slightly.

"I won't take much of your time," I said. "Five minutes."

Midori removed her sunglasses and narrowed her eyes. She might just as well have been looking at a crumbling, abandoned house some hundred yards in the distance.

"I don't want to talk to you. Sorry," she said.

The girl with glasses looked at me with eyes that said, She says she doesn't want to talk to you. Sorry.

I sat in the seat on the right end of the front row for the lecture (an overview of the works of Tennessee Williams and their place in American literature), and when it was over, I did a long count to three and turned around. Midori was gone.

April was too lonely a month to spend all alone. In April, everyone around me looked happy. People would throw their coats off and enjoy each other's company in the sunshine—talking, playing catch, holding hands. But I was always by myself. Naoko, Midori, Nagasawa: all of them had gone away from where I stood. Now I had no one to say "Good morning" to or "Have a nice day." I even missed Storm Trooper. I spent the whole month with this hopeless sense of isolation. I tried a few times to speak to Midori, but the answer I got from her was always the same: "I don't want to talk to you now," and I knew from her tone of voice that she meant it. She was always with the girl with glasses, or else I saw her with a tall, short-haired guy. He had these incredibly long legs and always wore white basketball shoes.

April ended and May came along, but May was even worse than April. In the deepening spring of May, I had no choice but to recognize the trembling of my heart. It usually happened as the sun was going down. In the pale evening gloom, when the soft fragrance of magnolias hung in the air, my heart would swell without warning, and tremble, and lurch with a stab of pain. I would try clamping my eyes shut and gritting my teeth, and wait for it to pass. And it *would* pass—but slowly, taking its own time, and leaving a dull ache behind.

At those times I would write to Naoko. In my letters to her, I would describe only things that were touching or pleasant or beautiful: the fragrance of grasses, the caress of a spring breeze, the light of the moon, a movie I'd seen, a song I liked, a book that had moved me. I myself would be comforted by letters like this when I would reread what I had written. And I would feel that the world I lived in was a wonderful one. I wrote any number of letters like this, but from Naoko or Reiko I heard nothing.

At the restaurant where I worked I got to know another student my age named Itoh. It took quite a while before this gentle, quiet student from the oil painting department of an arts college would engage me in conversation, but eventually we started going to a nearby bar after work and talking about all kinds of things. He also liked to read and listen to music, and so we'd usually talk about books and records we liked. He was a slim, good-looking guy with much shorter hair and far cleaner clothes than the typical arts student. He never had a lot to say, but he had his definite tastes and opinions. He liked French novels, especially those of Georges Bataille and Boris Vian. For music, he preferred Mozart and Ravel. And, like me, he was looking for a friend with whom he could talk about such things.

Itoh once invited me to his apartment. It was not quite as hard to get to as mine: a strange, one-floored apartment house behind Inokashira Park. His room was stuffed with painting supplies and canvas. I asked to see his work, but he said he was too embarrassed to show me anything. We drank some Chivas Regal that he had quietly removed from his father's place, broiled some smelts on his charcoal stove, and listened to Robert Casadesus playing a Mozart piano concerto.

Itoh was from Nagasaki. He had a girlfriend he would sleep with whenever he went home, he said, but things weren't going too well with her lately.

"You know what girls are like," he said. "They turn twenty or twenty-one and all of a sudden they start having these concrete ideas. They get super realistic. And when that happens, everything that seemed so sweet and lovable about them begins to look ordinary and depressing. Now when I see her, usually after we do it, she starts asking me, 'What are you going to do after you graduate?'"

"Well, what *are* you going to do after you graduate?" I asked him.

Munching on a mouthful of smelt, he shook his head. "What *can* I do? I'm in oil painting! Start worrying about stuff like that, and *nobody's* going to major in oil painting! You don't do it to feed yourself. So she's like, why don't I come back to Nagasaki and become an art teacher? She's planning to be an English teacher."

"You're not so crazy about her anymore, are you?"

"That about sums it up," Itoh admitted. "And who the hell wants to be an art teacher? I'm not gonna spend my whole fuckin' life teaching middle-school monkeys how to draw!"

"That's beside the point," I said. "Don't you think you ought to break up with her? For both your sakes."

"Sure I do. But I don't know how to say it to her. She's planning to spend her life with me. How the hell can I say, 'Hey, we ought to split up. I don't like you anymore'?"

We drank our Chivas straight, without ice, and when we ran out of smelts we cut up some cucumbers and celery and dipped them in miso. When my teeth crunched down on my cucumber slices, I thought of Midori's father, which reminded me how flat and tasteless my life had become without Midori and put me into a foul mood. Without my being aware of it, she had become a huge presence inside me.

"Got a girlfriend?" Itoh asked me.

"I do," I said, then, after a pause, added, "but I can't be with her right now."

"But you understand each other's feelings, right?"

"I like to think so. Otherwise, what's the point?" I said with a chuckle.

Itoh talked in hushed tones about the greatness of Mozart. He knew Mozart inside out, the way a country boy knows his mountain trails. His father loved the music and had had him listening to it ever since he was tiny. I didn't know so much about classical music, but listening to this Mozart concerto with Itoh's smart and heartfelt commentary ("There— that part," "How about *that*?"), I felt myself calming down for the first time in ages. We stared at the crescent moon hanging over Inokashira Park and drank our Chivas Regal to the last drop. Fantastic whiskey.

Itoh said I could spend the night there, but I told him I had something to do, thanked him for the whiskey, and left his apartment before nine. On the way back to my place I called Midori from a public phone. She actually answered, much to my surprise.

"Sorry," she said, "but I don't want to talk to you right now."

"I know, I know. But I don't want our relationship to end like this. You're one of the very few friends I have, and it hurts not being able to see you. When *am* I going to be able to talk to you? I want you to tell me that much, at least."

"When *I* feel like talking to *you*," she said.

"How are you?" I asked.

"Fine," she said, and hung up.

A LETTER CAME from Reiko in the middle of May.

Thanks for writing so often. Naoko enjoys your letters. And so do I. You don't mind if I read them, do you?

Sorry I haven't been able to answer for such a long time. To tell you the truth, I've been feeling kind of exhausted, and there hasn't been much good news to report. Naoko's not doing well. Her mother came from Kobe the other day. The four of us—she and Naoko and the doctor and I—had a good long talk and we reached the conclusion that Naoko should move to a real hospital for a while for some intensive treatment and then maybe come back here depending on the results. Naoko says she'd like to stay here if possible and make herself well, and I know I am going to miss her and worry about her, but the fact is that it's getting harder and harder to keep her under control here. She's fine most of the time, but sometimes her emotions become tremendously unstable, and when that happens we can't take our eyes off her. There's no telling what she would do. When she has those intense episodes of hearing voices, she shuts down completely and burrows inside herself.

Which is why I myself agree that the best thing for Naoko would be for her to receive therapy at a proper institution for a while. I hate to say it, but it's all we can do. As I told you once before, patience is the most important thing. We have to go on unraveling the jumbled threads one at a time, without losing hope. No matter how hopeless her condition may appear to be, we are bound to find that one loose thread sooner or later. If you're in pitch blackness, all you can do is sit tight until your eyes get used to the dark.

Naoko should have moved to that other hospital by the time you receive this. I'm sorry I waited to tell you until the decision had been made, but it happened very quickly. The new hospital is a really good one, with good doctors. I'll write the address below: please write to Naoko there. They will be keeping me informed of her progress, too, so I will let you know what I hear. I hope it will be good news. I know this is going to be hard for you, but keep your hopes up. And even though Naoko is not here anymore, please write to me once in a while.

Good-bye.

I wrote a huge number of letters that spring: one a week to Naoko, several to Reiko, and several more to Midori. I wrote letters in the classroom, I wrote letters at my desk at home with Seagull in my lap, I wrote letters at empty tables during my breaks at the Italian restaurant. It was as if I were writing letters to hold together the pieces of my crumbling life.

To Midori I wrote, "April and May were painful, lonely months for me because I couldn't talk to you. I never knew that spring could be so painful and lonely. Better to have three Februaries than a spring like this. I know it's too late to be saying this to you, but your new hairstyle looks great on you. Really cute. I'm working in an Italian restaurant now, and the cook taught me a great way to make spaghetti. I'd like to make it for you soon."

I WENT TO SCHOOL every day, worked in the restaurant two or three times a week, talked with Itoh about books and music, read a few Boris Vian novels he lent me, wrote letters, played with Seagull, made spaghetti, worked in the garden, masturbated thinking of Naoko, and went to lots of movies.

By the time Midori started talking to me, it was almost the middle of June. We hadn't said a word to each other for two months. After the end of one lecture, she sat down in the seat next to mine, propped her chin in her hand, and sat there, saying nothing. Beyond the window, it was raining—a real rainy-season rain, pouring straight down without any wind, soaking every single thing beneath. Long after the other students had filed out of the classroom, Midori went on sitting next to me without a word. Then she took a Marlboro from the pocket of her jeans jacket, put it between her lips, and handed me her matches. I struck a match and lit her cigarette. Midori pursed her lips and blew a gentle cloud of tobacco in my face.

"Like my hairstyle?" she asked.

"It's great."

"How great?"

"Great enough to knock down all the trees in all the forests of the world."

"You really think so?"

"I really think so."

She kept her eyes on mine for a while, then held her right hand out to me. I took it. She looked even more relieved than I felt. She tapped her ashes onto the floor and rose to her feet.

"Let's go eat. I'm starved," she said.

"Where do you want to go?" I asked.

"To the Takashimaya department store restaurant in Nihonbashi."

"Why *there* of all places?"

"I like to go there sometimes, that's all."

And so we took the subway to Nihonbashi. Maybe because it had been raining all morning, the place was practically empty. The smell of rain filled the big, cavernous department store, and all the employees had that what-do-we-do-now? kind of look. Midori and I went to the basement restaurant and, after a close inspection of the plastic food in the window, both decided to have an old-fashioned cold lunch assortment with rice and pickles and grilled fish and tempura and teriyaki chicken. Inside, it was far from crowded despite the noon hour.

"Man, how long has it been since the last time I had lunch in a department-store restaurant?" I wondered aloud, drinking green tea from one of those slick white cups you can only find in a department-store restaurant.

"I like to do stuff like this," said Midori. "I don't know, it makes me feel like I'm doing something special. Probably reminds me of when I was a kid. My parents almost never took me to department stores."

"And I get the sneaking suspicion that's all mine *ever* did. My mother was crazy about department stores."

"Luckee!"

"What are you talking about? I don't particularly like going to department stores."

"No, I mean, you were lucky they cared enough about you to take you places."

"Well, I was an only child," I said.

"When I was little I used to dream about going to a department-store restaurant all by myself when I grew up and eating anything I liked. But what an empty dream! What's the fun of cramming your mouth full of rice all alone in a place like this? The food's not all that great, and it's just big and crowded and stuffy and noisy. Still, every once in a while I think about coming here."

"I've been really lonely these past two months," I said.

"Yeah, I know. You told me in your letters," Midori said, her voice flat. "Anyhow, let's eat. That's all I can think about now."

We finished all the little fried and broiled and pickled items in the separate compartments of our fancy lacquered half-moon lunch boxes, drank our clear soup from lacquered bowls, and our green tea from those white cups. Midori followed lunch with a cigarette. When she was done smoking, she stood up without a word and took her umbrella. I also stood up and took my umbrella.

"Where do you want to go now?" I asked.

"The roof, of course. That's the next stop when you've had lunch in a department-store restaurant."

There was no one on the roof in the rain, no clerk in the pet supplies department, and the shutters were closed in the kiosks and the kids' rides' ticket booth. We put up our umbrellas and wandered among the soaking wet wooden horses and garden chairs and stalls. It seemed incredible to me that there could be anyplace so devoid of people in the middle of Tokyo. Midori said she wanted to look through a telescope, so I put in a coin and held her umbrella over her while she squinted through the eyepiece.

In one corner of the roof was the covered games area with a row of kids' rides. Midori and I sat next to each other on some kind of platform and looked at the rain.

"So talk," Midori said. "You've got something you want to say to me, I know."

"I'm not trying to make excuses," I said, "but I was really depressed that time. My brain was all fogged over. Nothing was registering with me. But one thing became crystal clear to me when I couldn't see you anymore. I realized that the only way I had been able to survive until then was having you in my life. When I lost you, the pain and loneliness really got to me."

"Don't you have any idea how painful and lonely it's been for *me* without *you* these past two months?"

This took me completely off guard. "No," I said. "It never occurred to me. I thought you were mad at me and didn't want to see me."

"How can you be such an idiot? Of *course* I wanted to see you! I *told* you how much I like you! When I like somebody I really like them. It doesn't turn on and off for me just like that. Don't you realize at least *that* much about me?"

"Well, sure, but—"

"*That's* why I was so mad at you! I wanted to give you a good kick in the pants. I mean, we hadn't seen each other that whole time, and you were so spaced out thinking about this other girl you didn't even *look* at me! How could I *not* get mad at you? But aside from all that, I had been feeling for a long time that it would be better for me if I kept away from you for a while. To get things clear in my head."

"What kinds of things?"

"Our *relationship*, of course. It was getting to the point where I enjoyed being with *you* way better than being with *him*. I mean, don't you think there's something weird about that? And difficult? Of course I still like him. He's a little self-centered and narrow-minded and kind of a fascist, but he's got a lot of good points, and he's the first guy I ever got serious about. But you, well, you're special to me. When I'm with you I feel something is just right. I believe in you. I like you. I don't want to let you go. I was getting more and more confused, so I went to him and asked him what I should do. He told me to stop seeing you. He said if I was going to see you, I should break up with him."

"So what did you do?"

"I broke up with him. Just like that." Midori put a Marlboro in her mouth, shielded it with her hand as she lit up, and inhaled.

"Why?"

"'Why?'!" she screamed. "Are you *crazy*? You know the English subjunctive, you understand trigonometry, you can read Marx, and you don't know the answer to something as simple as *that*? Why do you even have to *ask*? Why do you have to make a girl *say* something like this? I like *you* more than I like *him*, that's all. I wish I had fallen in love with somebody a little more handsome, of course. But I didn't. I fell in love with *you!*"

I tried to speak, but I felt the words catching in my throat.

Midori threw her cigarette into a puddle. "Will you *please* get that look off your face? You're gonna make me cry. Don't worry, I *know* you're in love with somebody else. I'm not expecting anything from you. But the least you can do is give me a hug. These have been two tough months for me."

I put my umbrella up, and we went behind the games area and held each other close. Our bodies strained against each other, and our lips met. The smell of the rain clung to her hair and her jeans jacket. Girls' bodies were so soft and warm! I could feel her breasts pressing against my chest through our clothing. How long had it been since my last physical contact with another human being?

"The day I last saw you, that night I talked to him, and we broke up," Midori said.

"I love you," I said to her. "From the bottom of my heart. I don't ever want to let you go again. But there's nothing I can do. I can't make a move."

"Because of her?"

I nodded.

"Tell me, have you slept with her?"

"Once. A year ago."

"And you haven't seen her since then?"

"I *have* seen her: twice. But we didn't do anything."

"Why not? Doesn't she love you?"

"That's hard to say," I said. "It's really complicated. And mixed up. And it's been going on for such a long time, I don't know what's what anymore. And neither does she. All I know is, I have a kind of responsibility in all this as a human being, and I can't just turn my back on it. At least, that's how I feel about it now. Even if she isn't in love with me."

"Let me just tell you this, Watanabe," said Midori, pressing her cheek against my neck. "I'm a real, live girl, with real, live blood gushing through my veins. You're holding me in your arms and I'm telling you that I love you. I'm ready to do anything you tell me to do. I may be a little crazy, but I'm a good kid, and honest, and I work hard, I'm kinda cute, I've got nice boobs, I'm a good cook, and my father left me a trust fund. I mean, I'm a real bargain, don't you think? If you don't take me, I'm gonna end up going somewhere else."

"I need time," I said. "I need time to think and sort things out, and make some decisions. I'm sorry, but that's all I can say at this point."

"Yeah, but you *do* love me from the bottom of your heart, right? And you never want to let me go again, right?"

"I said it and I meant it."

Midori pulled away from me with a smile on her face. "O.K., I'll wait! I believe in you," she said. "But when you take me, you take *only* me. And when you hold me in your arms, you think *only* about *me*. Is that clear?"

"I know exactly what you mean."

"I don't care what you do to me, but I don't want you to hurt me. I've had enough hurt already in my life. More than enough. Now I want to be happy."

I drew her close and kissed her on the mouth.

"Drop the damn umbrella and wrap *both* your arms around me — hard!" she said.

"But we'll get soaking wet!"

"So what? I want you to stop thinking and hold me tight! I've been waiting two whole months for this!"

I set the umbrella down and held her close in the rain. The dull rush of tires on the highway enveloped us like a fog. The rain fell without a break, without a sound, soaking her hair and mine, running like tears down our cheeks, down to her jeans jacket and my yellow nylon windbreaker, spreading in dark stains.

"What do you say we go back under the roof?" I said.

"Come to my place. There's nobody home now. We'll both catch colds like this."

"It's true."

"It's kinda like we just swam across a river," Midori said, smiling. "What a great feeling!"

We bought a good-size towel in the linen department and took turns going into the bathroom to dry our hair. Then we rode the subway, with the necessary transfers, to her apartment in Myogadani. She let me shower first and then she showered. Lending me a bathrobe to wear while my clothes dried, Midori changed into a polo shirt and skirt. We sat at the kitchen table drinking coffee.

"Tell me about yourself," Midori said.

"What about me?"

"Hmm, I don't know, what do you hate?"

"Chicken and VD and barbers who talk too much."

"What else?"

"Lonely April nights and lacy telephone covers."

"What else?"

I shook my head. "I can't think of anything else."

"My boyfriend—which is to say, my *ex*-boyfriend—had all kinds of things he hated. Like when I wore too-short skirts, or when I smoked, or how I got drunk right away, or said disgusting things, or criticized his friends. So if there's anything about me you don't like, just tell me, and I'll fix it if I can."

"I can't think of anything," I said after giving it some thought. "There's nothing."

"Really?"

"I like everything you wear, and I like what you do and say and how you walk and how you get drunk. Everything."

"You mean I'm really O.K. just the way I am?"

"I don't know how you could change, so you must be fine the way you are."

"How much do you love me?" Midori asked.

"Enough to melt all the tigers in the world to butter," I said.

"Mmm," she said with a hint of satisfaction. "Will you hold me again?"

We got into her bed and held each other, kissing as the sound of the rain filled our ears. Then we talked about everything from the formation of the universe to our preferences in the hardness of boiled eggs.

"I wonder what ants do on rainy days?" Midori asked.

"No idea," I said. "They're hard workers, so they probably spend the day cleaning house or taking inventory."

"If they work so hard, how come they don't evolve? They've been the same forever."

"I don't know," I said. "Maybe their body structure isn't suited to evolving—compared with monkeys, say."

"Hey, Watanabe, there's a lot of stuff you don't know. I thought you knew everything."

"It's a big world out there," I said.

"High mountains, deep oceans," Midori said. She put her hand inside my bathrobe and took hold of my erection. Then, with a gulp, she said, "Hey, Watanabe, all kidding aside, this is not gonna work. I could never get this big, hard thing inside me. No way."

"You're kidding," I said with a sigh.

"Yup," she said, giggling. "Don't worry. It'll be just fine. I'm sure it'll fit. Uh, mind if I have a look?"

"Feel free."

Midori burrowed under the covers and groped me all over down there, stretching the skin of my penis, weighing my testicles in her palm. Then she poked her head out and released her breath. "I love it!" she said. "No flattery intended! I really love it!"

"Thank you," I said with simple gratitude.

"But really, Watanabe, you don't want to do it with me, do you—until you get all that business straightened out?"

"There's no way I don't want to do it with you," I said. "I'm going crazy, I want to do it so bad. But it just wouldn't be right."

"You're so damned stubborn! If I were you, I'd just *do* it—and think about it afterward."

"You would?"

"Just kidding," Midori said in a tiny voice. "I probably wouldn't do it, either, if I were you. And that's what I love about you. That's what I really really love about you."

"How much do you love me?" I asked, but she didn't answer. Instead, she pressed against me, put her lips on my nipple and began to move the hand she had wrapped around my penis. The first thing that occurred to me was how different this was from the way Naoko moved her hand. Both were gentle and wonderful, but something was different about the way they did it, and so it felt like a totally different experience.

"Hey, Watanabe, I bet you're thinking about that other girl."

"Not true," I lied.

"Really?"

"Really."

"Because I would really hate that."

"I *can't* think about anybody else," I said.

"Want to touch my breasts, or down there?" Midori asked.

"Oh, boy, I'd love to, but I'd better not. If we do all those things at once, it'll be too much for me."

Midori nodded and rustled around under the covers, pulling her panties off and holding them against the tip of my penis.

"You can come into this," she said.

"But it'll make a mess of them."

"Stop it, will you? You're gonna make me cry," Midori said as if on the verge of tears. "All I have to do is wash them. So don't hold back, just let yourself come all you want. If you're worried about my panties, buy me a new pair. Or are they going to keep you from coming because they're mine?"

"No way," I said.

"Go right ahead, then, let go."

When I was through, Midori inspected my semen. "Wow, that's a huge amount!"

"Too much?"

"Nah, that's O.K., silly. Come all you want," she said with a smile. Then she kissed me.

In the evening, Midori did some shopping in the neighborhood and made dinner. We ate tempura and rice with green peas at the kitchen table, and washed it all down with beer.

"Eat a lot and make lots of semen," Midori said. "Then I'll be nice and help you get rid of it."

"Thanks very much," I said.

"I know all kinds of ways to do it. I learned from the women's magazines when we had the bookstore. Once they had this special edition all about how to take care of your husband so he won't cheat on you while you're pregnant and can't have sex. There's tons of ways. Wanna try 'em?"

"I can hardly wait," I said.

After saying good-bye to Midori, I bought a newspaper at the station, but when I opened it on the train, I realized I had absolutely no desire to read a paper and in fact couldn't understand what it said. All I could do was glare at the incomprehensible page of print and wonder what was going to happen to me from now on, and how the things around me would be changing. I felt as if the world was pulsating every now and then. I released a deep sigh and closed my eyes. With regard to what I had done that day, I felt not the slightest regret; I knew for certain that if I had it to do all over again, I would live this day in exactly the same way again. I would hold Midori tight on the roof in the rain; I would get soaking wet with her; and I would let her fingers bring me to climax in her bed. I had no doubts about those things. I loved Midori, and I was happy that she had come back to me. The two of us could make it, that was certain. As Midori herself had said, she was a real, live girl with blood in her veins, and she was putting her warm body in my arms. It had been all I could do to suppress the intense desire I had to strip her naked, throw open her body, and sink myself in her warmth. There was no way I could have made myself stop her once she was holding my penis and moving her hand. I wanted her to do it, she wanted to do it, and we were in love. Who could have stopped such a thing? It was true: I loved Midori. And I had probably known as much for a while. I had just been avoiding the conclusion for a very long time.

The problem was that I could never explain these developments to Naoko. It would have been hard enough at any point, but with Naoko in her present condition, there was no way I could tell her I had fallen in love with another girl. And besides, I still loved Naoko. Bent and twisted as that love might be, I did love her. Somewhere inside me, there was still preserved a broad, open space, untouched, for Naoko and no one else.

One thing I could do was to write a letter to Reiko that confessed everything with total honesty. At home, I sat on the veranda, watching the rain pour down on the garden at night and assembling phrases in my head.

Then I went to my desk and wrote the letter. "It is almost unbearable to me that I now have to write a letter like this to you," I began. I summarized my relationship with Midori and explained what had happened that day.

I have always loved Naoko, and I still love her. But there is a decisive finality to what exists between Midori and me. It has an irresistible power that is bound to sweep me into the future. What I feel for Naoko is a tremendously quiet and gentle and transparent love, but what I feel for Midori is a wholly different emotion. It stands and walks on its own, living and breathing and throbbing and shaking me to the roots of my being. I don't know what to do. I'm confused. I'm not trying to make excuses for myself, but I do believe that I have lived as sincerely as I knew how. I have never lied to anyone, and I have taken care over the years not to hurt other people. And yet I find myself having been tossed into this labyrinth. How can this be? I can't explain it. I don't know what I should do. Can you tell me, Reiko? You're the only one I can turn to for advice.

I mailed the letter that night with special-delivery postage attached.

REIKO'S ANSWER CAME five days later, dated June 17.

Let me start with the good news. Naoko has been improving far more rapidly than anyone could have expected. I talked to her once on the phone, and she spoke with real lucidity. She may even be able to come back here before too long.

Now, about you.

I think you take everything too seriously. Loving another person is a wonderful thing, and if that love is sincere, no one ends up tossed into a labyrinth. You have to have more faith in yourself.

My advice to you is very simple. First of all, if you are drawn so strongly to this person Midori, it is only natural for you to have fallen in love with her. It might go well, or it might not. But love is like that. When you fall in love, the natural thing to do is give yourself to it. That's what I think. It's just one form of sincerity.

Second, as to whether or not you should have sex with Midori, that is for you to figure out. I can't say a thing. Talk it over with Midori and reach your own conclusion, one that makes sense to you.

Third, don't tell any of this to Naoko. If things should develop to the point where you absolutely have to tell her, then you and I will come up with a good plan together. So now, just keep it quiet. Leave it to me.

The fourth thing I have to say is that you have been such a great source of strength for Naoko that even if you no longer have the feelings of a lover toward her, there is still a lot you can do for her. So don't brood over everything in that superserious way of yours. All of us (by which I mean *all* of us, both normal and not-so-normal) are imperfect human beings living in an imperfect world. We don't live with the mechanical precision of a bank account or by measuring all our lines and angles with rulers and protractors. Am I right?

My own personal feeling is that Midori sounds like a great girl. I understand just reading your letter why you would be drawn to her. And I understand, too, why you would also be drawn to Naoko. There's nothing the least bit sinful about it. Things like that happen all the time in this great big world of ours. It's like taking a boat out on a beautiful lake on a beautiful day and thinking both the sky and the lake are beautiful. So stop eating yourself up alive. Things will go where they're supposed to go if you just let them take their natural course. Despite your best efforts, people are going to be hurt when it's time for them to be hurt. Life is like that. I know I sound like I'm preaching from a podium, but it's about time for you to learn to live like this. You try too hard to make life fit your way of doing things. If you don't want to spend time in an insane asylum, you have to open up a little more and let yourself go with life's natural flow. I'm just a powerless and imperfect woman, but still there are times when I think to myself how wonderful life can be! Believe me, it's true! So stop what you're doing this minute and get happy. *Work* at making yourself happy!

Needless to say, I do feel sorry that you and Naoko could not see things through to a happy ending. But who can say what's best? That's why you need to grab whatever chance you have for happiness where you find it, and not worry too much about other people. My experience tells me that we get no more than two or three such chances in a lifetime, and if we let them go, we regret it for the rest of our lives.

I'm playing the guitar every day for no one in particular. It seems kind of pointless. I don't like dark, rainy nights, either. I hope I'll have another chance to play my guitar and eat grapes with you and Naoko in the room with me.

Ah, well, until then—

Reiko Ishida

eleven

REIKO WROTE TO ME SEVERAL TIMES AFTER NAOKO'S DEATH. IT was not my fault, she said. It was nobody's fault, any more than you could blame someone for the rain. But I never answered her. What could I have said? What good would it have done? Naoko no longer existed in this world; she had become a fistful of ash.

They held a quiet funeral for Naoko in Kobe at the end of August, and when it was over, I went back to Tokyo. I told my landlord I would be away for a while and my boss at the Italian restaurant that I wouldn't be coming in to work. To Midori I wrote a short note: I couldn't say anything just yet, but I hoped she would wait for me a little longer. I spent the next three days in movie theaters, and after I had seen every new movie in Tokyo, I packed my knapsack, took all my money out of the bank, went to Shinjuku Station, and took the first express train I could find heading out of town.

Where I went in my travels, it's impossible for me to recall. I remember the sights and sounds and smells clearly enough, but the names of the towns are gone, as well as any sense of the order in which I traveled from place to place. I would move from town to town by train or bus or hitching a ride in a truck, spreading my sleeping bag out in empty lots or stations or parks or on riverbanks or the seashore. I once got them to let me sleep in the corner of a neighborhood police station, and another time slept by the side of a graveyard. I didn't care where I slept, as long as I was out of people's way and could stay in my sack as long as I felt like it. Exhausted from walking, I would crawl into my sleeping bag, gulp down some cheap whiskey, and go right to sleep. In nice towns, people would bring me food and mosquito coils, and in not-so-nice towns, people would call the police and have me chased out of parks. It made no difference to me one way or the other. All I wanted was to put myself to sleep in towns I didn't know.

When I ran low on money, I would work as a laborer for a few days until I had what I needed. There was always some work for me to do. I just kept moving from one town to the next, no destination in mind. The world was big and full of weird things and strange people. One time I called Midori because I had to hear her voice.

"School started a long time ago, you know," she said. "Some courses are even asking for papers already. What are you going to *do*? Do you realize you've been out of touch for three whole weeks now? Where are you? What are you doing?"

"Sorry, but I can't go back to Tokyo yet. Not yet."

"And that's all you're going to tell me?"

"There's really nothing more I can say at this point. Maybe in October . . ."

Midori hung up without a word.

I went on with my travels. Every once in a while, I'd stay at a flophouse and take a bath and shave. What I saw in the mirror looked terrible. The sun had dried my skin out, my eyes were sunken, and some odd stains and cuts marked my bony cheeks. I looked as if I had just crawled out of a cave somewhere, but it was me after all. It was me.

By that time, I was moving down the coast as far from Tokyo as I could get—maybe in Tottori or the northern shore of Hyogo. Walking along the seashore was easy. I could always find a comfortable place to sleep in the sand. I'd make a fire from driftwood and roast some dried fish I bought from a local fisherman. Then I'd swallow some whiskey and listen to the waves while I thought about Naoko. It was too strange to think that she was dead and no longer part of this world. I couldn't absorb the truth of it. I couldn't believe it. I had heard the nails being driven into the lid of her coffin, but I still couldn't adjust to the fact that she had returned to nothingness.

No, the image of her was still too vivid in my memory. I could still see her enclosing my penis in her mouth, her hair falling across my belly. I could still feel her warmth, her breath against me, and that helpless moment when I could do nothing but come. I could bring all this back as clearly as if it had happened five minutes earlier, and I felt sure that Naoko was still beside me, that I could just reach out and touch her. But no, she was not there; her flesh no longer existed in this world.

Nights when it was impossible for me to sleep, the images of Naoko would come back to me. There was no way I could stop them. Too many memories of her were crammed inside me, and as soon as one of them found the slightest opening, the rest would force their way out in an endless stream, an unstoppable flood: Naoko in her yellow rain cape cleaning the birdhouse and carrying the feed bag that rainy morning; the caved-in birthday cake and the feel of Naoko's tears soaking through my shirt (yes, it had been raining then, too); Naoko walking beside me in winter wearing her camel's hair coat; Naoko touching the barrette she always wore; Naoko peering at me with those incredibly clear eyes of hers; Naoko sitting on the sofa, legs drawn up beneath her blue nightgown, chin resting on her knees.

The memories would slam against me like the waves of an incoming tide, sweeping my body along to some strange new place—a place where I lived with the dead. There Naoko lived, and I could speak with her and hold her in my arms. Death in that place was not a decisive element that brought life to an end. There, death was but one of many elements comprising life. There Naoko lived with death inside her. And to me she said, "Don't worry, it's only death. Don't let it bother you."

I felt no sadness in that strange place. Death was death, and Naoko was Naoko. "What's the problem?" she asked me with a bashful smile, "I'm here, aren't I?" Her familiar little gestures soothed my heart and gave me healing. "If this is death," I thought to myself, "then death is not so bad." "It's true," said Naoko, "death is nothing much. It's just death. Things are so easy for me here." Naoko spoke to me in the spaces between the crashing of the dark waves.

Eventually, though, the tide would pull back, and I would be left on the beach alone. Powerless, I could go nowhere; sorrow itself would envelop me in deep darkness until the tears came. I felt less that I was crying than that the tears were simply oozing out of me like perspiration.

I had learned one thing from Kizuki's death, and I believed that I had made it a part of myself in the form of a philosophy: "Death is not the opposite of life but an innate part of life."

By living our lives, we nurture death. True as this might be, it was only one of the truths we had to learn. What I learned from Naoko's death was this: no truth can cure the sorrow we feel from losing a loved one. No truth, no sincerity, no strength, no kindness can cure that sorrow. All we can do is see it through to the end and learn something from it, but what we learn will be no help in facing the next sorrow that comes to us without warning. Hearing the waves at night, listening to the sound of the wind, day after day I focused on these thoughts of mine. Knapsack on my back, sand in my hair, I moved farther and farther west, surviving on a diet of whiskey, bread, and water.

ONE WINDY EVENING, as I lay wrapped in my sleeping bag, weeping, by the side of an abandoned hulk, a young fisherman happened by and offered me a cigarette. I accepted it and had my first smoke in over a year. He asked why I was crying, and almost by reflex I told him that my mother had died. I couldn't take the sadness, I said, and so I was on the road. He expressed his deep sympathy and brought a big bottle of sake and two glasses from his house.

The wind tore along the sandy beach as we sat there drinking. He told me that he had lost his mother when he was sixteen. Never healthy, she had worn herself out working from morning to night. I half-listened to him, sipping my sake and grunting in response every now and then. I felt as if I were hearing a story from some far-off world. What the hell was this guy talking about? I wondered, and all of a sudden an intense rage struck me; I wanted to wring his neck. Who gives a damn about your mother? I lost Naoko! Her beautiful flesh has vanished from this world! Why the hell are you telling me about your goddamn mother?!

But my rage disappeared as quickly as it had flared up. I closed my eyes and went on half-listening to the fisherman's endless talk. Eventually he asked me if I had eaten. No, I said, but in my knapsack I had bread and cheese, a tomato, and a piece of chocolate. What had I eaten for lunch? he asked. Bread and cheese, tomato, and chocolate, I answered. "Wait here," he said, and ran off. I tried to stop him, but he disappeared into the darkness without looking back.

All I could do was go on drinking my sake. The shore was littered with paper flecks from fireworks that had been exploded on the sand, and waves crashed against the beach with a mad roar. A scrawny dog came along wagging its tail and sniffing around my little campfire for something to eat but eventually gave up and wandered off.

The young fisherman came back a half hour later with two boxes of sushi and a new bottle of sake. I should eat the top box right away because that had fish in it, he said, but the bottom box had only nori rolls and deep-fried tofu skins so they would last through tomorrow. He filled both our glasses with sake from the new bottle. I thanked him and polished off the whole top box myself, though it had more than enough for two. After we had drunk as much sake as we could manage, he offered to put me up for the night, but when I said I would rather sleep alone on the beach, he left it at that. As he stood to go, he took a folded five-thousand-yen note from his pocket and shoved it into the pocket of my shirt. "Here," he said, "get yourself some healthy food. You look awful." I said he had done more than enough for me and that I couldn't accept money on top of everything else, but he refused to take it back. "It's not money," he said, "it's my feelings. Don't think about it too much, just take it." All I could do was thank him and accept the money.

When he had gone, I suddenly thought about my old girlfriend, the one I had first slept with in my third year of high school. Chills ran through me as I realized how badly I had treated her. I had hardly ever thought about *her* thoughts or feelings or the pain I had caused her. She was such a sweet and gentle thing, but at the time I had taken her sweetness for granted and later hardly gave her a second thought. What was she doing now? I wondered. And had she forgiven me?

A wave of nausea came over me, and I vomited by the old ship. My head hurt from too much sake, and I felt bad about having lied to the fisherman and taken his money. It was time for me to get back to Tokyo, I decided; I couldn't keep this up forever. I stuffed my sleeping bag into my knapsack, slipped my arms through the straps, and walked to the local railway station. I told the man at the ticket window that I wanted to go to Tokyo as soon as possible. He checked his schedule and said I could make it as far as Osaka by morning if I transferred from one night train to another, then I could take the bullet train from there. I thanked him and used the five-thousand-yen bill I had gotten from the fisherman to buy a ticket to Tokyo. Waiting for the train, I bought a newspaper and checked the date: October 2, 1970. So I had been traveling for a full month. I knew I had to go back to the real world.

The month of traveling neither lifted my spirits nor softened the blow of Naoko's death. I arrived back in Tokyo in pretty much the same state in which I had left. I couldn't even bring myself to phone Midori. What could I say to her? How could I begin? "It's all over now; you and I can be happy together"? No, that was out of the question. However I might phrase it, though, the facts were the same: Naoko was dead, and Midori was still here. Naoko was a pile of white ash, and Midori was a living, breathing human being.

I was overcome with a sense of my own defilement. Though I returned to Tokyo I did nothing for days but shut myself up in my room. My memory remained fixed on the dead rather than the living. The rooms I had set aside in there for Naoko were shuttered, the furniture draped in white, the windowsills dusty. I spent the better part of each day in those rooms. And I thought about Kizuki. "So you finally made Naoko yours," I heard myself telling him. "Oh, well, she was yours to begin with. Now, maybe, she's where she belongs. But in this world, in this imperfect world of the living, I did the best I could for Naoko. I tried to establish a new life for the two of us. But forget it, Kizuki. I'm giving her to you. You're the one she chose, after all. In woods as dark as the depths of her own heart, she hanged herself. Once upon a time, you dragged a part of me into the world of the dead, and now Naoko has dragged another part of me into that world. Sometimes I feel like a caretaker of a museum—a huge, empty museum where no one ever comes, and I'm watching over it for no one but myself.

THE FOURTH DAY after my return to Tokyo, I got a letter from Reiko. Special delivery. It was a simple note: "I haven't been able to get in touch with you for weeks, and I'm worried. Please give me a call. At nine A.M. and nine P.M. I will be waiting by the telephone."

I called her at nine o'clock that night. Reiko picked up after one ring.

"Are you O.K.?" she asked.

"More or less," I said.

"Do you mind if I come visit you the day after tomorrow?"

"Visit me? You mean here in Tokyo?"

"That's exactly what I mean. I want to have a good long talk with you."

"You're leaving the sanatorium?"

"It's the only way I can come see you, isn't it? Anyway, it's about time for me to get out of this place. I've been here eight years, after all. If they keep me any longer, I'll start to rot."

I found it difficult to speak. After a short silence, Reiko went on, "I'll be on the three-twenty bullet train the day after tomorrow. Will you meet me at the station? Do you still remember what I look like? Or have you lost interest in me now that Naoko's dead?"

"No way," I said. "See you at Tokyo Station the day after tomorrow at three-twenty."

"You won't have any trouble recognizing me. I'm the old lady with the guitar case. There aren't many of those."

AND IN FACT, I had no trouble finding Reiko in the crowd. She wore a man's tweed jacket, white slacks, and red sneakers. Her hair was as short as ever, with the usual clumps sticking up. In her right hand she held a brown leather suitcase, and in her left hand a black guitar case. She gave me a big, wrinkly smile the moment she spotted me, and I found myself smiling back. I took her suitcase and walked beside her to the train for the western suburbs.

"Hey, Watanabe, how long have you been wearing that awful face? Or is that the 'in' look in Tokyo these days?"

"I was traveling for a while, ate junk the whole time," I said. "How'd you like the bullet train?"

"Awful!" she said. "You can't open the windows. I wanted to buy a boxed lunch from one of the platform vendors."

"They sell them on board, you know."

"Yeah, overpriced plastic sandwiches. A starving horse wouldn't touch that stuff. I always used to enjoy the boxed lunches at Gotenba Station."

"Once upon a time, before the bullet train."

"Well, *I'm* from once upon a time before the bullet train!"

On the way out to Kichijoji, Reiko watched the Musashino landscape passing the train window with all the curiosity of a tourist.

"Has it changed much in eight years?" I asked.

"You don't know what I'm feeling now, do you, Watanabe?"

"No, I don't."

"I'm scared," she said. "So scared, I could go crazy just like that. I don't know what I'm supposed to do, flung out here all by myself." She paused. "But 'Go crazy just like that.' Kind of a cool expression, don't you think?"

I smiled and took her hand. "Don't worry," I said. "You're gonna be O.K. Your own strength got you this far."

"It wasn't my own strength that got me out of that place," Reiko said. "It was Naoko and you. I couldn't stand it there without Naoko, and I had to come to Tokyo to talk with you. That's all. If nothing had happened I probably would've spent the rest of my life there."

I nodded.

"What're you planning to do from now on?" I asked Reiko.

"I'm going to Asahikawa," she said. "Way up in the wilds of Hokkaido! An old college friend of mine runs a music school there, and she's been asking me for two or three years now to help her out. I told her it was too cold for me. I mean, I *finally* get my freedom back and I'm supposed to go to Asahikawa? It's kinda hard to get excited about a place like that—some hole in the ground."

"It's not so awful," I said, laughing. "I've been there. It's not a bad little town. Got its own special atmosphere."

"Are you sure?"

"Absolutely. It's way better than staying in Tokyo."

"Oh, well," she said. "I don't have anyplace else to go, and I've already sent my stuff there. Hey, Watanabe, promise me you'll come and visit me in Asahikawa."

"Sure I will. But do you have to leave right away? Can't you stay in Tokyo awhile?"

"I'd like to hang around here a few days if I can. Can you put me up? I won't get in your way."

"No problem," I said. "I've got a big closet I can sleep in, in my sleeping bag."

"I can't do that to you."

"No, really. It's a *huge* closet."

Reiko tapped out a rhythm on the guitar case between her legs. "I'm probably going to have to condition myself a little before I go to Asahikawa. I'm just not used to being in the outside world. There's a lot of stuff I don't get, and I'm nervous. Think you can help me out a little? You're the only one I can ask."

"I'll do anything I can to help you," I said.

"I hope I'm not getting in your way," she said.

"I don't have any *way* for you to get *in*," I said.

She looked at me and turned up the corners of her mouth in a smile, but said nothing.

WE HARDLY TALKED the rest of the way to Kichijoji Station or on the bus to my place. We traded a few random comments on the changes in Tokyo and Reiko's time at the College of Music and my one trip to Asahikawa, but said nothing about Naoko. Ten months had gone by since I last saw Reiko, but walking by her side I felt strangely calmed and comforted. This was a familiar feeling, I thought, and then it occurred to me it was the way I used to feel when walking the streets of Tokyo with Naoko. And just as Naoko and I had shared the dead Kizuki, Reiko and I shared the dead Naoko. This thought made it impossible for me to go on talking. Reiko continued speaking for a while, but when she realized that I wasn't saying anything, she also fell silent. Neither of us said a word on the bus.

It was one of those early autumn afternoons when the light is sharp and clear, exactly as it had been a year earlier when I visited Naoko in Kyoto. The clouds were white and narrow as bones, the sky wide open and high. The fragrance of the breeze, the tone of the light, the presence of tiny flowers in the grass, the subtle reverberations that accompanied sounds: all these told me that autumn had come again, increasing the distance between me and the dead with each cycle of the seasons. Kizuki was still seventeen, and Naoko twenty-one: forever.

"Oh, what a relief to come to a place like this!" Reiko said, looking all around as we stepped off the bus.

"'Cause there's nothing here," I said.

As I led her through the back gate and the garden to my cottage, Reiko was impressed by everything she saw.

"This is terrific!" she said. "You *made* these shelves and the desk?"

"Sure did!" I said, pouring tea.

"You're obviously good with your hands. And you keep the place so clean!"

"Storm Trooper's influence," I said. "He made me clean-crazy. Not that my landlord's complaining."

"Oh, your landlord! I have to go introduce myself to him. That's his place on the other side of the garden, I suppose."

"Introduce yourself to him? What for?"

"What do you mean 'what for?' Some weird old lady shows up in your place and starts picking on the guitar, he's going to wonder what's going on. Better to start out on the right foot. I even brought a box of tea sweets for him."

"Very clever," I said.

"The wisdom that comes with age. I'm going to tell him I'm your aunt on your mother's side, visiting from Kyoto, so don't contradict me. The age difference comes in handy at times like this. Nobody's going to get suspicious."

Reiko took the box of sweets from her bag and went off to pay her respects. I sat on the veranda, drinking another cup of tea and playing with the cat. Twenty minutes went by, and when Reiko finally came back, she pulled a tin of rice crackers from her bag and said it was a present for me.

"What were you talking about so long over there?" I asked, munching on a cracker.

"You, of course," said Reiko, cradling the cat and rubbing her cheek against it. "He says you're a very proper young man, a serious student."

"Are you sure he was talking about me?"

"There is not the slightest doubt in my mind that he was talking about you," she said with a laugh. Then, noticing my guitar, she picked it up, adjusted the tuning, and played Antonio Carlos Jobim's "Desafinado." It had been months since I had last heard Reiko's guitar, and it gave me the old, warm feeling.

"You practicing the guitar?" she asked.

"It was kicking around the landlord's storehouse, so I borrowed it and plunk on it once in a while. That's all."

"I'll give you a lesson later. Absolutely free." Reiko put the guitar down and took off her tweed jacket. Sitting against the veranda post, she smoked a cigarette. She was wearing a madras short-sleeve shirt.

"Nice shirt, don't you think?" she asked.

"It is," I said. In fact it *was* a good-looking shirt, with a handsome pattern.

"It's Naoko's," said Reiko. "I bet you didn't know we were the same size. Especially when she first came to the sanatorium. She put on a little weight after that, but still we were pretty much the same size: blouses, slacks, shoes, hats. Bras were about the only thing we couldn't share. I've got practically nothing here. So we were always trading clothes. Actually, it was more like joint ownership."

Now that she mentioned it, I saw that Reiko's build was almost identical to Naoko's. Because of the shape of her face and her thin arms and legs, she had always given me the impression of being smaller and slimmer than Naoko, but in fact she was surprisingly solid.

"The jacket and pants are hers, too," said Reiko. "It's all hers. Does it bother you to see me wearing her stuff?"

"Not at all," I said. "I'm sure Naoko would be glad to have somebody wearing her clothing—especially you."

"It's strange," Reiko said with a little snap of the fingers. "Naoko didn't leave a will or anything—except where her clothes were concerned. She scribbled one line on a memo pad on her desk. 'Please give all my clothes to Reiko.' She was a funny one, don't you think? Why would she be concerned about her clothes of all things when she's getting ready to die? Who gives a damn about clothes? She must have had tons of other things she wanted to say."

"Maybe not," I said.

Puffing on her cigarette, Reiko seemed lost in thought. Then she said, "You want to hear the whole story, in order, I suppose."

"I do," I said. "Please tell me everything."

"TESTS AT THE HOSPITAL in Osaka showed that Naoko's condition was improving for the moment but that she should stay there on a somewhat longer-term basis so that they could continue the intensive therapy for its future benefits. I told you that much in my letter—the one I sent you somewhere around the tenth of August."

"Right. I read that letter."

"Well, on the twenty-fourth of August I got a call from Naoko's mother asking if it was O.K. for Naoko to come visit me at the sanatorium. Naoko wanted to pack up the things she had left with me and, because she wouldn't be able to see me for a while, she wanted to have a nice long talk with me, and maybe spend one night in our apartment. I said that would be fine. I wanted to see her something awful and to have a talk with her. So Naoko and her mother showed up the next day, the twenty-fifth, in a taxi. The three of us worked together, packing up Naoko's things and chatting away. Late in the afternoon, Naoko said it would be O.K. for her mother to go home, that she'd be fine, so they called a cab and the mother left. We weren't worried at all because Naoko seemed to be in such great spirits. In fact, until then I had been very worried. I had been expecting her to be depressed and worn out and emaciated. I mean, I knew how much the kind of testing and therapy and stuff they do at those hospitals can take out of you, so I had some real doubts about this visit. But one look at her was all it took to convince me she'd be O.K. She looked a lot health-ier than I had imagined and she was smiling and joking around and talk-ing in a much more normal way than when I had last seen her. She had been to the beauty parlor and was showing off her new hairdo. So I figured there would be nothing to worry about even if her mother left the two of us alone. Naoko told me that *this* time she was going to let those hospital doctors cure her once and for all, and I said that that would probably be the best thing to do. So then the two of us went out for a walk, still talking the whole time, mainly about the future. Naoko told me that what she'd really like was for the two of us to get out of the sanatorium and go live together somewhere."

"Live together? You and Naoko?"

"That's right," said Reiko with a little shrug. "So I told her it sounded good to me, but what about Watanabe? And she said, 'Don't worry, I'll get everything straight with him.' That's all. Then she talked about where she and I would live and what we'd do, that kind of thing. After that we went to the birdhouse and played with the birds."

I took a beer from the refrigerator and opened it. Reiko lit another ciga-rette. The cat was sound asleep in her lap.

"That girl had everything figured out for herself. I'm sure that's why she was so full of energy and smiling and healthy-looking. It must have been such a load off her mind to feel she knew exactly what she was going to do. So then we finished going through her stuff and throwing what she didn't need into the metal drum in the yard and burning it: the notebook she had been using to keep a diary, and all the letters she had been getting. Your letters, too. This seemed kind of strange to me, so I asked her why she was burning stuff like that. I mean, she had always been so careful about putting your letters away in a safe place and reading them over and over. She said, 'I'm getting rid of everything from the past so I can be reborn in the future.' I guess I pretty much took her at her word. It had its own kind of logic to it, sort of. I remember thinking how much I wanted for her to get healthy and happy. She was so sweet and lovely that day: I wish you could have seen her!

"When that was over, we went to the dining hall for supper the way we used to do. Then we bathed and I opened a bottle of good wine that I had been keeping for a special occasion like this and we drank and I played the guitar. The Beatles, as always: 'Norwegian Wood,' 'Michelle,' her favorites. Both of us were feeling pretty good. We turned out the lights, got undressed, and lay in our beds. It was one of those steaming hot nights. We had the windows wide open, but there was hardly a breath of wind. It was black as ink outside, the crickets were screaming, and the smell of the summer grass was so thick in the room it was hard to breathe. All of a sudden, Naoko started talking about you—about the night she had sex with you. In incredible detail. How you took her clothes off, how you touched her, how she found herself growing wet, how you went inside her, how wonderful it felt: she told me all of this in vivid detail. So I asked her, 'Why are you telling me this now, all of a sudden?' I mean, up to then, she had never spoken openly to me about sex. Of course, we had had some frank talk about sex as a kind of therapy, but she had been too embarrassed to get into anything specific. Now I couldn't stop her. I was shocked.

"So she says, 'I don't know, I just feel like talking about it. I'll stop if you'd rather not hear it.'

"I said, 'No, that's O.K. If you've got something you need to talk about, you'd better get it all out. I'll listen to anything you have to say.'

"So she went on with her story. 'When he went inside me, I couldn't believe how much it hurt. It was my first time, after all. I was so wet, he slipped right in, but still, my brain fogged over—it hurt so much. He put it in as far as he could, I thought, but then he lifted my legs and went in even farther. That sent chills all through my body, like I was soaking in ice water. My arms and legs went numb, and a wave of cold went through me. I didn't know what was happening. I thought I might die right then and there, and I didn't care one way or the other. But he realized I was in pain, so he stopped moving, and still deep inside me, he started kissing me all over—my hair, my neck, my breasts—for a long, long time. Little by little, the warmth returned to my body, and then, very slowly, he started to move. Oh, Reiko, it was so wonderful! Now it felt as if my brain was just going to melt away. I wanted to stay like that forever, to stay in his arms for the rest of my life. That's how great it was.'

"So I said to her, 'If it was so great, why didn't you just stay with Watanabe and keep doing it every day?' "

"But she said, 'No, Reiko, I knew it would never happen again. I knew this was something that would come to me once, and leave, and never come back. This would be a once-in-a-lifetime thing. I had never felt anything like it before, and I've never felt anything like it since. I've never felt that I wanted to do it again, and I've never grown wet like that again.'

"Of course, I explained to her that this was something that often happened to young women and that, in most cases, it cures itself with age. And, after all, it *had* worked that one time: there was no need to worry it wouldn't happen again. I myself had had all kinds of trouble when I was first married.

"But she said, 'No, that's not it, Reiko. I'm not worried about that at all. I just don't want anybody going inside me again. I just don't want to be violated like that again—by anybody.'"

I drank down my beer, and Reiko finished her second cigarette. The cat stretched itself in Reiko's lap, found a new position, and went back to sleep. Reiko seemed at a loss how to go on until she had lit her third cigarette.

"After that, Naoko began to sob. I sat on the edge of her bed and stroked her hair. 'Don't worry,' I said, 'everything is going to be all right. A beautiful young girl like you has *got* to have a man to hold her and make her happy.' Naoko was drenched in sweat and tears. I got a bath towel and dried her face and body. Even her panties were soaked, so I helped her out of them—now wait a minute, don't get any strange ideas, there was nothing funny going on. We always used to bathe together. She was like my little sister."

"I know, I know," I said.

"Well, anyway, Naoko said that she wanted me to hold her. I said it was way too hot for holding, but she said it was the last time we'd be seeing each other, so I held her. Just for a while. With a bath towel between us so our sweaty bodies wouldn't stick to each other. And when she calmed down, I dried her off again, got her nightgown on her, and put her to bed. She fell sound asleep right away. Or maybe she was just pretending to sleep. Whatever, she looked so sweet and lovely that night, she had the face of a girl of thirteen or fourteen who's never had a bit of harm done to her since the day she was born. I saw that look on her face, and I knew I could let myself fall asleep with an easy heart.

"When I woke at six in the morning, she was gone. Her nightgown was there, where she had dropped it, but her clothes and sneakers and the flashlight I always kept by my pillow were missing. I knew immediately that something was wrong. I mean, the very fact that she had taken the flashlight meant she had left in the dark. I checked her desk just in case, and there was the note: 'Please give all my clothes to Reiko.' I woke everybody up right away, and we took different areas to look for her. We searched every inch of the place, from the insides of the dorms to the surrounding woods. It took us five hours to find her. She had even brought her own piece of rope."

Reiko sighed and patted the cat.

"Want some tea?" I asked.

"Yes, thanks," said Reiko.

I boiled water and brought a pot of tea back to the veranda. Sundown was approaching. The daylight had grown weak, and long shadows of trees stretched to our feet. I sipped my tea and looked at the strangely random garden with its funny mix of yellow globeflowers and pink azaleas and tall, green nandins.

"So then the ambulance came and took Naoko away and the police started questioning me. Not that there was much to question. There was a kind of suicide note, and it had obviously been a suicide, and they took it for granted that suicide was just one of those things that mental patients *did*. So it was pretty pro forma. As soon as they left, I telegraphed you."

"What a sad little funeral it was," I said. "Her family was obviously kind of bothered that I knew Naoko had died. I'm sure they didn't want people to know it was suicide. I probably shouldn't even have been there. Which made me feel even worse. As soon as I got back, I hit the road."

"Hey, Watanabe, what do you say we take a walk? We can shop for something to make for dinner, maybe. I'm starved."

"Sure. Is there something you want to eat?"

"Sukiyaki," she said. "I haven't had anything like that for years. I used to *dream* about sukiyaki—just stuffing myself with beef and green onions and noodles and roasted tofu and greens."

"Sure, we can have that, but I don't have a sukiyaki pan."

"Just leave it to me. I'll borrow one from your landlord."

She ran off to the main house and came back with a good-size pan and gas cooker and rubber hose.

"Not bad, huh?"

"Not bad!"

We bought all the ingredients at the little shops in the neighborhood—beef, eggs, vegetables, tofu. I picked out a fairly decent white wine. I tried to pay, but Reiko insisted on paying for everything.

"Think how the family would laugh at me if they heard I let my nephew pay for the food!" Reiko said. "Besides, I'm carrying a fair amount of cash. So don't worry. I wasn't about to leave the sanatorium broke."

Reiko washed the rice and put it on to boil while I set up for cooking on the veranda. When everything was ready to go, Reiko took out her guitar and seemed to be testing it with a slow Bach fugue. On the hard parts she would purposely slow down or speed up or make it detached or sentimental, listening with obvious pleasure to the variety of sounds she could draw from the instrument. When she played the guitar, Reiko looked like a seventeen-year-old girl enjoying the sight of a new dress. Her eyes sparkled, and she pursed her lips with the hint of a smile. When she had finished the piece, she leaned back against a pillar and looked up at the sky as if deep in thought.

"Do you mind if I talk to you?" I asked.

"Not at all," she said. "I was just thinking about how hungry I am."

"Aren't you planning to see your husband or your daughter while you're here? They must be in Tokyo somewhere."

"Close enough. Yokohama. But no, I don't plan to see them. I'm sure I told you before: it's better for them if they don't have anything to do with me. They've started a new life of their own. And I'd just feel terrible if I did see them. No, the best thing is to keep away."

She crumpled up her empty box of Seven Stars and got a new box of cigarettes from her suitcase. She cut the seal and put one in her mouth, but she didn't light up.

"I'm all through as a human being," she said. "All you're looking at is the lingering memory of what I used to be. The most important part of me, what used to be inside, died years ago, and I'm just functioning by rote memory."

"But I like you now, Reiko, the way you are, lingering memory or whatever. And what I have to say about it may not make any difference, but I'm really glad that you're wearing Naoko's clothes."

Reiko smiled and lit her cigarette with a lighter. "For such a young guy, you really know how to make a woman happy."

I felt myself reddening. "I'm just saying what I really think."

"Sure, I know," said Reiko, smiling.

When the rice was done soon after that, I greased the pan and arranged the ingredients for sukiyaki.

"Tell me this isn't a dream," said Reiko, sniffing the air.

"No, this is one-hundred-percent realistic sukiyaki," I said. "Empirically speaking, of course."

Instead of talking, we attacked the sukiyaki with our chopsticks, downed lots of beer, and finished up with rice. Seagull came around, attracted by the smell, so we shared our meat with her. When we had eaten our fill, we sat leaning against the porch pillars and looking at the moon.

"Satisfied?" I asked.

"Totally," she groaned. "I've never eaten so much in my life."

"What do you want to do now?"

"Have a smoke and go to a public bath. My hair's a mess. I need to wash it."

"No problem. There's one down the street."

"Tell me, Watanabe, if you don't mind. Have you slept with that girl Midori?"

"You mean have we had sex? Not yet. We decided not to until things get straightened out."

"Well, now they're straightened out, wouldn't you say?"

I shook my head. "Now that Naoko's dead, you mean?"

"No, not that. You made your decision long before Naoko died—that you could never leave Midori. Whether Naoko is alive or dead, it has nothing to do with your decision. You chose Midori. Naoko chose to die. You're all grown up now, so you have to take responsibility for your choices. Otherwise, you ruin everything."

"But I can't forget her," I said. "I told Naoko I would go on waiting for her, but I couldn't do it. I turned my back on her in the end. I'm not saying anyone's to blame: it's a problem for me myself. I do think that things would have worked out the same way even if I hadn't turned my back on her. Naoko was choosing death all along. But that's beside the point. I can't forgive myself. You tell me there's nothing I can do about a natural change in feelings, but my relationship with Naoko was not that simple. If you stop and think about it, she and I were bound together at the border between life and death. It was like that for us from the start."

"If you feel some kind of pain with regard to Naoko's death, I would advise you to keep on feeling that pain for the rest of your life. And if there's something you can learn from it, you should do that, too. But quite aside from that, you should be happy with Midori. Your pain has nothing to do with your relationship with her. If you hurt her any more than you already have, the wound could be too deep to fix. So, hard as it may be, you have to be strong. You have to grow up more, be more of an adult. I left the sanatorium and came all the way up here to Tokyo to tell you that—all the way on that coffin of a train."

"I understand what you're telling me," I said to Reiko, "but I'm still not prepared to follow through on it. I mean, that was *such* a sad little funeral! No one should have to die like that."

Reiko stretched her hand out and stroked my head. "We all have to die like that sometime. I will, and so will you."

WE TOOK THE five-minute walk along the riverbank to the local public bath and came home feeling somewhat refreshed. I opened the bottle of wine and we sat on the veranda drinking it.

"Say, Watanabe, could you bring out another glass?"

"Sure," I said. "But what for?"

"We're going to have our own funeral for Naoko, just the two of us. One that's not so sad."

When I handed her the glass, Reiko filled it to the brim and set it on the stone lantern in the garden. Then she sat on the veranda, leaning against a pillar, guitar in her arms, and smoked a cigarette.

"And now could you bring out a box of matches? Make it the biggest one you can find."

I brought out an economy-size box of kitchen matches and sat down next to her.

"Now what I want you to do is lay down a match every time I play a song, just set them in a row. I'm going to play every song I can think of."

First she played a soft, lovely rendition of Henry Mancini's "Dear Heart."

"You gave a recording of this to Naoko, didn't you?" Reiko asked.

"I did. For Christmas the year before last. She really liked that song."

"I like it too," said Reiko. "So soft and beautiful . . ." She ran through a few bars of the melody one more time before taking another sip of wine. "I wonder how many songs I can play before I get completely drunk. This'll be a nice funeral, don't you think—not so sad?"

Reiko moved on to the Beatles, playing "Norwegian Wood," "Yesterday," "Michelle," and "Something." She sang and played "Here Comes the Sun," then played "The Fool on the Hill." I laid seven matches in a row.

"Seven songs," said Reiko, sipping more wine and smoking another cigarette. "Those guys sure knew something about the sadness of life, and gentleness."

By "those guys," Reiko of course meant John Lennon, Paul McCartney, and George Harrison.

After a short breather, Reiko crushed her cigarette out and picked her guitar up again. She played "Penny Lane," "Blackbird," "Julia," "When I'm 64," "Nowhere Man," "And I Love Her," and "Hey Jude."

"How many songs is that?"

"Fourteen," I said.

She sighed and asked me, "How about you? Can you play something—maybe one song?"

"No way. I'm terrible."

"So play it terribly."

I brought out my guitar and stumbled my way through "Up on the Roof." Reiko took a rest, smoking and drinking. When I was through, she applauded.

Next she played a guitar transcription of Ravel's "Pavane for a Dying Queen" and a beautifully clean rendition of Debussy's "Claire de Lune."

"I mastered both of these after Naoko died," said Reiko. "To the end, her taste in music never rose above the horizon of sentimentalism."

She performed a few Bacharach songs next: "Close to You," "Raindrops Keep Falling on My Head," "Walk On By," plus Laura Nyro's "Wedding Bell Blues."

"Twenty," I said.

"I'm like a human jukebox," Reiko exclaimed. "My professors would faint if they could see me now."

She went on sipping and puffing and playing: several bossa novas, Rodgers and Hart, Gershwin, Bob Dylan, Ray Charles, Carole King, The Beach Boys, Stevie Wonder, Kyu Sakamoto's "Sukiyaki Song," "Blue Velvet," "Green Fields." Sometimes she would close her eyes and nod or hum to the melody.

When the wine was gone, we turned to whiskey. The wine in the glass in the garden I poured over the stone lantern and replaced it with whiskey.

"How's our count going?" Reiko asked.

"Forty-eight," I said.

For our forty-ninth song, Reiko played "Eleanor Rigby," and the fiftieth was another performance of "Norwegian Wood." After that she rested her hands and drank some whiskey. "Maybe that's enough," she said.

"It is," I answered. "Amazing."

Reiko looked me in the eye and said, "Now listen to me, Watanabe. I want you to forget all about that sad little funeral you saw. Just remember this marvelous one of ours."

I nodded.

"Here's one more for good measure," she said, and for her fifty-first piece she played her favorite Bach fugue. When she was through, she said in a voice just above a whisper, "How about doing it with me, Watanabe?"

"Strange," I said. "I was thinking the same thing."

We went inside and closed the curtains. Then, in the darkened room, Reiko and I sought out each other's bodies as if it were the most natural thing in the world for us to do. I removed her blouse and slacks, and then her underwear.

"I've lived a strange life," said Reiko, "but I never thought I'd have my panties removed for me by a man nineteen years my junior."

"Would you rather take them off yourself?"

"No, go ahead. But don't be too shocked at all my wrinkles."

"I like your wrinkles."

"You're gonna make me cry," she whispered.

I kissed her all over, taking special care to follow the wrinkled places with my tongue. She had the breasts of a little girl. I caressed them and took her nipples in my teeth, then slid a finger inside her warm, moist vagina and began to move it.

"Wrong spot, Watanabe," Reiko whispered in my ear. "That's just a wrinkle."

"I can't believe you're telling jokes at a time like this!"

"Sorry," she said. "I'm scared. I haven't done this for years. I feel like a seventeen-year-old girl: I just went to visit a guy in his room, and all of a sudden I'm naked."

"To tell you the truth, I feel as if I'm violating a seventeen-year-old girl."

With my finger in her "wrinkle," I moved my lips up her neck to her ear and took a nipple with the fingers of my other hand. As her breathing intensified and her throat began to tremble, I parted her long, slim legs and eased myself inside her.

"You're not going to get me pregnant now, are you? You're taking care of that, right?" Reiko murmured in my ear. "I'd be so embarrassed if I got pregnant at this age."

"Don't worry," I said. "Just relax."

When I was all the way in, she trembled and released a sigh. Caressing her back, I moved inside her and then, without warning, I came. It was an intense, unstoppable ejaculation. I clutched at her as my semen pulsed into her warmth again and again.

"I'm sorry," I said. "I couldn't stop myself."

"Don't be silly," Reiko said, giving me a little slap on the rump. "You don't have to worry about that. Do you always have that on your mind when you're doing it with girls?"

"Yeah, pretty much."

"Well, you don't have to think about it with me. Forget it. Just let yourself go as much as you like. Did it feel good?"

"Just great. That's why I couldn't control myself."

"This is no time for controlling yourself. This is fine. It was great for me, too."

"You know, Reiko," I said.

"What's that?"

"You ought to take a lover again. You're terrific. It's such a waste."

"Well, I'll think about it," she said. "But I wonder if people take lovers and things in Asahikawa."

Growing hard a few minutes later, I went inside her again. Reiko held her breath and twisted beneath me. I moved slowly and quietly with my arms around her, and we talked. It felt wonderful to talk that way. If I said something funny and made her laugh, the tremors came into me through my penis. We held each other like that for a very long time.

"Oh, this feels marvelous!" Reiko said.

"Moving's not bad either," I said.

"Go ahead. Give it a try."

I lifted her hips and went in as far as I could go, then savored the sensation of moving in a circular pattern until, having enjoyed it to the full, I let myself come.

ALTOGETHER, WE JOINED our bodies four times that night. At the end each time, Reiko would lie in my arms trembling slightly, eyes closed, and release a long sigh.

"I never have to do this again," said Reiko, "for the rest of my life. Oh, please, Watanabe, tell me it's true. Tell me I can relax now because I've done enough to last a lifetime."

"Nobody can tell you that," I said. "There's no way to know."

I TRIED TO convince Reiko that taking a plane would be faster and easier, but she insisted on going to Asahikawa by train.

"I like the ferry to Hokkaido. And I have no desire to fly through the air," she said. I accompanied her to Ueno Station. She carried her guitar and I carried her suitcase. We sat on a platform bench waiting for the train to pull in. Reiko wore the same tweed jacket and white pants she'd had on when she arrived in Tokyo.

"Do you really think Asahikawa's not such a bad place?" she asked.

"It's a nice town. I'll visit you there soon."

"Really?"

I nodded. "And I'll write to you."

"I love your letters. Naoko burned all the ones you sent her. And they were such great letters, too!"

"Letters are just pieces of paper," I said. "Burn them, and what stays in your heart will stay; keep them, and what vanishes will vanish."

"You know, Watanabe, truth is, I'm scared, going to Asahikawa by myself. So be sure to write to me. Whenever I read your letters, I feel you're right there next to me."

"If that's what you want, I'll write all the time. But don't worry. I know you: you'll do fine wherever you go."

"And another thing. I kinda feel like there's something stuck inside me. Could it be my imagination?"

"Just a lingering memory," I said, and smiled. Reiko smiled too.

"Don't forget about me," she said.

"I won't forget you," I said. "Ever."

"We may never meet again, but no matter where I go, I'll always remember you and Naoko."

I saw that she was crying. Before I knew it, I was kissing her. Others on the platform were staring at us, but I didn't care about such things any-more. We were alive, she and I. And all we had to think about was contin-uing to live.

"Be happy," Reiko said to me as she boarded the train. "I've given you all the advice I have to give. There's nothing left for me to say. Just be happy. Take my share and Naoko's and combine them for yourself."

We held hands for a moment, and then we parted.

I TELEPHONED MIDORI. "I have to talk to you," I said. "I have a million things to talk to you about. A million things we have to talk about. All I want in this world is you. I want to see you and talk. I want the two of us to begin everything from the beginning."

Midori responded with a long, long silence—the silence of all the misty rain in the world falling on all the new-mown lawns of the world. Forehead pressed against the glass, I shut my eyes and waited. At last, Midori's quiet voice broke the silence: "Where are you now?"

Where was I now?

Gripping the receiver, I raised my head and turned to see what lay beyond the telephone booth. Where was I now? I had no idea. No idea at all. Where was this place? All that flashed into my eyes were the countless shapes of people walking by to nowhere. Again and again, I called out for Midori from the dead center of this place that was no place.

TRANSLATOR'S NOTE

Haruki Murakami was shocked and depressed to find his normal six-figure readership exploding into the millions when he published *Norwegian Wood* in 1987. Fame was one thing, superstardom another, and the craziness of it sent him back to the anonymity of Europe (he had written the book in Greece and Italy). In 1991 he moved on to the United States. Not until 1995 was he prepared to resume living in Japan, but strictly on his own terms, without the television appearances and professional pontificating expected of a bestselling Japanese author.

Norwegian Wood is still the one Murakami book that "everyone" in Japan has read, but Murakami's young audience has grown up with him as he has begun wrestling with Japan's dark past (in *The Wind-Up Bird Chronicle*) and the 1995 double punch of the Kobe earthquake and (in *Underground*) the sarin gas attack on the Tokyo subway.

Accustomed to his cool, fragmented, American-flavored narratives on mysterious sheep and disappearing elephants, some of Murakami's early readers were dismayed to find that *Norwegian Wood* seemed to be "just" a love story—and one that bore a suspicious resemblance to the kind of Japanese mainstream autobiographical fiction that Murakami had flat-out rejected since his exciting debut in 1979. As Murakami himself tells it, "Many of my readers thought that *Norwegian Wood* was a retreat for me, a betrayal of what my works had stood for until then. For me personally, however, it was just the opposite: it was an adventure, a challenge. I had never written that kind of straight, simple story, and I wanted to test myself. I set *Norwegian Wood* in the late 1960s. I borrowed the details of the protagonist's college environment and daily life from those of my own college days. As a result, many people think it is an autobiographical novel, but in fact it is not autobiographical at all. My own youth was far less dramatic, far more boring than his. If I had simply written the literal truth of my own life, the novel would have been no more than fifteen pages long."

The author may joke away its autobiographicality, but the book *feels* like an autobiography, it favors lived experience over mind games and shots at the supernatural, and it does indeed tell us much more straightforwardly than any of his other novels what life was like for the young Haruki Murakami when he first came to Tokyo from Kobe. Back then, in the years 1968–1970 that occupy the bulk of the novel, Murakami's experience centered on meeting the love of his life, his wife, Yoko, amid the turbulence of the student movement. The author is right, though: there is a lot of fiction here, and a lot of caricature and humor, and a lot of symbolism that Murakami's regular readers will recognize instantly. It is by no means "just" a love story.

Determined Murakami readers abroad may have succeeded in obtaining copies of Alfred Birnbaum's earlier translation of *Norwegian Wood*, which was produced for distribution in Japan, with grammar notes in back, to enable students to enjoy their favorite author as they struggled with the mysteries of English. Although the novel has appeared in French, Italian, Chinese, Korean, Norwegian, and Hebrew, the present edition is the first English translation that Murakami has authorized for publication outside Japan.

Jay Rubin